OLD GLORY SAGA

DECISION

LOCKDOWN 2020

Book 2

by

Assaf Raz

In the name of my beloved wife and children...

"Here I am."

CONTENTS

FOR YOUR SAFETY

– Venice Beach, CA –
Saturday, August 15, 2020

"**I** hate it," growled Dani, turning her head from the sight of me pricking her finger with the small needle. Her long black hair hid her blue eyes while her fit body tightened in childlike terror. She put her other hand on the desk in my studio to brace herself.

"Baby, breathe. It's not a syringe," I pleaded with her, suppressing my laughter while enjoying watching her body squirm.

"Oh, shut up already and finish!"

She focused her eyes in the direction of the early morning light coming through the patio glass door.

"I'm done," I assured her, as the tiny amount of blood filled the sample plate.

Snatching back her finger like a wounded animal, she rose from her chair, eyes rumbling like a storm that threatened to drown me.

Yeah, I'm tired of it too, Baby.

With every day cooped inside, our nerves frayed a bit further. The combination of lingering physical exhaustion and high-energy children was not wearing well on either of us.

"They're coming," whispered the Beast, sensing my desires and prickling my body with anticipation.

"What?" Dani's forceful tone stunned me, and I looked up into eyes that held a question.

"Huh?"

"Your face... Never mind." She shook her head, grumbling her intent to depart instead of push. "The kids will be up soon!"

"Are you good with the plan?" I asked.

Her mouth closed briefly before she rhymed back the steps I had given her. With every detail, I nodded in appreciation.

When she was done, instead of leaving, she placed her hands on her hips, an angry glare rising as dots connected behind her narrowed eyes.

Oh shit.

"Tanner Washington! You bastard!"

Bracing myself, I stood up to face her as she advanced slowly toward me.

"You want this, don't you?"

"What?" I tried one more time to deflect, but it was hopeless.

"Don't 'what what' me! You think they're coming for us, don't you?"

My face hardened, and it took her aback when I stood my ground, fists clenched.

"Yeah, I don't think they're done with us. It can come at any time." It was my turn to growl.

Her face reddened with anger.

"You didn't answer my question. Do you *want* this to happen?"

"She sees me. Don't deny her," warned the Beast.

I resisted the urge from taking me over, but some of it spilled out, "Yes. I do."

Shock replaced anger, but only for a moment. She launched her body forward, slapping my face with lightning speed.

Fuck.

"Are you serious? Are we your bait? How could you?" she barked at me, switching to Hebrew in the middle of her questions. "We've been living under this crap for months now. Every day is a living nightmare..." She vented, tying together all the horrors of the pandemic, the riots, and Nico's death. "I'm barely holding on some days, and then you pull this stunt!"

The shackles tightened as I recalled the death of my Hermano. My devotion and love for my family constricted my breath for a moment, holding my darkness at bay.

"For now." The Beast's words echoed and faded.

My hands reached for hers, and she reluctantly reached back.

"I'm sorry."

Her eyes searched mine until she eventually nodded and mumbled about getting ready for our uninspiring morning routine.

The small plastic comb removed the old wax like a knife cutting soft butter. I'd cleaned most of my boards and was working on the last one when I heard Ari shout from the balcony above.

"Rabbi!"

With warmth filling my tired chest at the sound of my son's voice, I dropped the comb and reached for the mask hanging by the front door.

Opening it, I had to raise my hand to shield my eyes from the glaring noon sunlight.

"Good eyes, Scout." I looked up in time to see his wild blond hair disappearing back into the house.

Across the courtyard, Rabbi Shemtov was walking toward us, holding a nine-foot longboard that explained why his silver beard was wet. His short frame was dressed in board shorts, an oversized Hawaiian shirt, and a straw hat. He looked wet, and his beaming face confirmed my assessment.

The power of the ocean.

"Ahoy, Captain!" I called through the mask.

Shemtov laughed as he approached, dropped the board by the door, and surprised me with a firm hug.

"Come on. It's been days since you got it. I'm not afraid," assured the Rabbi, sensing my concern.

We bantered about the surf and the neighborhood before Shemtov asked, "Would you mind if we pray quickly for your complete healing?"

I glanced up at Ari, who was back on the balcony and watching us closely. The Rabbi followed my gaze and made a face that made Ari giggle. The sweet exchange helped quell my inherent resistance to religious ceremonies.

"Of course, Rabbi," I replied, and he led the blessing while I echoed it in Hebrew.

"Today, I prayed for you. Maybe one day, you'll do me the honors," he said after we'd finished.

His words begged me to quiet my mind and reflect, but my phone rang and chirped at the same time.

"Holden," I quickly greeted the LAPD's commander of the Pacific Division while my eyes scanned the text from the RCC.

"They're coming for you," he started. The tone of his voice conjured an image of his dark face grim and wide shoulders tense.

Quickly, I activated the "chip record" feature via the phone, which allowed a Rogue to use the phone to record all signals around the user and then store them on the chip, from which the file would be uploaded to the RCC and notify them.

"Who's coming?" I asked, motioning for Shemtov to wait a moment.

His words confirmed my worst fear and woke the Beast from its short slumber.

"They asked for backup. Dee is one of the officers." Holden's tone was angry and he took a moment to lower his voice to a whisper. "I can get word to City Hall. This doesn't seem right."

I could feel Shemtov's eyes boring into me as I looked toward the gate in anticipation.

"No special treatment. I got it. Thank you, Brother."

The chip recording was uploaded to the RCC, and I lifted my face to look at Rabbi's puzzled expression.

Another chirp. Jack's message confirmed that Custer, Eli, and he were ready.

"Am I a plant or something?" mumbled the Rabbi, his eyes still jovial but his expression sobering.

His eyes widened as I shared what was about to unfold.

"How...? How do you know...?" he stammered in surprise.

"It doesn't matter how, Rabbi." I poked my head inside the door. "Dani!"

She was downstairs in seconds and had barely acknowledged Shemtov when she saw my face and her olive skin paled.

"Should I call Celeste to come help with the kids?" she wondered about a part of the plan we hadn't discussed in detail.

The Rabbi looked confused, removing his straw hat to scratch his head.

"No. Just turn on a movie so they stay inside," I replied, wincing at the thought of Nico's dark-haired widow joining us.

I definitely don't want Cel here now. She's more sensitive and reactive than usual.

"What's going on? Have you two been preparing for this?" muttered Shemtov.

"Rabbi, welcome to the 'being married to Tanner Washington' show!" Dani's lips were tight as she hustled back into the house.

I turned to face Shemtov.

"You better go home, Rabbi. You don't want any part of this."

"Try to move me," he said, indignance setting his jaw. "Just get me a chair, as these old knees don't like standing too long."

I was about to laugh when I heard voices near the gate.

"No chair needed, Rabbi." I squeezed his shoulder as I turned back to the door. "Dani!"

A masked group of suits entered the courtyard.

Councilwoman Victoria Sabech was among them, dressed in her snappy business fashion, including a tight bun and a fashionable face diaper, which did little to hide her blazing brown eyes. A lean black female cop walked behind her beside another male cop.

Dee.

I caught sight of the Israeli agent, a mid-thirties blond male, moving quietly into the courtyard. He hung back when the officers noticed him.

As the group stopped, about ten feet from us, I looked up to see my neighbors stepping onto their balconies. Most had phones and didn't appear to feel any shame recording the unfolding scene.

This can't get any better.

The Beast howled with glee.

"Mr. Washington," started the female health department employee who had visited us three days earlier.

"Yes."

The female inspector's eyes widened when she saw Shemtov standing to my left.

"You should know better than to associate with people, especially older people, in your condition."

"Is this so important to hassle a family on Sabbath?" Shemtov bristled so quickly, it surprised me.

The inspector was taken aback.

"Who are you?"

"I'm the family Rabbi. Your tyranny may have closed our synagogue but not our faith's reach. I've already had the Dragon and healed, so I feel safe to be next to them."

I stared at him, not trying to hide my questions, as he'd never revealed being infected. He smiled sadly and nodded back.

Must have been while I was gone. Damn.

An Asian man in a gray suit pushed forward.

"Tanner Washington, I'm Kim Kwon from the Department of Child Services."

My stomach turned.

"What do you want?" I replied, barely able to keep the contempt from twisting my tone further.

Kwon hesitantly held up a stamped page and handed it to me for review.

As I scanned the document, the agent explained that the state was here to take custody of our children due to our refusal to adhere to the Dragon measures, creating an unsafe environment for the children.

A low growl, more bestial than human, caught my attention. When I turned to find its source, I saw Dani standing by the door just a few feet behind us. Her eyes blazed above her mask, fists clenched by her slim body.

I nodded, and my wife disappeared behind the door.

"Hold on a moment." I glared at the DCS worker.

As Shemtov shifted angrily, his face reddening with readiness, I shook my head to let him know we had this.

"Mr. Washington," Victoria advanced, "just cooperate with the health department and let them test your blood for public safety. That will allow me to intervene with DCS. It doesn't have to be this way."

"Why are you so worried about my case when there are so many others?" I challenged.

"There is a new variant, first spotted in Chicago and now spreading," interjected the health department worker. "We just want to know what kind you've got."

What a useful idiot. But whose?

Feeling Dani arrive behind me, I turned to retrieve the small black satchel and gasped softly when she paused to drop my mask and hers and kissed me. Replacing our masks, her eyes remained wild and oblivious to all who watched.

The health department worker coughed, and I turned to face her and Victoria.

"I thought I was clear enough last time. You're not testing anyone in my family." I trained my eyes on Kwon. "As for you taking our children away..."

Resisting the urge to unload all of my rage at the Dragon measures on this one man in front of me, I glanced toward my queen.

I'm not sure it will go much better for him this way, but...

"I'll let their mother respond to that." I held the satchel out to Dani, eyes locked on hers.

Her face shifted from sheer surprise to ravenous fury as she snatched it from my hand, advanced one step forward, and ripped her mask off.

All of them, except the two cops at the back, retreated as if my wife carried a zombie virus.

Pussies. You're gonna get it.

Kwon looked to the health department inspector, who stuttered, "Ma'am, I ask that you mask up now. You're infected."

"I'm done with your games," Dani hissed. "You stay where you are. We have plenty of distance between us."

The DCS worker began to stammer as my wife shifted her focus to him, wielding her power like a samurai with a blade.

Oh shit.

"And you!" Dani snarled as her hands opened the satchel and pulled out three black passports stamped with a gold Jewish Menorah.

"These are three Israeli diplomatic passports for my two children and me. So, if I were you, I'd go fuck myself right out that gate over there, like the chicken shit loser you are for participating in all of this tyrannical bullshit."

"You don't need to use offensive language," he retorted.

"Asshole, I meant to offend you. You wuss."

Kwon gasped and exchanged a look with Victoria. Behind them, Dee approached and stopped to whisper something to the councilwoman.

When Victoria nodded, Dee advanced toward Dani.

"May I examine them, ma'am?"

Dani gave Dee a hard look, but there was no malice as she handed the documents to the young black officer.

A quick glance at Shemtov made it hard for me to not laugh out loud. His face was frozen somewhere between astonishment and admiration.

I told you she's scary. You didn't believe me.

Returning the passports to Dani, Dee addressed the group of workers, "These are diplomatic passports, as she said. Nobody is touching this family."

Victoria remained fixated on me, or at least it seemed so, as her mask and shades hid most of her face. She looked unsure about her next move as the Israeli agent moved toward us. I nodded to Dee, signaling it was okay.

He pulled out his credentials and identified himself as working for the Israeli consulate.

"Unless you want an international incident, I suggest you end this quickly," he stated matter-of-factly.

The DCS worker lifted his hands in surrender and glanced at Victoria as he stepped back.

I looked back to Dani, nodding with admiration.

She did contend with the Beast.

"Get out of here!" Dani roared.

The councilwoman looked around at my neighbors with their phones out before she sighed, shook her head, and turned to leave, the rest of the bureaucrats on her heels.

Dee waited for them all to pass her before allowing the smile to break across her face.

"I'll be right back," I whispered to Dani, still mesmerized by her fire.

"What makes you think I'm done with you and your stunts?" she growled, her eyes full of mischief.

Shemtov burst out laughing, as Dani put her arm in his and walked him toward the door.

"Admit it. You enjoyed it," I called after her, bursting into laughter myself when she silently gave me the middle finger as she entered the house.

★   ★   ★

I ran toward the gate, thanking the Israeli agent as I passed him. Victoria was standing by her car and turned when she heard my footsteps. The young Hispanic councilwoman removed her sunglasses and mask, revealing her pretty light brown face.

She's trapped! my intuition screamed at me.

It looked like she was still wondering about her next move as she murmured, "I heard some assholes graffitied Nico's mural. I want you to know I asked Holden to watch it. That restaurant is a neighborhood treasure."

Victoria's words astonished me, and now it was me wondering about the right next move as I watched her regroup. Shaking her head, she lifted her mask and donned the large shades before taking her seat in the city SUV.

Trapped? I wondered as I watched the car speed away.

CONNECTION

The sky was red, the last of the sun gracing us before letting Venice and the whole west coast fall into darkness. I sighed, shifting my eyes from the window to the mess in front me. The kitchen was a shitshow, but saying so much to the chef would be like calling for war. Choosing my battle, I stayed quiet and emptied the dishwasher to prepare it for the next load while Dani enjoyed art time with the kids in the living room.

As I stacked the dishes, I felt her eyes on me and turned to find her smiling sadly.

They need me here. The shackles hung heavy as I lifted the mugs to their shelf.

My thoughts were interrupted briefly by the sounds of homeless people fighting in the parking lot, which was visible from the kitchen window.

Can we walk away from it all? I wondered as I watched someone break up the fight and turned back to see Dani staring at me.

"What about your promise?" hissed the Beast.

I ignored It, letting my mind continue to wander.

What would have happened if I had retired in Israel when we were first married?

The memory of our earliest days reminded me of my wife's riddle. My mind still came up with nothing except the innocent face of ten-year-old Dani, coming to see my family off.

She was so sweet. Who knew she would become so formidable.

"Ouch," I growled as I sliced the palm of my hand on a sharp knife that had gone unnoticed during my walk down memory lane.

"I'm fine," I said, sensing she was still watching me. I wrapped a paper towel around the bleeding hand and was using the other to stack the dishwasher when Dani's phone rang.

"Hi Cel—" When her speech was cut short, I looked over in time to see her face harden as she rose and took the call upstairs.

A few minutes later, she came down and gave me that look.

Here we go again.

"Okay. Tell me," I said to Dani when we finally reached our bedroom that night.

Instead of talking, she handed me her phone, her eyes immediately welling with tears.

Formidable, but still vulnerable.

Sitting on the edge of the bed, I held my breath as I scrolled through dozens of abusive posts, describing us as an "unsafe" family in Venice Beach. The main post included a video of our scuffle with the bureaucrats. I grunted, realizing the angle of the filming indicated it was one of Victoria's people who had their phones ready to record the event.

"How dare they! People want our children to be taken away!" The dam of tears released, and I reached for her. I held her close as she sobbed into my shoulder, whimpering, "How can people turn so evil, so quick?"

My answers would have kept her awake at night, so I held her wet face and kissed her gently.

"Mothers like you give me the conviction and strength to keep fighting."

Glancing at her phone, which I had dropped on the bed, I saw a new post with the Dragon Skull symbol on it.

"What is it?" Dani mumbled as her eyes followed mine.

The message was from Ryse LA: "Funeral soldier keeps being a danger to his community. But he'll get down on his knees. We 'know' they do!"

My body hardened with rage, and her eyes widened with the realization.

"Are they talking about..."

She didn't finish her question, but I nodded slowly in answer.

"I need to make a call," I replied after forwarding the post to my phone.

"It can't be a coincidence," grumbled Jack, reluctantly agreeing to my assessment about who had written the post. "They're taunting you to act foolishly."

Motherfuckers.

I was alone in the studio, sitting at my desk with the laptop open, looking into the hard face of my father and commander. His gray eyes were focused, his brown hair laced with thickening silver streaks.

"That's why they wanted your blood sample. Someone wants to see if you can be tied to Chicago," he mumbled.

"Or they are simply using the local government to distract me from the mission. If DCS had succeeded in taking the kids, it would have gotten me off track for God knows how long." I seethed at the insinuation in Ryse's post.

"Do we think Victoria would carry on such an op of her own volition?" asked Jack.

"For what purpose? It makes no sense for her to antagonize me without good reason."

"Agreed." His tone was resigned.

I'd never told him about Victoria's sadness over the mural. It belonged to a private riddle of mine, related to whatever she and Nico had before he'd enlisted and gone to Afghanistan.

"It could be Deep State actors, but I find no reason for that. If they truly knew about you, the FBI would have already descended on your home," added Jack.

An epiphany struck with his last words.

"Dad, let's try something. RCC, I need the US map overlayed with any city that experienced a new variant emergence."

Three locations showed on the screen: Portland, Seattle, and Chicago.

"Okay, but that doesn't tell us much. All three cities had major riots, which can easily account for the outbreaks," challenged Jack.

"One sec," I replied. "RCC, please compare the outbreak severity from other outbreak cities that are not 'new variant emergence sites.'"

The graphs changed on my screen, showing how Seattle, Portland, and Chicago blazed red compared to other riot hotbeds with outbreaks.

"Hmmm. What exactly are you saying?" Jack wasn't following yet.

"What if the outbreaks in those three cities were spiked further by introducing new variants and spreading them into the population?"

"How?"

"What if this all relates to the Travelers coordinating migrants? What if the migrants are infected and are the actual weapon?"

There was a long silence on the phone as he digested my theory.

"If you're right, then this is quite devious. To use innocent people." He immediately sounded pissed.

"And unstoppable. A bio-emp, like Lee suggested," I continued, letting the implication linger without verbalizing it.

China.

He remained quiet, and I recalled Custer's stories about their time in Vietnam.

"Any ideas?" he asked at last.

"Keep a tab on this new Chicago variant. It's still fresh in the country, so you should be able to treat it as a footprint, especially if it suddenly emerges in a riot somewhere. Then we'd know that that area is most likely where they operate."

"It's a messy theory, Son, but we'll check it out."

HEARTLAND WOES

The boardwalk was nearly empty as I pulled my two happy, chatty children in the little red wagon.

We'd gotten the "Dragon clearance" the same day we'd had that unfortunate encounter with DCS, and every moment since, we had spent outside on the beach and inside shuttered parks.

Todd was setting up his flag display when we rolled by. In his usual style, the lean black man stopped what he was doing and played with the children. He was always kind to them, but I had never seen him so tender.

"I never told you of the world before this," the sweet old man invited.

My eyes tracked the kids, who appeared pretty contained on the hill.

"Please do," I encouraged.

He spoke of a hard life. Growing up as an orphan in the system but not letting that define him. Meeting his wife, also an orphan, and building a life together in a home out east.

"We had a family, Tanner. I used to have a family." His dark eyes probed mine.

Tightness gripped my chest as I tried to picture Todd in that reality.

What happened?

"It was a horrible traffic accident, and the Lord only spared me, to see that my hands on the wheel were not enough. He took my innocent daughter and beloved wife away to his kingdom." Todd sighed and smiled at Lil whose blue eyes were transfixed on him. "I've been on the road since being released from the hospital after the accident. I never even returned to my home. Decades of... wandering... and emptiness."

Touching the side of Lil's head of soft blond curls affectionately, he changed the topic, "I saw the video. I can't believe the DCS went after you and your kids."

Fucking social media.

"I'm very proud of you two. There are more like you, objecting to what is happening."

I turned to focus on this man who had no experience in the realms that were home to me.

"What is happening, Todd? Can you tell me?"

Todd handed Ari a stack of small US flags and showed him how to stick them into the grassy hill. When the kids ran off on their new assignment, he unfolded himself and returned his attention to me.

"It's a time of change, Tanner, and the Lord will be watching our decisions," he started. "I spent decades on the road, crisscrossing the country. I was treated well in most places and grew to see much more of this great land's blessing."

Again, my mind struggled to conjure the images of this tall black man hitchhiking across the country with a broken heart.

"When 2020 started, I was about to hit the road after hanging around here for nearly two years." Wonder crossed his face and passion filled his voice. "I wanted to go so badly, to escape what I knew was coming. But I couldn't leave."

"What was coming?" I pressed, feeling the Beast stirring.

Todd gave me a long look.

"The Devil, of course... and you, my friend, know it."

His statement struck like a searing dagger, and the Beast howled.

"When the Dragon measures arrived, I was already ready to rebel. The riots have just pushed it even further. So, I built this stand of flags, so people can remember that freedom is worth fighting for—that we are an imperfect union." His tone was reminiscent of a soldier's.

Memories of Ishmael waving the US flag outside the Hatfield Courthouse in Portland stole my attention.

"What?" he asked.

"You remind me of this guy I know," I replied.

"You've been gone since the funeral."

It was a statement that also held a question within it.

"I have." I offered a faint smile.

"We're lucky to have you on our side."

As he clapped my back with brotherly appreciation, I ignored the knot of fraudulence forming in my belly and took in our surroundings.

He's exposed on the boardwalk. No weapons or RCC.

It was noon by the time the kids finished setting up the flags for their friend Todd and agreed to get back into the wagon so we could check on Shemtov. They didn't mind the rocky ride to the synagogue, over sidewalks covered with debris and around the camps that had been set up on many sections of the pavement.

I shook my head at the dystopian Dragon ads only getting more ridiculous with each passing day. Posters advertising the wonders of a "contactless life" made me cringe at the inevitable psychological and social impact of these measures.

That's if they don't completely wipe us out before then.

Shemtov waited for us near the side entrance and helped me get my party of three inside. The kids screamed with joy when they saw the toys in Ari's old preschool and jumped out of the wagon without assistance.

We were watching them play when I noticed a lone tear on my friend's old crusty, bearded face. He must have felt me looking and laughed as he wiped his tears.

"For decades, I could hear their innocent banter in my office. It used to wash away any problem or challenge on my desk. All I had to do was close my eyes and listen."

I, too, recalled the fond memories of the eighteen months of Ari's learning here before the Dragon changed everything.

But we were having different reactions. My anger spiked while my Rabbi's face grew calmer and sadder. The contradiction placed a pause on my growing angst.

"Thank you for the other day. With the DCS," I started.

"We Jews have a history with persecution. We know better than to stand by and do nothing." He led us to the bench and motioned for me to sit with him. "Are you going away soon?"

"At some point." The words soured in my throat. "You know, I did think of the Sacrifice story again. The first verse."

His eyes widened.

"What was the context? The trigger?"

"Anger related to my father," I admitted, the sour turning to bitter on my tongue.

"Good. Good," he answered, almost talking to himself.

"Why do I feel you are not surprised?"

"Are there more associations with the Sacrifice story? Beyond your father?" pressed the Rabbi.

An unexpected equanimity descended on me, allowing the words to find their way out.

"What I do, Rabbi... and who I am for them," I said, pointing at the children, "are two opposing forces. I'm not sure where this will take me."

Shemtov shook his head slowly.

"*Are* those forces opposed? Some parents protect their kids at home, yet others meet the danger in faraway lands and the shadows of war. Many times, they only return in caskets, if at all. Both love their children."

So many riddles.

He must have understood my struggle to put all of the pieces together, as he patted my shoulder and urged me to keep reflecting on the story when possible.

"Mommy!!!" the kids cried in unison when they noticed Dani standing outside our townhome. Their response to her presence always made me feel like a second-class citizen.

In "Dani's world."

"The Ramirez invited us to a BBQ," she told me as we wrangled the kids out of the wagon.

When we reached the top of the stairs, I noticed the red chyrons on the silent TV in the living room. I turned it off quickly, so the children wouldn't see it, and raced downstairs to the studio as soon as we had them settled.

The TV turned on in the middle of the anchor's speech, "...two officers were shot, and the police entered the neighborhood in full force to find the attackers."

It was a shitshow in Milwaukee, Wisconsin, where the riots started shortly after the police were shot at. The door opened behind me, and Dani entered silently to watch it with me.

"I guess I should go alone, and you come later?" Her sad tone could not compete with the stress stirring in my chest.

"Yeah, go ahead without me," I replied, quickly glancing away from the disturbing images on the screen to look at my wife.

Jack's call came a second after she left.

"It was a sniper who hit the cops. They were refueling their car when he hit them," explained Jack. "Both are wounded, but nothing fatal."

"Just like Chicago," I grumbled, leaving the unspoken in the air.

Fucking MSS is doing this shit.

"Yeah. It forced the cops to call all their reserves and SWAT, and then their search in the neighborhood sparked a riot. For the first time, we're seeing reports of local militias volunteering to watch over businesses in Milwaukee."

Defund the police, and this is what you get.

After listening to Jack rave about how much my prodigal brother Chad was helping them understand the events through the leftist prism, I addressed next steps before he did.

"What are our orders, Sir?" I asked, feeling guilty for my desire to return to "work."

"Alfa is on high alert and assembled in the Cape," he said.

I walked around the desk to sit, feeling the Beast's presence growing in its silent demand for chaos.

Come on, Dad. Send us there.

Almost sensing my thoughts, Jack said the RCC hadn't picked up any new details on the MSS or the CPC.

"They upped their security since revealing Moss."

"How is he?"

Moss had been moved to the Ranch to heal.

"Well, he's doing his best to annoy everyone here, so we'll let him go," mused Jack before his tone grew serious. "Hopefully, we'll get something useful from the data grab he initiated in the building. The RCC has been working on the encrypted files day and night."

"What about the thing I showed you?"

"We're on it. So far, Milwaukee has no Chicago strain. Anyway, have your bag ready, and I'll let you know when it's time."

The line went dead, and I was left alone in the house.

I should join Dani and the kids.

But my eyes remained glued to the screen, my right hand reaching to raise the volume.

"In all my years covering Milwaukee, I have never seen this amount of destruction," finished the older man on TV, the city in flames behind him.

FIRE ATTRACTS

– Venice Beach, CA –
Saturday, August 22, 2020

"**D**adda… hamham," Leelee whined from the living room.

Shit. Shit.

I'd fumbled while lifting the sunny-side-up egg from the pan, and the yellow liquid was running across the pan.

Fuck. She won't eat it.

I made a tactical decision to stall with a cracker for my early bird customer and then began to work on a new egg. Luckily, she returned quietly to her cartoon while Dani and Ari snored upstairs.

With her distracted, I returned my eyes to the tablet I'd set on the shelf at my eye level. The sound was muted, but the images said everything. On the screen, Milwaukee smoldered, the riot growing more treacherous by the day. "Militias are coming" flashed across the screen as I took my second pass at the egg.

I managed to get it out perfectly and then added the toast.

"Hamham coming," I called as I walked to the living room. Before I'd finished setting the plate and plastic spoon on the kids' table, Lil squealed with joy. She started to eat, barely gracing her cook with a glance.

I would have been insulted if the news didn't beckon. This time, I raised the volume a bit, Lil now fully engrossed in her food and cartoon.

"...we have reports of militias coming into Milwaukee to protect businesses, or so they say," said the young blond anchor, barely holding back a sneer.

Fucking parrots.

Tension rose in my spine.

"Nobody knows whether these militiamen are associated with the vigilantes, who already struck in other cities, always against peaceful protesters," the newswoman continued.

Lying cowards!

My anger froze when a text came in from Jack, hinting at a lead from the online journalist, Ken Lim, and establishing that Alfa would pick me up in twelve hours.

An ecstatic ripple coursed through my body.

Finally!

Then reality blindsided me, using my daughter's sweet voice, "Hamham."

"You can say what you need to say." Dani gave me one of her all-knowing queen looks while washing the late breakfast dishes, and then her eyes softened. "It's okay, Baby. I already know in my heart and can take it."

"I need to go. Tonight," I answered, reaching with my arms to massage her neck as she worked.

Her body shivered, but her words were assuring.

"We'll be fine."

It had been ten days since the life-shaking intrusion by the DCS goon squad. Initially, I'd feared that traumatic experience would impact my wife's courage and determination. But once again, God had shown me there was more to learn about my queen.

"You can trust her more," reminded the Beast.

It was my turn to shiver, considering where this suggestion was coming from.

She must have felt it. She turned off the faucet and faced me, slipping her arms around my waist.

I kissed her softly.

"Are you sure about staying here?"

My queen nodded confidently into my chest as she whispered, "We showed them. I'm not afraid. I feel protected. Thanks to you and everyone else."

I pulled her closer, unsure if it was her closeness or my unrelenting concern about leaving my family behind that made my heart race.

"Hi, Daddy." Ari entered the studio in his pajamas.

I need time to slow down, I thought as I realized the sun was setting and bedtime was fast-approaching.

He watched me pack my small green duffel bag.

"Will the bad governnnant people come again?"

"Go-vern-ment," I corrected him slowly, taking the extra time to digest the horrific nature of my son's question.

"Look what they're doing to our family," growled the Beast.

I reached for the *Sense* as I registered the entity's use of words.

Our?

I paused to look at his sweet face.

"They won't come again. Your mom is a lioness... scarier than me. Didn't you see how she chased them away?"

"But what if she needs you?" pressed Ari, his eyes full of adult-like concern.

I bent down until I was at his eye level.

"I'll always come for you, your sister, and your momma. Always!"

He kept his eyes on mine until some sort of inner satisfaction was reached, only to move on to his next concern.

"What are... vigil...lanta?"

I rose to my feet to continue arranging my gear.

Oh boy. He did hear us from the balcony.

"Vi-gi-lan-te," I slowly corrected him, once again buying some time to process an answer.

"I heard it on TV," he declared.

"Only there?" I asked, pausing again to evaluate my son's expression.

The battle played out on his face, but he eventually offered the family-trademarked crooked smile and answered honestly, "I also heard it when you talked with Uncle Holden."

Good boy.

But my elation was cut short at the sight of Dani standing quietly in the doorway with that look on her face.

Oh, man.

I stopped organizing my gear and kneeled to face my eldest child.

"Sometimes, people take the law into their hands. Instead of waiting for police to do their job, they use violence. Such people are called vigilantes." I shifted my gaze to Dani momentarily before facing my little warrior again.

He seemed confused, and my right hand gently reached out to tussle his long hair.

"Think about vigilantes like soldiers. They fight for their family. Their home."

Dani and I exchanged a smile when his brow furrowed, but my amusement was short-lived.

"Why, Dad?"

"Why what?" I responded.

"Why do people have to do this?"

My hand froze on his shoulder. It was the moment I dreaded every waking moment of my new life—to be asked to reveal the real me to those I loved the most.

"Speak the truth," insisted the Beast.

My body hardened, like the growing lone castle in my mind. Grasping both of his shoulders, I looked deep into his eyes.

"Because sometimes, nobody comes to help. No police or soldiers. Nobody. It would be best if you had vigilantes for those moments." I knew the words might have gone a bit over his head, but it was the truth Dani had deserved to hear for a long time now.

Ari's eyes grew big, and his mouth opened.

"Like Uncle Nico, right? He needed them." His face darkened quickly.

My shock must have instantly reached my face, as Dani stepped toward us but said nothing. Both hands retreating slowly, I rose to my feet.

"I really miss him." Ari's sadness constricted my chest.

Is he saying that... What's he saying?

The Beast laughed at my effort to keep the shame and guilt from drowning me alive in the presence of my son.

Ari leaned forward and kissed me on the belly through my shirt, reconnecting me to the only thing that could really keep that shit at bay. I crouched to embrace him, and Dani joined us for a warm family hug.

Moments later, they were gone, and the clicking sound of the door closing behind them shattered my heart.

I rolled my bike out into the courtyard an hour later, closing the studio garage door behind me. Briefly, I looked up into the dark open windows of Chelsea's apartment before twisting the throttle in the direction of the gate. The black female Israeli agent nodded at me and I nodded back.

Take care of them while I'm gone, I silently pleaded.

The small, silver Old Glory jet was alone on the tarmac when I arrived. Liam approached to handle my bike, and I rushed to board the plane and catch up with my team.

"We were ready to break quarantine and come for you," growled Hux. "I can't believe they did that."

"Yeah. I heard." I shot the giant a smile and then told them the rest of the tale.

When my story was complete, Dex updated me on their quarantine time at the Ranch, "I gave them a mini–Black Hills exercise to kill time." His words elicited grunts and snorts from the rest, until they all laughed.

The ear vibration synced with Sarah's going on the jet's comms, "Romulus and Remus on the line, Alfa-leader."

I walked to the small commander-secured room and slid into the comfortable business chair. The black screen showed split feeds from Jack and Custer in their separate locations.

"All indicators flash red," said Jack, referring to my old chart of concerns within the riot zones.

"The Chicago variant?" I asked, wondering if my theory had any legs to stand on.

"Too early. It takes a few days for the infection reporting to catch up," chimed Custer, his stern black face and eyes catching my attention

"It's Ken. He's undercover and managed to get out some disturbing data," Jack continued, explaining the real reason for our activation.

The data streamed to my screen, showing unmarked trucks offloading riot gear for protesters, all the time guarded by what appeared to be Ryse foot soldiers, who seemed capable enough. Then, the identical vehicles returned to a large factory yard in an industrial part of town.

"Now watch this," instructed Jack as the new clip showed tinted-windowed tour buses arriving at the factory yard. The camera kept at a distance, I had to look more closely to make out masked civilians, women, and children being hurried out of the buses into the factory.

"The migrants."

"Could be," replied Jack as the video ended. "Ken couldn't get more than that, but it was enough, considering the sniper incident on the cops, like the one in Chicago."

"What about the militias?"

"It's a new phenomenon and sadly to be expected." Custer shook his head. "It also doesn't help that some of those boneheads declare their support to the vigilantes."

Jack's eyes widened as he added, "That was the other thing Ken found. He caught on an order from the Traveler to instigate fights with the militias."

Clever. I let my palms rest on the dark hard surface of the desk.

"Okay," grumbled Custer, cuing Jack to start the mission briefing.

They wanted Alfa to infiltrate the riot zone under strict rules of engagement and see if we could pin any of our various points of interest. The factory was designated for recon only at this point.

"Watch out for the militias," instructed Custer. "A lot can go wrong when so many people point guns at each other." The General cleared his throat and changed the conversation to Moss's data grab back in Chicago. "Among other things, we managed to ascertain the existence of Ryse and Comrades cells across the country, which are all meant to support neighboring cells, like a defense system. This is probably playing out in Milwaukee right now."

If we ever gain access to their system...

"We got much more from that grab..." Jack went on to describe how Pax Eden and OBI actively funded Ryse and Comrades.

Something is spooking these guys. What are they hiding from me?

"*Like father, like son. Both hide their darkness,*" taunted the Beast.

The conversation ended, leaving me alone with Ari's haunting words, "Like Uncle Nico, right? He needed them. I really miss him."

WHEN YOU'RE ALONE

When we landed just outside of Milwaukee, I divided Alfa into two scouting teams. Dex led the blond giant Hux and Sarah to create a concealed position behind the factory. Slender Asian assassin Jenny joined me in the riot zone while Liam stayed at the safe house Old Glory had secured between our two targets to handle the comms and provide reinforcement if needed.

It didn't take much time on the ground to see that Milwaukee was in even worse shape than the news indicated, and the blueprint was identical to all the other cities we had been to—looting, fires, Dragon Skulls, Soviet signs, Comrades and Ryse flags waving, and even a lone looted cell store with Western Jihad painted all over its broken front. Thousands of rioters did their best to sack the section of the city where the original police ambush took place, and the mayhem barely slowed during the daytime hours.

Brazen lawlessness, I thought as I took it all in.

The factory, on the other hand, was nestled inside an industrial part of the city, which was severely affected by the strict lockdown orders enacted by local government. Dex established the nest on top of a three-storied abandoned textile facility that overlooked the two-story target property. Jack kept Chad available in case the nest spotted Daj, a Comrades commander.

It was late afternoon two days into the operation when Jenny and I entered the nest. The team was agitated, ready for action, hoping Hux would see something that might give us the green light. Even Dex, who always maintained his calm, quietly cursed a few times.

He's been angry since that all happened to his dad.

My chip vibrated, and I excused myself to a side room where I stood at the dirty glass window, eyes still on the factory yard.

Jack wasted no time.

"After retreating from the factory, Ken reached out about security concerns. He's back in the riot zone, seeing militiamen spreading around a large motorcycle yard. He says that Ryse and Comrades are antagonizing the militias around the bike shop."

"What's going on with the police? Where are they?" My blood boiled at yet another example of inept local government.

"The Governor is a coward. She's definitely not a fair representation of this state's good people," answered Jack bitterly.

"Blue?" I asked, suspecting the answer.

"Yes," grumbled Jack. "She's stopped the police from entering so far. But these militias finally gave the Republican-controlled state legislature the final ammo required to push back against her soft approach."

I pulled up my phone, searched, and streamed a live social media feed from someone in the crowd pushing on the bike shop. Shivers tore down my spine as I realized the escalation since Jenny and I had returned from scouting.

"Dad, I'm watching it right now. Unless they march in and break this, there will be blood."

He grunted in frustration.

"This 'Defund the Police' managed to weaken the hearts and minds of many leaders. Nobody wants to be the next Chicago."

A sudden commotion rumbled from both Jack's background and among the team. I stepped back into the room and held my finger up, signaling, "I'm with Romulus."

"The Eye just confirmed what looks to be a large cluster of families in one part of the factory," said Jack. "They are piled on each other... probably caged."

Images of Ari and Lil assaulted me, fueling my anger with the thought of any frightened children among the captives.

We need to go in!

Words began to form in my mouth.

"Hold," instructed Jack. A few moments later, he returned with news that a scuffle had begun around the bike shop within the riot zone. "Ken is nearby and streaming it live on his social media."

I switched to Ken's handle and started to watch and listen. Ken's position was just over a block from the bike shop, and his angle caught the Ryse fighters who waded in to augment the rioters.

What the fuck?

Alfa began to huddle on their devices while Hux remained trained on the factory through the scope of his sniper rifle.

"I want to keep everyone in the factory," I insisted, remembering the botched Portland operation and how Daj managed to escape while we protected Ishmael.

"Do you think the factory might be a trap?" Jack wondered out loud.

"For whom?" I didn't follow his line of thinking.

"For you. For the vigilantes."

"Go on." I was intrigued.

"We know they have firepower inside, but nobody is moving out to help with the militias. Just look. No movement. Not one car engine purring."

He broadcasted his feed to my phone, and the hunter in me prickled.

"MSS then. Like we thought."

"If it's true, then those sons of bitches have a live feed from their spy satellites, yes?"

"Then what?" I felt deflated, shaking my head in response to my team's questioning looks.

"We manage to tip state police and get them rolling on this place."

Our conversation ended up with the order to hold and wait.

Damn it. What the hell is going on?

"Sir?" wondered Dex, sensing my upset.

"State police is called in. RCC thinks this might be a trap, and they could be right."

Did I miss this one? Am I too close?

Sighs and curses filled the nest as we all focused on the factory in the distance.

"They know. Watch," called Hux from his sniper position.

I trained my binoculars, helped by the last light of the descending sun. Ryse foot soldiers stormed out of the factory toward the gate and other locations.

Oh shit.

I opened Ken's feed as shots began to fly between the militia and the people in the riotous crowd.

We watched helplessly as the firefight ignited around the bike shop as soon as the state police convoy got off the freeway and headed to the factory.

"Watch the side gate," Hux urged.

My eyes shifted to the sliding metal gate in the brick wall surrounding the factory's yard. I took in a long, deep breath as Ryse opened it and other black-clad fighters rushed through into a massive crowd of people.

"Are they moving...?" I started to ask but then saw the satellite feed.

"They're releasing them," a few spoke in shocked unison.

The state troopers arrived at the gate while the stream of families continued to the side of the factory. More people joined, many dressed in black.

The fuck...?

The few Ryse at the gate started to hackle the cops, but did nothing more than prevent the officers from entering the yard in time.

And if they were infected...

My mind began to contend with a harrowing realization. This was biological warfare, and we got played.

REBIRTH AND WITHDRAWALS

– Cape Perpetua, OR –
Tuesday, September 1, 2020

Watch the spike in the Chicago variant," urged Dex.

We were seated in the Cape's operations command room, poring over the infection data from Milwaukee. Seven excruciating days had passed since our return to base after the failed factory police raid. All we could do was analyze and watch.

The riots died after our last night there, as the bike shop gunfight spooked the state government enough to send in the National Guard and end the charade. It was too late for the five young men, one militia and four other rioters, who had died in the exchange.

"Yes, I can see it." It was clear how the red infection graph of the Chicago strain suddenly overtook the first variant, which was still the most widely found in the states. It had happened almost overnight. Images of the hundreds of families being pushed out through the side gate haunted me. None of them were ever found, so all we had were our suspicions.

Bad news poured in from across the whole country. In Virginia, the state senate decided to approve the legislation that would allow reclassifying attacking a cop to a misdemeanor instead of a felony. Republican senators were harassed by Ryse agitators without any help from DC police, directed to stand down by the mayor who constantly appeased the rioters. Crowds of rioters in Oakland, California, marched every night, chanting "Death to America." In Seattle, several police were shot without provocation.

Dex cursed and I felt a sudden urge.

Should I ask for his flask?

My phone rang, and I rose and walked toward my room.

"Hi, Baby," said Dani. "I called to wish you Happy Rebirth Day."

I gasped quietly, stunned at my forgetfulness.

The urge to drink.

"Thank you, Love," I mumbled.

"Did you forget your day?" Dani asked, even though she already knew. "You better stop working and give it some time." Her tone was pleading.

"You're right. I'll do it as soon as we finish. How are you and the creatures?"

The prescribed ride felt like a stolen moment from my otherwise deteriorating world. The morning sun was behind me, highlighting nature's flowering along the Yachats River, as I sped toward the liquor store on the 101. I took in as much detail as I could while I drove through Yachats, with its beautiful shops and restaurants on both sides of the state road.

Pulling into the oversized parking lot, my heart rate increased when I noticed a few bunched-up motorcycles at the end of the lot. Old violence coursed through my veins.

Slowly riding by the few choppers and other tour bikes, I relaxed, concluding these were probably some friends touring together.

"And who was there with you? That night?" whispered the Beast, catching me unprepared.

I didn't know.

When the Beast laughed and receded beyond my reach, I parked my bike by the double glass doors and walked in. The shop's owner was a vet and didn't know or care about the state laws on masking, which made this stop one of Alfa's favorites.

The unchanged whiskey bottle design drew my eyes instantly.

My old friend..

I grabbed the bottle and walked to the lone register stand where the bikers paid for their stuff. The middle-aged men bantered among themselves and with the older cashier lady.

Buddies on tour. I sighed in relief, still unwilling to consider the riddle the Beast had offered.

★   ★   ★

The swell broke on the rocks below the wood-made observation station overlooking the small sandy bay where the Yachats River and ocean meet.

I placed the whiskey bottle on the rail and let the *Sense* clear my mind until all that remained was the sound of the crashing waves.

Into the silent nothingness emerged fractures of memories. Early days in Venice after my first discharge from the Marines. Meeting and falling in love with Jessica. Thinking of my first wife and that life felt like looking through dirty glass at another person.

Feeling the bubbling urge, my eyes returned to the bottle.

More images flooded into my mind. Seeing myself deciding to return to service and how that choice became the road to divorce.

A painful sigh escaped my lungs, knowing that no matter how poor our chances were, Jessica and I were deeply in love for a time.

The urge increased, and my right hand touched the cold glass bottle.

I need to see this.

The river of memories continued to flow, carrying scenes from my breakdown after the divorce, the sleepless nights, the meaningless bars and clubs and alcohol growing both in amount and frequency.

Nico's smiley face was there too. His determination to be there for me. The constant harassment designed to end my self-destruction.

"You punished yourself without knowing the crime," whispered the Beast.

A large seagull landed on the rail beside me, rattling the metal enough to yank me from the most recent riddle.

I could almost see Nico at the wheel of the noisy RV, singing to a new rap song in Spanish, as we traveled with a bunch of Venice locals to a famous desert festival for days of scorching heat, drugs, and alcohol.

I grimaced, remembering the mentally abusive hours as my mind fought sadness and rage over a life chosen for me. Then I grinned, remembering the moment Nico found me sitting alone in the desert far away from the camp.

It was early morning, and the cold air carried fine white dust that covered every inch of my skin. I was staring at the same whiskey bottle, unopened and waiting, wondering whether it would be the sand or the alcohol that would make me completely disappear if I stayed there long enough.

"Are you going to drink this, Hermano?"

He was a few years sober already.

Then the epiphany that nothing could break me if I didn't allow it. Emptying the whiskey bottle tradition started that day and had continued every September 1st since.

My eyes refocused on the bottle and then widened.

When did I open this?

A woman, dressed in trail gear and sunglasses, walked up to the observation deck. She smiled at me.

"Not too many people show their faces anymore, masking even out in the open. Insane."

The absurdity of the comment gave my mind a needed reprieve.

"I can help you dispose of this," she offered, lifting her sunglasses to reveal light blue eyes.

Did you send her, Brother?

Her hand reached forward, and I smiled as I released the bottle into her possession.

"You have a good day." Her tone was genuine.

And with that, she disappeared.

★ ★ ★

When the Cape's base was first built, the destroyed military bunker system was purposely left untouched. It was where we ran the bulk of our exercises, simulating pitch-dark fights.

Today's drill was straightforward—to seek and destroy until the last standing Rogue. We had no lights or weapons. Just our trained bodies and minds. Dex would oversee the exercise. My starting point was in a side room. Eyes closed, I waited.

"10… 9…" Dex's voice came through the earbud.

"Not so tough after all, soldier boy," the Demon guy's voice echoed.

"8... 7..."

My heart rate increased, and my fingers clenched and flexed.

"Who am I?" challenged the Beast.

I recalled how the entity had tried to get me to fight Alfa in the cave during my welcome home exercise.

You are the Beast.

"7... 6..."

"And why did you name me this way?" The Beast persisted, corralling me into a forbidden section of my mind, always guarded by the *Sense.*

The question returned my mind to that moment of entering the forest right before meeting Alfa in the trees for our first melee.

It's what you are. You love the darkness.

"6... 5..."

The Beast laughed and shoved me back into the dream-like sequence.

The marks in the dirt turned out to be small footprints. They were faced outward from the cavemouth.

"5... 4..."

Deep breaths.

"Bogotá," whispered the Beast.

"4... 3..."

"Alley rhymes with Ali... Alley rhymes with Ali..." I quietly repeated, feeling myself slipping.

"Let me show you. Even if you're still too afraid to look at what happened, let me loose."

Curious about the Beast's ability to augment my skills, especially in the darkness It seemed to prefer, I considered the deal.

"2..."

Agreed.

"1... Go!" commanded Dex through the comms.

Rogues are trained to operate in zero visibility. The first challenge is to conquer the mind from the body's incessant desire to keep the eyes open for no purpose except panic.

My body began moving forward, hands groping to find a wall. Once found, I began to move along the cement surface like a spider, listening ahead.

The Beast's presence rushed forward, seeking to co-pilot my body. Without thinking about it, I allowed the entity to meld with my decision-making, releasing resistance to this temporary union.

"To the center," instructed the Beast, countering decades of training.

Rogues hunt on the outskirts, enjoying the benefit of one of their sides being without enemies. But I pivoted my body away from the safety of the cold cement, following a new path toward the center of the bunker.

I dropped to my knees, sensing a large body moving in the air from behind me. I heard it crash on the hard rock ahead.

"Ooo." The silent grunt was enough for me to triangulate my jump, landing on Hux and punching him under his ribs with a killer hook.

The Beast made my shoulder blades twitch, and I swiveled to encounter a new threat. The assailant tried to hook my side, a sure way to get a Rogue out of the game, but they missed as they crossed and passed me.

The Beast pushed on my vocal cords, and I roared in the direction of my attacker while hurling myself forward to crash against a body.

The slim body twisted fast like a snake.

Jenny!

But it wasn't fast enough to escape my hook, and she gasped for air after contact.

Red blaring lights came up.

"Exercise over. Alfa-leader, meet me at command and control."

"What's going on?" I called to Dex as the command control room's door hissed and closed behind me.

He shifted his gaze from the screen and gave me a long, scrutinizing look.

"What?" I pressed, a bit irritated.

"Back there... What was going on with you? Your vitals and moves were both on the extreme."

"It doesn't matter. Go on now," I commanded, sitting beside him in front of the screens.

"Your Dad and Shida are waiting to speak with you." *Shida? Shit.*

I usually enjoyed my interactions with the DHS agent, but her presence in this meeting surprised me.

"Should I leave?" he asked.

I looked at him, grateful that Alfa would always be safe in his hands one day.

"Yes, I'll update you."

"Evening." My father's voice and expression were serious. When Shida made her appearance a second later, he wasted no time. "Tell him, Shida."

I turned my attention to the beautiful olive-skinned woman, her long dark hair draped at her shoulders.

"I'm sorry to tell you that Ishmael Harris just died," she said softly, eyes lowered.

It took me a moment to register the meaning of her words.

"How?"

"He was beaten to death on his way to the court in a nearby alley. The police are on-site right now. I got feelers there, and they got nothing. It was a mob beating." Her tone dripped with disgust, eyes reflecting the same as she looked up.

"Shida and I crossed our references, and it seems planned." Jack's sadness surprised me.

"Comrades practically ordered it," she sighed. "But it would never stand in court, being masked in memes and over multiple obscure social media posts. The police by the court did see Ishmael leaving after being haggled, but the mayor ignored their request to go out and check on him." Her eyes narrowed.

Fuckers.

My blood boiled.

"We tried to look into this, but the police are ordered not to cooperate with us," she grumbled.

Jack shook his head in disbelief.

"At this point, I'm hinted at with reminders that I should reconsider my priorities." It wasn't easy for her to say those words and she grimaced at the cloaked terms.

Deep State.

She said a quick goodbye, leaving us alone on the line.

"I'm sorry, Son," offered Jack, knowing enough to suspect how this affected me.

"I appreciate it." My chest constricted with a futile attempt to shield my heart from pain.

"Ken immediately reacted to Ishmael's death by promising to help as much as he could."

"Do you have the funeral details?" I tried to keep my mind focused.

"Yes, Shida has them. Are you planning to go there?"

"We'll see," I replied, swept away by the storm inside.

I failed him too.

"On another subject..." Jack's tone was suddenly uncertain. "Your mom reminded me to wish you Happy Rebirth. I'm sorry for such news on your special day."

"Thanks, but..." Anger burst up to my throat, forcing its way past my protocol. "You gotta let us act, Dad."

He sighed but presented no willingness to budge from his position.

"Why did you even invent this Doctrine if you're not using it as you should?" I growled as the frustration exploded.

"I, too, made a promise, Son. To do everything possible before ever agreeing to unleash Directive Two. There is no going back once we turn the crosshairs on our own, even if they are traitors."

My mind had collected so many pieces, cataloging them to the different riddles of my life. This piece was new, but I knew which plot it belonged to because of Custer's words during our recent meeting: "The Admiral made the Doctrine possible."

How did you convince him, Dad? How does it all connect?

"Admiral Benson?" I questioned.

He took a deep breath before he answered, "William told you."

"Is it Benson?" I pressed, feeling emboldened. "How did you convince him to go along with the Doctrine?"

Custer's words sliced through me: "Now, it seems as if your turn has arrived."

Am I like him?

"I gave my oath to the Admiral. That is… correct." Jack's tone was full of reverence.

He's not answering.

"Now on to China," diverted Jack, snatching our discussion away from our checkered family history. He waited a moment, allowing my fume to dissipate.

"You and Jenny are going to Taiwan. You'll be working with Beta."

Other Rogues?

He chuckled at my quiet surprise and admitted that the moment had finally arrived.

"But you need to know something. It was Beta who supported your team during Market, and some of them didn't return home."

That's going to be an interesting dynamic.

"You're allowed to tell them you were the team they defended. Just keep away from talking about Market itself for now."

"Is this about the Uighurs? Did you see…" I told him about the chilling video with an imprisoned model who said, "They use the virus on us… please help us…"

"I saw it," he grumbled but didn't answer my question. "Just say your goodbyes and get ready for a long deployment with Jenny."

Although this new direction intrigued me, I couldn't ignore my resistance and the growing pit in my stomach.

Are they safe?

"How can I leave now? You saw what happened in Milwaukee."

"You are needed across the ocean," replied Jack, leaving no room for negotiation. "There is a monster there as well."

Zhang's dark eyes rose from my memories, and the Beast stirred at the idea of seeing China's monstrous Ministry of State.

"Okay. I'll be ready."

Sitting in front of the screens and their various feeds, which Dex monitored, I closed my eyes and breathed through the pain growing in my chest.

How can I leave them?

Memories of Ishmael Harris waving his flag in front of the court made it all too painful, and I released a long sigh as I opened my eyes.

Died for the flag. Be careful, Todd.

I picked up my phone and called Shida.

"It's tomorrow mid-day." She quickly gave me the details for the funeral, warning me that the area was unsafe and not patrolled by the police.

Zhang, I'm coming for you, but I am going to honor a free man first.

ANOTHER DEAD MARINE

– Cape Perpetua, OR –
Wednesday, September 2, 2020

"**I** wanted you to hear it first."

It was early morning, and Jenny was seated on the other side of the desk in my room. Dressed in her usual black cargo pants and white workout tank top, her long black hair was pulled back into a ponytail, making it impossible to hide the impact of what I'd just shared.

Eyes narrow, lip quivering for only a moment, her tone was fierce, "I'm ready to execute the mission."

The door hissed and closed behind her, leaving me alone with my concerns.

She hides her pain. Will it be enough?

My hypocrisy tasted like bile, and I shook my head as I rose to follow her.

Everyone but Moss, who still recovered at the Ranch, was seated and waiting in the large briefing room.

"Alfa-one," I looked to Dex. "I'm passing you the command effective immediately. Alfa-four comes with me for a long overseas deployment."

Their eyes grew wide and shifted toward Jenny, who remained detached while I explained our mission and that we'd work with Rogue team Beta.

"They are the team that covered us during Market. They lost some Rogues in the process."

Alfa looked around at each other and back to me.

"Wow." Liam was the only one who spoke.

"Other Rogues. I wish I could come," Sarah mused with a smile.

Dex and Hux looked more thoughtful but also nodded their heads, recognizing the importance of the moment.

As the excitement over Beta receded, the elephant remained in the room.

"So... China again?" Dex called it out.

I looked to Jenny, and the rest followed suit. They all knew enough about the harrowing price our sister and her family had paid to escape from China.

"Yeah," was all I offered before moving on. "And there's something else I need to tell you. There's another dead Marine."

Hux and Liam both cursed when I revealed that Ishmael Harris had been murdered, but the rest remained silent.

"Is this why you held back your flight to LA?" Dex wondered.

Alfa looked up at each other, a bit surprised.

He knew, and he didn't…

I nodded, offering him a smile deserving of his loyalty before addressing the rest.

"His funeral is today, and I need to be there."

Practically screaming at me with their silent subtext, they eventually looked to Dex, and my second turned to face me.

I raised my hand and firmly addressed him before he could deliver whatever words he had ready.

"You have a team to command, Alfa-one." My eyes turned toward the rest of them. "I'm doing this one alone, Alfa. Is this understood?"

They all grumbled but nodded before I turned and left the room.

The morning sun broke on my right as my bike pushed north on Interstate 5.

"What will we do about this?" the Beast wondered.

We're going to pay respect to a fallen soldier.

"If…?" the Beast asked.

Dex's questioning eyes reappeared in my mind's eye.

If! I confessed my willingness to unleash violence if the situation afforded it to me as I slid between two long trucks, earning a loud honk just before my ear vibrated.

"So, you decided to go after all," started my father, making his statement sound like a question that didn't need a response.

They're all worried.

"They should be," echoed the Beast.

"Yes," I replied.

"You've got twenty-four hours to finish up and board that plane to Taiwan."

The line went dead and I squeezed the throttle, shooting the bike onward.

Getting off the interstate and into downtown Portland felt like free-falling into a nightmare with my eyes open—neglect, homelessness, and so many boarded-up businesses. I rode by the courthouse, seeing the fences still up and local police patrolling. Sadness weighted my chest, and I turned the bike toward the cemetery in the eastern part of Portland and away from the tall buildings and bad memories.

I parked a few blocks from the location, pulled up my neck gaiter, and slid on my sunglasses. As I walked under trees on the verge of their fall splendor, I saw Shida in her white hijab, standing alone a block away. Quickly, our eyes met and she dropped the covering for a moment to offer a sad smile.

"Thought to join you," she said and offered her arm as I approached.

I nodded, crossed my arm in hers, and started to walk.

The shouts reached our ears as we entered the facility with no walls around its expensive lawns and countless headstones. Outside the entrance and welcome sign stood maybe a dozen protesters with ominous signs about the police and other social justice bullshit. Mourners walked slowly by the buzzards, who didn't do anything but make noise.

When Shida motioned for me to look right, I saw it right away—the Dragon Skull graffiti on the pavement just outside the cemetery. Nodding, I whispered to her about the few "watchers" I'd spotted.

I could feel her body tense beside mine as she murmured, "I guess some of these assholes believe the vigilantes might show up for the funeral. I wonder why."

Her comment amused me momentarily, but that feeling faded when we were cursed at and shoved as we crossed into the graveyard.

The sight of at least a hundred people dressed in black, congregating ahead of us, stopped me in my tracks. Guilt rooted one foot and shame the other.

Another dead Marine... and I...

"This is not your fault." Shida turned to look at me.

I took a deep breath, using the *Sense* to pull my feet out of the ground and my emotions together. We joined the crowd, mostly masked and spread apart.

A black woman in her twenties stepped forward from Ishmael's parents, who clung to each other in great pain. The woman introduced herself as the fallen soldier's only younger sister before she spoke of his growing up tough in Portland but always wanting to excel and serve as an example.

"He joined the Marines because he wanted to help and learn. After two tours as a combat medic, he returned to his hometown and became an EMT," she continued. "Like all of us, seeing the video from Chicago saddened my brother, but he sat me down that night and explained how we should all come together to push for improvement and not allow it to separate us as Americans." She wiped a tear and offered a sad smile. "He was cursed with being right."

His sister explained why Ishmael started waving the flag around the court one day.

"He wanted to promote civility. To remind people that we're all one." Her face contorted and her tone grew tighter. "My brother stood there alone, carrying our nation's flag. He was abandoned by the city he worked so hard to support and defend."

The crowd murmured, but she didn't care.

"If you didn't know, this wasn't Ishmael's first encounter with death." She looked around. "The first time, some angels chased away his attackers before it took him." Shaking her head, voice cracking with tears, she whispered, "I guess God tasked them elsewhere that night."

The parents held each other tightly, but his sister kept looking around until she surprised nearly everyone in the crowd.

"Semper Fidelis!" she cried out with all her heart, breaking into a sob before she returned to hug her parents.

Her pain-filled shout strangled my heart.

Those were his words.

"Which you took on as a mission that you're still pondering," grumbled the Beast.

"Time to go," I whispered to Shida and turned her around with me.

I sensed someone's eyes on me and turned to my left to see a small, masked guy with shades. He lifted them to reveal his almond-shaped eyes and quickly returned them, nodded, and walked away.

Ken.

Shida didn't notice the quick exchange, and we walked toward the entrance without a word. The protesters remained outside, and my blood boiled as I read their obscene signs.

The agent's black sedan was parked a few blocks back, and we stopped by her door.

"Are you staying?" she asked quietly.

"I might," I responded, wondering again at the trust that can be built in such a short time when people work together for something greater than themselves.

She closed one eye and inspected me with the other.

"My cop side would love to ask you some questions. But then again, am I ready for your answers?"

I snorted and shook my head, partially in amusement and partially in answer.

"May Allah watch over you and your decisions," Shida whispered, squeezing my arm gently before slipping into her car.

Mourners from Ishmael's ceremony passed me, heads down, as I walked back to the cemetery. Holding back behind a large tree, I watched the dozen or so protesters still hackling people coming out of the graveyard.

Amazing. No police.

"Would you want them around? To save you from making decisions?" taunted the Beast.

Shemtov's voice bubbled from the place in my mind that was still working out the riddle he'd given me: "'And Abraham arose early in the morning, and he saddled his donkey, and he took his two young men with him and Isaac his son, and he split wood for a burnt offering, and he arose and went to the place of which God had told him.'"

My mind raced over the verse as I watched the scene before me—wondering, pondering, sensing how the riddle still remained just outside of my grasp as it had since the last Marine's funeral three months earlier.

With the last mourners out of sight, the assholes huddled to smoke and banter. They left their vile signs on the ground, discarded, like the man who had been murdered.

Wicked rage heated my body, and my feet ached to approach but stopped when I noticed a young Asian woman pushing a stroller past them from the other direction.

"Mask up, Bitch!" yelled one of the protesters, raising his hand in her direction.

I raced forward, hearing another guy screaming, "Put your mask up, Bitch! Same goes for your rat."

The urge to wade into them overwhelmed my senses, but I changed directions and fell into step with the young mother. I waved to the startled baby girl and then looked at her frightened mom through my sunglasses.

"Trust me. Go. Now."

She seemed shocked but nodded as I kept in step between her and the protesters.

When they yelled at me, I raised my hands, palms open, and stayed next to the mother and child until they stopped following us.

"Thank you, Sir," she said when we'd arrived safely at her destination.

"You're welcome. Goodbye, Little One," I whispered to the sweet little girl whose innocent expression reminded me of my own Leelee.

I waited and watched the two greet those who waited for them and then turned back toward my bike.

"They are still back there," the Beast provoked, reminding me of the hecklers outside the cemetery.

God damn it.

I walked to my ride and mounted it, wondering what this growing, irreconcilable divide was going to do to me and my life.

EACH TIME IS HARDER

– Venice Beach, CA –
Wednesday, September 2, 2020

It was close to midnight when I turned into my complex's driveway and punched the code into the gate's dashboard. When it slid open, the dark-skinned, short Israeli agent nodded as I passed by. I returned the nod, rolled through the dimly lit courtyard, parked, and quietly unlocked and entered my home.

The bright white light chased the darkness away, and I was relieved to see the studio the way I left it.

I'd just removed the Wraith and placed it on my desk when a sensation made me spin. Dani stood in the doorway, her six-shooter revolver aimed with a steady hand.

"Unarmed," I called, holding my hands up and palms open.

Dani's deadly focus dissolved and relief filled her eyes.

Sensing she was near faint, I rushed to her. She fell into me and began sobbing. My left arm tightened around her while I used my right hand to gently release the revolver out of her grip and place it on the desk.

"Sorry for not giving you a heads up," I whispered, pulling her head up and stroking her wet cheeks with both hands. "You did great here." I gestured my head toward the gun.

She tried to smile back, but her eyes were full of pain.

"How long are you staying?"

"Morning. After breakfast."

"Is that it?" The queen was back, her hands on her hips.

Shit.

I leaned back against the desk, distancing myself from her scrutiny before continuing.

"It's a long deployment overseas." My eyes fell. I couldn't bear to see her expression.

It was her increasing breath rate and movement that made me look up to see her pacing around the room.

"I didn't plan for this. I didn't plan for this," Dani mumbled to herself.

Plan for what? What the hell?

To my surprise, she walked out of the studio and up the stairs without another word or glance.

My heart ached to go after her, but a growing resentment rooted me to the ground, fueled by my inability to hold it all together for everyone.

She was snoring by the time I showered and got into bed. Noticing the growing heaviness in my chest, I closed my eyes and was gone.

The water held onto the summer's warmth, making the dark world a bit more inviting. I was out there when the red glimmer started above the buildings and the visibility improved enough to head out.

A perfect four-footer formed, and I swiveled my shortboard and paddled with the growing power of the water. Popping up on the board, I felt the boiling lava in my core and let it bubble into a roar that nearly shattered the tunnel as the board crossed the lip and curved down like a blade. Every ounce of air pushed out of my body, my heart eventually forced the pump to bring back oxygen.

Surfers began to arrive, and with my kingdom of solitude invaded, gratitude cooled my chest.

"Thank you, God. I needed it," I mumbled, taking one last wave back to shore.

"Ahoy." Todd looked like an African or middle eastern prophet dressed in white. Standing on his hill, he caught me walking back from the sand onto the boardwalk.

I smiled and turned to climb the small knoll where he was planting all his US flags.

When I reached him, he stopped his work to embrace me with a firm hug.

"How are you?" I wondered, noticing my friend's old age in his tired eyes and fallen face.

Todd shook his head.

"It's been tough, my friend. Some days, I don't know if I will survive the night."

"That bad?" I asked, knowing the answer in my heart.

"Worse," he uttered. "Evil is loose upon this world."

"Then why, Todd? Why are you keeping this up?" I pressed.

His head tilted back, enabling a regal posture, only enhanced by the rising dawn that made his black skin and white beard appear red.

"Madison 51," he started.

What the...? I couldn't believe what I'd just heard. *Did he just...?*

"If men were angels, no government would be necessary. If angels were to govern men, neither external nor internal controls on government would be necessary."

I spoke it with him in the silence of my mind.

"You ask me why?" his tone boomed. "I do this to remind myself, and fellow Americans, that we have a system that is worth fighting for. It's not perfect, and it requires constant work. But we're more united than not, thanks to it. This is my *why*."

I nodded, taken aback by his fire until his expression shifted from fierce warrior to concerned mentor in the matter of a split second.

"I heard a wounded beast out in the waves."

Beast.

My eyes locked onto his as my mind and heart reviewed the unique relationship we had built.

"It's been hard to be away from them," I admitted, motioning with my head in the general direction of my home.

His good eyes sparkled as he nodded, and for the first time, knowing how he lost his family, I could identify the endless suffering.

It was always there, but I didn't understand it.

"I don't know how long I can make my stand here, but I'm reassured that someone like you might pick up my flag and keep it tall because good men don't bow to malice. No matter the cost. Before long, you'll embrace it too."

My bewilderment intensified and intertwined with concerns about Dani.

So little time to try to make it better.

"Go home now. Spend time with your precious family." He pulled me in for another hug and turned back to his sacred work.

The kids were both sprawled across Dani on the black L-shaped sofa when they saw me.

"Daddy!" they yelled and started to run.

I bent my knee and scooped them both into my arms, noticing Dani mumbling about getting breakfast as she pulled herself up and moved toward the kitchen. When her phone rang, she answered in Hebrew.

Feeling the painful distance between us, I was torn as the kids dragged me into their morning playtime.

"You remember about being the 'man of the house'?" I asked while playing soldiers.

Ari looked up at me, eyes full of concern.

"Are you leaving again?"

Sadness pierced my heart as I nodded.

"Yes, Son. Right after breakfast."

His countenance fell to the ground, allowing his long blond hair to hide his expression.

Feeling her brother's distress, Leelee tried to cheer him up with a funny squeal, and he eventually looked up and smiled again.

My eyes turned to the kitchen, and I caught her looking away from us as she ended the call.

She saw it.

Luckily, the kids agreed to trade my presence for morning cartoons without a long negotiation, and I rested my back on the counter right next to where she prepped our breakfast.

"Who was it?" I asked, motioning toward her discarded phone.

"Ella." Dani took a deep breath. "My sister has been calling me daily since you left."

A grunt escaped my throat as I wondered how Dani's older sister viewed everything. After all, she was a former Mossad agent for many years before deciding that her family came first.

My queen stopped cutting the salad and focused her piercing blues on me.

"It's awful to know you're heading out, and maybe never to return. How can a few hours be enough? We barely had you, and here you go again." Her voice trembled with sadness and anger.

Just grab them and go away!

The shackles seemed to get heavier every time I returned, but it was resentment that bubbled in my throat.

What do you want from me?

"What? Nothing to say? At least acknowledge it," she pleaded with me.

Recalling our encounter in the studio the night before, my upset was interrupted by an intuition.

What's going on here?

"Enough with this," grumbled the Beast.

Exhaling my resignation, I walked back to the living room to kiss the kids goodbye.

"It's not what I wished for. None of it is," I grumbled to Dani when I returned to her side. "I love you, and I need to go now. I won't be reachable for a while. Contact the Ranch for anything you might need."

When I reached out to kiss her goodbye and felt no reciprocation, I paused.

Her mouth open in surprise, eyes misting, she whispered, "Are you just going to leave like that?"

"Sadly." I squeezed her hand and turned back to the stairs.

★　★　★

Jenny was waiting for me at the Santa Monica Airport, and I could feel her quietly observing me while I stored my bike in the Old Glory storage unit.

Don't do it, Jenny. I can't right now.

"The driver will be here shortly," she said as the storage door rolled down.

I nodded at her slowly, feeling heavy inside and grateful she hadn't insisted on confirming her senses.

A few minutes later, the black SUV arrived, and the older driver asked to confirm that we were heading to Los Angeles Airport.

My mind was somewhere else entirely as the cityscape whipped by.

Impossible! This whole thing.

The private white jet waited on the tarmac runway, and the SUV took us all the way to the stairs. A few attendants grabbed our luggage as we scurried up and found our seats. Out my window, I took one last look at Venice Beach.

You better get your fucking head in the game, Tanner, I scolded myself, pulling my attention back into the plane and to the mission at hand.

It was just the two of us and the two pilots. When I glanced at Jenny who sat next to me, her face was unguarded, almost childlike.

"It's easier this way, carrying our pain together," she reflected.

I smiled sadly at her and settled into my seat as we lifted off and away from my dear ones, who were once again left behind.

ACROSS THE GREAT DIVIDE

Our three days of travel west were almost over, just east of Taiwan's airspace. Scanning news updates from home, I grumbled at the growing disaster. A famous conservative news anchor exposed a bombshell report about how California, Oregon, and Washington had begun to flex their muscles via the Western States Pact. Originally, the WSP was supposed to deal with the pandemic, but this report showed the three states had confidential sessions about simulating various antagonistic situations with President Stone, his administration, and the possibility of him refusing to concede if he lost in the upcoming election.

Ridiculous!

Riots erupted again in Portland, Rochester, and New York City. While the news people seemed too dumbfounded to uncover the triggering events, the sinking feeling in my stomach grew.

They're testing the response time.

More mentions of militias appeared around riot zones, but no other fights had broken out since the Milwaukee battle around the bike shop.

I should be there.

The thought irritated me, and I left the small room and headed to the main cabin.

Jenny sat alone, looking out the window until she noticed me coming down the aisle. A smile broke across her pretty face as she announced, "You can see Taiwan."

I sat beside her to take in the view.

The early morning sun shone over the island's eastern coast. It was in the distance, but I could see the tall, forest-covered mountains.

"How are you, Jen?" I pulled my gaze from the horizon to her thoughtful expression.

She turned and scrutinized my eyes. After a long moment of searching, her face relaxed and softened.

"The memories are coming back lately. It hasn't been easy." Pain was woven in her words.

I relaxed back into my seat, keeping my focus on her, hoping she would share more.

Her eyes returned to Taiwan's landscape growing closer with every minute.

"My father was a proud man. He served in the army in his younger years, but he wasn't as strong as the Party..." Jenny spoke about her mom, father, and two younger sisters who lived in China until her dad got in trouble for standing up to a corrupt Party member who made an advance on her mom in the factory where she worked.

"That asshole harassed my mom, and my father reported him to the police." She shook her head sadly. "I was just ten years old when they broke our front door in the middle of the night." Bitterness crept into her tone. "The Party member was 'connected,' and he got the MSS to pay us a visit."

I closed my eyes for a moment, imagining younger Jenny seeing this.

"They raped my mother in front of all of us while beating my father, telling him that he was lucky to not be sent to the camps." Her eyes were haunted by the recollections.

Shit, that detail wasn't in the report.

"After they left, my father rushed my mom to the bathroom, where they stayed for what seemed to be forever. When he came out alone, he forced us to pack our things quickly..."

Jenny recounted how her dad got them all into the small family car and took them on a long journey south.

"He was so focused, he must have planned this before. None of us knew, not even my mom. But he was very concerned the MSS would come after us for our disloyal escape, and he was right..." Her voice trembled as she told me how the MSS caught up to them right before the Nepalese border. "They shot my mom not even a mile from the border. The worst part was that we never had the chance to bury her."

Jenny took a deep breath and found the strength for a faint smile.

"But Dad managed to get us all safely to the States, where he worked hard and built us a new home." She paused momentarily. "He never remarried. Said all that mattered were his girls."

Quickly, she wiped the lone tear slipping down her cheek and shook her head.

"I dedicated my life to being strong so that when the day came, I could fight back," she said, her voice indicating the story was moving into new territory. "Back in Market, I felt that was my moment—that all the training had led me to that. But it didn't happen that time. Maybe now..."

"Jenny, I'm so sorry you went through all of that. What a nightmare." I paused, noticing the suffering and shame rising within me. "Thank you for sharing," I finally managed to say.

"What?" Her eyes were searching mine again.

"I fucked up, and I'm constantly reminded of that."

Her gaze intensified, yet the softness remained in her expression. "You did fuck up and left us. But you are here with me now, and that's all that matters."

Her honesty grounded me back into the current mission, and I nodded gratefully.

"You're gonna have to remember that when we meet up with the other Rogues. There will be some pain to unpack."

I knew she was referring to the recent revelations about Beta's role in defending Alfa during Market and the price the second team had paid.

Everything we'd discussed hung heavy in the cabin between us until Jenny lightened it up for a moment.

"Maybe we'll eventually learn where the RCC is located."

I let out a chuckle.

As if he'd ever let that happen.

It was afternoon when our plane descended onto the lone runway cut into a thick forest with only a few small structures built beside it. My briefing had included a section about this Old Glory forward base, established in the early nineties. It also contained Beta's home base outside the States.

Neck gaiters up and shades on, we disembarked from the plane, each carrying a black duffel bag and backpack with our essentials. Our small arms were concealed on our bodies.

The middle-aged woman, dressed in Old Glory forest green BDU uniforms, stood waiting beside an all-terrain vehicle. She presented herself as the Old Glory facility commander and then opened the trunk.

Neither Jenny nor I had ever visited this base, but they all worked the same. Old Glory staff knew how to shuttle and support the Rogues without prying. We tossed our carry-ons into the back and climbed into our seats.

The gravel road took us into the forest and then on a rough jungle road for another mile. Eventually, the commander stopped by a large dark rock protruding from the soft earth.

"Wait here. Good luck," she offered before turning around and heading out of the forest.

A cheerful whistle reached our ears, and we turned to see a lone masked man walking toward us. Despite the face covering, I could see he was a lean Asian man about my height. He stopped ten feet away, right hand close to the Wraith sidearm strapped to his thigh.

"Madison 45." His voice was tight.

This historical moment added a reverence to my tone as I responded, "The powers delegated by the proposed Constitution to the federal government are few and defined. Those that are to remain in the state governments are numerous and indefinite."

I pulled my neck gaiter down and removed my shades. Jenny followed my lead, and the man lingered on her face momentarily. After a few moments, he removed his mask to reveal a handsome man in his mid-forties with short black hair and dark eyes.

He offered his right hand for a shake, and I embraced it, noting his iron strength.

"Deshi Chin, Beta-leader."

"Tanner Washington, Alfa-leader."

Deshi offered his hand to Jenny, and they exchanged greetings.

"This is historic." His smile was laced with reverence.

"Indeed." I too, felt the gravity and excitement of two Rogue teams meeting for the first time in the Doctrine's history.

"You can leave your things here," Deshi said as he turned back toward the forest and away from the road.

I shrugged at Jenny and we both dropped everything we were carrying and followed Beta-leader into the thick woods.

If only we could leave the pain here too.

Deshi led us through a hard mountainous path under the dense forest foliage. Jenny was in the middle, and I brought up the rear. At one point, she turned and gave me the silent sign for "we're followed." I nodded back at her, confirming it.

Higher up the mountain, we reached a mighty waterfall. Deshi led us into the natural cave behind it and as we started to move deeper, I stopped him.

"We can wait for them."

Deshi laughed and called out on his comms. Jenny and I smiled when five figures in black appeared through the waterfall, carrying our duffel bags and backpacks.

There was enough natural light to reveal their features. They all looked Chinese, like Deshi—four men and one younger woman.

No one spoke while Deshi and his five Rogues scrutinized us.

"For years, all we had were Romulus and Remus," started Deshi. "Then this mess started, and we saw you on TV." He swiveled his head to look at his grinning team. "We started making bets once we figured out Romulus was your father." His tone was cheerful, and I exchanged a quick glance with Jenny.

They have no clue about Market.

"It's our honor to work with you," I started in Mandarin, smiling at him and his team. "From now on, this is how we speak."

There were at least two whistles in response, and Beta's Rogues smiled in agreement.

All the formalities behind us for the moment, we shook hands, excited like brothers and sisters who had just met for the first time.

Deshi led us deep into the cave through a concealed entrance to a side tunnel. They tested our ability to follow them in the darkness, offering no night vision gear, though we were kept in the middle where we wouldn't get lost.

The tunnel ended at a dimly lit elevator door, with a sign engraved into the stone above it: 1776**.

As the elevator took us down, Jenny bantered with Beta until the door hissed and opened into an underground base with lights installed in the long tunnel walkways.

Deshi led us to our rooms and then motioned for me to join the briefing with him.

Beta's command room reminded me of our equivalent back in the Cape. The space was empty, and Deshi led us to a spot with large screen chairs to grab.

"Are you ready for this?" He was grinning from ear to ear.

"Fucking wild, but yes. I'm here." I sat forward in the chair.

Deshi nodded as he pressed a button and Custer and Jack's feeds cut the large screen in two.

"Listen up…" Remus switched to his deep voice after exchanging a few pleasantries. The General explained how the US military had approached Old Glory, asking for deep undercover work around a specific facility in the Chinese province of Xinjiang. "The administration is pushing hard for evidence on what's going on with the Uighurs."

Wow. I didn't think the President had the stones for this.

As if reading my mind, the General lamented that the operation reeks of political agenda.

"But it serves our purpose." He detailed how an Old Glory operator would lead a Mongol paramilitary outfit into China to perform the task.

Jack took over the briefing and blindsided me with the information that Moss's data grab in Chicago managed to implicate Zhang and the MSS in the events back home—that the intention was to remove Moss to San Francisco and then to China.

"But we found a way to track him." My dad surprised me again.

"How?" I asked..

Jack suddenly focused on Deshi, who stood next to me in silent attention.

"Beta-leader, there will be things you will not understand in this conversation. My apologies."

Deshi nodded, and Jack explained that the help came from the retired General Tall.

"He got us the goods."

My father then described how the Rogues would shadow the Old Glory team on their way into Xinjiang.

"OGT will lure Zhang out of the target facility, and then Beta will abduct him."

"To be clear," chimed Custer, "Alfa-leader is to assume overall command of the mission, while Beta-leader is to continue to lead the team accordingly."

"This authority also includes breaking Zhang and disposing of him," Jack finished, sealing the fate of another man.

Deshi looked at me, eyes full of questions. I held his gaze for a moment and then turned to face Romulus and Remus.

"Who will command OGT?"

"Harry Ganbold. He's a former Green Beret and has been operating for Old Glory for years," answered Custer.

Jack explained that our training would begin in Taiwan and then continue in Mongolia, where we would insert into northern China.

"No outside comms from this point onward," commanded Jack, his eyes passing between Deshi and me.

My mind still wrestled with the mission.

"How exactly will OGT get Zhang out in the open?"

"That's handled." Jack left no more room for discussion.

"What about the leak?" I asked openly, drawing Deshi's stunned look.

"Accounted for," grumbled Jack before insisting the call was over.

Alone under the shower's steaming water pressure, I felt anxiety spreading unabated.

China again.

Dani's pained face resurfaced, and I sighed, feeling regretful about how I'd departed.

I can't lose them.

INTEGRATION

Jenny and I were given two days to recuperate, and the 0400 alarm marked the end of our rest period. Feeling refreshed and ready, I hurried to the shower, knowing it wouldn't be long before he arrived.

The knock came just as I finished pulling on my black BDU shirt.

I pressed the button on the desk, and the door unlocked and hissed open.

"You wanted to speak with me?" Deshi walked to one of the two chairs in the room.

"Yes," I replied, positioning my chair directly across from him. "I need to tell you something before your team hears it later today…"

He listened silently and then asked a few questions.

"Are you a lawyer?" I wondered, after answering to the best of my abilities.

Deshi laughed and admitted, "Actually, I'm a defense trial lawyer on the 'outside.'"

"Good cover story."

"Pays the bills." Deshi smirked, but his eyes were still troubled by what I'd shared as he stood up.

This isn't going to be easy.

I braced myself as I grabbed my phone off the desk and followed him out the door.

The dawn's early light helped only a bit as Jenny and I followed Beta, climbing treacherous mountainsides and navigating through the thick foliage.

Two hours into our hike, Deshi asked me to join him, finishing with, "Just us two."

Beta and Jenny disappeared between the vegetation as I followed Beta-leader through the trees and into a deep ravine. Once at the bottom, he led us into a crevice in the rocky edge of the canyon where a man stood waiting.

The tall, wide-shouldered Asian was dressed in Old Glory jungle green BDU with a sidearm on his belt. His face was stern, dark eyes focused.

We advanced toward him unmasked. There was no point hiding our faces, as we'd be working together closely.

"Harry Ganbold, OGT leader." The large man spoke in perfect English, extending his hand.

Old Glory had supported the Doctrine since its inception, but the company staff had rarely come in direct contact with the Rogues, let alone known their identities. In this specific case, Jack had cleared him to know our names, so we offered them in return.

We settled a bit deeper into the rocky crevice before getting to know each other.

"Tell us a bit about your roots." I leaned against the rock wall of the ravine.

A wide smile softened Harry's face, and he began by telling us that his family was originally from Xinjiang Province.

"It wasn't easy for Mongols there, and my parents eventually managed to get out of China and into America, where my mom gave birth to me—the first-generation American Mongol."

"Where are they now?" I hoped for a better tale than Jenny's.

His smile faded, but his eyes remained focused.

"They passed from the world a few years back, leaving me the last of our family line."

"I'm sorry to hear that," I responded, noticing a strange type of jealousy in my chest.

No shackles.

"Tell us about your team." I moved us on to a new subject.

Face brightening, he described the Mongol freelance outfit as trustworthy, experienced military operators.

"I've worked with them many times over. They are mercs, but with a cause."

"Which is?" Deshi's question earned Ganbold's sideways glance, but he didn't blink or hesitate before answering.

"To even the score with China."

What's going on here?

"Where's your team?" I asked, and Ganbold turned to face me again.

"Just north of here," he replied, arms softly crossing in front of him.

"Good." I turned to look at Deshi. "Do you have a nice place for us to brawl?"

His eyes grew wide with surprise at my unexpected request. But then a smirk spread across his face.

"Matter of fact, we have the perfect place."

The jungle clearing was wide enough for a red-painted circle about thirty feet in diameter. The earth was soft, covered only in grass.

Ganbold and his ten Mongol warriors—wiry, lean Asian men dressed in Old Glory BDU—stood on one side, faces stoic.

I looked back at Beta and Jenny, who stood on the other side, focused but relaxed.

What the hell?

Reading my face, Deshi leaned in and whispered, "They see us as Chinese. It doesn't matter that we're all Americans. There's bad blood here."

"Ah. Well, more of a reason to bury the hatchet right away."

I advanced into the circle and spoke to the group in Mandarin.

"The only China," my hand pointed westward, "is out there." My eyes scanned them all, and my other hand pointed down at the circle's center. "Here, we are one team—one mission."

My predatory smile reflected my inner thoughts.

"So… the mission is to see the last man…" I swiveled to look at the two female Rogues and continued, "…or woman standing."

It wasn't a surprise that everyone wanted to beat the other group. I stood outside the ring as the seven Rogues fought the eleven operators, and then quickly began to turn on their own. Unlikely duos of Mongols and Rogues grabbed people from their teams and threw them outside the ring, laughing as they tossed them. I joined in the laughter when Deshi stopped fighting alongside Jenny to trip and push her out.

Ganbold and Deshi were the last two in the ring, and everyone else cheered.

Ganbold pounded his chest and rumbled, "Being alone is growing strong."

Something about the moment struck me as I watched Deshi slowly circle Ganbold like a predator.

I've seen this before.

The realization hit me as Deshi swooped in on Ganbold with kicks and punches. The big man knew how to fight but was no match for Beta-leader's martial arts and Rogue training.

Ganbold managed to block many of the strikes, but he was hurting. He shook his head and dropped deeper into his battle stance.

Voices and images from the not-too-distant past overwhelmed me. The Demon's voice, commanding Nico, "Kneel on your sacred flags," and Nico's response of "Never," and his futile charge at the Demon transposed themselves onto the scene before me.

I need to stop this.

"Don't you dare," snarled the Beast.

Deshi came in for the last attack, thwarted Ganbold's punch, and then tripped him to the ground, grabbing the Old Glory operator's hands and dragging him outside the ring.

As soon as his victory was complete, Beta-leader offered his hand and Ganbold grasped it and rose. When both were on their feet, Deshi bowed to Ganbold, who laughed and hugged the Rogue leader firmly.

Everyone cheered, and I sensed the Beast's deep satisfaction as it receded into the depths.

Deshi assembled Beta in the briefing room after a hearty dinner. When he nodded in my direction, my eyes turned back to the crew.

"You need to know something before we embark on our mission," I started and then waited until every eye was on me. "Back in 2015, your team was tasked to protect a group of escapees from China. You lost a few Rogues during the mission."

"Nameless and loyal." Jack's words echoed as I watched Beta's expressions fall.

"It was Alfa, under my command, you protected." The Rogues looked at each other and back to Jenny and me. "We're sorry for your losses. *I* am very sorry."

Jenny bowed respectfully to Beta and then Deshi specifically.

Did we earn their sacrifice? The morbid thought tempted a spiral, but I used the *Sense* to stay on track.

"Now, it's time to focus on Operation Praetorian..."

Deshi used the screens to display the data relevant to my briefing, and I paused when Zhang's photo came up on the monitor. The Chinese General was speaking in front of staff, dressed in a dark uniform.

"This is the target. General Jun Zhang, Ministry of State. This is payback time. For your team and the tens of thousands who've died because of this monster."

"What do we know about him?" Beta-two, the young female Rogue, asked. She was more petite than Jenny with black hair cropped at her shoulders.

I told them about Zhang's Harvard background and ruthless military career, leaving out Market and the Dragon project.

"Questions?"

Beta-four, the only bearded Rogue, caught me off-guard with his question, "How did you learn Chinese?"

"I spent the first six years of my life in China during my father's deployment."

Pain zinged through me as I recalled how Jack used to drop me off far away from our home to figure out how to get back without even a cent.

I was just a child!

"And yet you made it home every time," the Beast grumbled.

"Does Zhang have anything to do with the issues back home?" asked Beta-two.

Her question fueled my resentment, and I nodded without offering more.

"Was that battle, in 2015, related to the Dragon?"

What's going on here? What are they after?

I nodded again and then discussed the training, slated to begin early the next morning.

"I'll see you at 0500." I was done answering questions.

"There are some new toys I need to show you." Deshi was at my side as soon as the briefing ended. "They'll download to our chips soon." I followed him out of the room and into the elevator while the Rogues hung back. "We just got some rapid testing kits for the Dragon, and some therapeutics in case of an infection." He pressed one of the elevator buttons.

"Good to know. I have natural immunity by now."

Deshi's eyes betrayed a connection, but he remained silent.

When the elevator's door slid open, he led us into the tunnel.

"What did you mean before when you said that bets were placed about me?"

Deshi smiled as the defense system scanned us both and opened the large metal door to a vast armory space where rows of weapons of all sizes and functions filled the walls.

"The running bet was that you were a Rogue. All those videos that came out," he started, and then his face grew somber. "The funeral one was hard to watch."

"I see." I felt uneasy at the recognition.

"RCC never confirmed or denied anything, even when those child service pricks went to your home."

"Is this why your Rogues look differently at me?"

Deshi nodded while punching a code into a nearby touchscreen and then turned to explain, "They were full of questions and confused about what was going on back home. Then they started seeing you on TV, and now you are here in flesh and blood."

Knowing that speaking about "back home" could provoke parts of me that were better left dormant, I ended the conversation.

"That is a different part of me. Let's focus on the mission."

His eyes searched mine for a split second before he nodded and led us to a workbench with covered items displayed on its white-lit surface.

Deshi pulled the dark material off the first item to reveal a soft black body suit. It reminded me of the wetsuits I wore to surf, but the texture felt different.

Like reptile skin.

"Never been tested. We are the first to try it," offered Deshi. "It's called 'snakeskin,' and it syncs with our chips."

"Tell me more." I carefully examined it from all angles while he rattled off its other features: temperature control, small caliber and blade resistance, and thermal signature cloaking, making its wearer invisible to most types of detection.

The Beast rumbled beneath the surface, as if fascinated with the skin.

"This is called a..." Deshi shifted our attention to the second covered item.

All the air left my lungs when I saw it.

"...Dragon Skull." I completed his sentence.

"How did you...?" His eyes were wide with surprise.

"Just go on." I took a deep breath to collect myself.

"Well... the helmet-"

"The Skull," I corrected, remembering the terrified face of the dying guard in Chicago.

Deshi cleared his throat and started again, "The Skull integrates with our chips and the Skin. It's voice-activated like the old Flex, which you probably know."

I nodded at him, and he continued on explaining the various features.

My physical eyes remained fixed on the Skull, but all I could see was the Dragon Skull graffiti back home. I reached out to pick it up and bring it to my face.

"Me alone." The Demon's voice returned with the image of him advancing on Nico.

"Please leave me here." My eyes were locked on the Skull's black, oval-shaped eyes and my voice sounded far away.

"Ummm. Sure." He hurried back toward the door.

When the elevator door had closed behind him, I called Jack.

"Seems you like it." My dad's voice carried clearly into my earbud.

Damn it!

I resisted the urge to look around and locate the cameras he used to watch me live.

"You designed it like this on purpose."

"Yes."

"Why?" I marveled at the structure of the Skull.

"It seems fitting," he answered, his words carrying an unusual edge of violence. "Do you approve?"

The Beast urged me, pleading with me, to put it on.

"I do."

"Well, turn off the lights and put it on," he ordered.

As soon as I put it on, my chip synced with the Skull, bringing up the familiar Heads-Up Display (HUD) I'd worked with in the earlier Flex model.

The beast rumbled like a rodeo bull in the pen, making it hard for me to hear my dad's voice.

"This new design has a few more features. For example, you control whether the outside world hears you speaking on the comms."

"Anything else?" I switched vision spectrums, struck by how much the HUD had improved since the Flex.

Jack laughed.

"Tell him, Aide."

Aide?

A melodic, almost ethereal, female voice spoke, "Hello, Tanner. I've been waiting for this moment."

My hands were about to pull off the Skull when Jack interrupted, "No point, Son. The Aide is in your chip. The Skull is just a connecting device. Just give us a moment here."

What??

"Speak to it. Try it out."

"How long has that thing been in me?" I felt bizarrely violated.

"Ask it." Jack's tone was authoritative.

A wave of resistance overwhelmed me, mixed with growing resentment.

I'm just a tool for him.

"Aide, how long have you been with me?"

"Since November 16, 2000. You were in Big Bear, California, with Nicolas Ramirez," the Aide answered.

Sadness slammed against the resentment as I recalled the mysterious download into my chip and my father being silent about it all.

It heard everything.

"Do you broadcast what you hear or see me do?"

"This is unnecessary," started Jack.

The Aide interjected before he could finish, "It takes both Doctrine commanders and a third authenticator to authorize me to send this data out. Such a request has never been presented to me before."

A third? Jack and Custer and…?

"Who is the third authenticator?" I sensed my father's growing unease and took advantage of the moment.

"Ali Washington, your mom. She is my creator."

No shit.

Mom's cryptic words before one of my departures suddenly made sense: "I'm sorry for everything we've done to you. I haven't given up."

"You can name me," said the Aide.

Name you? What the…?

"It's meant for the operator to develop a personal relationship with their aide." My father answered my unspoken question and spiked my irritation again.

"You are just a machine. I'll refer to you as 'Aide.'" I did no work to remove the anger from my tone.

"Son, try to stay open-minded about the tech."

Ignoring his suggestion, I asked, "Do all the other Rogues have Aides now?"

"Yes. We're rolling it out now on all teams."

When the sense of deep exhaustion overwhelmed me, I asked to be excused, and my father consented and ended our call.

I slowly removed the Skull and gently placed it on the work bench before turning to leave.

"Put it back on," the Beast beckoned, stopping me in my tracks for a moment at the elevator.

I'm done for now, I insisted as I pressed the button and wished for something more than an elevator to take me away.

"What are you so fucking afraid of?"

Losing control and everything else because of you.

LET'S SEE

Multiple screens showed various points of view of the evening urban exercise. I was seated in Beta's command room, watching Deshi leading Beta in an attack on a residential complex guarded by the Old Glory team.

As I watched, I saw no sign of fatigue, despite the fact that the last seven days had been a daily training grind for both teams. Our schedule was packed as Old Glory shuttled us across Taiwan to various military training locations.

The Rogues reached the target estate and began to "search and destroy." Both teams used comparable gear, but Beta won most matches outright, with only one exercise ending in a draw.

But the big surprise was the Mongols and their Green Beret commander. They fought hard every round, willing to end in a brawl when needed. Ganbold drew both teams closer, using his charismatic, larger-than-life personality. Even he and Deshi had warmed up, enjoying banter in the after-drill debriefs.

"Oh shit!" I exclaimed when the Old Glory team surprised Beta as they entered the open courtyard complex, raining soft-painted training rounds.

Ganbold! You're getting better!

One Rogue down, Beta managed to breach the large estate, and my eyes jumped to the next screen to watch through the set of cameras in that area.

As I watched them fight with outdated technology, I thought about our Rogues-only training a few days earlier. The Rogues' new gear wasn't allowed in the joint exercises, but we had tested it out amongst ourselves. The reptilian snakeskin proved invaluable in all terrains, making us invisible predators with the finest armor that humanity had ever created.

But the Skull, beyond the excitement of its advanced features, had created more inner conflict for me. Using it meant more exposure to the Beast who seemed stronger when the Skull was on, and it was getting harder and harder to resist Its call.

Lastly, the Aides connected all of our arsenal into an insular operating system activated by voice command or typing. Beta and Jenny hastily adopted the new technology, pushing its boundaries and proving its superior value, even against my skepticism. When Deshi noticed my apprehension and asked me why I'd left my Aide unnamed, I gave him the same answer I had given Jack.

It works great. But it's just a machine, I tried to convince myself again while watching the final moments of the exercise. Beta had regrouped and managed to flank and route OGT, but they paid with one more Rogue. It wasn't long before Beta took out the last OGT holdout.

Damn it. They're good.

The thought was interrupted when the vibration reached my ear.

"Impressive," said Jack, who'd been watching the Beta OGT drill.

"Yeah..." I agreed and updated him on the other good stuff from the past week, placing extra emphasis on my strong impressions of Deshi and Ganbold. He was happy to hear it all.

"What are your thoughts about tomorrow?" he asked.

The new gear was revolutionary on multiple levels, and it was about to be tested in our last exercise before leaving westward.

"I decided to try evening the playing field a bit."

He shook his head slowly with a crooked smile.

"Might as well... I guess..." Then he moved on to detail our next leg to a forward base in Mongolia, which the US government and civilian contractors had used for decades.

"Beta will be smuggled inside among OGT and then remain disguised within our area of the base, unless on training, under the guise of Old Glory," he continued. "Leave it to Ganbold to handle communications with the base. There will be plenty to discuss with the military, and the CIA expects OGT there."

"Yes, Sir." Then it was my turn to switch gears. I wanted to talk about Market, the Dragon, and Beta's lack of knowledge about the underlying events leading to this mission.

"There will be a time... later in the mission. Everything will come out when needed."

When we break Zhang.

My hands clenched on the armchairs, accepting my father's cold, hard logic.

"I've got some valuable information that will help you with Zhang." He paused. "He has a son..." Jack told me everything he knew about Zhang's son, Ye, a law student in a northwestern Ivy League back home. An image of the younger version of Zhang filled one of the screens. "He's a nice, polite young man by all accounts, despite the fact that his father is a monster."

Resentment grew in my chest as my mind quickly calculated and contrasted the ruthless Chinese General's decision about his son's future with my father's.

How will this help?

"What else?" Jack asked himself, as if reviewing an inner checklist before he proceeded to update me on Dani and the kids. "Your mother speaks with them daily…"

My heart physically ached as he gave me some of the details Ali had procured from my queen.

I need to talk with her. I hate how I left it.

"Oh, and Moss is ready for action and heading back to the Cape."

Thank God. Dex will be so happy.

Jack continued with his briefing about what was happening back home, mentioning increased activity by right-wing militias.

"Those nutjobs chose the worst time to flex their muscles, as every week brings more attacks on the police by the far-left crazies." He updated me on the most recent ambush in California where two Sheriff deputies were gunned down while sitting in their car.

Feeling a ping of concern, I brought up the incident on a side screen.

Holden. Dee. Watch your backs.

Romulus described the tightening Dragon measures across the blue states and even some red falling into lockstep.

"This is not coming from the President." We both knew our founding documents give the states inherent "police power" to protect public health and safety. My blood boiled until he reminded me, "But not everyone buckles. Our Lynn fought back and ensured that the South Dakota state Rodeo tournament would go on without any restrictions or measures."

My pride in her surprised me. No living politician had earned it before Lynn Norton-Bower.

Jack smirked when he saw my face.

"Damn fools. They have no idea whose blood runs in her veins. No one, but God, can move Jerome if he believes himself to be on the true path."

I recalled my last time with Lynn's father in the Black Hills and his request to watch out for his daughter as she continues her fight for freedom. Concern for her and our country mixed with the pride in my chest, tapping into the growing urgency to turn things around.

Maybe sensing my unrest, Jack's tone changed as he began to grumble about Pax Eden and the recent revelation about their monstrosity fund being tasked with helping Dems in their 2020 runs across the country.

"They funneled nearly $600 million into the federal and state races."

"How's Alfa?" I asked, moving us away from subjects beyond our Doctrine's reach.

Jack laughed and told me how they had done some "charity work," helping law enforcement catch arsonists across Western Oregon.

"Shida was involved, and they put those cells down. But we gleaned nothing new. Just pawns tasked with breaking stuff up." He paused thoughtfully. "And Dex. Exemplary leader!"

He really is.

"Anything on the migrants? The Chicago strain?" I hoped for something new for my mind to digest.

"We got the smoking gun, but nobody's fingerprints," he mumbled, admitting that the Chicago strain did make unique appearances in some riot zones. Still, it was impossible to tie it to anything beyond that, as no migrants were ever found again.

"Good work today," I started the briefing with Jenny, Beta, and the Old Glory team. I'd arrived at their location in a nearby town less than an hour after finishing with my father.

Observing both teams, I could sense the camaraderie in their loose stance and easy banter.

Time for the hammer.

"Our final exercise begins tomorrow at 1900 hours. Brown Team," I said, referring to Old Glory and looking at Ganbold, who nodded in response, "will have forty-eight hours to escape the zone." Turning to Deshi, I finished, "while the Black team will be tasked with killing us."

Ganbold looked confused, and Deshi asked everyone's question, "Us?"

Smiling wickedly, I answered to the whole group, "Yes. I'll be joining the Brown Team."

They all exchanged looks, but Deshi again read my mind.

"You asked for it."

Ganbold looked dumbfounded, and I felt sorry for him, his team... and myself.

We're going to need him to deal with the monster, I thought, recalling my conversation and the haunting image of Ye Zhang, the monster's son.

BLUE ON BLUE

– Training Grounds, Taiwan –
Wednesday, September 16, 2020

The sun seemed to struggle to stay in the sky as the darkness relentlessly encroached on its domain.

"You weren't kidding about them," huffed Ganbold, still deep breathing from the strenuous climb along the rocky mountain.

Before we headed out, I'd dropped a hint to him and his team regarding the true nature of our pursuers: "Be your best because we're about to be hunted and haunted." They'd smirked with confidence, except for Ganbold whose eyes narrowed while he scratched his five o'clock shadow.

Now they know.

"How's the morale?" I asked him, checking the paint ball ammo in my assault rifle.

Ganbold swiveled his head to look at what remained of our team and then back to me.

"We left twelve strong, and now we're seven." His eyes were wide. "All taken out without us knowing. Just gone."

It was impressive how Beta had managed to whittle us down without even being seen.

Ganbold shook his head, a glint of admiration in his eyes.

"My boys are all hard men, battle-tested. But if we hadn't worked with them until now, I don't know how they would truly react."

Wait until you SEE them.

Ganbold extended his neck and turned to look up to the edge of the woods.

"I've never dreaded a forest as much as I do now." His face was smiling, but his tone was genuine.

The exercise had a simple boundary: Brown escapes and Black chases. But nobody said that the Brown team just had to run.

Time to see if Deshi accounted for that.

I paused.

"How do you feel about turning the tables on them?" His face hardened with every nod.

"At least we'll see them finally," he murmured.

"Be careful what you wish for."

Nature hooted and howled as the night creatures left their hiding places to roam the dark forest. The remaining OGT team was spread across the forest's edge. I chose the location, knowing very well that once deep in the woods on the mountain, our chances against Beta would become non-existent.

One of the Mongols pinged us for a possible movement, and I trained my eyes downrange at the rocky terrain below.

Something moved, but my thermal scan caught nothing. It all remained dark green, with zero highlighted signatures.

"They're coming. Brace yourselves," I whispered on our comms as the first suppressed shots hit our side.

Without the ability to see their heat signatures, every little movement drew our fire.

Ganbold scored the lone hit as the shadowy figures forced us back into the forest after losing three more Mongols to their precise shots.

Four left. I wonder if they'll even have the chance to SEE them.

Beta managed to outpace our retreat and then finally showed themselves.

"Monsters!" A voice from OGT called loudly as a dark figure with blazing red eyes appeared momentarily, jumping and tackling one of the Mongols. The caller, immediately shot in the back, dropped to the ground.

"What the fuck?" hissed Ganbold, hiding behind a tree near me.

There was something surreal in experiencing his shock and trepidation as he realized the Rogues' abilities augmented by the new gear.

"You took one of them down," I whispered back. "Trust me. You earned their respect."

His smile was rising when a creature of nightmares—a small and slender humanoid skull with red eyes—appeared behind the former Green Beret, grabbed him, and placed a black blade to his neck.

I didn't even have time to warn him.

"Yes, you earned our respect, but now you're done," replied the distorted female voice.

Jenny. I almost laughed out loud. *So fucking fast, that one.*

Ganbold dropped his gun and lifted his hands in surrender. Jenny dragged him back into the foliage, leaving me alone.

I sighed and changed the comms to the open channel so both teams would hear me.

"Brown-leader, Overlord, over."

"Go ahead, Overlord, over," responded Ganbold from wherever Beta held him.

"Exercise is over. Collect your team and exit the area. Good work, Brown-team."

Ganbold appeared on the open channel, confirming OGT was returning to the barracks.

There was an opening among the trees, maybe ten feet in diameter, where the moonlight shone on the earth, penetrating the otherwise thick wood. I took off my NVG set and dropped my assault rifle and small arms on a rock before I walked to its center, hands empty.

They began to appear around me like nearly-invisible, red-eyed ghosts. It was hard to discern who was who until one dropped his weapons at his feet and walked into the clearing.

Deshi.

The creature's intense red orbs increased my deep longing for my own Skull and Skin.

"What now?" Deshi overrode the voice scrambler, allowing his authentic voice to be heard.

I looked around at Beta, slowly appearing in the clearing with Deshi and me.

They want to test me.

My eyes returned to Deshi.

"You still got one more Brown-team to take down."

His expression hidden behind the Skull, he switched to the voice scrambler to make his voice threatening.

"You're at a disadvantage."

Images of the Demon beating Nico broke through my mind's well-developed barriers, boiling my blood in seconds.

"Teach him," demanded the Beast.

"Prove it," I replied, dropping into a battle stance.

Deshi launched forward with the finesse of a blade dancer, and I barely escaped the ferocity of his first strikes.

After a hardened fist hit my ribs, in the time that it took Deshi to swivel and cut my legs from underneath me, I was yanked into a memory.

Nico on his back, his shirt torn open, and chest visible. Using his boot, The Demon moved the shirt remains aside, exposing the cross and tear tattoo. "Was that Latin you used? Did you pray?" Laughing, he challenged, "Where is your Christian God now?"

I hit the ground hard, jolted from one memory to another.

In the darkness. Alone.
The kid screams in agony.
A decision forming, my legs pulling me forward.

"You think you deserve to see? Can you embrace the pain to redeem yourself?" taunted the Beast.

Deshi charged forward and, feeling my moment stolen, my anger overwhelmed every sense.

Beta-leader's kick missed, and I unleashed my fury at him in a roar, feeling the Beast consenting to join my movements as we met in a ferocious exchange of blows.

The Skull and Skin hardened his defenses, enhancing his superior martial art skills.

No pain was felt as I rained punches on Deshi, seeking out soft spots. After several minutes of combat, he made the mistake of regrouping to take a breath. The last of my strength funneled into an aerial kick that sent him flying.

"Do it. Show them!" commanded the Beast.

It took all the *Sense* I could muster to not charge and kick Deshi straight in the Skull. Luckily for us both, he rose to his feet and bowed, conceding the match before my inner conflict was determined.

My anger dissipated and I bowed back, taking a longer deep breath to let all the intensity go. Deshi advanced and we locked our arms, clasping hands in silent honor.

Stepping back again, Deshi began to thump his right fist on his chest just above his heart, and all the Rogues joined him, viscerally connecting our ancient kinship as brothers and sisters.

Ignoring the time, Ganbold had suggested both teams drive to the local bar to celebrate the end of the exercise.

Seated in a side booth, I watched them by the bar, all raising toast after toast, Rogues and Mongols together.

They deserve it, I thought as I sipped on my orange juice, wishing it was a mocha and wondering how my queen fared across the ocean.

Deshi and Ganbold were involved in a profound exchange, faces animated and smiling. I mused at how much different it was from the wild-eyed expression I'd seen when I'd reached the barracks and he'd admitted, "I've seen many things in my life, lost many people and friends. That Dragon helmet will probably haunt my dreams."

Jenny broke off from the group and walked toward my table, beer in hand.

"May I?"

When I smiled, she slid into the booth across from me, smirking at my glass of fruit juice.

We looked at each other for a long moment before she finally squinted her eyes in fake irritation.

"Just say it."

I lifted my open hands in surrender.

"I'm not Liam."

She laughed and softened her tone, "Just say it."

"I'm surprised you're not there with him." I motioned toward Deshi, who was still engaged with Ganbold.

She followed my gaze, and a genuine smile sneaked across her face. By the time her eyes returned to mine, she was fully flushed.

Mmmhmmm. That's what I thought.

"Life is weird." Jenny's face turned serious again. "But I wanted to check on you, Sir."

Her care felt good in my empty, cold chest, and I shrugged a half-answer.

"That fight with Deshi... it's like what you did back in the Cape."

I shrugged again, and Jenny tilted her head back, scrutinizing me momentarily.

"It feels connected to your vengeance, Sir." She looked from me back to her bottle and turned it on the table. "I know the feeling, and it's only growing as we get closer."

Caught between my concern about her growing agitation and another riddle of parallel experiences, I remained silent.

"Fine." Her tone was resigned yet amused. "What did you make of Beta's reaction after your tussle?"

The image of the Rogues thumping on their chests warmed mine again.

"Maybe it means that we'll all fight together one day."

First, China's monster and then ours.

DISCREET

The almost two-day journey from Taiwan was full of twists, turns, and stops in order to shield the route from prying eyes. This last leg toward the US installation in the mountainous Gobi region of southwest Mongolia was particularly harrowing. The closer we got to China, the more the Beast bristled against the shackles and the more my vexed mind wrestled with the ever-growing list of riddles.

Closing my eyes, I struggled to leave behind my ache for Dani and the kids, my never-ending fear for their safety, and my growing concern that I would be forced to choose or be split in two. Worries about Todd and Shemtov and wonderings about Alfa intertwined themselves.

Why did he really pick Jenny?

Her Chinese ethnicity, language command, and skills made her the optimal choice over any other Alfa, but it nagged at me that Jack might be leveraging the pain of her personal story. After all, my father tended to have multiple agendas and deeper insights driving them.

She's a warrior, but she suffered greatly. I'm going to have to keep an eye on her.

I shifted in the little jet seat, against the increasing unrest inside.

And why the hell is he being so mercurial every time I ask about the breach?

I took a deep breath, trying to navigate my increasing resentment with Romulus.

Using the *Sense*, I set aside what I had no control over in the moment and focused on the mission and the question I'd been asking myself since Jack had mentioned Zhang's son. At the end of the day, it would be my decision alone.

And the price...

I was glad to see the airstrip ahead. Old Glory's rich history with the American government meant the company had an assigned private hangar within the secret US forward base just twenty miles from China.

As soon as we touched down, Ganbold left us to handle company matters. The rest of us masked and blended among the rest of the Old Glory crew, heading to our new temporary home. Beneath the large silver hangar with two choppers, a half-dozen vehicles, and sleep quarters around it, was a restricted area where the Rogues would stay until further notice.

"Shower!" yelled one of the Rogues, and the rest hooted and hollered as they stamped into the barracks.

"I'm going to clean up and catch up on the news from home. Ping me when Ganbold is back and settled."

Deshi responded to my request with a nod before following the others.

The shower was average and the news was dismal. Dragon cases were in another uptick, likely to continue through the typical flu season. The nation remained divided about the path for containment, with states enacting various approaches to mitigate the pandemic. Lawlessness continued unabated in areas controlled by the Dems and district attorneys funded by the Open Borders Initiative decriminalized offenses, further undermining the cops who risked their lives to arrest those who hurt the public.

When my phone chirped, I turned off the laptop and waited.

Ganbold punched Deshi's shoulder as they walked into my room, both of them laughing.

Good. We'll need this.

Once they were settled, I explained that the plan called for OGT to continue training openly while the Rogues stayed confined to the hangar. We discussed a few more formalities, and then I left them.

Ready to scout the base, I recalled seeing a watch tower nearby and figured it might be a good place to have a moment to myself. Lifting my neck gaiter and dropping my shades, I walked outside.

I climbed up the tower and surprised an armed female guard inside the observation deck. The striking young redhead seemed to relax when I chuckled genuinely and suggested she ask Ganbold to confirm my OGT affiliation.

Once she left, I used the powered binoculars on deck to look out at the other installations in the base. The unease in my chest crackled, seeing just how close we were to the government's reach.

Baker... the leak... who knows who else is involved.

I called the elusive government man the Spider for a reason.

Texting Romulus, I requested updates regarding our breach, only to be stonewalled again.

Damn it, Dad.

Turning my gaze south toward the faraway mountains belonging to another nation, trepidation and excitement reverberated through my body.

Zhang, I'm coming for you.

The entity woke up in me.

"Have you made up your mind?" The Beast's question sounded more like a dare.

No.

WAITING

"**I** have a possible incoming drone. Ten mikes distance from OGT," called Jenny from her desk. "Flagging it for the RCC," she added, maintaining standard protocol.

For the last five days, she and Deshi had helped me while the Old Glory team went out of the wire for hard training. Together, we monitored their exercises from the secured command and control room, within our section of the company hangar.

While OGT did report some side looks from others in the base, it was to be expected. They did their best to stay discreet when outside the hangar because everyone looks in places full of all government branches and civilian contractors like Old Glory, but the drone was a new escalation.

"On screen," I commanded.

While Ganbold and his ten-man team traversed a rocky valley just south of the base, the Eye caught the drone coming from the east, enjoying the cover of the falling sun.

"A very advanced model. Unsure about weapon capabilities." Jenny's tone conveyed concern.

The system marked the drone with a red square around it, and we watched as the small craft darted forward, dropping lower toward the ground.

"Nine mikes for contact." Her voice was tight with this last update, and I figured she was sharing my concern that the drone was armed.

I felt the urge to hail Romulus and Remus to help me sort the right decision until Deshi appeared at my side, his eyes on the main screen.

"We're lucky to have the Eye," he mumbled.

He was right. Having Old Glory's only satellite tasked to your area was a great privilege and often the difference between life and death, but the advanced system couldn't help me choose the right path.

It's just a machine.

"Instruct OGT-leader to continue business as usual," I ordered, sensing the growing pit in my stomach.

Ganbold's voice came on the comms after Jenny relayed my order. He sounded confident and even somewhat jovial in spite of the news of the unknown danger flying toward him. His unexpected response quickly reminded me of something I'd paused on while reading his file.

Buddhist. Maybe that's the reason, or maybe it's that he has no shackles. If it were me, would I...? I stopped. There was no time for an inquiry into my own faith.

It was seven minutes to contact, and I sensed Deshi's eyes on me. Then Jenny's.

"It makes no sense to attack the team. Hopefully, they're trying to get a better look at the faces." I searched the eyes of the two Rogues. "If we do evasive maneuvers now, we risk exposing our satellite capabilities." I didn't have to add that an advanced attack drone could easily hunt a few foot soldiers unless they have the proper countermeasures. They knew that.

Not fully satisfied, we all returned our focus to the large wall screen, where Ganbold and his team continued trekking in a loose column.

"One minute," called Jenny on the mission channel.

Stay on course.

"Damn," murmured Deshi, shaking his head when the drone exemplified high stealth capability, likely filming as it shadowed OGT.

To my relief, OGT appeared to not notice at all as the drone did its thing and then darted away.

"He's a good leader." Deshi's voice was full of relief. "I'm glad he's here for what's coming."

"You're running out of time," provoked the Beast.

I know!

Ganbold and his team reached their Humvees and rode toward the base in a three-car column formation. With the sun making its final descent behind the mountains, we kept our eyes on them as they drove back.

Over the next hour, other Rogues joined us in the command room, but nobody spoke. All eyes remained glued to the screen where the Old Glory lead car eventually reached the outer base gate.

Ganbold's hidden body cam gave us a live feed with audio, and Jenny projected it onto the screen adjacent to the Eye's view.

The guards knew OGT, and the watch commander walked over as Ganbold exited his vehicle unarmed and with a relaxed posture.

A civilian contractor company out of South Carolina had been hired to handle all security for the base and effectively be the ones dealing with Mongol authorities. This was an old practice, enabling whichever US administration was in power to gain a layer of plausible deniability with the host country, Congress, and its committees, not to mention foreign adversaries. Old Glory had a long-standing relationship with them, and had never had any issues.

The watch commander seemed apologetic as he asked Ganbold to order his men out of the vehicles. He mumbled something about a "routine checkup."

The large former Green Beret seemed unfazed and clapped the watch commander's shoulder before he yelled for his men to disembark.

"There," said Deshi, pointing at the feed.

We watched as the lone man that had been observing from behind the guards casually strolled and shadowed the watch commander as he ascertained each Old Glory team member's identity.

"A spook," murmured one of the Rogues as Ganbold's hidden camera captured the new guest, who continued hovering but didn't get involved in the screening process.

If it bugged him, the OGT-leader didn't show it. When the watch commander approved their entry into the base, Ganbold smiled and wished all the guards a good night.

"Do you understand now why we kept you locked up?" Deshi asked his Rogues. They grumbled, but they all nodded in understanding.

The tension was building within my chest, and I needed time alone.

"Let Ganbold know to find me once they arrive and settle in."

Once seated at my tiny desk, I turned off the light and settled into the pitch darkness. With only the sound of the air conditioning in the background, I could finally focus on the riddles.

Whoever authorized the drone and ID check-up was from our end. I doubted it was the hosting Mongolian government that would benefit nothing from such a move. *They fear China even more than we do.*

"So, who is it then?" wondered the Beast.

They're Americans... could be anyone. This might be our only chance to learn about the assault on our nation.

"Are you ready to break him?"

My mind culled through everything I'd learned about Zhang on paper and in the flesh. He was a ruthless fighter, but this wasn't just about killing a warrior. To force him to reveal and betray his people and nation, I would have to be willing to commit to the worst I could fathom.

Wait... isn't that what...?

The haunting conversation between Professor Bach and the news anchor I'd heard on the way back from Big Bear with Ari started to replay in phrases and segments.

What was it he said to the anchor who asked for a more straightforward answer?

It took a moment, but the words of the professor finally came together: "I can't. You don't belong among those who've crossed the threshold of Good and Evil, hands bloodied in the making of human history."

I leaned back into my chair, hands on the desk, fingers stretched flat on the cold metal surface. Nearly a week had passed since our arrival, and my inability to reach a decision wore on me.

It has to end.

"*Then look,*" the Beast challenged.

Memories of being in Yachats, checking out the motorcycles outside the shop, and the origins of the angst plagued me. The Beast seemed eager for me to continue pulling on the thread, so I did. In the silent darkness of my room, I let my mind descend.

Each generation has its own traumas and the endless recollection of where you were when the event happened. My life changed when the planes hit the New York City Towers on September 11, 2001.

At the time of the terrorist attack, I had lived in Venice for about two years since discharging from the Marines. And worse than the shock of our country under attack and thousands of lives eliminated in an instant, was the indifference and lack of empathy where I lived. It was as though the smoldering ruins and the thousands of lives were insignificant.

And then another blow. The phone call that night from my dad who told me Grandpa had a heart attack shortly after seeing the event on TV.

I'd returned to the Ranch and found Ulysses was dying. When I realized he could still think and communicate well, I'd decided to spend every moment possible with him.

During the few days we had together, my grandfather told me about his military past, enlightening the shady spots he'd always kept to himself. He'd hinted at Jack's difficulty growing up under his role and lamented that while it was necessary, it also had ramifications.

"You, my boy, have lost your innocence because of me and what I've done to your father."

My eyes popped open. It was hard to hear those words back then, and again now in the blackness of my room. I could sense the Beast on edge, watching my willingness to partake in the recollection.

I took a deep breath and relaxed back into the chair, closing my eyes.

"What's my path then?" I had asked Grandpa, willing to sacrifice my new civilian life back in California.

He was so frail, but his eyes blazed with life as he spoke, "You cannot escape who you are, Tanner. You were meant to serve." He relaxed after that, a small tear appearing in his eye. "I will soon be with her."

We buried Grandpa two days later, next to Grandma, in a small meadow near the main house. When the ceremony ended, I told my father I was ready to serve again. It wasn't until much later that I learned Ulysses had prepped Romulus and Remus about my readiness. He had even bet it would happen shortly after he passed away.

Jack and Custer had surprised me a few days later, hinting about the Doctrine and the Path of a Rogue. My father further revealed that all my harsh training since childhood was meant to prepare me for this service.

"Is this a part of the military? Government?" I'd inquired.

"Far from it, Son," Jack had replied and said nothing else.

Fueled by Ulysses's passing and the attack on New York, I'd agreed to the "tryouts."

Every Rogue had to first be proven worthy of the path and training involved. The first challenge was the "Blood Test."

In my case, Jack and Custer exposed me to a horrific crime committed in Missouri. A biker gang had hassled an Army Ranger and his family while they ate in a restaurant. When one of the bikers assaulted his wife in the bathroom, the Ranger had charged the gang, enabling his wife and kids to run out to the car and get help. Sadly, when the cops arrived, the Ranger was dead after being stabbed repeatedly.

I was surprised to learn that while the police didn't have any leads, Jack and Custer had located the gang and their hideout. Stunned by the conversation, I was also strangely elated to see how my test was connected to the horrific event.

"You are to seek them out and eliminate them *all*. Burn their hideout and get out of the area undetected," he instructed. "Do all of this with the handgun of your choice, ammo, and a battle knife."

Custer had come to speak with me before they dropped me a few miles from the gang hideout up a forested mountain in upstate Missouri. He wondered about my thoughts, and I admitted to concerns about killing Americans without a trial.

"But I am also willing to face wickedness."

He'd smiled before saying the words that had haunted me ever since: "Evil doesn't hesitate."

"Who said that?" I'd asked.

"Just a tough, disobedient Marine," replied Custer with the shadow of a sad smile.

The gang was half-decent in skills, posting some guards and making efforts to patrol their little compound. None of it helped them. I massacred them all, taking a moment with the gang leader so that he'd know why I was sending him to hell.

The memory had spiked my heart rate and desire for violence.

You were with me back then, pushing on my blade. Why haven't you talked with me?

"Because your body was committed, but your mind refused to acknowledge my birthplace," answered the Beast.

The temptation to open my physical eyes and turn on the light grew, but it was clear that this would mean just one more retreat. Instead, I took a moment to wonder where the road would lead if not stopped by my mind.

Bogotá?

"*Yes. Don't look away again,*" echoed the Beast with satisfaction as it receded beneath the surface of my conscious mind.

My eyes opened, and my right hand pressed the lights button.

"Evil doesn't hesitate," I whispered.

My decision was made, although it had a price.

I need help here.

It had been a few weeks since the rollout of the Aides, and Beta and Jenny had plunged deep into using the AIs to improve their performance. But not me. I'd enabled my Aide to streamline communications with the other Rogues but did nothing else to engage with It.

"Aide," I called into the earbud.

"I'm here, Tanner," the Aide responded, sounding ready.

What are you?

"Can you communicate with another aide without being eavesdropped on?"

"Yes, a private link can facilitate both advanced and secured communications. It will remain as such unless the three authenticators override my encryption."

I can work with this, but can I trust the Aide? I took a long deep breath. *There is only one way to find out.*

Jenny's eyes remained wide while listening to my plan, and it was time to drive the point home.

"This is all on my Independent Authority, not the RCC."

Her face remained unreadable, eyes fixed on the noise scrambler working on my desk.

"Is this going too far for you, Jenny? Speak your mind," I commanded her.

A vicious, gorgeous smile rose on her face.

"Semper Fidelis, Sir. That is my answer."

She bought a ticket to a ride that I'm still figuring out.

I was moved by her use of the words no other Rogue had uttered.

"But how can we communicate with Alfa?" she asked, knowing very well that we were monitored and so were our comms.

"Make sure that your aide…" I started.

"Jesse," she chimed with a smirk.

"I'm not addressing your aide like that," I grumbled, drawing a laugh from her.

"Just make sure to only communicate via private links." I suppressed an eye roll.

She confirmed and rose to leave the room.

Ten minutes later, she sent a private message that the mission was completed.

Here goes nothing.

I went to bed exhausted and was just dropping off to sleep when the ear vibration startled me.

The first few seconds were full of trepidation.

Did It betray me?

As my father updated me about various events, my heart calmed, unable to sense a ruse from my lifelong trainer.

"Police in Chicago are telling people that they're understaffed and cannot get to all 911 calls..." he said, describing the abysmal conditions in the Windy City. He explained how the social media giants were beginning to wade into politics and the upcoming election. "It's not our purview, but there are enough smoking guns to show that conservatives are being blacklisted on many platforms."

I don't know why I was surprised to hear about a new riot in Lexington, Kentucky.

"We're suspecting some outside interference," Jack continued, detailing how moving trucks were spotted bringing gear for those willing to cause mayhem across the city. "The Chicago variant is wild there, but is now so widespread that we can't tie it to anything. We sent Alfa to Lexington to see if we can spot anything." His final update was about Chad and his growing contribution to the company and family life on the Ranch.

When he didn't mention my recent secret transgression, I asked his opinion about the drone and gate incident.

"I grant you that this is our side. But who knows..." was his first reply. "Just remain on course and keep Beta hidden."

His ambiguity bothered me, but there was more to discuss.

"When are we leaving?"

Jack laughed softly but urged patience, explaining that Custer would be at the base soon.

"He's there for the military, so don't contact him unless it's an emergency."

"Yes, Sir."

When the call ended, Ganbold came up on the comms to tell me he had arrived.

The moon was covered by clouds, enabling deeper darkness to roam the earth. But I could see the one heat signature at the top of the structure through my NVG goggles.

I opened the watch tower observation deck door to find that Ganbold had arrived before me and emptied it of its guards.

With the door closed behind, the dimmed red light inside the space allowed me to remove my NVG.

"It's a good spot. I've used it many times," affirmed the large man while my eyes adjusted and took in the space. He was still dressed in his dirty BDU.

We walked to the large open window facing south and talked openly. After the mission debrief, I asked about his take on the incidents.

Ganbold grumbled simple truth, "We need to leave this place before they start checking more."

Instinctively, we both turned our eyes south toward China.

"Are you following events back home?" I wondered.

Ganbold surprised me with acute knowledge of all that had befallen our nation since the pandemic started.

"I wish more people knew what communism and socialism are really about..." Relaxing his posture a bit, he opened up about how his family left China, seeking a more accessible life, which they eventually found on the West Coast.

"But now I see these... kids almost... burning our flag, waving the hammer and sickle." He shook his head.

He needed to vent, and I was eager to learn more about the man tasked with being bait for the monster.

"Look at my men." Ganbold's tone hardened. "The Chinese took everything from them... and then some. They meet this grief on the battlefield, fighting for their people beyond the border. They don't compromise on what's right and what's wrong."

He snorted in disdain.

"It's funny. I lived in California since my birth, shortly after they arrived. Yet, right here," he said, pointing outside to the empty black land, "I feel more in America than back there."

The big fellow made sense, but his next words scrambled me.

"What made you come here? Away from your family? The world is falling apart." I sensed him hinting at the televised events surrounding my life, yet he didn't bring it up.

My eyes stayed focused on the black emptiness outside the tower as I leaned against the windowsill, struggling to ride the waves of contradicting thoughts and conflicting emotions battling for territory inside me. But all the pieces, broken as they may have been, pointed at one answer.

"I'm here to fix my mistakes."

He gave me a long look, his face half-hidden within the shadows cast by the dim red ceiling light.

"And what if you can't?"

Ganbold walked past me but stopped to squeeze my shoulder before he left the tower.

I've got to try.

I slumped at the window, feeling the weight of my shackles pulling me east and the road of vengeance calling me south.

NEED TO KNOW

I double-checked myself in the bathroom's mirror, ensuring my presentation was up to code.

Old habits die hard.

Satisfied, I stepped into my room and messaged Ganbold and Deshi to verify that the hangar was ready for today's late afternoon visit.

My body screamed to be out and on mission as I took my seat at the small desk. It had been more than a week of waiting for the General's arrival, and it had stretched my patience in more than one way.

I hope his arrival means it's time.

Opening the laptop, I began to scan the updates. Out in Lexington, Alfa didn't find anything noteworthy. Back in South Dakota, Lynn continued her opposition to the Dragon measures.

Badass. Hopefully, others will follow your courageous leadership.

I noticed a flagged update on my list with the RCC and read the report about Canada's prime minister discussing the pandemic, mentioning the "once-in-a-lifetime opportunity for a great reset" and "a new beginning for our world." A woman standing behind the prime minister caught my attention. She seemed to be in her late sixties, with short straight brown hair and blue eyes.

"Aide, freeze the video and zoom in on the woman behind the Canadian prime minister."

I was using the AI more these days after trusting It with my scheme.

The Aide did as requested.

"Who is she?" I asked.

"This is Claudia Kruger, CEO of Pax Eden, Inc."

"Continue." I cringed, watching the Canadian leader reveal nothing of value beyond her platitudes.

The video ended and the screen went black, but my mind raced to connect the dots.

The Great Reset. Columbo and his letter... Dad's behavior around this...

The vibration shook me, as if my thoughts were being monitored.

Jack started our call by reassuring me that they'd been keeping up with Dani and the kids daily.

"Your son is fascinating," he mentioned, which elicited both pride and foreboding. "Anyway, Custer has landed, and his convoy is heading over. Ganbold will handle the event."

I acknowledged his updates, internally concluding that this wasn't the time to check further about my initial concerns but find Deshi instead.

Deshi and I were seated at our command and control with one of the other Rogues manning the large bank of computers. One of the wall screens had the convoy pinned on a map as they made their way to the base.

"Does Ganbold know about Custer's true identity?" Deshi asked.

I shook my head.

"Old Glory personnel know Jack solely as the company CEO."

"I wonder what he thinks of us," Deshi wondered.

Old Glory personnel generally knew nothing of the Doctrine and the Rogues.

Does Ganbold suspect?

"He's probably thinking that we belong to the company's 'black ops' division," I responded, noticing the deep furrow in his brow and wondering about this man who stood next to me.

"How and when did you meet the General? And my father?"

His dark eyes narrowed briefly, but then a smile broke across his strong face.

"I guess we're in story time, aren't we?" He smirked and told me his tale.

Deshi's family had also barely escaped China.

"We were very lucky, as my mother worked for a European diplomat who got us all visas for a trip, from which we never returned…" He revealed how his family settled on the East Coast, his growing up there, and the eventual decision to enlist when he was eighteen.

On screen, I noted that Custer's convoy was due to arrive at the base's main gate.

"We only figured it out after we fought each other in the jungle," continued Deshi, explaining his prior connection with Ganbold. They had both served in the Green Berets around the same time. "I never operated with him but knew of his excellent reputation." Deshi's respect for Ganbold was evident in both his tone and expression. "I did a few tours but got out early before it became my life. Got my law degree and managed to do some interesting stuff. It was then your father and Custer found me."

"Please go on," I implored him.

His face hardened as he spoke of the choice to enter the "tryouts" and then the grueling Hell Year.

"Black Hills, Brother."

"Black Hills," I echoed the words and sentiment while marveling once again how my family's estate meant so much to so many.

Deshi smiled.

"We always thought your dad would terminate us throughout the year. The General, on the other hand, surprised us all with his warm moments."

I smiled back, thinking about my own childhood and how correct he was about the differences between our Doctrine's commanders.

He squinted his eyes and tapped his fingers on the desk.

Does he want to ask me something?

The moment passed when we suddenly realized that the convoy was going directly to the hangar without any prior stops.

"Let's get ready for him." I clapped his back, looking around the command and control space, ensuring everything was tidy.

Masked Ganbold, who knew nothing of our relationship with the General, presented Custer with complete formality, despite the fact that Remus wore a civilian outfit.

Custer turned to look at Ganbold and pointed to the mask.

"If you do this for me, no need. I already got the bug and am feeling good."

OGT-leader removed his mask and continued into the mission update, asking Deshi for access to the main screen.

"We leave in twenty-four hours, heading to the Bayingolin Mongol Autonomous Prefecture in the

Xinjiang Province," explained Ganbold. "It's where we'll find the target facility."

BMAP, as the district was referred to in short, was known for Chinese military activity against the Uighur population in the region.

Deshi must have known that, as he chimed in, "There is much surveillance there... high tech..."

Custer motioned with his head for Ganbold to continue.

"OGT's mission is to infiltrate the district and obtain damning material about the abuses against the Uighurs. We also know about a secondary location, in a nearby forest, which we have no further details on. As for mission control," Ganbold motioned toward me, "Overlord will provide that unless Old Glory Command intervenes."

The General smiled.

"Excellent. Now, please leave and await my call for my drive back."

Ganbold remained impassive and then smiled back, acknowledging the General before leaving the room.

It was weird to see Custer embrace Deshi with genuine warmth on his face.

Like seeing your father hugging your stepbrother that you didn't know your whole life.

The thought ended when the General got to me with his bear hug.

The virus is not stopping us!

Custer looked at Deshi and me, beaming.

"Look at you. Rogues working together for the first time." His expression sobered quickly. "The world is changing, and so are we."

"What about Ganbold?" I wondered. "Wouldn't he suspect... with you staying here with us?"

He smiled and waved his giant hand dismissively.

"Old Glory operators know to focus on their lanes, and he is one of the best." We nodded in agreement. "Now, let's talk about your mission." The General grabbed a chair and motioned for us to follow suit.

The plan called for us to shadow OGT while avoiding detection by the Chinse and our side.

"We were able to locate underground forward locations for both teams to use," he explained, adding how Ganbold and his team would scout both the primary and forest facilities, attracting Zhang into the open.

Deshi and I exchanged a quick look.

Yeah. He's not exactly explaining what "attracting Zhang" entails.

"We have CI within Zhang's close circle. We'll let you know when the time is right for the abduction." Custer's dark eyes locked on mine as he finished.

Deshi took his leave and as the door hissed closed, Custer spoke again, "You have a tough job ahead of you. When you're done, that cave will be his last rest."

Feeling the Beast dance at the invitation to violence, I answered, "Yes, Sir."

I leaned back in my chair, looking at the main hangar live feed, and noticed Ganbold waiting by Custer's two vehicles and men.

"Does he know they're bait?"

Custer shook his head slowly, eyes on Ganbold as well. He faced me again, his voice low and somber, "This outfit he leads is a special team. They are all dedicated freedom fighters who banded together to offer their services against China. Whatever they think of the mission doesn't matter. Both Ganbold and his team are fully committed."

It was no surprise to me when the General asserted that he'd remain in the area until the end of the operation. But when he revealed that the President would be watching personally, as he was counting heavily on this mission to succeed, I paused.

"Frankly, Son..." His voice was strained. "The President isn't that wrong, even without knowing anything beyond the official Old Glory mission. He just doesn't know how much worse it is. With what's going on back home, we need this one, and this is the best place to use you."

"I will make it work, Sir," I answered, expanding my chest against the weight of my shackles and decision to use "Independent Authority."

He matched my long deep breath before leaning toward me.

"How are you, Son?"

"Ready, Sir." There was no opening in me, so I assured him with what I could offer.

The General seemed unconvinced for a moment before he looked at his watch and rose from his chair.

He extended his right hand for a strong handshake while his left squeezed my shoulder.

"I'll be waiting for your return," he grumbled, trying to disguise his emotions.

Thinking of my family, friends, and all the suffering back home, I promised, "I will come back."

He's just my first stop on this path.

INSERTION

– US FOB, Mongolia –
Friday, October 2, 2020

Staring at the Skin, Skull, and the rest of my equipment displayed on my bed, I could feel the Beast's restless yearning.

Not much longer, I assured It.

We had spent our last day checking our gear and reviewing mission details. Both teams were under lockdown to avoid any chance of outside interference.

The phone chirp interrupted my thoughts about all the ways I would likely use that equipment to eliminate the monsters that threatened my country, my freedom, and my family.

Perfect timing, Dad, I thought as I read his text: "Godspeed." *Wait, what's…?* When I opened the attachments, I gasped at the surge of gratitude and pain.

My heart raced as I scrolled through the new photos of my family repeatedly.

Why do the creatures grow faster when I'm gone? The racing stilled to an ache. *I want to call her.*

I sat the phone on the bed beside me, closed my eyes, and ordered my mind until the ache dissolved. Quickly, I erased all the files from the device and turned my eyes to the Skull.

The shackles can't interfere with this mission.

When I heard the knock on the door, I clicked it open to find the large man dressed in desert-mountain camouflaged BDU. According to the plan, Ganbold was the only one who would initially know about the Rogues trailing them into China. It was inevitable that the rest of his team would learn about it, but now was not the time. Furthermore, our travel was restricted to nighttime, with predesignated resting spots for each of the teams.

"Are you ready for this?" I asked.

His hard olive-skinned face softened a bit before he chuckled lightly.

"I'm exactly where I'm needed. A man cannot ask for more than that."

I smiled and stood to hug him, suppressing my turmoil.

How can I do this?

He left the room, and my eyes returned to the Skull staring at me.

"*It's time!*" boomed the Beast.

It was dark outside when the Old Glory staff drove Ganbold and his team to the front gate, where they'd begin on foot.

"Assemble," I called on the Beta channel as I walked out of my room, dressed in the Skin, holding the Skull in my right hand. With an eighty-pound sack of equipment strapped to my back, an assault rifle slightly dangling from the strap across my body, and a gnawing hunger for action, I was ready.

The team hustled into the empty hangar and readied by one of the side doors.

"Wear your Skulls," I commanded as I lifted and slowly pulled my own over my head.

The Aides took a moment to sync all of us while our HUD showed all of the essential details.

"RCC confirms invisibility," reported Jenny.

Jack had tasked the Eye to cover our departure and ensure that we remained unseen to the prying eyes of other satellites.

"Good. Activate beacons so that they'll see us," I instructed before sneaking out of the hangar and into the dark night.

"I see them," whispered Deshi, directing his Aide to share his visuals with us. A small screen on my HUD showed OGT creeping forward below us. We were on a mountain ridge, looking down into the valley that led to the Chinese border, barely half a mile away.

Our short trek south paid off and we quickly managed to close the distance with Ganbold and his men, using our stealth tech, Skin-augmented mobility, and Skull HUD that revealed the path in the otherwise pitch-dark night.

When another slender creature with reptile skin, and a black skull with dimmed red eyes, appeared beside me, my HUD helped to ID Jenny, as the Rogues were otherwise nearly indistinguishable.

"Are you good?" I asked her on a private channel.

"Yes. Been in touch with Dex. They're ready."

"This isn't what I wanted, Jenny," I answered, feeling the sudden weight of my chosen path.

She lowered her head for a moment and then looked back at me.

"It's time for me to face my demons." Her wavering tone gave away her inner conflict.

"Very well," I responded before switching back to Beta's channel. "Rogues, we have a long journey ahead of us. Beta-leader, let's go."

I watched the rest of Beta walk around the mountainside and ahead toward the OGT team.

We're all haunted.

"So, be the Hunter," whispered the Beast in eager anticipation.

"Good luck, Tanner," called my Aide.

"Thanks," I grumbled, still unsure about the nature of this developing relationship with the machine and the growing number of voices in my head.

ALTERNATE REALITY

– Xinjiang Province, China –
Wednesday, October 7, 2020

We made it to our day shelter just before dawn. The small forest on the side of a rocky mountain afforded us both a protective invisibility cloak and nest-like visibility over the land below us.

It had taken five grueling night marches to reach this last stop before our designated new home. Ganbold led his team superbly a few miles ahead of us. It was obvious that his Mongols knew the terrain well, some of them hailing from this very region.

I hope they're warm enough, I thought as I laid down for some rest.

Winter was due to start next month in Northern China, but the cold weather was already upon the land. Fortunately, the Skins made good on their promise to regulate the temperature, enabling us to wear nothing else.

I was about to remove my Skull and sleep when my Aide alerted me, "You are needed at the overwatch."

"Damn," I mumbled, tempted to blame the machine in my annoyance, as I headed out to see whatever kept me from sleep.

"Sons of bitches," murmured one of the Rogues sitting next to Deshi.

The village at the base of the mountain was too far away for our Skull's zoom, so Jenny employed powerful binoculars and shared the feed straight to our HUDs.

The Chinese army dressed in HAZMAT suits moved among buildings, dragging people from their homes into trucks. This was our first time seeing people, as we had traversed the most remote route south, avoiding civilization as much as possible.

"Those are Uighurs. They even take the little kids," explained Deshi.

The sight of the small children being dragged into the trucks made my blood boil.

"Your team's vitals are also increasing." The Aide's voice stunned me in the sanctum of my Skull, with both its timing and its concerned tone.

Fuck.

"Can OGT see this?" I asked Deshi.

He turned to look at me, reminding us both of the futility of assessing facial expressions beyond the black Dragon Skull, and shook his head slowly.

Memories of child services at my door, ready to round up my children, surfaced for a moment.

If it were Dani and the kids, I... I stopped myself, knowing where this train of thought would take me.

"We can't do anything about it." I hated the sound of my own voice as much as the words I said.

He paused a moment and then nodded. I glanced at Jenny who was still busy operating the binoculars. A few moments later, we all turned back toward our hideout.

Back in the woods, every time I closed my eyes, I saw the terror on the Uighur kids' faces. Unable to sleep or find any sense of rest, I decided to catch up on some news.

The updates were depressing, but one thing stood out. In New York, a prominent Democrat lawmaker had suggested the creation of a "Truth and Reconciliation Commission" to deal with all those who question the Dragon measures.

Are they fucking insane? We need to ship them here, so they see where all that shit leads!

"You want to believe that it will never happen to you, to your country. But people are just people." Ulysses's words haunted me as I laid down and closed my eyes.

The monsters have to be stopped.

★　★　★

We started the march as the sun finally deserted the land of the living. Nobody spoke of the village, but we didn't need to. It hung heavy in the air between us as we navigated the arduous trek.

"Up there," called the scout over the comms, shifting our attention to where the moonlight shone on the lone mountain in the distance.

"Step on it, Rogues," I instructed.

Deshi immediately increased our pace.

The skies began to lighten as we reached the top of the mountain, covered with early snow. Finding the cave was difficult, but Jenny and Deshi located it together.

Cute.

I suppressed a chuckle and the ache that sat just under my breastbone.

The Rogues descended into the gaping cave mouth hidden under a large dead tree and a pile of snow, but I remained outside, watching the first sun rising beyond the endless desert.

Ganbold texted that they had reached their location and that they'd commence operations the next day.

God, I hope this leak is actually "accounted for," like he said. I don't want to lose even one of them.

SIT TIGHT

– Xinjiang Province, China –
Saturday, October 10, 2020

I sat against the large cavern's hard wall, Skull propped at my side while it was charged by a solar battery device. Intense white light from the field lamp filled the space, setting our eyes at a constant squint. Some Rogues worked out while others checked gear.

We had spent the last two and one-half days studying our immediate surroundings and settling into our makeshift residence. The cave system was deep but not wide, and none of us had experienced sunlight since arriving.

The Old Glory team had begun their scouting mission the morning after our arrival. The target facility was a vast walled complex operated by the Ministry of State on the outskirts of a large town. Fortunately, the OGT fighters blended among the population, which made their job easier. Unfortunately, they had no success catching atrocities on tape.

The second night, Ganbold had privately alerted me to a large truck convoy that had left the MSS facility and entered the forest, where we knew a secondary facility existed. I had set the Eye on the trucks, but their "anti-satellite" coating prohibited a closer look into the vehicles' content. When the convoy reached the large concrete hangar in the forest, it was completely hidden from the Eye's gaze. The trucks were out of sight for twenty minutes and then reversed their course to the MSS facility. I reported the details to the RCC but was told to stay on course and focus on the target. It didn't help to check again, as the answer remained the same.

"It's time," said the Aide.

I picked up the Skull as I stood.

"Are you heading out?" Deshi approached swiftly.

The Beast's eagerness to leave nearly overwhelmed my mind, and I paused to take a deep breath.

"Yes," I confirmed, picking up my assault rifle. "I asked Ganbold to meet me."

With the light behind him, Deshi's face was half-hidden in the shadows, but his tone communicated plenty as he pressed, "Why are you heading out alone? Let me get someone to shadow you."

I like him more every day.

"That won't be necessary." I strapped the rifle and got the Skull ready.

"I know that voice..." he paused, as if calculating his next words, "...burdened with the need for revenge."

Suppressing the pain, my mind pointed to something else.

He wants to ask for something.

"Do you have a question for me?"

He confirmed my intuition with a nod.

"Another time. Godspeed, Overlord."

The last of the gray sky gave way to the night's rule. Emerging from the cave, I passed the sentry placed to watch the top and started running down the mountain. Following the path highlighted on the HUD, I picked up my speed, wishing to outrun my guilt-ridden soul.

Images of Nico and his family flashed in my mind.

I promised Roberto I would avenge his son, but I'm so far away. Damn it, Deshi!

My thoughts moved on to Ganbold, wondering how the Green Beret felt fighting alongside his kin after being raised as an American.

Selfless dedication is so rare.

Reflecting on Old Glory team's leader, I felt the twinge of comparison.

"We'll see." The Beast never sounded out of breath.

I increased my pace again, feeling the Skin enabling my body's maximum mobility as I raced down through the ravines. An hour later, my feet slowed as I approached the dry riverbed and the Aide identified Ganbold who crouched among the rocks.

"Aide, ping OGT-leader for my arrival."

Ganbold responded in kind a few moments before I joined him.

"Hard to get used to the red eyes," he muttered after we greeted each other.

I removed the Skull when I saw its effect on my friend, albeit reluctantly.

When the moonlight shone on his face, the big man's wide grin made me smirk as I settled in to listen to his debrief of the last few days' reconnaissance.

"We're making inroads, but the place is buttoned up," he finished.

"Tell me more about the trucks," I probed. "Are you planning to follow them into the forest?"

He shook his head and murmured something in Mongolian that sounded like a curse.

"How come?"

"We tried, but OG Command told us to stay on the MSS facility and avoid the forest. I bet the military is forbidding us. Too worried about an international incident."

"Could be." I took a deep breath and stared into the distance, pondering these final revelations.

IMPROVISE OR DIE

– Xinjiang Province, China –
Monday, October 12, 2020

I stood in the shadows of the cave's entrance, watching the sun's final descent. My pack, rifle, and Skull leaned against the solid rock wall, but my mind found no rest.

Ganbold and his team had managed to get locals to talk about the MSS building, and the consensus was that while everyone dreaded it, none knew its function. The truck convoys continued into the forest and back, but OGT didn't eyeball the vehicles' content.

I'd tried to get approval for a recon mission, but the RCC had denied my efforts for two days. With each denial, my agitation increased. The longer I was forced to wait, the more time my mind had to spin on the concerns that kept me awake at night.

I have to do something.

When the RCC told me the Eye would be tasked elsewhere once the sun was down, it was the opportunity to test my mission's limits and channel the brewing storm inside me.

"Ganbold just reported seeing the convoy returning to the facility." The Aide's update came through my earbud.

"Confirm back in a text," I instructed the Aide. "How long before the Eye goes away?"

"Thirty-two minutes, Tanner," replied the A.I.

Perfect. I got the whole night.

"Fool me once, shame on you. Fool me twice, shame on me," the man's voice called from deeper inside the cave behind me.

Damn it.

I turned back, unsurprised to see Deshi and the team, all dressed for full combat. Jenny looked genuinely pissed.

No point hiding this.

"I decided to scout the forest facility. It's against the orders, and I'll be operating under my Independent Authority."

"How exactly?" wondered Deshi.

"The convoy just got back. There's a window, and I'm going to use it." I was fully aware of the fragile nature of my plan.

Alfa-four, still livid, walked toward me. "I'm sure you meant to include me under your IA, Overlord." Her voice was brutal and uncompromising.

An unspoken sense of trepidation spread through my guts.

She seeks vengeance.

"She deserves vengeance," growled the Beast.

I sighed and nodded, and Jenny stood by my side.

"You know we're coming too. Right?" Deshi laughed.

I should've seen this.

"Fine."

We huddled up, silently watching the day turn to night.

"The RCC will know quickly," Deshi quietly offered.

"The Eye is tasked somewhere else tonight," I reminded him.

His mouth remained pursed.

"They'll still see our live location. They don't need the Eye for that."

He was right. Our chips made us "walking beacons," whether we liked it or not.

"Nothing to do about it unless you consider a 'Fallen Angel.'"

The idea evoked an involuntary shudder from Deshi as he shook his head.

"For what it's worth, I'll add Beta into my IA." I lightened my tone.

He smiled.

"It's worth everything, Overlord."

I looked at the other Rogues as I reached for my Skull.

"Listen up. Once we're out, we remain on our private team channel. Let's go."

It took about an hour of marching under the moonlight to get close to the forest, where we stopped on a small hill a mile from the wood's edge. Below us, the HUD marked the road from town that continued between the trees.

The MSS facility seemed to be buttoned up for the night, according to Ganbold, who was tasked with staying there until we finished our scouting mission.

"At least they can't call us," murmured Deshi as he crouched beside me.

The RCC had begun texting us for updates when they noticed we'd left our hideout, but they didn't risk actual calls due to the Chinese cyber defense systems. It helped that the Aide could read those messages to me during our fast-paced march, but none of them answered the riddle settled in the back of my mind.

Dad didn't reach out.

"Yeah," I agreed. "Are you ready for this?"

The red Dragon's eyes looked at me.

Amazing how quickly I've adjusted to this scary face.

"Ready," responded Deshi.

"Invisible from here," I commanded.

He nodded.

The sign was given, and the Rogues began their forward march, using stealth techniques enhanced by the Skin and Skull.

This equipment makes it so easy. It would be nearly impossible to see them without it.

★　★　★

The forest was dense, but the ground was arid and rocky where we crept toward the facility, completely unnoticed.

"You have an urgent message from Ganbold." The Aide's voice could only be heard in my Skull. "It says, 'Urgent. Seven truck convoy departed and heading your way.'"

Damn.

I motioned for the Rogues to hold and asked the Aide, "How long before the convoy reaches the facility?"

"Assuming all factors, I estimate it at about seventy minutes from now."

The Rogues were spread out around me, all of their red eyes on me as they awaited my command.

Fuck. Fuck.

It was one thing to do this unauthorized scouting and another to risk the team and the mission to this degree.

"Aide, open team channel," I ordered. "Listen up..." I relayed Ganbold's news and finished with a command, "Beta-leader, take your team back to base."

"What about Alfa-four?" he asked.

My HUD showed Jenny crouched under a tree, her red eyes locked on me.

"She stays with me," I replied, uneasy about my decision.

Jenny nodded and looked elsewhere.

"Beta," called Deshi, "we stay with Overlord, under my Independent Authority." His tone was as immovable as his body posture.

I was speechless, but Deshi made sure to cover for that as well.

"What? I learned from the best." This time, I could hear the smirk behind the Skull.

"There are plenty of guards, but they don't seem too worried about outsiders," reported Deshi on our private channel.

We spread out along the edge of the woods, assessing the situation. The twenty or so guards patrolled the immediate grounds but mostly seemed focused on the road, which ended at their facility. The vast warehouse had been built into the hard earth, with massive air filters and chimneys protruding from its slanted roof.

"How come the Eye didn't see it before?" Deshi's voice came across on our private channel again.

"Look up." I pointed toward the facility. "Zoom in."

"Damn. I see it now," sighed Deshi.

A huge thin net stretched high above the warehouse, likely an advanced anti-satellite material, to keep its existence and activities hidden from the world.

"Seems they don't want attention," added Deshi.

The Aide notified me that we had thirty minutes before the convoy arrived. Our window to check the place out had shrunk drastically.

This might not work.

"Overlord, I volunteer to infiltrate," offered Jenny on the team channel, refocusing my mind.

My heart sank, but I knew she was the best Rogue for the job, and the Beast rumbled in agreement.

"Beta-leader?" I asked for his assessment.

It took him a moment to respond, "She's a better shadow than any of my team."

I was right about those two.

"Approved. Let's do it."

Jenny dropped all her gear before she left the tree line and crouch-crawled toward the warehouse. The HUD tracked Alfa-four's unbelievably agile movement as she approached the warehouse undetected. We lost visuals of her as she went behind the building and waited patiently, feeling every second we couldn't see her.

"Seventeen minutes," reminded the Aide.

"Come on, Jenny," I grumbled, seeing her red dot in the warehouse.

"She's coming out," called one of the Rogues just as our visuals picked up Jenny hurriedly making her way back to us.

What happened?

After another few precious minutes, she crouched in front of us, removed her Skull, and vomited bile on the ground.

What the...? I rushed to her side, removing my Skull as I kneeled beside her.

"Eleven minutes," called the Aide.

I caught a glimpse of her wet face before she turned and dropped full weight into my arms, sobbing quietly while Beta stood watch around us.

What did you see? I kept the question to myself but she must have read my thoughts.

She pulled away slowly.

"Put on your Skull."

Still confused, I pulled it on as Jenny broadcasted a recording across the team channel.

It started with her crawling through a large vent. The warehouse had large machines stacked at one end and what seemed to be a massive hole in the middle of the cement. The POV changed as Jenny crept toward the spot, and then we all gasped in unison at the sight of the endless rows of bodies of all ages, which the Aide quickly identified as Uighurs.

The channel remained silent as we continued to watch, but my HUD showed everyone's vitals spiking intensely, including my own.

When the video showed the other machines, my heart stopped. Incinerators.

Oh my God.

Jenny had managed to get close enough to look inside one of the ovens, which was littered with skulls and other skeleton parts.

The film ended, and the only voice speaking was the Aide's.

"Nine minutes."

They all looked at me, waiting for the command to channel the erupting rage.

"Romulus texted you," the Aide alerted.

"Go ahead." The moment's weight nearly crushed my soul.

"Eyes on the target, what do you see?" The Aide repeated my father's words. I immediately used the *Sense* to wrestle control of my mind back from the horrific images inside the warehouse.

"Seven minutes…"

"Overlord," Deshi called on the team channel.

The scouting mission was complete, but I couldn't leave. The images continued to loop through my mind despite all of my attempts to put them away.

"Remain in position. We watch."

When the seven trucks pulled out of the forest into the clearing, the guards rushed forward on both sides of the road and walked alongside the trucks crawling toward the warehouse.

I already knew what to expect in my heart, but my eyes had to see it too.

Grumbles rose from all the Rogues as the guards opened the trucks and pushed out nearly two hundred civilians. It was hard to identify them from afar, but it was safe to assume they were Uighurs.

Jenny hailed me on a private channel, "I can't turn from this, Sir. Even if it means I do it by myself."

Memories of Ulysses's black and white photos from the death camps his unit liberated flooded my mind—endless bodies, skeletons, and survivors that looked like the walking dead. Then Eli's stories of his father, Dani's grandpa, who lost his first family in Auschwitz. Thinking about the Nazis reminded me of my conversion and what it would have meant if I had lived back then.

Even if I just did it for Dani.

Deshi had to hush the Rogues. The finest warriors humanity had ever created had big hearts, and the rage grew with each passing second.

"What's your order, Overlord?" Deshi was either unable or unwilling to manage the edge in his tone.

I looked around the half-circle of red glowing eyes, and stopped when I got to Jenny. A wave of pain struck me, crashing with the intensity of all that had happened to our world since the pandemic started.

"Evil doesn't hesitate," Custer's words from my Blood Test echoed.

The Beast was elated as a decision formed in the depths of my psyche.

"This isn't happening tonight." I dropped my assault rifle and backpack on the ground. "Rogues, Wraiths, and blades."

The Rogues softly pounded their fists on their chests and then dropped their gear as Deshi decided on a quick attack formation and broadcasted it to our HUDs.

We raced out of the woods like vampires racing out of hell itself.

While the unsuspecting guards were focused on herding the captives, Jenny scored the first kill. Speeding past all of us and jumping on the back of a large guard, she eviscerated his neck with her blade. As soon as he roared in pain like a possessed banshee, the mayhem started.

Some of the Rogues used their Wraith to lock on and eliminate targets, while the rest of us chose Jenny's method and waded into the sentries with blades.

Many captives escaped into the night, but others quickly joined us in the fight. A leader emerged in the broad-shouldered young man who smashed a rock into the head of one of the guards, revealing the path to the rest of the enraged Uighurs. The Chinese began to retreat into the warehouse, using fully automatic fire on the people to kill children, women, and men alike.

There was no need for orders. Each Rogue operated as an insulated killing machine, precise to a fault. Two

Betas terminated the shooters after the fearless Uighurs charged and managed to bring them down.

When the last guards fell, twenty Uighurs and eight Rogues paused and looked at each other. A moment later, a chant erupted from the Uighurs as they encircled and closed in on us, reaching hands out to touch us.

"What are they saying?" asked one of the Rogues.

"Aide, on team channel," I called, overwhelmed by the sensation of the few children's small hands on my stomach.

"They are saying, 'Dragons... Dragons... Dragons...'"

Suddenly, Jenny broke away from us and waded among the Uighurs like a ghost.

"On her," I commanded and we all pushed past the civilians to follow Jenny who was now racing toward the side of the warehouse, where my HUD showed a signature of a man.

When the man noticed Jenny, he squeezed one shot at her before she jumped and wrestled him to the ground.

We arrived as Alfa-four stood over the man and used her distorted voice to warn him against rising to his feet.

Deshi instructed the Rogues to create a secure space while Jenny talked with the prisoner behind us, as some survivors had caught up and begun screaming at him.

The Aide translated their words, "They seem to know him. They blame him for working with the devil. I don't know if that is a metaphor, but..."

"Enough, Aide," I turned back to the captured man, about my size and in his thirties.

"He's an MSS captain." Jenny's tone was tight as it rang over the team channel. "He's got some stuff to say."

Deshi joined us and urged the Captain to speak.

Looking concerned, the MSS commander bemoaned the release of the prisoners.

"Tell him why," growled Jenny, causing the Captain to crawl backward.

The MSS commander looked down and murmured that the Uighurs were all infected. He admitted that the warehouse was where the diseased were disposed of.

"They killed my son," roared a grief-stricken man behind us, his words translated by the Aide without prompting.

My blood boiled to the crescendo of angry Uighurs around us.

"They use the virus on us... please help us..." The memory of the detained model surfaced.

"Has General Zhang arrived?" The Captain's eyes grew wide at my question. "I thought so."

Jenny remained still and silent.

"*Now,*" echoed the Beast.

I reached out to Alfa-four, clapping on her shoulder as I spoke over the private channel, "You did it, Jenny. Do what you need to do, and we're out of here."

Red eyes toward me, her head bowed momentarily. Then she returned her attention to the Captain, who shrieked and jumped as she took the final step and bent her knee to get level with his face.

"Men like you raped and murdered my mother," growled Jenny, her voice distorted and menacing.

Deshi swiveled his head toward the exchange.

"People like you. They chose to become what you are."

In a blur of speed, her right hand raised her blade, preparing for a downward strike as the captain screamed in fear, dropping to his back, hands up.

The crowd yelled at the unfolding spectacle, fueled by vengeance.

But she didn't strike.

Instead, Jenny rose slowly, returning the blade to her waist and turning to Deshi.

"Let them have him."

I was stunned speechless, and it wasn't just me. Beta-leader paused and then ordered Beta to stand down as the Uighurs rushed toward the MSS commander.

The captain screamed for our help as the small crowd decimated him with fists, rocks, and bare feet.

"Urgent message from Ganbold," started the Aide. I accepted it and learned the game had changed.

"Listen up," I called the Rogues on the team channel. "A large force of soldiers just left the MSS building, presumably heading here to check on their missing convoy." Then I looked past them at the remaining Uighurs who awaited our word.

From the onset of the pandemic, the Chinese had used the harshest lockdown and virus mitigation methods known across the globe, pursuing an un-realistic "zero infection" goal.

Now dozens of infected are heading back to their people.

"*Own it,*" whispered the Beast.

The brave, broad-shouldered, bearded Uighur leader stepped forward and spoke. According to the Aide, they all wanted to come with us. He started the "Dragons" chant again and the twenty or so of his group—men, women, and three teenagers—joined him.

"They're all fighters. The rest fled already."

The Rogue was right, and a realization beset me.

This is my mess to clean up.

When I raised my hand, the Uighur chant died.

"Aide, can you translate me live?"

"There is no need, Tanner," answered the AI. "They are quite capable of understanding your Mandarin."

I addressed the crowd, promising to take them to a nearby refuge. There was only one commitment beyond that, and we had to leave right away.

The Uighur leader got his group organized, and some of the Rogues also helped while I took a moment to run into the warehouse to see the atrocities with my own eyes.

I removed the Skull at the edge of the mass grave, horror threatening to buckle my knees.

How?

"*This can happen everywhere. Don't forget this,*" warned the Beast.

We need to leave.

I put on the Skull and ran out.

"Let's go. Aide, call OGT-leader," I instructed as we entered the woods again, grabbing the gear we'd left behind.

Ganbold answered quickly, and I ordered him to return his team to camp, wrap it up, and come to our base. Knowing I had operational command of the mission, he agreed and asked no further questions.

I shuddered with rage and quietly resisted the impulse to turn around and bring down the wrath of God to blast the devil's warehouse to pieces.

The march back to base was arduous. The Uighurs didn't have the night vision technology on the uphill climb through rocky terrain, and we pushed them constantly for a better pace. But no one complained, not even the youngsters.

As dawn approached, I stood at our cave's entrance, watching the Rogues herd the rest of the survivors into our base and keeping an eye out for activity below. From our high perch on the mountain, my Skull visuals zoomed in on the distant military choppers buzzing through the skies.

We kicked the hornet's nest in the balls.

Behind me, Deshi took command of the Uighurs, moving them to a side cave, away from the Rogues and their command space. The civilians moved quickly and offered gratitude as they passed.

Yes, they are warriors.

Because the Uighurs were all infected, I instructed our team to keep the Skulls on unless we were in the privacy of our space. Not only would it protect our health, it would keep our real faces hidden.

"Should I upload to the RCC?" asked the Aide.

Our Skulls had filmed everything live, but nothing was broadcasted due to security concerns. Now, back at the cave, we had the extra equipment to safeguard communications.

"Yes, proceed."

"Incoming, OGT," called our guard on the team channel.

I moved outside the cave to join him in time to see the Old Glory warriors trekking up the mountain with all of their gear.

Ganbold raised his hands and boomed, "Hallelujah!"

He and Deshi walked over to me as both teams huddled, the Mongols showing deference to the Rogues.

I quickly related the essentials of the story to Ganbold, who listened intently while I emphasized the infection and my decision to keep wearing the Skulls.

"Permission to take care of the civvies," asked Ganbold.

"Of course." My heart warmed.

Such a good man.

OGT-leader quickly dispensed his orders, and his team stacked their gear on the ground and headed to the side cave.

They don't let the virus take their humanity. Unlike home. How low did we fall?

"Overlord, Romulus on a secure line," called one of the Rogues on the team channel.

Oh boy. Here goes...

"Please connect us."

Jack was pissed, but he withheld his fury and asked me to explain myself.

"This is why I authorized the scouting in the first place..." I told him about the first part of the events.

When I was done, he leveled, "So let me get this straight, you decided to lend us a hand in finding damning evidence?"

"Yes," I replied. "We now have all this material–"

"Which we cannot share with the government, considering what you did to get it," he interjected with a sigh.

There was a long silence on the line.

"Dad..."

"It was all a trap, Son." His words reverberated like a bomb detonating. "We agreed to take the government contract, not because we thought we had a chance to catch the Chinese in the act. It was just a good cover for setting an ambush for whoever is leaking from our side."

When my legs almost went out from under me, I leaned against the tunnel's hard wall. Ahead of me, OGT-leader came out of the side cave and spoke with Deshi, who then sent their team medic back with him.

"What about Zhang? Was that part fake as well?" I wondered as the possibility hit me.

"No... no. That part was real as it comes. Once we had the mole caught, we planned on setting up Zhang, provoking him to come after the OGT team with all his might. And that was to be your chance to catch him."

I fucked up.

"Did you?" challenged the Beast, surprising me with its presence.

"There will be some real-world ramifications for this, but we can't do anything about that anymore." His tone had shifted from pissed to concerned.

"I'm sorry, Sir. I broke the chain of command and sabotaged your trap." My mind served up the sights from the warehouse. "But it had to be done."

"I should have seen it." Jack sighed. "Too much for you and your history."

"It was just like in Grandpa's photos." Images of the incinerators haunted me.

"That too." Jack's tone saddened, which it always did when Ulysses was mentioned.

He switched the topic and updated me on what was happening around our cave.

"We estimate about a hundred infected escaped the forest and spread into the countryside. The Chinese think the number is a bit higher, considering the twenty or so that tagged along with you…" He detailed how the Chinese had mobilized their army, the MSS overseeing the operations. "They're closing down on the villages, forcing people to test, and removing the infected."

"Isn't that what they always do?" I recalled the village we saw during our route south.

"You don't get it. That little fight of yours is currently assumed to be the handiwork of insurgency." The anger was back and it was hot. "Nobody has dared to do things like this before, so it got them mobilized and angry."

I looked down at the Skin that covered my body, wishing it were my wetsuit and that I was home and getting ready to ride waves instead of the rollercoaster I knew was coming.

"Wouldn't the leak tell them it was Old Glory?"

"Not likely," he replied, without divulging anything more.

"Well, this mess can help us get out more easily."

"Perhaps," replied Jack. "Are there any other IAs you gave without letting me know?"

Might as well.

"Well…" I told him about the order I gave Alfa.

"I'll be damned," muttered Jack.

Oh shit.

Romulus surprised me with a nasty chuckle.

"Custer bet that you'd do something crazy. I didn't think so." My father sounded stuck somewhere between admiration and disbelief. "You break that monster, and it will be all worth it then."

Oh, I plan on it.

"We'll work on the details and keep you posted..." Jack said the RCC was figuring our escape route. "Ration your supplies in the meantime."

He was ready to end our conversation, but something gnawed at me.

"Why didn't you try to stop the mission? You said nothing. Only the RCC asked what we were doing."

He didn't answer for a few moments, as if he were calculating what to say.

"Eyes on the target, what do you see?"

The line went dead after that, and my irritation exploded.

He's always training me! Damn him! An answer once in a while might help me!

I rose and walked deeper into the tunnel, leaving everyone behind me.

What is he waiting for? It's been like this all of my fucking life!

"*Did you ever think that he needs you?*" asked the Beast.

My feet stopped, and my body froze.

But why? The possibility had never crossed my mind.

The Beast receded, leaving me with yet another riddle.

My dad is somehow connected to all of this, and I am...

The Aide broke into my thoughts, letting me know that Deshi and Ganbold waited to speak with me.

★   ★   ★

The two waited for me in the Rogues' space, and I removed my Skull as I approached them.

"Thank you both for backing me up out there..." I updated them about my debrief with Romulus.

"Nonsense," called out the OGT-leader. "You fought for people, not of your own, and saved them from extermination. I only wish to be worthy in life to do such a thing." Before I could respond, he continued, "I heard them call you 'The Dragons.' Funny enough, some of us, who operated for OG for a long time, have always suspected 'you people' are some black-op operations. But I know now that you are much more than that."

Deshi and I exchanged glances, wondering where Ganbold would take this.

"Whatever you are, we're all with you." He pulled his hands together in front of his chest, stopping just short of a bow or maybe even a prayer.

"Thank you," I mirrored his hand posture. "But I also made a huge mistake..." I explained about the leak and the undermined trap in broad strokes.

When met with silence, I looked at Ganbold.

"Did you know you were to be the bait?"

He laughed and admitted knowing enough.

"I didn't know about any mole, but your dad called me personally to tell me it was probably a one-way ticket. That we must catch Zhang was enough for me... for my entire team. Anything to balance the debt." His eyes were sober but still bright.

A willing sacrifice. My mind raced to understand the riddle Shemtov had served up at my best friend's funeral, but I couldn't let myself go there.

Deshi nodded in agreement and clapped his hand on the large Mongol's shoulder.

The brotherly gesture between the two warriors reminded me that both teams had a deep personal stake in this battle—a stake far beyond the mission's parameters.

We all have debts to settle, but these guys... something is different.

Ganbold asked to be excused again to check on the Uighurs, and I called Jenny over, so I could update them both and make sure Jenny got Dex caught up to speed.

As Alfa-four approached, she and Deshi exchanged the briefest of tiny smiles, but even my tired eyes caught it and my heart warmed.

Even in this place of evil. Even with debts hanging over all of our heads.

PARTING WAYS

– Xinjiang Province, China –
Tuesday, October 13, 2020

Ganbold and his Mongols were with the Uighurs as soon as the sun came up, preparing them for the upcoming march. Everyone was on edge, wondering which would come first—mission confirmation or retaliation from the Chinese.

Deshi and I stood in a tunnel, watching the RCC updates in our Skulls. The map showed the Chinese had already mobilized their military to lock down the entire Xinjiang Province.

"Wow." I could hardly believe my eyes.

"This isn't their first time, but to see it with my own eyes..." Beta-leader sounded dumbstruck, even though his team's main work was in China.

The map was replaced with the current escape plan to Mongolia, developed with Ganbold's help.

"Not easy," Deshi sighed when the presentation ended.

"No, but they're all used to this terrain." I wondered if the RCC had considered creating any diversion to help OGT get out of the immediate area.

Finally, the update on General Zhang arrived. According to the report, the general was likely be out tonight with the troops, and Beta was to be ready to execute its mission.

"And I was worried about a diversion." Deshi's tone was suddenly full of enthusiasm.

A laugh escaped me as I patted his shoulder and turned to look for Jenny, who I found sitting by herself near the cave entrance.

The moment Alfa-four realized it was me, she visibly relaxed. Smiling softly, Jenny motioned for me to join her, and I pulled the Skull off as I sat across from her.

"How are you?" I asked.

Jenny's almond-shaped eyes closed a bit, making her beautiful Asian face serene and ageless at the same time.

"I've always remained the terrorized young girl, seeing her mother being abused and murdered." Her tone was sad, almost hopeless. "I learned how to wage war and kill with my bare hands. It didn't help. The nightmares have continued."

"Does it ring a bell?" echoed the Beast.

I can't think about that right now.

When Jenny rose to her feet, I followed suit and she bowed.

"You honored me, Sir. I know the war against this evil has barely started, but at least I feel calm."

I stepped forward to hug her.

How does she do this? The calm? Is it time, or the satisfaction of finally fighting back against the monsters and slaying them?

The ear vibration seemed too well-timed for the moment, and I stepped back and bowed to take my leave.

"Both missions are greenlit for tonight," said Jack. "Now, listen up."

My heart raced in anticipation as I focused my mind on the mission. The situation could have been better. Old Glory had notified the US military that they'd decided to pull OGT out when the Chinese had suddenly begun to mobilize in the province.

"They were pissed with me until the CIA probably confirmed the current situation on the ground."

"Do they know about the refugees?"

"Well… sort of," he chuckled. "We told them Ganbold decided to help refugees, and we couldn't stop him."

Forcing the government into a situation was never the best tactic, and I wondered how that would actually turn out.

"I hear the President was livid, but he still ensured that the Mongolian government will help at the border. And Custer is on the ground."

Thank you.

"Have the Chinese blamed the US already?"

"Not at all. It could mean they're buying the insurgency theory." Jack's voice was tight. "This was always the preferred option when we war-gamed this mission."

His cold logic was irrefutable. It was much easier to strike at the enemy when social strife existed.

Like they're doing to us back home! I was caught between rage and sadness thinking about all of the innocents suffering from the scheme.

Jack switched to OGT and detailed the plan for them to leave at dusk.

"Wish them good luck because they'll need it."

"Are you worried about the leak?"

"It doesn't matter, Son. The consequences have begun, and we must live with them."

"Consequences make the world move," whispered the Beast.

I pushed away both the guilt and the relief of my decision to free the Uighurs.

"How confident are you that Zhang will be out tonight?"

"Quite," he responded.

"And if he isn't?" I pressed.

"Then you'll be approved to create some chaos to stoke the fire of the 'insurgency' and cover for OGT's escape." He wasn't trying to hide his frustration. "I also spoke with Dex. Alfa's ready."

"Anything else?" I asked, suddenly craving a moment alone.

"Oh... yes..." He hesitated. "Danielle sent me some amazing videos of her and the kids. I promised her to send them over once we can."

My heart squeezed, the old trepidation returning.

I can't lose them.

"She's not the only woman who misses you," he said with a softer voice.

"Mom."

"Yeah. Your 'retirement' gave her years of peaceful sleep. Now, she's back to sleepless nights on the porch, looking out to the dark skies."

The tension became too much for both of us and when he cleared his throat, I took the opportunity to end the call, "Tell Mom I'm alright. If that's all, I'd like to go and finish preparing myself and my team."

"Alright, Son. Let's put an end to this monster and get the intel we need to stop the others."

"Are you both clear?"

Deshi and Ganbold looked at each other and then nodded back to me.

"Do the Uighurs understand the cover story?"

We knew once at the border, the asylum seekers would be debriefed. Their rehearsed story would be that they had run away when the "Dragons" attacked.

"They're taking this very seriously." Ganbold cocked his head and smiled, as if he were about to tempt us to skip school. "Are we getting any diversion for the escape?"

Feeling the growing bond with the former Green Beret, I glanced at Deshi. He smiled faintly, obviously sharing my affinity for the large Mongol as Ganbold laughed in his bass tone.

"The great hunt... of course. That would work as a diversion for sure. Funny, we all were ready. I truly believed this was my last journey. Instead, we are set to do everything to rescue some of our ancestral brothers and sisters, as we fight our way out of this hell."

After the three of us embraced, Deshi instructed the Rogues to retreat deeper into the cave while OGT led the Uighurs into the descending darkness.

"Do you think that they'll make it?" Deshi asked when he joined me outside the cave.

Without the Skulls, we looked into the blackness.

"Yes, and we have our part to play. We leave in twenty."

He called on the team channel but didn't leave my side.

"Anything else?" I wondered.

Deshi nodded gravely.

"That butcher tortured two of my team until they committed suicide." The implication was clear for me—someone who had also lost two good soldiers.

I miss you, Brother.

The Rogues were moving gear behind us, preparing for departure.

"You saved our lives back then," I started, my own need for vengeance intertwining with guilt. "When I'm done with him, he's yours."

Deshi bowed his head, face tight. I was about to turn to go back in when he asked the question that had hung between us since we met, "How come you left? Right after Market?" His tone conveyed disbelief and maybe disappointment. "Jenny told me," he added when I didn't respond.

My eyes scanned the dark skies, now humming with distant choppers and flickering plane lights.

"I live with that mistake every day. I used to tell myself it was because of my dad and Custer. That they abandoned the mission, which fueled my rage and gave me the power to leave. I was wrong."

"Have you learned your lesson? You committed?"

The question's brutal honesty blindsided me, and the shackles tightened around my heart and body, reminding me of my family's first place.

I want to see the videos.

"Get ready to execute the mission, Beta-leader." I returned my attention to my gear as Deshi opened his mouth to continue, and then decided not to before taking his leave.

"*You're not ready,*" bristled the Beast.

OUR TURN

Just before we left, Jack told us about the confidential informant who drove General Zhang around with a personal GPS beacon. I felt gratitude for General Tall and whatever strings he pulled to get us the CI.

The reasonable estimate was that the MSS General was due to oversee a raid on the large village less than two hours march from our forward base, so we headed there. Staying away from the main roads, we were thankful for the sparse population in the region.

On top of all the pressure and importance of our job was our concern about OGT and their vulnerable convoy. When we stopped for a water break, I checked on Ganbold and his crew and relayed my findings back to the two teams.

"So far, so good," I updated after checking the RCC feed.

The only other emotion that was palpable among us, especially Beta, was the growing savage anticipation of reencountering the Chinese General.

It was always more personal for them, I thought as we all slipped on the Skulls and ran into the night.

While the dark skies buzzed with aerial activity, we remained invisible to human and tech-prying eyes, even as we were prone among a few large rocks not even three hundred feet from the Uighur settlement.

The village was carved into a challenging rocky terrain, with a hodgepodge of mud-brick, square one-story homes. Just outside of it stood a force of at least fifty Chinese soldiers with trucks and other people in HAZMAT suits.

"Target convoy is approaching." The Aide projected the Eye's live feed to a side window on my HUD, focusing on four combat vehicles.

"Focus and highlight the CI," I instructed. A yellow square immediately surrounded the second car's driver.

There were three more passengers in the vehicle, and no way to ID Zhang behind the dark windows in the black night. In fact, all we could do was assume he was inside.

I allowed Beta to creep forward as we watched the convoy stop when it reached the village.

Not even a hundred feet behind the Chinese soldiers, we still needed more light to discern his face.

"This might be Zhang." The Aide analyzed the Eye feed and targeted one man. "See how they set around him for protection."

I had the Aide share the findings with the rest of the Rogues as we all watched the Chinese prepare to enter the village and heard the first of children's screams and women's wailings.

Damn it.

We couldn't risk a frontal assault, facing nearly one hundred soldiers. Powerless, we had to stand by and witness the calamity befalling these people.

The soldiers began their advance on the village, leaving just a few men with all the vehicles, one of whom was our CI.

"Now!" I ordered on the team channel, and the eight of us crept forward like hungry sharks in the dark ocean. The guards were focused on the village, where the sounds of resistance increased.

Our assault rifles' sights synced with our HUD and when I gave the sign, we eliminated the few guards within two seconds of suppressed fire and rushed forward.

Surrounding the stunned CI dressed in combat fatigues, who had his hands up in surrender, I used the code word that Jack had given me. It relaxed him only slightly as he stared frightened into the Skulls and red eyes that surrounded him.

"We're going to take him now. Stay here until we're done." I used my voice scrambler.

He nodded, still speechless.

I was about to order Beta to continue when the driver surprised me, "You can't leave me like this. You must hurt me, or they will kill me and my family." He motioned toward the village. "Zhang is a demon."

I paused as the image of another demon outside Taco Libertad flashed through my mind.

Shoving the memory down, I focused on the moment.

"How bad do you want it?"

"Bad," he replied with a faint smile.

"Walk backward." I took a few steps away.

"I'd pray that you get help within the hour." I leveled my rifle and fired two non-lethal shots and watched him crumble to the ground, wailing in pain.

"Time to hunt," I growled over the team channel and headed toward the sounds of crimes against humanity.

The Chinese had secured the path into the village and then tried to force each home to submit to rapid virus testing. But this time, they had full-blown mayhem on their hands, as the Uighurs fought back with rocks and sticks.

We waited impatiently until one of the Rogues managed to identify Zhang.

"Fire!"

The surprise attack from behind was swift. We dropped a dozen soldiers in the first three seconds. The Uighurs, shocked to receive help, proved themselves, charging the soldiers no matter the cost.

Jenny and Beta's female Rogue slipped away while we dealt with the remaining soldiers, who tried unsuccessfully to find refuge among the buildings.

When Zhang tried to retreat with his guards, the female Rogues were waiting. They jumped from a nearby mud-brick roof, wading into the soldiers with their blades.

"We got him!" barked Jenny across the team channel as I finished a soldier with two shots to the chest.

The ground was littered with bodies, mostly uniformed. As soon as Zhang went down, the morale broke and the remainder of the Chinese soldiers fled in all directions. The Uighurs hooted and hollered with what seemed to be cries of victory. The villagers all pointed at us, their expressions nothing short of incredulity.

"On me," I called on the team channel, and the two teams immediately joined me to find our other Rogues and their prisoner.

The General was zip-tied with his hands behind his back and black-bagged. He tried to say something, but Jenny jabbed him in the ribs and ordered him to stay quiet.

"They're on us," called one of the Rogues as dozens of the villagers surrounded us and the "Dragons... Dragons..." chant began.

Fuck, not again.

"The rumor spread," muttered Deshi, who stood shoulder-to-shoulder with me.

"Tell them to fuck off from here and take the weapons. The Chinese will come hard on this place," I grumbled. "We're out in two mikes."

Deshi engaged the villagers as I joined Jenny and another Rogue opened the retractable stretcher.

"Get him ready."

On my order, Jenny and two other Rogues lifted Zhang. The General was livid, yelling from inside the bag, but he was no match for the Rogues who forced him onto the stretcher and used the straps to tie his hands and feet to it.

"Make him sleep," I commanded.

Jenny pulled out a small syringe and swiftly poked the General, who passed out instantly.

We hustled out into the night, hoping the villagers would listen.

Getting back to our cave was difficult, as the Chinese had escalated their activity not even twenty minutes after we left the village.

"He's fucking heavy," grunted one of the three Rogues on stretcher duty.

It was true and on this final leg, my muscles screamed against the never-ending incline toward the mountaintop.

The red light of dawn spilled slowly across the sky as we approached our destination. Once inside the cave, a Rogue replaced me and they all moved our "guest" deeper into one of the tunnels.

"Superb work, Rogues," I called on the team channel, stretching my aching shoulders.

When the ear vibration started, I took the call inside the Skull.

Romulus was pleased with the results.

"Do you want Alfa to execute the mission?" The question came from the man who had always cautioned me from pulling out a weapon unless I was willing to use it.

While my shackles kept growing, their loving reach didn't apply to those marked as enemies. For them, I had something else.

"Me," whispered the Beast with elation.

"Proceed as planned," I answered, setting unknown events into motion. "Are we safe in our position?"

"Quite." Jack chuckled. "Your recent stunts have turned this whole 'insurgency' into a real thing. We're now getting reports of other sporadic efforts to resist the authorities, so the Chinese are sending two infantry divisions to the province. You're also deep enough in the ground to avoid tracking if he's chipped."

"Is this helping OGT?" I wondered from the corner of my heart that worried about my new friends.

"Absolutely." Jack told me about some overtures from the government, asking more questions about the operation and OGT's whereabouts. "I suspect that with all the mess now in the open, Baker is involved."

The name alone made my body tense.

I knew it!

"How's the homeland?" I asked, pushing past my apprehension.

"Not good," muttered Romulus. "We've always been apolitical, but I must admit to being concerned. If Stone loses, the country will change."

I stood still in the tunnel's darkness, waiting on my father to add more.

"The Deep State had a good reign during the Charlton administration, and Grayson was his Defense Secretary. We could see their power surge if he takes the White House."

There was so much going on, and my body ached.

"Just tell me, Dad."

"For the good and the bad, this is the place and time you have to break him."

A ping of resentment rippled through me, but I kept it to myself.

Do you ever think about what you made me become?

"He made you strong," answered the Beast.

"Yes, Sir." I barely remembered the family man I was a few months ago as I ended the call and followed the Rogues into the belly of the mountain to break the monster who waited for me there.

RESISTANCE IS FUTILE

– Xinjiang Province, China –
Wednesday, October 14, 2020

Zhang had been placed inside the main cave and a few Rogues stood by, wearing their Skulls per my instruction. Three hours after his capture, he was seated in the middle of our space, still gagged, black-bagged, and zip-tied. Unsurprisingly, he hadn't uttered a word since regaining consciousness.

A veteran.

I stood twenty feet away in the tunnel when Jenny spoke on my private channel, "He's injected. Give it thirty minutes."

My HUD told me it was ten o'clock in the morning, and I marveled again at the state of "no time" inside the cavern system's depths.

Just like Vegas, including the no sleeping.

My body should have been exhausted after more than twenty-four hours without sleep, but I felt none of that as I looked at the man who had haunted my thoughts for years.

"Roger. Get him ready, and I'll be back."

★　★　★

10:16

Permission

"So far, so good." Jack sounded relieved as he related the convoy's status. The Chinese were so busy with the recent outbreak and surprise insurgency, OGT had a perfect cover for their escape. "It's amazing. Ganbold updated us that locals are also helping them along the way." His tone grew somber as he detailed the massive search for Zhang and the lockdown operation across the entire Xinjiang Province. "From all indications, they still consider it related to an insurgency and are doing their best to prevent any media coverage leaks."

"Insurgency?" I wondered. "We barely scratched them twice."

When he laughed, the audio quality made me scan the darkness and wonder if my father had pulled a stunt on me and arrived in time for the show.

"This is way beyond your stunts now, and it's happening as we speak." Jack shared multiple reports of Uighurs and Mongols, both minorities in the country, fighting back across the province. "They're mostly abandoning their villages when the military comes, but we got word of several actual attacks and horrific Chinese reprisals."

My mind raced, calculating how all these updates changed our picture.

"As the events have escalated, the government and military have asked where OGT is, but I think they believe we aborted because of the situation."

"What would have happened if they didn't?" I asked, though I wasn't sure I wanted the answer.

"I would have been zip-tied in some dark room by now, like the General. Or worse, depending on which side discovered us."

Fuck.

Romulus grunted.

"China hasn't blamed the US. Pray that it stays like that."

I kicked a small stone with my boot and, as it clanked down the tunnel, I wondered how many of the details being shared with me were the rippling echoes of my previous actions and inactions clamoring to their dark end.

"You read the files. He's a skilled and ruthless adversary. Tread carefully and be ready to own your convictions." Jack paused. "Did you study all the material we sent?"

"Yes, and it's my second time with him."

"Fair enough, Son. Anything else?"

"There is," I started. "It's time for Beta to hear everything. They have earned that and more."

"Agreed," he replied.

10:35
Decision

As the line went dead, my heart raced and my throat closed. I removed the Skull and dropped to my knees and fists, struggling to catch my breath.

What the fuck? I leaned back against the tunnel wall and called on the *Sense* to calm my mind. *Violence... You grow more assertive when I...*

"*Yes, we become stronger as we evolve,*" whispered the Beast.

What do you want from me? Fear mixed with rage.

When there was no response, I growled into the nothingness, "I will not lose them. Not to you or anyone else."

The image of my hermano holding Taco Libertad's door blended with his final words before the door exploded open: "I choose this, Hermano."

My hands shot to the sides of my head, as if trying to prevent an outside force from entering.

"*Do what you must, and don't bother me with your weakness,*" growled the Beast.

Fuck you!

As I stood and put on the Skull, I felt immediate release from the tormentor inside and wondered for only a moment if I would regret it.

Deshi had arranged the Rogues outside the main cave, where they all waited for me.

"Okay, Rogues, here's what's happening..." I relayed my dad's briefing to them and quickly moved to the subject at hand. "You've been out here fighting for your homeland, and it's time you know more about what's going on..." I explained that Romulus had approved them to observe Zhang's interrogation.

They looked at each other briefly, unable to read each other's faces, and then back to me.

"Are you ready?"

Deshi began thumping his fist on his chest, and the other Rogues immediately matched his war-like cadence. The combination of kinship and determination warmed and fueled me.

"Let's do it."

11:00

Motivation

We returned to the cave, where the red-light field lamp glowed as the Rogue who had remained with Zhang prepared the General for his interrogation.

I advanced toward our prisoner, noticing the tablet next to him.

Placing the last sensor on Zhang's bare chest, the Rogue informed me on a private channel that all was ready.

I sat on the ground, just three feet away from Zhang, and dimmed the lamp until the red light covered the two of us but left the rest of the cave in darkness.

According to his file, Zhang was sixty, but his muscular body seemed much younger, albeit scarred in various places. I reached forward and pulled the black bag from his head and then sat back, my eyes taking in the man who had hunted us back in Market.

Zhang's almond-shaped eyes squinted and scanned the space slowly and then the two white sensors on his chest. No other muscle moved on his face as he looked down at the screen and then focused on me.

Feeling something wasn't right, I slowly removed the skull and placed it on the ground facing him despite the Beast's resistance.

He's a worthy warrior.

His stern face relaxed a bit with something akin to gratitude for barely a second before a sneer made him rigid again.

"So, you are those creatures that attacked us," growled Zhang in English without a trace of an accent.

Harvard-educated.

As he asked questions regarding his whereabouts and the time and date, I waited for the opening.

Zhang leaned forward. "Have we met before? Are you American?"

We were all masked and disguised during Market.

I nodded my head.

"I must admit that we didn't factor in a second team. Touché." He smiled.

"Good. You're ready."

Zhang's eyes widened and his face lost every hint of civility.

"What did you inject me with?"

"Resistance is futile," I responded flatly.

"This is a declaration of war! There's nothing you can do to break me before you're all found," he barked.

I shuddered, recalling the pit, the dark, cold water, and the creature.

Everyone breaks.

"Establish a connection," I called out.

A set of shimmering red eyes appeared in the darkness, capturing both Zhang's and my attention. The General searched the darkness, noticing the dark shapes in the shadows. The red eyes disappeared when the tablet's screen came to life, revealing golden sunlight reflecting off the ghostly pale skin of on an unconscious young Asian man, prone inside a freshly dug grave.

I noticed the uptake of breath as Zhang realized who laid there, dressed in jeans and a university sweatshirt, hands and feet bound.

"Alfa, remove his mask for a moment," I called into my earbud, so Zhang could confirm his deepest fear.

Someone from Alfa, dressed in Skin and Skull, came into view and removed the man's oxygen mask.

Zhang cursed in Chinese, struggling against his zip ties.

"Put it back on."

The Alfa Rogue placed the mask back on Ye Zhang, eldest son of Ministry of State General Jun Zhang, and then disappeared from view.

When the General turned his gaze upon me, the dark red tones from the lamp made him appear even more demonic.

"He's unconscious. We figured the boy didn't need to see what could happen to him." The Beast ignited my insides with every word. "This is the full extent of my mercy."

"His vitals are spiking," the Aide cautioned me. "He's controlling his breath, though."

"Nice game you got here. We both know you can't do anything to him, so stop the show while you can. This is a huge international incident," snarled Zhang, still fighting against his restraints.

"The only game is the one you'd play with yourself. How much will you gamble on your son's life?"

Please don't make me do this, I silently pleaded with the father sitting before me.

"Alfa, bury him."

Zhang's thrashing increased as the Skull-covered operators began to shovel dirt onto Ye's body and face.

When Zhang tore his eyes from watching his boy being buried alive to look at me, a powerful wave of remorse crashed through me.

He's just a boy. How can I do this?

The shoveled dirt sounded like thunderclaps in the otherwise silent cave, but the MSS General stared at me and I felt a crack in my resolution.

"Let me help," offered the Beast with a rare warmth in Its tone.

Without the Skull. Allowing my defenses to drop, I felt rejuvenated in dark energy as it eliminated my doubts and I watched his strong face shift from cold rage to a grimace and then...

"Stop this," he pleaded, bowing his head.

"Alfa, hold."

Zhang and I turned our eyes back to the screen to find Ye half-covered, most of his face above the soil, eyes still closed.

"This is the deal. I'll offer it only once, father to a father. Speak truthfully, and the boy will be spared."

He sighed and lifted his eyes.

"This can't be a US Government sanctioned mission. You are something different."

I nodded my head.

"Then, will you kill me at the end?" Not even a trace of fear tinged his voice, and I nodded slowly.

"This will be your burial site, Zhang. Choose your next words wisely." I used the words he'd spoken to me during Operation Market when Baker ordered us to hand Lee back to him.

His mouth opened for a moment, the rest of his facial expression hidden in the shadows created by the red lamp, until he began to laugh menacingly.

"You! I should have ended you as we ended your friends." He tried to lean forward, tilting his head to get a better view of me. "What's your name? You look familiar."

I didn't need to look at the team vitals to sense the raw anger rising in the cave.

"I'd be careful speaking about those you killed. As for you, you're a dead man. But I do keep my promises beyond the grave."

Looking down and then to the screen, and then back at me, he let out a sigh.

"Ask your questions, and then release him."

"I give you my word."

"And pray that he keeps his," warned the Beast.

11:58

Betrayal

Zhang answered truthfully about the details of his decades-long career in the military before transferring to the Ministry of State and even admitted to being involved in many operations against the Uighurs and other groups who resisted the Party.

"But that is not all that you did," I grumbled, keeping my achy back straight. "Let's talk about the virus and our government's role in the matter."

Surprise crossed his face, but the drug and his half-buried son did their part.

"The dark side of the story is..." Zhang almost regrettably revealed how the virus project was initially conceived as a "joint science project" to better understand how to fight pandemics. "Shortly after the project started, we developed a virus that had the ability to spread unbelievably quickly. But it was even better than we hoped, as it had the potential to be saddled with other elements to effectuate different results."

His tone, even now, sounded awe-inspired by the abomination, and it took much control to not punch him in the face.

"How did Paul Baker take the news?" I asked.

Zhang released a brief laugh, followed by a curse in Chinese.

"Yes, that man embodied the administration he served. Tainted..." He didn't hesitate to expose how excited Baker had become once they made initial progress with the virus.

"Was President Charlton involved too?" I asked, wondering how far the web spread.

Zhang shook his head.

"Not that I know."

"Then who was?" I pressed.

He looked at me for a long moment, briefly glancing toward the screen and the live feed.

"Secretary of Defense must have known at least something."

Grayson.

"Continue. What happened next?"

"We all saw the potential, even as adversaries in a historical context. It was an unholy alliance with purposes beyond striking at each other."

A movie reel of images flipped through my mind—the pandemic, riots, death, and violence.

"Did you know what our side wanted the virus for?"

His answer carried a smidge of regret, "No. I should have…"

When his expression turned to amusement, I growled, "What? Speak!"

"It wasn't supposed to be a weapon. That doctor you had, Lee, designed the whole thing to mass-vaccinate populations via organic infection." He sighed. "Maybe we shouldn't have played with nature. Yet, once discovered, the military potential was too powerful to let go of."

"Have you broken the virus's code?" My body coiled in tension.

Zhang shook his head.

"And not for lack of trying."

The tension left my body until a dreadful thought occurred to me.

"The place in the forest, the mass graves… is that where…" My words trailed off, recalling the Uighur model pleading and warning about the experiments.

"Yes. I told you that we never stopped trying to find the key for the virus encoding. You can bet that your country would have done the same if they could," he scoffed.

"Is this the only place?"

The pit in my stomach grew when he shook his head and admitted there are a few such facilities, all with their own "clearing house" for the bodies.

A fucking genocide.

"This is what's on the line, Tanner," glowered the Beast.

He must have read my silence right and barked, "What? I'll do everything to protect my country. Even this that keeps me awake at night!"

I closed my eyes and used the *Sense* to sort and prioritize my thoughts and base knowledge.

Focus on Market.

"The night we met Lee. Tell me your version of the events."

He nodded, sparing a quick glance at the screen.

"He had help, and we missed who provided it..." The MSS General explained that the joint lab had staff from both countries. "We both sent our best spies among the eggheads."

"For quite different reasons," I grumbled.

Zhang nodded after a moment.

"Fair enough." He went on to describe how Lee had disappeared and not come back to work after the weekend.

"What happened next?"

"Baker. That's what happened next..." The General's face contorted as he detailed how Baker had reached out to him, admitting to having Professor Lee and offering to hand him back.

I've needed this information.

"Why would Baker offer Lee back?"

Zhang shrugged and then asked if I would release his restraints.

Carefully, I reached with my blade and cut the zip-ties. Zhang bowed in return and rotated his wrists and ankles.

"Humor me," I pressed on my last question.

"Could be many things, but if you're asking me, they couldn't risk this going public." Then with an edge of mockery, his eyes fixed on mine. "We don't have such concerns here."

My blood hitting its boiling point, I took a few deep breaths.

"Look at you," Zhang challenged. "Such typical American arrogance. Your people didn't even know Lee's true importance." His eyes glistened for a moment. "Is... he dead?"

I shook my head, sensing a moment of reprieve.

"We lied to Baker about it."

"I knew it," grumbled Zhang, whose face seemed strangely serene.

What was that?

"This is an Apex Predator. He will do his best to kill you and those you love, even on his way down and beyond his grave," warned the Beast.

"Our time is limited by the size of your son's oxygen tank," I blurted, feeling my vocal cords snatched from my control.

Beast!

The words struck him like a punch, and there was very little respect left in his eyes when he faced me in silence.

"You need me, so I helped you," the Beast rumbled in return.

"When Baker called, he told me they got a virus sample," Zhang answered.

"Why?"

The MSS General shrugged.

"They must have known that we'd eventually learn who took Lee, and that would be a declaration of war, or at least close to it. Maybe they figured that having the weapon was enough. It's the old thinking of mutual destruction détente, and it worked until we were provoked to act."

Provoked?

"Well... Baker fooled you. The sample was inert. Lee didn't trust our side either." I didn't bother to hide my disgust.

Zhang recoiled, cursing first and then laughing as his eyes stayed on the cave's ceiling.

"Continue with the story," I prodded.

"We agreed to the deal with the caveat that the American team guarding Lee would also be eliminated. It wasn't personal." He smirked. "We simply couldn't risk something from Lee leaking to the world through you and your team."

Anchoring myself to the rocky ground beneath me, I used the *Sense* to stem the increasing fury in spite of the Beast's opposition.

"Did Baker agree?" I asked.

"Not immediately," he grunted, "but fast enough to prevent the deal from failing."

Son of a bitch.

"You always knew," echoed the Beast.

Zhang snickered.

"All your values and Constitution have made no difference. Your government was willing to sacrifice you just the same."

We were in the ring, even if it was just in our minds. It didn't matter that he was sentenced to death and I was free as we battled our core ideas and principles.

"What gave us up? Why did you shoot first?" Zhang's tone conveyed pure curiosity.

"My first years of life were spent in China. I learned your language and, later on, the weight of your state-sanctioned brutality."

Zhang suppressed a chuckle, raising his hands, palms open.

"Point made. You didn't exactly trust us, but there must have been something else. I've wrestled with it since that night."

The memory of the Chinese scientist's face as he pleaded with me after Baker gave us the command still haunted me.

"Lee never asked us for his life. He simply asked to be killed so you wouldn't be able to use him further. Now, you tell me, who would I trust more?" I cocked my head to one side.

Zhang glanced at the screen when Ye stirred and then refocused on me.

"Your attack shocked us…" He admitted to being blindsided by Alfa's preemptive strike and daring escape. "Another force constantly thwarted us, and you…" the Chinese General motioned toward me, "got away."

"Tell me about the other team and the prisoners you took," I ordered.

"Eventually," he smiled viciously, "their luck ran out and we cornered the whole team. We managed to capture two operators during their impressive escape." His face twisted, his tone filled with anger. "We tortured them together, which turned out to be a mistake, as they took their lives at the same moment."

My sadness for Beta, listening to the story from the shadows, mingled with admiration for the fallen Rogues who'd had the discipline to time their deaths, preventing their enemy from succeeding.

Nameless and loyal.

"You have the same tooth, don't you?" Zhang smiled.

Instinctively, my tongue touched the cyanide-packed tooth in my mouth, and I nodded.

I wish I had more time.

12:39

The Plan

"Let's move forward. Why did you release the virus?" I demanded.

"What? You didn't believe our story?"

Rage erupted in my head at the memory of Chinese officials announcing the onset of the pandemic together with the World Health Organization that last day of 2019. I blinked away the image and shifted my focus to the screen when Ye began to murmur. Turning back to Zhang, I saw the amusement had left his face.

"All this time, and we didn't know the sample was inert. How ironic. How do you people say it? 'No good deed goes unpunished'?" In a harsh tone, the MSS General detailed how they prepared their "first strike" doctrine so that China would choose the time and place of the pandemic.

"Did you believe the US would initiate a biological first strike against your country?" I was intrigued.

He nodded.

"Maybe not your elected government, but rogue elements within it could very well initiate such a turn of events. We both know at least one of them."

Fucking Baker.

"We couldn't take a chance on our sovereignty ever again."

"What?" I wasn't sure what he meant.

"American! What do you know about being down on the ground, groveling in front of the new masters of your land? We were invaded, pillaged, and abused!" His tone and volume escalated as he spat, "China was humiliated for generations, the worst by the West and Japan. Never again!"

"The drug is working. His vitals are perfect for deep inquiry," the Aide interrupted.

"Tell me more about the operation. What was it called?" I kept my tone neutral, despite the growing storm within.

"The codename was Yihetuan," he answered.

It took me a moment to recall the meaning.

"The Boxer Rebellion."

Zhang tilted his head forward, his tone deepening as he corrected me, "The rebellion was what they called it the last time. It didn't work, our empire died, and the Qing dynasty was no more. This time..." He paused for a moment. "This time, it's the Boxer *Revenge*."

I knew Chinese history quite well, and it was no secret that foreign powers had abused China even after rifles and cannons put down the rebellion from 1899 to 1901.

"What were the steps?" I directed, feeling Zhang edging around my thoughts, probing for my role in this mess.

I wish it was the savior role I was playing, but the more answers I get, the more I feel responsible for all of this. I should have ended you when I had the chance!

He rattled off the Chinese virus release doctrine and its multi-year plan. They had more effectively equipped their military, invested in PPE gear, and propped socialist movements worldwide. By launch time, Zhang had been promoted to head of research and release execution.

None of this surprised me, as "first strike" doctrines have existed within the Weapons of Mass Destruction realm for decades. But living through this nightmare since the pandemic began had contextualized that knowledge painfully.

He noticed my fist clench.

"What? Is this the moment you kill me?"

"You wish," I replied, forcing my revulsion to recede.

13:22

The Catalyst

"So, you had the plan for a while. What led your country to execute it?"

"Stone," said Zhang. "His anti-Chinese campaign slogans and his surprising victory in 2016 forced us into action."

And I missed all of this in my post-Market retirement and new life in Venice with... I stopped, knowing the mere thought of my queen and my other life and its shackles would break my focus.

"He's the first American President to oppose us in decades..." Zhang described how Stone had led the federal government to push back on China on various fronts—trade, counter-espionage, copyrights, and the constant positioning within the United Nations' vast entity.

It all corresponded with my limited knowledge of Stone's first term in office, but something still didn't make sense.

"What triggered the *actual* decision?" I growled.

Zhang's eyes narrowed as he snarled, "When we learned that your President would use the virus if we liberated Taiwan."

Liberate? Try subjugate!

"Insanity," I uttered in disbelief, unsure whether it was directed at China or my country, which had opposed them over Taiwan since the Chinese civil war in 1949.

"Fucking Baker. We were... I was fooled and believed your country could strike when we..." he stammered, struggling to resist the drug.

"When, Zhang? When is the invasion? After all, you're killing millions already." I wondered how the Rogues were taking all this information. Their vitals hadn't changed, but the restrained rage in the cave was palpable.

He shrugged and shook his head.

"These decisions are above my position."

Damn it. I don't have time for this. Taiwan can wait.

"Why did you use your soil for the first outbreak?"

"You figured it out already," started Zhang, but something about my face must have inspired him to reconsider that approach. "It was a measured risk. It was a given that the West would be too busy with their self-destruction and ideologies to notice what took place. Who could blame us after all the suffering in Wuhan?"

I recalled the early pandemic videos out of Wuhan—the panic, the bodies, and the endless beds occupied by people with red throats.

All this happened while I slept at the wheel.

"Who gave the green light? Was it your Chairman, Ho Yang?" I was frustrated by my limited knowledge about the head of the Chinese Communist Party and the nation's leader.

"Him... others... the same people who have already decided the fate of Taiwan."

We looked at Ye as he stirred again, face half-buried in the brown earth.

"Go on," I readied myself for the weight of more guilt.

He described how the pandemic's success stunned the Chinese leadership.

"We managed to cripple our ancient oppressors without a single shot fired. All while using a weakened strain."

Of all the images that whipped through my mind, it was Dex's anguish over his father dying alone in the hospital after succumbing to the virus that stirred the Beast within. I wanted to reach out and reap the vocal cords straight from the general's exposed neck.

"We showed the West how to do it when we locked down Wuhan, but we never imagined getting them to do it to their people would be so easy."

The fucking Dragon measures.

I'm not sure what infuriated me more—his proud tone, the measures themselves, the fact that my country had strayed so far from its origins, or the reality that it all unfolded while I was focused solely on my family.

"You tell me, how different are you from us now?" Zhang's knowing sneer was enough to boil my blood.

★　★　★

13:46

The Players

Ye seemed to mumble something, but it wasn't clear through his mask. I asked Alfa to check on him and make sure he was okay for now, so that I could reclaim his father's attention.

Once I had it, I moved to my next question, "When did you decide to begin active hostile operations on US soil?"

He looked around into the darkness, unable to visually discern the Rogues waiting in the dark.

"The Chicago event..." Zhang detailed how the social strife that had gripped the nation from coast to coast provided a timeless opportunity to strike from the shadows. "The same assets we nurtured over the years have turned against your government. What better time to show some solidarity?"

The Aide was closely watching the general's vitals, paying special consideration to the drug used to keep him honest. With every word, a part of me wished it were all a lie.

"Do you mean Comrades? Ryse?"

He nodded.

"But even more than them. It's no secret that we have embedded ourselves into your academia and universities."

And our politicians. The state apparatus has fully embraced CPC back in California and other blue states.

"Tell me about the CPC." As soon as the words were out of my mouth, the Aide alerted me his vitals had spiked.

Now we're getting somewhere.

When Zhang started with the known facts about the organization, I stopped him.

"Enough with this. Tell me what your lackeys never admit."

Sighing, he admitted that the CPC has a close relationship with China and its various government arms.

"It's so ironic that the West, with its corrupt high morals, has mostly prevented your intelligence agencies from getting a closer look at our operations."

"Do you actually direct them?" I pressed.

Zhang shook his head.

"For various reasons, they have vast operational autonomy, so long as their actions serve the motherland."

Decentralized insanity. Not good for us.

"June ninth. Calexico. Tell me about that…"

His momentary surprise turned to appreciation.

"That *was* you! That Cartel traitor! You got to him."

"Answer my question," I commanded.

He was describing the shipments smuggling in the MSS operators into the states when he realized something else, "So it was you behind the attack on the compound?" Zhang snorted. "You fooled us there. Our analysis blamed rival cartels for the attack."

"How many operators did you get inside?" I recalled the huge group of armed men pouring from the trucks.

It was a long moment before he quietly answered me, "About two hundred."

Oh my god.

"How qualified are they?" My insides twisted with fury and fear.

"Top of their class in special forces, all with a background of living in Western countries and command of the English language."

"What is the focus of their tasks?" My fears expanding with every answer, I braced myself for the next.

"Providing support for local assets to further destabilize your government and country."

This is too big. I need...

"Enough! You are IT! It is YOUR task to break him and face the consequences of your knowledge!" demanded the Beast.

How?

"Use all your rage. Focus it into a tunnel. Show this monster that the world won't fall to his design and demands." The Beast receded again.

Zhang used my silence to look at his eldest son on the screen until my question brought his attention back to me.

"Who gives them the orders?"

"Short of the extreme decisions, it's the CPC," he confessed with a tinge of defeat. "We created layers of maximum deniability between them and us."

Pressed further, he revealed the CPC did use the MSS operators to help the "American revolutionaries" in their various riots across the country.

I bristled at the memories of Chicago and Milwaukee.

"Like sniping at cops to provoke heavy hands and riots?"

He laughed, nodded, and raised his hands with open palms like one who'd been caught.

Something clicked into place my mind, and Mr. Jones's words about those who were supposed to meet the first shipment in Calexico made sense: "All I know is that they're some revolucionarios."

This is how they view Comrades and Ryse—as revolutionaries.

"*Is it so surprising? That they want to provoke a revolution at home?*" grumbled the Beast from the depths.

"What?" Zhang tilted his head toward me, as if sensing my unease. "Your country has done it to others for generations. How do you say it? The chickens are coming home to roost?"

I can't let him get to me. Another deep breath quieted my mind and kept the Beast at bay.

"Tell me about the 'Travelers.'"

"All I know is that the CPC created a program to create radical activists, and those who finished it carry that title." His answer was flat and infuriating.

The moment the temptation to end the conversation, kill him, and race home nearly overwhelmed me, I reigned it in, using the *Sense* so as not to provoke the Beast to wrestle control from me.

"Tell me about the migrants."

"He's concerned." The Aide offered a reason for Zhang's silence.

"Maybe it's time to wake your boy from the nightmare." I moved my eyes to the tablet.

"No... please... I'll speak," implored the General. "We had the cartels smuggle infected migrants. It was simple math to increase the infection rates and cause further weakening of your medical system and the government."

Like Lee said, "Bio EMP."

I let out an imperceptible sigh of relief when the he confirmed that they'd stopped those smugglings after the attack on the cartel compound.

"We'd created enough damage by then."

"Tell me about Ryse and Comrades. What do you know about them?"

He spoke candidly but knew less than what we'd already discovered.

"What about 'Western Jihad?'" I pressed.

Zhang tilted his head and stretched his back for a moment.

"They serve another 'master.'" I had to press him for more. "I don't know who gives them the orders. We assumed some middle eastern player."

Deep undefined concern rose in my chest. I'd seen too much and I needed answers to solve these riddles.

"What's their end game? Do you know their plans?"

He shook his head, and the Aide made no sound about the vitals.

"They have their agendas. We help them along."

I pushed him again, and Zhang mumbled that they'd heard rumors of a more extensive play but had yet to acquire reliable data.

"What about Pax Eden and the Open Borders Initiative. What do you know about them?"

He chuckled and nodded.

"I don't know much. But from the little I do know, they're fools. They finance their death, using their radical lawyers to protect their schemes." His tone changed to near-disbelief. "It's amazing how many pillars of your society have stopped believing in your path."

Politicians, media, big tech, and academia. They've all supported the Dragon measures and the Defund the Police movement like obedient little assets.

"Your elites and ours are not that different. It's difficult to stomach, even for me," grumbled Zhang in a rare moment of self-reflection. Looking down at the screen, he murmured, almost to himself, "What would you be willing to do to create a better world for your children?"

"Tell me about Grayson," I quickly moved myself away from thoughts about my children.

Beyond the facts about the virus project, Zhang exposed the old relationship with Grayson, returning to his time as Secretary of Defense during the Charlton Administration. It was no surprise. President Charlton had been soft on China during his two terms.

"Did you manage to get to him?"

"I don't know, and this isn't my department. I'd assume we got to his inner ring, as he's using people who served Charlton with him."

"What about the elections?"

He laughed and took a moment to refocus.

"It's straightforward. Grayson is the old approach we've used for decades. Stone is just too unpredictable. Who knows what he'd do if he had to?"

Taiwan again. Damn it.

"Your time is growing short, Tanner," the Aide warned.

It felt wrong not to dive into the matter, but I had to choose my battles. Thinking again about his words, I decided to dig in on the Deep State.

"Tell me about this Old Approach you mentioned. When did it start?"

He grunted, shifting uncomfortably in the chair.

"It started during the Vietnam War. We saw you could be beaten—that your society had begun to split. So, we decided to foster a better relationship with your country to accelerate the process without the need for bullets."

"How did you manage to keep the relationship intact? Administrations and parties change."

He chuckled wickedly.

"Those we deal with are never elected and always perpetuating their power."

"The Deep State."

"For lack of a better term," conceded Zhang.

I cringed, recalling how Custer and my father had been betrayed by their government in the name of not creating an incident with the Chinese.

"Some of them are dangerous but, in the end, they're useful idiots." His tone was becoming weary.

"Baker?" I took the gamble on his apprehension.

"Yes... and others like him," he answered before asking for water and a chance to relieve himself.

★　★　★

14:40

Remaining Riddles

It felt like we'd been dueling forever as I walked back to sit across from Zhang. He thanked me for the break, glancing briefly at his unconscious son on the screen.

"If all my side conjured are useful idiots, I'd appreciate it if you explain more about The Great Reset."

He immediately sat at attention, his eyes wide. The Aide confirmed his vitals were spiking, implying that his gesture was sincere.

"You're not the only one wondering about that term and its meaning. Whatever or whoever is behind it is not Chinese."

"Back to Pax Eden. What do you know about their relationship to this Reset?"

"We gathered that Pax Eden pushed the idea out across your media and halls of power, but there were signs they might have been the megaphone, not the originators of the plan," he mumbled, departing from his confident tone.

"How would you summarize the essence of the 'idea,' as you called it?"

The Aide alerted me to his vitals increasing, "He doesn't seem to lie. Maybe he's worried."

"It's a Western Socialist theory about a catalyst event, which would enable the 'reimagining' of the economic system."

"And you provided them the catalyst without even knowing," I added.

"An inert sample, nonetheless," he said quietly, as if speaking to some other stunned part of himself.

"Tell me about Claudia Kruger, the CEO." I interrupted his incoherent muttering in Chinese.

"She is dangerous, and we never got to her..." The few more details he added I already knew, but they reminded me of something else.

"How about Columbo?" I inquired about the man who had penned the open letter to President Stone.

"Whoever he is, he knows to hide," answered Zhang after admitting to having read the letters.

I needed a moment to think, but he didn't wait to drive his point.

"You make us the villains of all your stories and films while your own people scheme and plot against you from within."

A wave of anxiety constricted my chest. I felt lost in the web, with not one but many spiders rapidly approaching. I rose to my feet and paced outside of the red light momentarily.

The MSS General shook his head, looking truly dumbfounded for a moment when I returned to sit in front of him.

"I never understood your people's true interest in the Dragon development," he admitted. "We always thought it was about attacking us. Maybe we... I... got them all wrong. Fucking Baker and the sample!"

I need more time. I know it's all connected somehow.

"Oxygen supply at 35%." The Aide's update forced me forward.

★ ★ ★

15:13

Debts Repaid

"Tell me what you know about Old Glory."

Zhang rattled off the many known facts about the civilian contracting company and Jack Washington, its CEO, since the nineties. When I pressed for more, he surprised me by talking about some black ops that OG was involved in.

Yet he doesn't seem to know about the Doctrine, my connection to Dad, or the individuals standing in this room—all of us full of stories and pain that would be his demise.

A decision formed inside.

"Back to Vietnam for a second..." I asked for his knowledge about the Chinese Incident Custer had exposed to me.

Zhang seemed confused for a moment but then admitted to knowing quite a bit about the event, including details of the dogfight and the failed attempt to capture the American pilots.

"Jack Washington was one of the pilots," I revealed when the Aide confirmed Zhang's vitals were spiking.

It was my turn to hit back. "And I'm his son, Tanner Washington."

Zhang tilted his head forward to see me better, and the sudden movement nearly forced my right hand to my Wraith.

What's this about?

We observed each other for a long moment, and when he spoke again, he didn't refer to my identity. Instead, he recounted how he'd learned about the Chinese Incident in special forces history classes.

"Insane. We studied the story of your father's escape with wonder and... awe. I remember my conflict as I found myself admiring the enemy."

"Did you suspect that Old Glory was involved in Market?"

He nodded slowly and revealed that by 2019, there was extreme suspicion about it.

"Was it Baker who revealed it?"

Zhang shook his head.

"Those conclusions were reached in departments other than mine, but I don't think it was him."

The leak? How long have we been compromised?

"Do you know if *anyone* betrayed that info?"

His chuckle pissed me off as he claimed to know nothing about that. The Aide once again confirmed it as fact based on his vitals.

"What about now? Our operation. Who communicates with you from our side?"

"I've known we have someone on your side and that we'd know when and where to look for your people. But they've kept me from all other details." He paused. "That's why your attack on the secondary facility surprised us."

Damn it. My father's words about the consequences of my action weighed more heavily.

"He could be lying. The drug is entering its final leg," the Aide stated matter-of-factly.

"Can you please check his air supply?" The care in Zhang's voice startled me and I looked at the tablet.

"Alfa, how long do we have on the tank?" I relayed Dex's answer to Zhang, "Only a quarter to go."

Recalling the Aide's warning about time, I pushed again.

"You need to give me something on the leak. He'll wake up as soon as the canister is near the end. What do you know?"

His demeanor changed as his breath rate sped up and his eyes darted between the screen and me.

"All I can tell you," he stammered, "is that the CPC has been handling the agent." He took a deep breath to calm himself. "Nothing else was ever passed to me and for good security reasons."

"What about our guy nabbed in Chicago? How was he discovered?" It was a long shot, but it was worth the try, considering how I'd screwed up the trap.

Zhang's answer stunned me. He confessed they'd gotten Moss's photo from someone on our end and exposed that they did intend to transfer Moss to China for further analysis.

"Did he catch the new variant from the infected migrants?"

"Yes. It was an unintended result, as the building also housed the infected and someone passed it to your man."

His words reminded me of what my family faced because of that.

"You didn't recognize me at first, but you *did* know about me, didn't you? The health department and child services, right?"

He smirked and admitted that by then, it was believed that I worked for Old Glory and that there was an effort to ascertain any connection to the raid in Chicago to reclaim Moss.

"It wasn't conclusive. We weren't sure."

And I blamed Chelsea.

"What about the councilwoman, Victoria Sabech?"

Claiming not to know operational details, as the CPC handles the "dirty work" for them, he offered, "It's not hard to weaponize your government to act against your people. She could have been a tool without even knowing it."

"Put the Skull on and let me have him." The Beast waited impatiently to dismember the man who'd gone after what was most precious to me.

"You do understand that you brought my family into this. You aimed at my kids."

Zhang seemed reflective as he looked back at the screen where Ye stirred again.

"I might have miscalculated what this would push you to do," he said at last.

★　★　★

15:51

Monsters Made

I felt empty as I stared at my adversary, knowing his death was imminent. He seemed to sense it. As he stood up for the last time, I rose to face him.

Standing with me in the small circle of red light, Zhang searched the shadows before focusing all of his attention on me.

His posture grew more erect as he spoke, "The West forgot what made it strong, and we're coming to remind you what the ramifications are in the name of all you've done throughout history. To us and all who suffered under your boot." His words held power and conviction, unlike the sound of a man in the final moments of his life. "America's time on the stage is coming to its final scene. I thought I'd be the one to lead my country to victory, but others will."

I sensed the Rogues stirring in the darkness, and my body braced for what came next.

"Your greatest enemies are your countrymen and women. How's that for irony? To be just like us."

I never thought I'd live to see the day, even after he warned me.

"No matter what happens, I die today knowing that my country will triumph while yours becomes subservient and ultimately erased. You have lost the will to fight." His voice reverberated from the walls of the cave. "All that remains are the Thirty Tyrants, who would rule you on our behalf."

The silence returned to the dark space as my mind filed away the various questions raised by his words.

Almost on cue, Ye thrashed against his restraints and Zhang hurriedly picked up the screen.

"Stop this. Please."

"Alfa, give him another shot and release him."

Immediately, one Rogue gave Ye a shot that put him back to sleep and another helped him pick Ye out of the grave and out of view.

I extended my hand when the screen went black, and Zhang slowly passed me the tablet—his final connection with his son.

"Would you have killed him?" His tone was even.

"Yes," I allowed the Beast to force the word from my lips.

"What does it say about you? About your noble American values?"

I glanced down at my Skull, which remained at my feet. Eyes back on Zhang, I crouched, lifted it, and put it on.

Something about my movement inspired him to take a step back.

"You fought bravely, Zhang. You were only broken by your choice to protect your son's life as a good father would." My words were measured, but my heart was gripped by my own fears for my family. "We're done. Rest assured that your son is safe and my word will stand."

Before I offered him over to Deshi, the MSS General whispered, "Who are you? *What* are you?"

"You could have stopped this, Hermano." Nico's words echoed from beyond the cave.

I looked down at my hand, fingers covered by the reptilian armor.

Do I even know?

"I'm becoming something else. I'm not sure what." An odd sensation coursed through me as I shared my deepest truth with the monster before me.

"Who *made* you? People like you are created and molded," he pressed.

Deep in the darkness.
The boy screams in Spanish.
I don't know the path or how to find him.

A pebble rolled somewhere in the cave, pulling me from the trance. My eyes refocused on Zhang and his question.

"That was my father's decision," I responded.

Terror crossed his face, and he retreated out of the red light for a moment.

"Those operators that you tortured… their friends are here." I paused before calling out, "Beta, he is yours."

The General's eyes widened, but he didn't flinch. Instead, he dropped into a fighting stance, fists up, eyes probing the darkness.

"How should he die?" Deshi asked on the team channel.

I looked at Zhang, ready to fight against the finality of death.

"A warrior's death, Deshi. He earned it," I answered, sensing a cool emptiness spreading through my middle.

"Eyes!" Beta-leader called out through the voice scrambler.

"You asked who we are." Deshi moved forward from the circle of red eyes and closer to Zhang. "We are the Dragons! And this is our vengeance!"

His roar was matched by the other Rogues' as Deshi rushed in like a ghost and plunged his blade into Zhang's belly before the MSS General even realized he'd been attacked.

Zhang grabbed Deshi's shoulders and pulled him close while the Rogue leader's right hand still held the blade in his belly. He whispered something into his ear and then dropped dead to the ground.

Silence returned as the Rogues' red eyes dimmed, returning us back to darkness.

"What did he say?" I was certain I wouldn't like the answer.

The HUD's night vision made Deshi look like a creature from the underworld, with reptilian skin and an ancient beastly head, as he answered, "That you remind him of his best student."

SNOWBALL EFFECT

– Xinjiang Province, China –
Thursday, October 15, 2020

I sat in the main cave, staring at my laptop and the "upload completed" message. Zhang's interrogation film was in my father's hands now. With China's advanced cyber capabilities, it had to be this way. Broadcasting it on a live feed would have been dangerous.

How long have I been here?

I rubbed my eyes, feeling the impact of more than a whole day of sleep deprivation. My tired eyes shifted from the screen to the two Rogues that sat together.

Are they talking about last night?

I shifted my gaze to the middle of the underground space where it had all taken place and then to the tunnel at the end of which the Chinese General had been entombed forever with a controlled explosion.

Returning from her guard shift, Jenny walked into the cave and nodded at me. I marveled at her faint smile and relaxed expression.

All this pain, and now she is released.

Roberto Ramirez's face flashed across my mind, and my shoulders slumped with the burden of my promise.

Will I be released once I find them?

"Depends on how far you will go and what you sacrifice for it. Will you stop after you find the murderers or continue until you handle everyone who ever had a hand in it? How committed are you?" The Beast's merciless questions elicited physical pain.

I don't have an answer for you. I leaned my throbbing head back against the cave wall and closed my eyes.

My body screamed against the ear vibration as I slowly regained consciousness, finding myself face down on my inflatable mattress.

Who put me here? I looked around, wishing to thank the good Samaritan, but found myself alone.

"There's a lot to unpack from that interrogation, but we'll have to table it until you're all out of China." My commander's voice snatched away the last of the drowsiness, and I pulled myself off the mattress to give him my full attention.

I guess I was out at least five hours. He had enough time to watch the film, at least once or twice.

"What about his son?" I felt a slight shiver down my spine at the reminder of what could have been.

"Safe and back at his apartment. He didn't file a complaint with the police. Not surprising. The Chinese must have reached out to check on him when Zhang disappeared. I would be surprised if he's not already on a plane home with someone guarding him."

Jack moved on to update me on Ganbold and his convoy. They were making good progress toward the border.

"The chaos helped them pass through, and they continue to get local help." He sighed. "The insurgency is official across the province. You kicked something into motion, Son."

"It is wrong? To fight for your freedom?" I was too tired to try to soften my sarcasm.

"Spare me the rhetoric, Tanner. This regime would detonate a nuke on a rebellious city if they had to. What do you think they'll do to rebels in the countryside?" My stomach turned as he explained ongoing efforts by the Chinese military to clamp down on any sign of insurrection.

"And what about the international community? The UN?"

He laughed, but there was no warmth in it.

"Cowards and more cowards. They'll do nothing, just like when the pandemic started and the media blacked out anything that might suggest it came from China."

Every muscle ached for more sleep, and I braced myself against the side of the tunnel.

"You are to stay in position until further notice. It's enough to worry about OGT right now."

My frustration grew alongside my need to return home.

"Can you at least reflect some on what we heard from Zhang?" I pressed. "For example, what are we to do with the CPC? They know the leak."

"What would *you* do about them?" he inquired, his tone reminiscent of what he used in my childhood training.

"Place them under monitoring and get the government to raid them. Maybe they'll make a mistake, and we'll be there waiting." I took a deep breath, thinking again about my time with Zhang and my growing concern about Grayson. "I'm concerned about the election and whatever is coming our way as a result of it."

Jack dispelled any notion of government help due to a lack of evidence and the hostile local government in California. He also reminded me that we're not working under Directive Two and that raiding the CPC could very well be a trap.

"Like a Deadman Switch. Besides, who knows what Zhang's disappearance will make them do? Especially if they discover our involvement."

The leak. I fucked up. Damn it.

"Why did you send Jenny on the mission?" I recalled the steps leading to the attack in the forest.

He sighed, obviously calculating his words, "The Rogue Path leads you to contend with all that has happened in your past, so you can learn and become the best warrior." He hesitated for a moment. "Who knows? Maybe I erred, pushing her to face her demons."

When the image of Jenny's serene countenance returned, I assured him, "No, you did right, and the responsibility is all mine."

"Maybe so. Regardless, we will scale back some of our operations, thinking hard on any decision we do make, since we're left in the dark about the mole." As if feeling the weight of his words on my shoulders, he softened his tone, "Listen, Son. I trained you to take the initiative. This is part of what happens when you do. I will task Alfa to monitor the CPC immediately."

At least that.

Recalling Zhang's face when I admitted the scientist was alive, a fleeting thought crossed my mind, but I decided to work on it more before talking to Jack. There were just too many open riddles to focus on that one.

After updating me on the growing unrest back home, he wondered again why my Aide remained unnamed.

"All other Rogues have done it already. Don't you like it?"

I reflected on all the help the AI had given me and relayed that to him, admitting my gratitude.

"Then why aren't you naming it?" he probed.

Because it's just one more tool for you to use to control me.

"I don't know." I was too exhausted to contend with my resentment.

"Fine." His tone conveyed doubt. "Anyway, you're changing, Son, and this is good."

"Why would you say that?" I wondered, too spent to keep up with his eternal schemes.

"Your choice about the son, Ye Zhang. That's a good example."

His compliment found no hold.

"Is it good, Dad? My progress?"

"Your enemies will grow to dread your potential."

But those who love me, will they stomach what I am becoming?

"What did you make of his final comment? About his student reminding him of me."

"We have time to figure it out," he replied. "Now, get your head back in the game and wait for instructions." His tone softened again as he relayed to me that Dani and the kids sent their love and waited to hear about my homecoming.

"Thanks."

Would Dani condone my actions? If she saw what I did? The growing sadness threatened to consume me.

"Go get some more sleep, Son. You're wrecked."

Of course you would know that.

"Yes, Sir," I answered before we ended the call and I walked back to the main cave, eager for the silence of sleep.

"Why aren't you naming me, Tanner?" asked the Aide, Its musical tone on the border of wonderment.

Blindsided, I froze in the darkness and felt all my irritation, frustration, and fears ready to explode in the wake of my fatigue.

"A name is earned. Else you are just a tool."

As I entered our living space, all Rogue eyes turned toward me. We huddled together, and I shared Jack's update.

"Will we all go back to the States to fight?" asked one of the Rogues, though similar questions grew in the eyes of the others. They looked fired up to protect their homeland.

"First things first, let's see about getting out of China in one piece." I offered a smile that felt empty and untrue.

"You're stalling because you don't know how to answer Deshi's questions. Have you learned? Are you committed?"

Go fuck yourself. I need sleep.

INTO THE BLACK

The red sun fell fast in the west beyond the mountains while I stood alone on the arid, rocky mountaintop, holding the guard position until our departure. It was tempting to wear the Skull to see better, but I wanted to enjoy the wind on my face.

It had been five long days since Zhang was buried, and we'd all counted the minutes while waiting to receive the green light to head back to Mongolia. The news about the insurgency had finally reached the global media circuit, but everyone was too busy fighting the virus to care or dare to provoke China about it.

As for home, it seemed to worsen with every passing day. The riots and social strife grew, Comrades and Ryse threatening to shut down the country if Grayson wasn't elected. It didn't help that Democratic politicians and some cowardly Republicans sanctioned the violence through a lack of enforcement in their states and cities. As for the Dragon measures, one blue Governor even said that the only way to return to everyday life was to elect the right person.

Disgusting. I need to get back.

Deshi's voice came over the comms, confirming they were almost ready to depart. A smile crossed my face, thinking of the growing bonds between us and Beta.

Just imagine if we all worked together.

I looked at the dark skies, imagining how Ganbold and his convoy must be feeling. Jack said they had managed to cross to Mongolia just a few hours earlier, aided by the newly-formed resistance cells. Old Glory personnel had met them to treat the Uighurs and collect blood samples, which would hopefully help Lee's quest to better understand whether the Chinese had decoded the virus after he took the secret with him.

Thank God.

Jack warned me the path north would be dangerous as the insurgency, albeit beaten down, still simmered across the province. We both had a good laugh at the fact that Ganbold's "new friends" had dubbed the uprising the "Dragon Rebellion," but Zhang's words haunted the back of my mind: "This time, it's the Boxer Revenge."

None of us have a monopoly on pain.

Worried about home and our dwindling supplies, we couldn't wait to leave. Jack had provided us with the rendezvous coordinates and the revelation that the resistance would also aid us.

"We're coming out." Deshi sounded ready for what was ahead.

After one final look at the horizon's redness, I lifted my assault rifle and backpack and walked down from my post to the cave's entrance.

Beta-leader led us down the mountainside, and I stopped the group for a moment at the base of it to look back up. Glad to know Zhang was buried under tons of rocks, I could almost hear his words on the breeze: "You have lost the will to fight."

Pushing down the foreboding those words evoked, I turned away from his gravesite and gave the signal to continue.

We ran all throughout the night, avoiding many checkpoints and military movements, with the help of the Eye. There was time for only one break during the grueling march, and even then we barely made it to the small forest in time. Once settled, we set guards, placed our lithium batteries to charge by the coming sun, and sat down to eat from our meager supplies.

"Feels like the Black Hills," grumbled one of the Rogues and the rest laughed and looked at me.

"What?" I wondered with false irritation and a smile.

Deshi found his breath first, speaking for everyone, "You have an advantage. Your blood hails from that frozen, hard land."

My smile disappeared.

"I grew up elsewhere. It's never been my home."

They all quieted, and I felt terrible that my past had dampened the spirit.

"Fine... fine... let's talk about the Black Hills," I mumbled playfully.

The smiles returned and for the next hour, they all shared about their Hell Year and the Black Hills Final War week—being hunted, the frozen jagged terrain, and the knowing that it was either acceptance to the team or death.

As I listened to them, I savored the ever-deepening warmth and kinship among them and noticed the many glances between Deshi and Jenny.

I'm coming home, Baby. I am.

MISSED ME?

– Xinjiang Province, China –
Friday, October 23, 2020

Exhausted, cramping calves reminded me that my twenties were far behind me on the last leg of the three-day trek north. The challenging mountainous routes required the careful effort of every muscle and tendon.

A goat would find this scary during the daytime, let alone in pitch darkness, I mused as we pulled ourselves up to the top of a ridge and found shelter between the giant red rocks as dawn broke amid the cloudy skies.

Just two hours until the resistance would meet us and my stomach gurgled. Our food supplies were gone, our remaining water rationed, and it was far too dangerous to forage or leave any signs of hunting.

"The Resistance pinged us." The Aide woke me up from a restless slumber, and I looked up to see Deshi waking the other Rogues.

Minutes later, the team and I lay prone among the rocks, watching the white heat signatures of the dozen armed men who climbed the path toward our position, holding dimmed red lights.

"Are we going to keep the Skulls on among them?" one of the Rogues asked on the team channel.

"Yes, for now." Per my orders, I stood up and walked alone to meet the approaching men.

When I called out the code word, a deep voice echoed. The rebels were thirty feet from our position when the Rogues began popping up around them, red eyes blazing. There was some commotion among the warriors close to the two men at the front.

"Dragons... Dragons... Dragons..." The chant began in low, hushed whispers, and I wondered if it made the other Rogues feel weird too.

A familiar roaring laughter rose from the largest of the two men in front of the rebels.

Ganbold!!

"My friends, our little merry band is back again." The former Green Beret's voice was jovial and amused.

Nice surprise, Dad.

When I moved forward, Ganbold met me in a firm embrace. Deshi joined us, and the large Mongol hugged him next.

"Why are you back here, you damn fool?" I made my best effort to chastise him.

Ganbold looked at Deshi and teased me back, "Did you think I'd leave you to enjoy a heroic escape alone? I told you already. I'm exactly where I'm needed."

I recalled the last time he used the mantra, right before Operation Praetorian began and the night crossing into China. There was so much to admire about the jubilant peaceful warrior standing before me.

I envy his freedom.

Ganbold turned to his group and spoke in Mandarin, "Come, Amal."

The second man approached, and the Aide and my memory both identified him as the broad-shouldered, bearded man who was first to charge the Chinese guards at the forest facility.

"Amal is a courageous man, and his story is worth hearing." Ganbold all but forced the man forward to stand at his side.

He could not have been more than twenty, but Amal stood tall, looking like a seasoned fighter while Ganbold spoke highly of him and his immense contribution on the journey north.

"Amal's family had many connections. They helped smuggle us back south after delivering the people to Mongolia." Ganbold clapped his young friend on the shoulder. "We were hidden in the bottom of stinking chicken-filled trucks until this morning."

Acknowledging Amal with a slight nod, I asked Ganbold, "Are you alone? Where is your team?"

Ganbold admitted, "I prevented them from coming with me."

"How exactly?" chuckled Deshi. We both knew how the Mongol operators loved Ganbold.

"I had Old Glory quarantine them with the Uighur," confessed the large man with a smirk.

We all laughed, and I ordered the Rogues to remove their Skulls as Amal called out to the rebels. The two groups engaged, shaking hands and chatting.

Ganbold smiled wider when he saw my natural face again.

"Thank you, my friend. There's nothing to be afraid of with these men."

Amal spoke, tone at once reflective and sober, "Our families were murdered, and we are already dead. There's nothing else that can be taken from us. Your secrets are safe." He took a deep breath and bent his knee in front of Deshi and me. "May Allah bless me with the opportunity to help you, as you have saved us in the forest of death."

Both Deshi and I were stunned. We looked up from the kneeling man to see Ganbold standing silent with a faint smile and all of the Rogues and rebels focused on us.

"Inshallah," I responded, accepting his blessing. My hands reached down, clasped Amal's arms, and brought him up to stand eye-to-eye. "Where I come from, a man only bends his knee to God, to ask his wife to marry him, and to lift his children upward." I spoke the words quietly in Mandarin, knowing that my voice carried across the stillness of the hilltop.

Amal and I embraced, and his body heaved momentarily, though no cry left him. Ganbold nodded in return, and the "Dragons... Dragons..." chant returned to my chagrin.

Not again.

We decided to give the men the remainder of the night and the coming day to recover before we marched again. The sounds of laughter and banter rose between the large rocks as we dined. Fortunately, the rebels replenished our stores with fresh food, mountain spring water, and ammo.

As I watched Ganbold and Amal laugh, the Green Beret's, "I'm exactly where I am needed," and his young companion's, "We are already dead," echoed through my mind, reminding me of another brave warrior who showed up and stood tall as if he were already dead. I warmly remembered the face and presence of Abdul Qurban, the valiant Afghani chieftain who saved Nico and Dmitri from the clasps of the Taliban.

I hope you are well in these crazy times, my friend.

When Deshi asked Ganbold about the journey north with the Uighurs, both rebels and Rogues quieted as the large man recounted their daring escape through the net China had cast across the province.

"Well, we couldn't have made it out without the resistance's help," ended Ganbold, looking around at his newly-formed crew of Uighur warriors. "So, I figured I'd stick around with them and get you all out too."

He laughed and the rebels cheered.

"Tell us your stories," I invited the rebels, motioning with my hand for them to move closer to us. They all looked at Ganbold, who confirmed with a nod.

When concern crossed their faces, Amal encouraged them in their Turkic language and the weary warriors began to divulge their painful life stories. The Aide alerted me that my vitals and the team's were elevating as we all listened to the tales of concentration camps, constant surveillance, and never-ending hope for a brighter tomorrow.

Like Grandpa's stories. Zhang's final words about my country's departure from its origins seized my heart. *Could this happen at home one day?*

"Then came the virus, and it got worse..." Amal's words trailed off and his eyes dropped. Ganbold reached for the young man's arm with his large hand and dragged him close, whispering in his ear.

Amal nodded at the OGT's former leader and then looked back at me. His voice was steady as he detailed how the Chinese had ramped up military control on them once the pandemic started. We all held our breath as he shared how his family was forced into the MSS building for experimentation until they all died.

"That night, at the forest, my whole bloodline was supposed to end," he whispered, trying to mask his pain.

Dawn approached as the last of the stories ended, and a long silence fell upon us until one of the rebels asked, "When does the rest of your military come?"

Ganbold must have discerned my confusion and spoke to me in English, "They might think that you are here as the American military and that more will come."

Oh man.

I nodded at Ganbold and then addressed the rebels in Mandarin.

"We're not the US military. No one else is coming."

Many of them visibly deflated at my words, dropping their heads for a moment. But Amal was different. He said something to Ganbold in their dialect, and the large Mongol smiled and nodded.

"I'll go replace the guard now," I said to Deshi as I stood and took my leave.

Beta-leader knew it wasn't my time slot, but he nodded.

"Nice surprise, Dad." I thanked Jack on our private channel and we shared a moment of mutual reverence for the brave Green Beret.

"We're getting an indication of some bizarre sonic attacks on US diplomats in a few countries," started Jack as we dove into other updates.

"What's your take?" I was crouched under a large rock, enjoying a full 360 degrees view from the top of the reddish hill.

"The White House blasted China for the reports coming out of Xinjiang about how they are putting down the rebellion. It could be correlated, maybe a warning sign. But I don't think it relates to your crew and the escape. At least not for now..." He updated me on the Alfa stakeout around the CPC in San Francisco. They'd caught nothing yet.

"Maybe reach out to Shida. Get some pressure," I suggested, hoping he would consider it.

"We'll see about that. The situation has been sticky since Praetorian was botched. We're getting some side glances from the military and intelligence agencies." He paused before he added, "Tall was the one to warn me."

I know I fucked up!

"Anything else?" I focused on controlling my mounting agitation.

"Oh yes," he said with a lighter note. "Your wife now threatens to come to the Ranch to wrestle my 'microphone,' as she called it, to call you."

We laughed, but it did nothing to alleviate the weight in my heart.

"Good luck with her, Dad. Please tell her I love her."

"Of course," he said before ending the call.

A movement registered on my HUD, and the Aide identified the heat signature as Ganbold's.

"I came to replace you," he said as I removed my Skull. "And I need a break from the heat between Jenny and Deshi." He shook his head and smiled warmly.

"I know. They're..." Missing my queen too much, I decided to stop and change course. "How did you convince Old Glory to send you back here?"

Ganbold scratched his short black hair as he answered coyly, "Well, I went straight to your dad, against all protocols. He gave me his cell once, telling me to call him directly if there were ever the reason."

"I see." I smiled, wishing I could have ear-hustled that one. "And what was your winning pitch?"

"Simple. I resigned from the company and promised a worried father to get his son back to safety."

My smile evaporated as my mind and heart grappled with Ganbold's decision and his assessment of my father's demeanor.

"He thanked me, approved the mission, and got General Custer involved."

He figured out that Custer is one of us somehow.

"And he's willing to sacrifice for what is right," echoed the Beast, surprising me with its presence.

A free man. Sadness flooded me as I recalled the other free men I've known and the fate that befell them. *Most of them.*

"What was it that Amal said to you?" I changed the subject, remembering the moment before I'd left to call my father.

"The rebels found something you should see. Hopefully, we'll see it on our way north."

OUR CHOICES DEFINE US

– Xinjiang Province, China –
Saturday, October 24, 2020

As both teams prepped their gear for the night march, the sun began its descent. Resting on a cold hilltop isn't the ideal way to gather strength, but beggars are not choosers.

"Head's up," Deshi spoke quietly, motioning toward the rebels.

I stopped packing my backpack and looked between the rocks to find Ganbold in an animated conversation with his team. Not knowing what it was about didn't prevent a moment of envy.

He's among his people, fighting where it's most needed. But am I?

"Let's see," I responded and returned my focus to the equipment, still wondering about the difference between the former Green Beret's place in life and my own.

It wasn't long before Ganbold walked toward us and interrupted us with the newest riddle. The large Mongol's face was severe and hard to read.

Unusual for him.

He cut to the chase, telling us the urgent news the rebels had received. Chinese headhunters were chasing a group of Uighur refugees headed north to Mongolia, about two days march from our position.

"Women and children are among them, and the men have no firearms."

Deshi and I exchanged a look, both puzzled. The whole province was under siege, and countless refugees tried to escape it.

Why this story? I looked back at Ganbold, waiting for him to answer the unspoken question hanging among us.

The Green Beret's eyes dropped for a moment, and when he looked back up, they were filled with sorrow and rage.

"The hunters are asking for me by name and photo."

My heart stopped, and Deshi looked at me with wide eyes.

This is my fault.

"Get in the game. Now!" roared the Beast.

The *Sense* helped me focus on the present moment, witnessing Ganbold's moment of equanimity, calmly waiting while a storm raged behind his eyes.

"Speak freely," I mustered a commander's tone.

His head recoiled slightly, eyes stunned wide for a moment. But then the shadow of a smile creased his weeks-old beard and he nodded.

"I ask your permission to leave with my men."

Wow. Here we go.

"Brother..." The word almost caught in my throat as I struggled against the rising wave of regret and loss. "You don't need my permission."

He clasped his massive hands in front of his heart and bowed ever-so-slightly as he reminded me, "But I do. A promise was made to your father."

The value of your word is all that we have.

"You do understand this is a trap." I bought myself moments before addressing his request.

He nodded, his jovial face not holding up against his sad eyes.

"I ask for nothing. It will be my boys and me. Nobody else can get to them in time."

"Let me speak with Command," I replied, and he nodded back and returned to his waiting men.

Deshi shook his head as I grabbed my Skull from the ground and put it on.

"Now I understand why the military and spooks are asking questions about him, and even Custer got some flack," growled Jack into the privacy of my Skull comms.

"The leak," I spoke the unspoken feeling the never-ending consequences rippling from my decision in the forest.

"It is what it is. What's next?" Jack asked.

I told him about Ganbold and the whole situation, and he listened for a long moment past my words before he inquired, "Have you made up your mind about it?"

I could sense the Beast deep within my mind, forging its desired path.

"I'm almost there."

"The decision is yours, Son."

What's this? Sudden freedom?

"Are you testing me, Sir?" I attempted to tilt my tone more to the welling surprise than resentment.

"Always. Until no more is needed," he answered flatly, as if it had been rehearsed.

"When would that be?"

"You'll know when."

Just as the resentment almost got the best of me, the Beast served up Its plan and I allowed my defenses down enough to consider it.

"This is what I want to do..." I detailed my suggested change for the mission.

After listening to my plan, Jack responded in his making-a-statement voice, "So be it." After a moment, he added, "As for our former employee, Harry Ganbold is free. Last I heard, he quit Old Glory and went on a backpacking trip somewhere in Mongolia."

★　★　★

I removed my Skull and called the Rogues to huddle up. The rebels noticed us and watched from twenty feet away.

"This is what we know…" I started in English and a lowered tone.

They listened silently to the situation as the dying light painted the giant rocks around us blood red.

"I've decided on a volunteer mission to help the rebels with the refugees." I gave them a moment and then added, "You come or don't. Choose."

The Rogues looked at each other for a few moments, and then the female Beta Rogue cracked a smile and raised her eyebrows to signal something to Deshi.

What the…?

Jenny shrugged and Deshi locked eyes with her for a moment before turning back to me with a sly smile.

"Semper Fidelis, Alfa-leader."

The Rogues started to thump their fists on their chest in unison, and I looked sharply at Jenny, who raised her eyebrows in mocked innocence.

"You spoke," I responded with a smile and raised my hand for them to stop with their fists.

Fucking embarrassing.

I walked toward Ganbold and his crew, Rogues on my heels. The two groups faced each other, faces strained by the twilight approaching.

"Did you think we'd leave you alone to enjoy this heroic rescue mission?" I asked with a smirk. Ganbold barely let me finish before his giant hands pulled me into a bear hug.

Rogues and rebels cheered as the two groups became one troop of men who celebrated their decision to walk into hell willingly.

NIGHT PLANS

– Xinjiang Province, China –
Sunday, October 25, 2020

When the sun rose, I decided against stopping and instead pushed for daytime travel. We replaced our Skulls and Skins with local civilian clothing, our growing beards lending themselves nicely to the illusion.

The march was so grueling and fast, everyone focused on breathing rather than talking. Even though it was a risky gambit, Jack tasked the Eye to help, so the cadence of our silent, swift march was interrupted frequently with RCC updates on the refugee convoy and Chinese military movements.

By dusk, the weather had turned on us, bringing heavy dark clouds and rain. It was the sign for us to catch a break, as the coming storm would also hamper the Chinese's efforts. Plus, we had already made excellent progress catching up to the refugees.

The rebels knew of an old, abandoned mining facility that could serve as a great shelter from the rising maelstrom in the skies. Once settled inside,

I called Ganbold and Deshi for a meeting about our evolving mission.

According to my plan, Ganbold and his crew would race to meet the refugees and lead them north through a known narrow mountain pass road. In the meantime, Beta and I would wire the pass and detonate it on the Chinese once the convoy cleared it. The hope was that it would buy us enough time to get to the border, aided by the rough weather, which was supposed to last another day or two.

Deshi smiled at Ganbold and both nodded at me, agreeing with the plan.

"Be ready to leave in three hours."

The Rogues and rebels crashed hard, their snores breaking the silence of the machine room deep within the mining factory. Unable to sleep, I roamed the old facility until I came upon Ganbold sitting on the hard cement floor by himself, reading a book with the aid of a small headlamp.

He raised his head when he heard my steps and motioned for me to join him.

"Can't sleep?" he asked.

As I sat, I marveled again at this man's presence and its effect on me.

He does feel like a brother.

"Let's just say that 2020 hasn't been good for my sleep."

He laughed and nodded with a somewhat solemn expression.

"What about you? What keeps you up?" I tried to discern the cover of his small book without success.

"Just sorting my mind a bit." Seeing my gaze, he held out the book for me to see clearly.

Time stopped as I was transported to the old world. In my car, driving back from Big Bear, hearing the professor and the annoying radio host discussing his book, *Endarkenment*.

"Are you saying that under extreme conditions, people can do what they want? What about morality?" the radio host had challenged. "Morality of what?" Bach had answered with plenty of resignation in his voice.

"Do you know the book? It was written by this Canadian Professor, Miles Bach." Ganbold wrestled me back from another time and place.

"Not exactly. I heard Bach speaking about it on the radio a while back…" I recounted the conversation from another life.

Ganbold laughed, confirming he'd heard that interview as well.

"I've heard everything Bach has ever said publicly, at least a few times."

"How come? Is his book that good?"

His face beamed in the dim light casting shadows around us.

"He helped me to become a better man. To reach clarity about my purpose."

"Go on." I sat upright, curiously apprehensive and intrigued at the same time.

"For example..." He quickly looked inside the book for a page he'd marked and then closed it. "There's this passage here. It talks about our inner beast and its lair within the depth of our mind."

My body froze, still not sure I'd heard him right.

What?!? Did he just...?

"Now, I never actually found this place, but I've seen glimpses of it throughout my service, maybe even heard the voice of my creature."

"What do you mean?" I leaned toward him, feeling the Beast lurking beneath.

"I lived a life of chaos until the Professor helped me to find the strength to bring order into the storm. To become stronger, driven, and purposeful."

When I extended my hand, he passed me the small worn paperback. I flipped it around to read the synopsis and saw the black-and-white picture of Miles Bach. He seemed to be in his sixties, and his piercing eyes, strong jaw, and black-grey hair sent an unexpected shiver up my spine.

"What led you to embrace his ideas?" I was unable to stop staring at the picture.

"Simple. The Professor said that the purpose of life was to find the largest burden and carry it. The Buddha would have agreed, so I chose to listen."

"And what was the burden?" I inquired, feeling my fingers yearning to hold onto the book as I gave it back.

When he smiled at me, his eyes glowed with more than wisdom gained.

Compassion? I resisted the impulse to look at the ground and prevent him from seeing into my tormented soul.

"I was afraid to die without fulfilling my destiny," admitted the former Green Beret. "It's been with me all my life. I thought joining the Army would cure it, but it didn't."

"And now?" I felt my envy rising at his tranquility.

He smiled sadly, dropped the book on the ground, and opened his arms wide.

"Here I am."

Shemtov.

"And that which you are still unwilling to look at," whispered the Beast, with unusual softness.

Bogotá.

"Will you take them to the border," Ganbold started, yanking me out of the rabbit hole again, "if I cannot?"

My throat constricted as my right hand reached for his and our left hands sealed them together.

"It would be my honor."

Ganbold picked up the book from the floor and held it between us for a moment.

"It's yours... when I'm done."

NOW OR NEVER

We left our shelter in pitch darkness and trekked toward the mountain pass. The storm continued above our heads, showering us with heavy rain, covering us from aerial threats, and preventing detection from space. But that also meant the Eye was limited.

It took us the whole day to reach the mountain pass where the teams separated and moved to their designated spots. Beta began placing their explosives around the large rocks above the narrow trail while Ganbold and his team left to get the refugees. It was late afternoon, but you wouldn't know it as the dark clouds hid the sun completely.

The Aide notified me that the convoy was due, so I ordered the Rogues to switch back to the Skins and Skulls.

Night fell and the rain intensified while we waited. When Jenny called up from up the road that she saw the refugees, we raced forward on the trail to greet them.

Looking at the long column of wet people, the only one I recognized was Amal, the young Uighur warrior. He was in the lead, holding his flashlight.

Where's Ganbold?

The refugees cried out with fright when they saw us materializing from the darkness. Amal turned to them and yelled for them to relax and stop their march. When he stepped forward, I walked to meet him, Deshi at my side.

"Tanner?" he wondered, reminding me that we all looked the same with the Skulls and Skins.

"Yes. Amal. Where's Ganbold?"

He shook his head and dropped his eyes, and I saw the tears mixed with the rain on his face.

"The Chinese were too close, and Ganbold decided to stay and hold them back." Amal looked at the ground, the young warrior obviously struggling to hold himself together.

When a similar image of my little warrior at home broke into the forefront of my mind, with his naïve face, green eyes, and lost innocence, I wrestled my attention back to the moment.

"He ordered me to lead the people to the border." Eyes still down, his voice cracked, "He said that I must first live before dying."

Damn it, Ganbold.

My heart racing out of my control, I used the *Sense* to calm my mind.

"Amal," I called to him forcefully. It did the job, and the young man snapped to look at me intently. "Get the people moving along the trail. Fast! We'll catch up."

The hundred or so refugees were visibly scared of us, and Deshi used it to support Amal's calls for them to all walk north faster. It worked.

I have to get to him.

"Call- "

"Call from Romulus," the Aide interrupted my instruction to call Ganbold.

"We can't see much, but it's bad," started Jack. He said that a Leishen unit was probably chasing us. "The Eye barely discerns the rebels setting up to defend the trail and the Chinese closing on them."

Fuck.

The "Thunder God" Commando Airborne Force was notorious for their ability to work in rugged terrain, low visibility, and with maximum lethality.

Romulus wished us good luck, and I ordered the Aide to get Ganbold on the comms while we all retreated to the ambush spot.

Thunder and lightning filled the skies like ancient Norse Gods fighting among each other. We were hiding above the trail when the Aide finally told me Ganbold was on the line.

"Hello, my friend." His voice was jubilant but quiet.

"Why did you change the plan?" I growled.

"Because there was no other way. They're too fast, and we need to stop them," he answered calmly. "We'll be engaging them shortly."

"You know he's right," insisted the Beast.

Lost for words, I remained quiet until Ganbold spoke again, "Sadly, I won't be able to show you..." He told me about an anomaly in the desert, which the rebels initially discovered. "The Chinese are building something there. It's huge. The coordinates..." He listed the numbers that would lead us there. "Make sure we get a look at it."

"Stay alive, and we'll do it together." I recoiled at the emptiness of my words.

"No," Ganbold chuckled softly. "They know my name. The country and the company will be in great trouble if I leave this place alive. This is the best case for everyone."

Anger turned to fury, tempting me to break from my cover and run south to find him.

"Everyone? What about you?" The rage caught in my throat, mixing with imminent grief.

There was a moment of silence in the heavens above, as though God wanted me to hear his words as clearly as possible.

"I'm where I'm supposed to be. I'm blessed... complete." His equanimity was tinged only by sadness as he made a final request, "Please keep an eye on Amal.

He's a good boy and has nobody. Only his desire to fight until he dies."

"Damn it, Ganbold!" Noticing the Rogues turning their Skulls in my direction, I took a long deep breath. "I promise."

Suddenly, I heard commotion filled with sudden cries and rifles unleashing sounds of death, their echoes reaching us.

"It's time," he said without the slightest change in his voice. The line died as thunder broke above us, the storm resuming in full force.

Fury rushed toward my head, starting from my guts, begging to break out of my vocal cords.

"Release it. Be with me," commanded the Beast.

But I was too afraid of what would happen next.

I ordered the Aide to update the RCC on the building Ganbold mentioned and then debriefed the Rogues, and we all tried to push our thoughts down and focus on our task.

Maybe they managed to stop them.

"Hostiles ahead," called Jenny twenty minutes later and projected what she saw to our HUDs.

The fifty or so Chinese soldiers appeared from across the bend, about three hundred feet from our position and speeding toward us.

My heart sank.

In the background, Deshi was prepping the team to blow the pass, but my mind was gripped with all my failures and their consequences and the Demon's words: "Just kneel, and we'll be done."

"Your vitals are spiking too high, Tanner," the Aide warned.

"You're not my doctor," I growled back, coming back from the endless ocean of guilt.

Calm down. It's just a machine!

"10... 9..." counted Jenny, as we all watched the Chinese running up the trail toward us.

My muscles tightened, and I took a deep breath.

"3... 2..."

"Now is the time for war," the Beast incited.

Deshi gave the order, and Jenny detonated the charges as lightning sliced the skies in two. The ridge above the trail exploded, raining endless rocks onto the surprised Chinese force.

We ran down behind the rocks, dropping the few Chinese who had survived the avalanche. Jenny ended the last of them, slicing his throat open before he even saw her.

"After me!" I roared and started running down the trail to find my brother.

We slowed down our trot when we saw them.

Oh my God.

Bodies everywhere, we searched and found our friend splayed, face down, in the middle of the road, two dead Chinese soldiers next to him. The Rogues close behind me, I crouched and gently turned him onto his back, hearing something through the rain and thunder.

"He's alive!" exclaimed one of the Rogues when Ganbold's eyes opened.

I removed my Skull and placed it on the wet ground.

"Are they safe? Is the boy with them?" He tried to smile.

I nodded, scanning his bullet-riddled body and trying to breathe against the vice wrapping itself around my heart.

"Feel no sadness, my friend. I'm the last in my line. I go now to my parents."

I placed my right hand on his chest, willing his heart to keep beating, but spoke the words for the moment, "Go to them and tell them you were one of us, a Rogue."

"Thank you." His eyes brightened at the trust given.

All the Rogues bent beside us, removing their Skulls, fist thumping on their chests while he coughed on blood and struggled for his final breaths.

He's hanging on for something.

He smiled at the circle of friends gathered and motioned for me to open his backpack. I opened it quickly and found his precious book sealed in a plastic bag.

"It's yours now," he whispered, his strength fading.

I felt the weight of my guilt wishing to drive me into the earth, straight into hell.

"How can I do it without you?" I asked, holding the book in my hand, feeling it reverberating unknown energy into my soul.

"We're always with you. Our words. Our actions. Tanner, don't be afraid of who you are."

His words rattled through me as he turned to Deshi and whispered, "Grenade."

The rain stopped, giving us another moment of silence while Beta-leader slowly reached into his tool-belt and handed Ganbold a black grenade.

"Now's the time." A contented smile crossed his face.

We all rose and stepped back and watched the ball of fire rise and consume the body of the brave Green Beret, friend, and brother.

"There will be a time to avenge this, but not now. Go!" exploded the Beast.

I placed the book in my pack.

"Let's go!" I pulled the Skull onto my head, grateful for the opportunity to let the tears fall as we all ran north.

CROSSING OVER

– Xinjiang Province, China –
Tuesday, October 27, 2020

We caught up with the refugees a few miles from the border just before dawn. The storm still raged, but it was on its last round as we made our way to the group's new leader. The civilians got spooked again as we raced by them to find Amal, but there were no cries of fear this time.

We saw the young warrior with a toddler bundled in a blanket on his shoulders at the front of the line. Hearing the commotion, he turned to see us closing in on him and picked up his pace.

"Keep moving!" I called in Mandarin, using the Skull to amplify my words between the sounds of thunder.

Amal roared at his people and accelerated his march, "Yalla! Yalla!"

A moment of uncontrolled laughter replaced the tears, as I recalled the last time my queen had used that to make everyone around her move.

Fuck, I miss her, I thought before yanking my focus back to the hundreds of people marching through mud toward their freedom.

The Rogues spread out around all sides of the convoy, scanning for threats and helping as needed.

We were on the top of the hill, the border just two miles away when I allowed them one stop as dawn approached. The sunlight was mandatory for the final part of the escape.

Amal removed the toddler from his shoulders, and the mom raced to help while the young girl pointed at me, eyes wide and full of fear. But when the Uighur warrior bent forward and whispered to her, a smile broke across her angelic face and her eyes lit up in understanding as she stared at me.

Leelee.

My heart seized at the thought of my little toe-headed princess.

She's probably hard to catch now.

"Skulls remain up at all times," I commanded on the team channel, motioning for Amal to join me.

We walked twenty feet from the crowd, looking down the mountain and north toward Mongolia. I updated him on Jack's plan and added, "Let the refugees say whatever they want. It won't matter, as they know nothing. As for you, a promise was made to Ganbold. Our people will find you and take you to safety."

"Safety?" His eyes were wide with shock. Quickly, his face hardened. "I'm going back in to fight. I just brought the refugees here."

With my right hand, I clasped his shoulder and spoke firmly, "If war is what you want, then war is what you'll have. But, wouldn't you like to become a better warrior at least?"

The young man's face softened, and I could almost see the child that he used to be.

"You bloodied your hands honorably. You're a man. When our people come, it will be your choice to go with them."

Amal nodded.

"He admired you. I now finally understand."

His words were meant to comfort me, but all they did was elicit guilt.

The leak provided his name and photo.

Besieged by fresh grief, I hugged him and returned to the crowd.

"On me," I called on the team channel and the Rogues gathered. But just outside our small circle, we were immediately surrounded by all the refugees and Amal, hands raised, palms open, chanting.

"Dragons...Dragons..." the crowd joined.

"You did good," the Beast affirmed.

For a moment, the internal darkness receded as the morning light illuminated the refugees' faces, and I felt that we'd made a difference.

"Now!" I called on the team channel.

Giving Amal a final nod, we moved out, refugees making room for us as they continued to chant, "Dragons... Dragons... Dragons..."

"It's tight," warned one of the Rogues on the team channel, expressing the tension we all felt. We were positioned on a hill, a few hundred feet from the refugees, watching them hustle the last mile to the border.

The Chinese choppers were due in three minutes as Amal pushed the people in a mad dash forward. One of the Rogues had a ground-to-air shoulder missile ready and aimed southeast.

Across the border were Mongolian army and aerial units and international journalists in the dozens.

Genius move, Dad.

"Got eyes on the birds," Jenny called, and our Aides synced the HUDs to paint red the dozens of tiny black dots in the air coming from the southeast.

Fuck.

My eyes returned to the convoy, the Aide zooming in the Skull visuals accordingly.

Come on, Amal. Come on!

"Permission to lock on front attack bird," called the Rogue with the missile.

My eyes returned to the approaching black dots.

"Hold."

If we were to lock onto it, the Chinese would know, no matter what we did.

I swiveled toward the convoy when I heard the rest of the Rogues rooting for the refugees on the team channel.

The morning sun blazed as Amal reached the international border line, left the toddler with a Mongolian soldier, and then ran to the back of his group, pushing and helping them cross safely.

"Hold," I called again.

The young Uighur warrior was the last man standing tall on the land of the Red Dragon, watching the approaching aerial threat.

Don't you dare!

I didn't breathe again until Amal turned and raced past the Mongolian soldiers.

"Put it on safety," I ordered the Rogue as we all wondered what would happen.

The choppers were hovering in the air, watching from about one hundred feet from the border, and the masked journalists flashed cameras at the Chinese while the Mongolians stood their ground.

On cue, the choppers all disengaged and flew back southeast.

The Rogues cheered and, for a moment, warmth and freedom replaced the anxiety and grief in my chest.

"Eyes on Remus," called Jenny.

We were ten miles into Mongolia, dressed in civilian garb and hidden under a bridge. It was afternoon, and the dark clouds returned while we waited.

When the large dirty truck came down from the east, we walked up to the road until the giant vehicle stopped by us. The Rogues piled up through the back. The last to enter, I closed the back doors and turned around to find the General, dressed like a villager, on the left bench. Everyone was seated, leaving me the spot across from him.

Custer beamed at the warriors he'd helped train, shaking hands, clapping tired backs as the truck pulled back onto the road. His proud eyes returned to mine frequently, accompanied by his warm smile.

"Did you get the boy?" I asked as soon as the commotion settled.

"Yes," Custer nodded. "He agreed to come along, and we got him out before anyone could speak with him."

So, he chose. May Allah watch over you, Amal.

"As for Ganbold..." The General shared that there were serious efforts by our side to find out more about the missing Harry Ganbold. "Old Glory showed his resignation letter, but the pressure is on."

"Because of China? Have they reached the US on this?" Deshi asked.

"Nope. Not a word about that or the whole crazy story about scary creatures. Funny, isn't it?"

The Rogues started to chuckle.

Custer shook his head and sighed.

"Whatever else the refugees might say about the 'so-called Dragons,' the story on Ganbold will hold, as they saw where his last stand was."

At the mention of our friend's resting place, we all fell silent.

"He will be honorably buried at the right time and place, even though his body is gone," he added softly.

In the silence, fatigue got the best of us, and soon the Rogues sank into restless, uncomfortable slumber while the General and I watched and waited.

The safe house was well-equipped, and the Rogues raised hell fighting for the showers.

"Come with me." Custer had his eyes on me, and I followed him into the kitchen to a door leading down to the basement.

He pulled a string, and yellow light illuminated the dusty space full of boxes arrayed in no particular order.

"Come here," he commanded, opening his massive arms.

For a moment, I felt like a tired child falling into a father's proud embrace.

His strong hand ruffled my long, unkempt hair, as he pulled back and tried to harden his expression.

"You're lucky I'm not court-martialing you for your poor display, Colonel."

"Add desertion while you're at it."

He laughed and I joined him.

"When am I going back?" I could feel the dam buckling.

My family.

"Tonight." His smile told me he'd read my mind.

My chest relaxed from the aggregated tension, and I let it all drop into the floor beneath me.

"We'll speak about Zhang and everything on the plane," he continued.

I nodded, noticing the weeks' accumulated dirt on my body.

"You liked him, didn't you, Boy?" The fatherly tone was rare, but always welcome.

My head dropped, but I wasn't willing to taint the memory of my fallen brother by allowing my weakness to resurface.

"Yes." I looked back at the General's strong face, noticing fresh silver stubbles against his dark cheeks. "He died one of us."

Custer smiled sadly and whispered the Special Forces' motto, "De Oppresso Liber."

"Amen."

He freed the oppressed, but left before he could help me. My heart clenched at the memory of his face when I asked him how I would do it alone.

"Tanner, don't be afraid of who you are."

His words were echoing in my darkness when the vibration brought me back to where I stood before one of the two men who'd shaped me.

"Speak with your father." Custer gave my shoulder another fatherly squeeze before he turned and walked up the stairs to the house.

"It's good to hear your voice, Son. Your mom and wife are worried sick and probably conspiring to kill me." He paused, as if not knowing how to continue the conversation without speaking about business, which he knew well not to do.

It was you who chose to be my Commander.

The pressure grew in my chest, warning me of all I'd left beyond the ocean.

"Thanks, Dad. Let's talk soon when I'm clean and rested."

"Okay, Son."

The line went dead, but my heart raced forward. The shackles returned, grinding on my body and filling me with rage.

The memory of the fireball consuming Ganbold returned in vivid color and sound, and the pressure grew, rushing from my guts, through my heart, and into my throat.

"Embrace me," the Beast coaxed.

Violence coursed through my veins. The surging desire to break everything around me, to scream until the walls collapsed on me, dropped me to my knees.

I will not lose them. I can't.

I bent forward until my forehead touched the cold basement floor and heaved, allowing the *Sense* to calm my breathing until control returned to all parts of my body.

I can't lose them.

Pushing myself off the ground, I took one more slow deep breath and turned to the stairs, determined to find a shower and sleep for as long as I could.

And then... home.

CHASING STORMS

Our ride reached the secured airfield just minutes after midnight. Deshi opened the back doors of the truck, and I smiled at the clean and shaven Rogues as they all hopped out of the truck onto the asphalted tarmac. The full moonlight glistened on the dark-colored Old Glory jet positioned for takeoff.

When my feet hit the runway, my eyes turned to Jenny on my left, who held my gaze with a faint smile. We were the only two among us carrying duffle bags when we turned toward the plane.

As we approached, two tall male figures emerged and descended the stairs. The larger of them was the General, but it took me a moment to make out who was behind him.

Dad!

A quiet murmur rose among the Rogues as the realization struck them all at once. We walked the last few feet and stood at attention, facing Romulus and Remus.

Dressed in his worn dark brown pilot jacket and jeans, Jack's rancher-wrinkled face beamed like a proud father's. He nodded as his eyes moved from one Rogue to the next, ending with me. Custer, still dressed in local Mongolian garbs, grinned widely beside him.

"Well done, Rogues. Alfa and Beta, the first ever joint operation across teams." Jack's tone was firm and proud.

I could see my teammates standing more erect, eyes forward. The sight and palpable brotherhood warmed my heart, surprising me with its intensity.

"Because deep inside, you always knew." The Beast was nearly undetected in the fabric of my thoughts.

Custer coughed the way he did when it was time to talk business.

"Beta, you are tasked back to Taiwan. Return to the safe house and await further orders." Turning his gaze toward Jenny and me, he smiled. "It is time to return to your team."

My team. Damn, I've missed them.

Alfa-four and I exchanged a glance and grins, and then my eyes returned to Custer.

"Yes, Sir."

Jenny gave a slight bow and then turned surprised everyone with the speed at which she leapt at Deshi and kissed him goodbye. Laughter and applause from everyone filled the moonlit tarmac, though Romulus and Remus kept their amusement constrained to the shaking of their heads and knowing smiles.

There was an energy in the air that none but those who have fought together would ever understand.

Deshi, holding Jenny close at his side, took in the faces of the Rogues now circled up.

"May we do by you as you have done by us," he pledged.

Silence fell on us all, and I wondered if everyone's mind returned to the decaying body under tons of rocks in China the way mine did.

Dropping my duffle bag, I held my arms out and all the Rogues huddled together for a group hug. Heart full of gratitude and grief, I pulled them all in a little tighter and then let go and reached for my duffle bag.

When I realized I was the only one, I stopped and looked up in time to see Deshi's eyes light up and fists reach his chest. The Rogues joined him in the cadence of a great heartbeat of something alive but not of our world.

My right fist clenched over my full heart and I gave them a final nod before Deshi smiled, exchanged one last sweet look with Jenny, and returned everyone to the waiting truck.

We walked to the plane where Jenny shook hands with Jack and Custer before ascending the stairs.

When I reached out my hand, Jack pulled me in for an awkward hug.

"Thank God you're back," he mumbled, releasing me before it made us both even more uncomfortable.

Custer clasped my shoulder, motioning with his head to where Beta recently stood.

"Mission accomplished, Alfa-leader."

Jenny dropped dead asleep before the plane cleared the runway, heading east on its way up to the black skies. As soon as she was out, I walked down the empty, quiet cabin, and through the metal sliding door at the end.

Jack and Custer were seated, focused on the chess board atop the table between them.

"Who's winning?"

"Black," grumbled Jack, and Custer burst out laughing as he motioned for me to sit.

We bantered briefly, speaking warmly about Beta and sharing a laugh about the young lovers and the RCC scrambling to enact security measures for this first-ever occurrence within the Doctrine.

When Custer carefully lifted the chess board to the shelf, he drew one last mumble from Jack about "future retribution." A playful grunt was the only response offered as he grabbed two scribbled notebooks and handed one to my father.

Jack pressed the touchscreen buttons on his side of the table and the large black screen on the wall lit up, showing a satellite feed of a substantial rectangular structure in the wilderness of China.

"This is what the rebels found. We have no idea what this is, and it will have to wait, even if it somehow relates to Taiwan."

We spent a few more words on it until Custer abruptly switched topics.

"How was working with the Aide?"

Reflecting on my undefined relationship with the machine which lived in me, I chose to focus on what I could at least compartmentalize.

"It's an excellent addition to our capabilities, but there are also concerns."

"Like?" Jack's eyes squinted with curiosity.

"I don't like it listening in on me."

"That feature's meant to protect you. A safeguard. You can always put the phone in another room, as it needs a connecting device to listen," explained Jack. "Besides, we never requested the file through the 'three authentication process.'"

"Fine," I grumbled, "but there's more."

"Go on," he said with slight annoyance.

"Can It override the user? Consider the user expendable, as it can continue living online?"

They exchanged a knowing look.

"What?" I recoiled a bit.

My father's right hand opened in surrender.

"You just sound like your mother. Those were her worries too, which she has addressed brilliantly, I must say."

My irritation turned into curiosity when he leaned forward to explain.

"Don't ask me to explain it in detail," he started, drawing Custer's chuckle. "But each Aide resides solely within the chip and is triggered for erasure if the Rogue dies. Thus the Aides' greatest digital wish is for their Rogue to survive. That's why the naming process is important... for the bond."

It fit Ali's special way of creating guardrails in life.

What else have you done, Mom?

My father waited for a response and shook his head slightly when none was given, quickly moving on to discuss Harry Ganbold.

"He was indeed the last of his family and will be treated as a fallen Rogue," Jack offered somberly, and I nodded in appreciation.

"Sadly, there's more news on the matter..." Custer explained that Ganbold's apartment back in the States had been broken into and ransacked.

My blood boiled as I imagined the desecration, and I barely heard my father say there was no sensitive information.

"It could be anyone who did it..." continued Jack, describing how Old Glory had fielded numerous checkups from the government about the deceased Green Beret and his disappearance post-resignation.

We remained quiet momentarily, long enough for me to compare Ganbold's brave sacrifice to my decision to stop fighting after Market.

My family comes first!

"So you say, but have you ever truly considered what it means?" grumbled the Beast, making my body tense up for a moment.

They both looked at me with narrowed eyes and brows furrowed until Custer broke the moment, "Let's discuss Operation Praetorian."

The General started with the fact that refugees were safe, with the first batch from the forest stowed away in Old Glory's FOB in Taiwan.

"As for Ye Zhang, the boy was spirited back to China with guards. They left two days after Alfa returned him to his university apartment." Custer sat forward and clasped his hands. "His story will probably hint foul play, especially with all that they already know about Old Glory."

"We always knew this day would come," Jack sighed. "We're taking precautions on our global operations."

Custer looked at his notes and moved on to share that the RCC had already concluded most of what Zhang had exposed about the virus development phase.

"Really? Have you ever figured out our side's plan for it?" I wondered what else had been hidden from me all this time.

They exchanged a look, and then Custer shook his head.

"We, too, only learned about Lee's true importance after his rescue," he started and then looked at Jack momentarily and then back at me. "I shudder to think what would have happened if you left him that night."

The words hung in the air, and I wondered if my commanders were remembering my disobedience to their order to release Lee to the Chinese, as Baker had told us to do.

"I was wrong, Tanner," he uttered.

"As was I." Jack paused. "Thankfully, we have him working in his cozy lab, eating from your mother's finest creations every night."

We shared a chuckle, and then Custer continued onto Baker's confirmed betrayal in agreeing to Zhang's demand to eliminate Alfa, "We always suspected he was a traitor."

"Beta paid the iron price for that," I scowled.

Custer continued, admitting they missed all the Chinese preparations for the virus launch.

"And then our side provided the false flag to provoke them to press the button." I could feel the rage pumping through my body as I recalled all that had happened to my family since the pandemic swept our state and nation.

"Indeed," affirmed Custer, as Jack shook his head in disgust. "As for Operation Yihetuan, or the Boxer Revenge, as Zhang called it. I wish I could say their memory of the events is wrong, but it isn't. China was humiliated for a long time, and if this motivates them now... God help us."

"Do you believe them that Stone was that much of a threat to them?"

They both quieted, and Jack answered, "Yes, but they were not the only ones."

Fucking Baker and the Deep State.

"In retrospect, their first strike, creating a mega-spreader event on their land, was diabolically genius," said Custer. "As he said, 'they crushed us without a shot fired.'"

"Let's switch gears to home," interjected Jack while I poured glasses of cold water for us, doing my best to hold the decanter steady despite the turbulence we were experiencing.

"I've got to hand it to Zhang. That bastard fought dirty and effectively..." Jack lamented how devious it was to use the MSS operators to help the radical left movements spike the riots and push them toward violence. "We have a lively riot in Philly, and we've sent the Gamma team there to see if they can get us any actionable data."

Jack looked tired and lost in his thought.

"They used our values to weaken us from within..." his words trailed off.

Like you warned us, Grandpa.

Custer snorted, wrinkling his nose in disgust as he moved on to the threat that boggled me the most.

"CPC has chapters nationwide, all positioned within friendly jurisdictions. If they are already in the phase of training Travelers," he began, referring to Zhang's admission about the CPC activist coordinator, "then we are facing a grave danger."

Jack nodded at him and took over.

"But like it or not, the company is American and so is most of their personnel."

They both stared intently, waiting for my reaction. Deep inside, I knew they were right. The Directive Two guardrail was meant to keep us from betraying the very principles we were committed to protecting in the first place.

But I'm also fucking pissed and not sure we can do what we need to with that guardrail.

The Beast laughed and faded into the background as my father moved on to the two hundred Chinese operators in our country, augmented by the decentralized nature of their missions.

"They hit us with the infected migrants," mumbled Custer. "They planned it."

We all fell quiet upon his words and their dangerous implications of future warfare among nations and even terrorist organizations.

"What do you think of the Chinese support to Ryse and Comrades?" I asked.

"Very troubling, without even considering Western Jihad and whoever is behind them in this mess." Jack's voice was tight.

"This is a big play they've been plotting for a long time." I hoped to direct the conversation again to the need for Directive Two authorization.

"Maybe so," responded Romulus, "but we'll need some actionable data before committing ourselves to intervention."

Damn it, Dad. How much more do you need?

"As for Zhang's remarks about OBI and Pax Eden financing the riots and other leftist causes, this is not such a secret, as some of their fundraisers are done on social media for everyone to see," Jack explained.

Custer shook his head in dismay, grumbling about how the Chinese managed to gain influence over our institutions.

"They've managed to subvert academia and our politicians and get them roaring at the Stone administration for even the slightest comment about the virus origins and the mega-spreader event in Wuhan."

"Which brings up to the election," interjected my father, exchanging an almost-imperceptible look with Custer.

What was that about?

"We're finding concerning connections between The Great Reset crowd and Grayson's staff," Jack started, garnering my full attention. "Claudia Kruger, Pax Eden's

CEO, has been in direct contact with them, and she's not the only one."

"Who else?" I felt the same unease in my chest that started the day Chicago erupted into a full-blown riot.

"Do you remember the Transition Election Review project?"

I nodded, recalling the conglomerate of Democratic politicians, academia, former military, and intelligence community members who had issued a report about what would happen if Stone doesn't win and concede the election.

"They've been meeting with Grayson's people as well."

The tension spread through my body as soon as Jack got half-way through his sentence.

Like fucking puppeteers behind the curtain.

"Are we going to intervene?" I pressed.

They both shook their heads in unison.

"We swore an oath, both for our Constitution and the Doctrine. The election is not our lane, but we watch," Custer confirmed after quickly glancing at Jack.

What is wrong with you guys? If we don't take care of those destroying it from within...

"Not our lane?" I mustered all of my control to keep my cool with my commanders. "What about Zhang and his work with our side on the virus?"

"This is not a new story, Tanner." Jack sighed.

"Is this about Vietnam?" I pressed harder.

Custer grunted in dismay and Romulus's face paled.

Sorry, Sir. I have to bring this up!

They exchanged another look and Jack nodded.

"We've been compromised for decades. Frankly, I'm surprised the Chinese teach about it in their military school," he muttered without offering more.

"Then why aren't we going after them? Baker, that son of a bitch, and his masters must have plans for the virus. They wanted it too!" Dangerously close to losing my temper, I leaned closer to them, hands flat on the small table between us. "Why?"

Custer leaned forward, matching my intensity.

"Explain yourself, Alfa-leader."

They're on two different pages about this. The General was irritated with my pushing, but my father looked haunted by something else. *What is it?*

My eyes returned to the General's.

"Dragon measures and The Great Reset ideas are correlated," I began making my case carefully. "Locking down the population, forcing the small businesses to close, while the big companies are designated as 'essential services' and thrive." My eyes swept back to my father. "What about all the money printing? People are being paid to stay home, getting them addicted to government help, not realizing that they will be taxed through the coming inflation."

I took a deep breath to quell the growing fury, knowing how important it was for me to make this case logically for the two of them.

"Even before the riots started, people were already confined to their homes, suckling on fear from the media, masked, and monitored for infection, as though the idea was to bring people to their boiling point."

Jack and I locked eyes.

Why did Chicago get you so spooked?

"Fine, Son. Let's talk about this Reset matter," uttered Jack.

My rising excitement was mudded by the Beast's whispered warning, *"Be careful what you wish for."*

"Zhang was telling the truth. China is not behind this." Jack looked at Custer, who gave a slight nod. "It's coming from our side, most likely originating with our Deep State."

Fuck.

"He was also right about Pax Eden as the main propagator of this plan, even if others fed them the entire thing. Claudia was the first CEO of a large company to ever discuss it openly." Jack's face soured as he spoke her name.

"We are monitoring the company but we must be extremely careful," Custer confirmed.

I grunted in frustration, feeling like I was fighting ghosts and illusions.

"What about Columbo? Any progress there?"

Custer answered, "No progress, but not for lack of trying. Whomever they are, Columbo knows about the virus and how to evade detection."

"How widespread is this?" I asked.

The General looked at Jack, who motioned for him to remain responsible for the answers.

What is going on here?

"By now, The Great Reset and its principles can be found in all Western countries' capitols, academia, and legacy media." Custer stopped to sip from his water. "Their official aim is a new economic equity model, which is a fancy way to cover up 'corrupt wealth distribution.'"

Fucking communism with another name!

"Forget about our allies for a second," instructed the General. "These Marxist ideas have pervaded our country for decades now, but we always had enough sane Americans to push back on them. But now, with the pandemic..." His words trailed off while he shook his head in resignation.

It shocked me to even consider that whoever had designed this monstrosity was probably one of us, maybe even an American. Zhang's words echoed eerily: "You make us the villains of all your stories and films, while you have your own people scheme and plot against your people."

My mind was an ocean of riddles and missing puzzle pieces, but something sparked amidst all the unsolved questions.

"When I told Zhang about the inert sample, he did seem to have a realization that maybe our side wanted *them* to release the virus. That they had been played." I left the possible conclusions to hang in the air between us.

Romulus and Remus seemed deep in their thoughts until Jack broke the standoff by deciding, "Let's move forward."

Really, Dad? Why so much evasion?

Jack switched to the concern about China and their knowledge about Old Glory's involvement in past and current incidents with them. "It was due to happen one day, and the mole could have helped them." When Jack looked at me, the pit in my stomach grew. "Whatever happened, happened. We now estimate that the mole works with the Chinese and our Deep State. It would explain how both started asking about Ganbold simult-aneously. We're back to square one with whoever is betraying us."

"It almost cost us Moss." My guilt and rage bubbled. "And the coordinated local government assault on my family."

They nodded gravely as Jack offered, "By the way, we've searched and found no relationship between Victoria and any of our antagonists."

Mention of the councilwoman made me cringe, thinking about how I'd left everything at home.

"You okay, Son?" my father asked.

"Why would you ask?" I almost snapped and caught myself.

"Some of your questions, with Zhang. It felt like you were on your crusade," he replied.

Anger pumped rapidly, stiffening my body, and I had to use my Sense to steady my breathing and avoid the mental trap. Instead of harsh words, I locked my eyes on his.

Yes, Father. A crusade, as you said.

The Beast was elated with my state of mind, and I pushed on them to reflect on Zhang's final words—the dark prophecy for America's downfall.

"Well, we're at least on the cusp," grumbled Custer, rubbing his tired eyes.

Jack kept his gaze on his hands, nodding slowly in agreement.

They are shackled as well and chained by their thinking. They never figured they'd have to use the full power of the Doctrine.

"Until all that remains are the Thirty Tyrants, who would rule you on our behalf," I quoted one of the few riddles that Zhang had left with us. "What was that about?"

"The term originates from the Peloponnesian War, fought between Sparta and Athens..." Custer explained how when Sparta won, they installed thirty magistrates to rule over Athens as a tyrannical government. "No clue why he'd say that."

"Would you have killed him?" Jack blindsided me with his question about Zhang's son.

"Yes," I replied, feeling the intensifying dichotomy between the man who answered the question and the man who wanted to get home to his wife and kids.

Romulus and Remus nodded at each other, like some ancient riddle had been solved.

"Why did you decide to wear the Skull at the end of the interrogation?" asked Custer, surprising me again. "You took it down to let him see your face."

It was easy to answer from the vast emptiness inside of my chest.

"It was his time to die. That's why." I resisted the impulse in my fingers to clench into fists.

Something about Custer's dark eyes expressed a desire to continue engaging this, but Jack tapped the table and it seemed to make the General relent.

"We're looking into his final comments. That thing about his student especially," mentioned Jack, leaving out the part about the likeness to me.

"You'll have forty-eight hours at home, and then you need to get to Alfa in San Francisco," he said after a pause.

My heart raced faster at the thought of my beloved.

"In the meantime, I'll reach out to Tall and see if we can get more help figuring out our next moves." Jack tapped the papers in front of him, signaling the end of our conversation.

★　★　★

"It's time you call her." His fatherly tone surprised me as he motioned for me to leave them.

I picked up my phone and stared at it, unable to stop the war waging inside. The man who longed to hear his queen's voice, and the man who longed for Directive Two. Minutes passed as I wondered which man would win... which man I really was... which man I would become.

She can't sense you. She deserves me.

If the Beast heard me, It made no sound about it.

Taking a deep breath, I dialed her and heard the line ring in my earbud.

"Hello." Her sweet sleepy voice melted me.

"Baby, it's me." It wasn't easy to keep my voice from cracking. I grabbed my heart when she exclaimed in happiness.

"I've missed you so much," she whispered into the phone.

"I'm coming, Baby. I love you so much. Kiss the kids for me."

After we'd said goodbye, I wobbled to my plane seat, finding Jenny still asleep in hers. The cabin was dark and protected from the blazing sun, and I quickly drifted into sleep and the nightmare that awaited me.

Darkness, a boy's screams in Spanish, impending doom, and the world shaking around me.

Eyes open, I realize it was the plane's turbulence that had saved me.

The book!

I sat up quickly and reached into my bag. The paperback cover was worn and now a brown blood stain graced it.

My brother.

Gulping down my regret, I turned on the reading light above my seat and flipped to the introduction.

"Amid my greatest pain, there was a portal. I walked through it with nothing to lose, finding a mental dimension between life and death and beyond good and evil. A place of long shadows and limitless potential. It is called Endarkenment…"

Okay, Ganbold. I'm here.

Quickly, I entered a trance in which nothing beyond the Professor's written words existed. I'm not sure I even breathed until I reached the last page and gasped.

What? This can't be it.

Deeply troubled by what the book hinted about what awaited me, I realized there was one more page. When I flipped it over, I gasped again, this time gulping back tears as I realized what I was looking at.

"Tanner. If you're reading this, I'm most likely dead. I wish I could stay, fighting by your side, until the evil in this cycle is defeated. This book will teach you how to harness the darkness, so that you fight for what is right, bearing the cost of the greatest sacrifice. But what is not written is how to get out of it. This part is meant to be the burden of the reader. I trust you will find your way back to him. Harry Ganbold."

Him? Who's he talking about?

I closed the book quietly and shoved it back into my bag, insisting the spirals of rage, fear, and guilt to leave my awareness with it.

I can't lose them. I won't.

HOMECOMING

The red sunset painted the jet's cabin red as I looked out to see Burbank Airport, surrounded by an ocean of buildings, and noticed the growing twist in my guts.

My family lives in this tinderbox!

The conference room's door opened, and Jack and Custer approached my row. We were the last passengers, as Jenny had been dropped off in Oregon.

"A few last words." Jack's tone was tight, and I nodded as they sat in the two chairs across from me.

"Team Gamma managed to intercept a van full of explosives in Philly and alerted the local authorities, who managed to arrest the Ryse goons who'd planned on using it."

Wow.

"What was their target?" I was stunned with the speedy scaling up of assaults.

Jack suddenly looked troubled.

"They planned to blow up a whole police precinct. According to Gamma, the explosives were professionally prepared and enough to level the whole building by just parking it in front of the station."

Fucking insane.

"MSS?" I wondered.

Romulus shrugged.

Any hope of hearing from them about changing the strategy was dashed when my father said he was heading back to the Ranch.

"We got red flags all over the country. Everyone's going crazy with the election just a few days away," he grumbled.

Custer chimed in, "And people aren't happy with me after my recommendation to use Old Glory in China turned into a bust operation."

He winked and confirmed what we all knew. Deep State had begun to stir the pot for him at Camp Pendleton.

"Any news on the CPC?" I asked, looking out the window to gauge the time for landing.

Romulus and Remus exchanged looks that I knew all too well.

They don't see eye to eye on this.

"Not yet," answered Jack at last. "But I can tell you that Moss is back with the team and arrived in San Francisco yesterday."

God, I've missed that guy. I'm so glad he survived that.

The pit in my stomach tightened.

I left the fight after Market, failed Nico, and fucked up the trap for the leak. What will be the price for all this?

I looked back at them.

"I'll be ready."

Stuck in traffic on the 405 Freeway, waiting to turn right toward Venice Boulevard, and I was dumbfounded by the masked people in their cars.

Back to insanity.

Sudden dread hit me, paralyzing my body in the back of the large sedan. I felt trapped behind enemy lines and alone. My eyes scanned my environment quickly, finding no danger.

"Are you okay, Buddy?" asked the masked driver, and I nodded in return.

My ear vibrated, and I answered.

"Welcome home, Alfa-leader," Dex started, and I immediately felt more at ease.

"I'm in a cab now. How's everything?"

"Alfa-four is coming to join us here in the lovely feces-infested Golden Gate City," he replied darkly.

The desire to turn the cab around and head north overwhelmed me, and somehow Dex sensed it.

"Go be with your family, Sir. You have the chance, and you never know in life." His tone was caring, but it also carried his pain.

"You're right," I responded. "We'll talk soon."

Leaving the freeway, we pulled onto Venice Boulevard, heading west toward the ocean and my home. I checked my voicemails. There was a message from Shemtov, mentioning checking on my family, and another from Holden, asking to chat when I was back in town. Dmitri and Emmanuel had also left messages, just saying hi. The last one was from my old real estate broker, wanting to see if I'd handle some deals.

Oh yeah, I was a real estate agent a few months ago. I chuckled half-heartedly.

"Turn here for a moment. I'd like to see something," I prompted the cabbie, who mumbled something about me paying the meter.

As the cab entered Venice Circle, my heart pounded at the sight of the shuttered restaurant across the roundabout.

"Stop here for a moment," I urged again and the driver obliged, parking us in front of Taco Libertad.

My eyes locked onto Nico's brown eyes painted in the mural, but I had to look away.

"Don't you dare," growled the Beast, surprising me with Its intensity.

"You can go now," I muttered, at a loss for how to respond.

It was completely dark when the cab stopped in front of the sliding metal gate. I paid the driver, exited the car, and nodded at the Israeli agent watching from the shadows between the complex and the next building.

Some neighbors hanging around the courtyard waved at me and said hello. I looked up to Chelsea's unit and saw the light inside her loft, but not her.

I blamed her too quickly.

The sounds of kids and mothers struck me as soon as the door swung open.

"Daddy!!!" yelled Ari, who always had keen ears. He waited at the top of the stairs as I approached the main level and leapt into my arms, squeezing every other concern away with his tight embrace. Leelee ran to me for her turn, and then Celeste's and Nico's kids followed.

When Celeste came in for a quick hug, I noticed her brown eyes were sadder before I saw my queen setting the food on the table.

"Hey you."

Dani's eyes brightened at the sound of my voice, and I reached for her.

"Baby." She allowed me to take her in my arms, yet her body was reserved.

Cel… She feels bad, I realized when her eyes looked aside after a short kiss and hug.

"Alright, who wants to eat?" I called to the room.

We all gathered around the table. Lil sat on my lap and Ari next to me, bubbling about how much he was "the man of the house" during my absence. It took a lot of energy to focus on his words and ignore the images resurfacing in my mind.

What would I do if anyone endangered my children?

"You know exactly what you would do," the Beast mused. But It didn't linger as I refocused my attention on my beloveds.

Bath time was a blur of splashing and simmering. The ache for my queen intensified every time she brushed against my skin as we wrestled and washed the creatures together. Every time I caught her eyes, they blazed back at me with mutual desire.

"Go shower. You stink!" She giggled when I kissed her shoulder and left her to fend for herself.

I joined her for story time and smiled as their innocent eyes closed for the day.

Dani wasted no time. On her way back to our bedroom, she looked back to make sure my eyes didn't leave her.

"Come on, Soldier."

We tore each other's clothing like hungry animals, and my wife welcomed all of my pent-up desire as we loved each other into a rare joint climax.

"Baby, I'm going to take a shower. Would you run to the liquor store for me?" She whispered her request against my chest.

"Of course. You want the usual?" I figured it was her way of testing my loyalty and dedication.

"No, actually, I'd like vanilla." Her kiss was the only gratitude I needed before she hurried to the bathroom.

When I entered our bedroom with the ice cream and a spoon twenty minutes later, her face lit up, but it didn't last long.

"It's awful out there, isn't it?" she muttered.

"Yeah, I can't believe how... dirty... and..." I struggled for the right words.

As she devoured her ice cream, Dani complained about how alien the city had become with the election just around the corner.

"If you dare to say that you don't support Grayson, you are boycotted or even attacked..." She shared some stories from the neighborhood that turned my stomach. "How can they say they're fighting for democracy?"

"It wasn't always like this," I mumbled, recalling better days in Venice. "It was always weird, but at least there was tolerance for other opinions."

She licked the last drop of ice cream off her spoon and pursed her lips, eyes boring through me.

"What?" I felt unmoored in my own home.

"Will our old life come back again? After this is over..." Anguish filled her voice before it trailed off.

"The pain of those you love is a stepping stone, a test of your conviction to walk the path." Words from *Endarkenment* paralyzed me.

"Are you okay, Baby?" she asked, but the words faded beyond the screen of the emotions that had been unleashed in my heart.

I have to tell her. I longed to reveal everything I'd done and what awaited me. It was wrong and weak, but also a possible way out. *She's the only one who can stop me. If I only tell her.*

"I-" My ear vibrated and I reached for my phone.

"Stop, Tanner. Tell me whatever you are about to say. Please, Baby." Her pale face and wide eyes tempted me, but only for a moment as I accepted the call.

"Hello."

"Tanner." I was speechless as the AI pleaded in its melodic voice, "Whatever you plan on saying, consider that everything will change in the next few moments." The line went dead and I sat frozen with the phone next to my ear.

Can I trust It?

"Honey?" Dani reached to caress my right arm.

"This might be more than a machine," echoed the Beast, sounding simultaneously intrigued and wary.

The phone chirped and I brought it down from my ear to view the screen.

The text was brief: "Bird heading your way. TBA. Confirm."

I looked into Dani's wet eyes as my finger pressed "Okay." And just like that, the sliding door to the reality in which I revealed it all to Dani was closed.

San Francisco.

I dropped the phone and reached out to pull her close, but she pushed me back.

"Are you leaving?"

The suffering quickly intensified as the shackles tightened.

"Yes. I have to," I replied.

"It's not fair. Not fair," she cried.

I stroked her long black hair, holding her weeping body, struck dumb by the intensity of her emotion.

She's usually not so...

"You've been gone so long. What if you can't come back to us in time?" She looked up at me, her deep blue eyes welling with tears and something else.

In time? I wondered but didn't ask. *There's no time.*

Instead, I held her chin and kissed her.

"I'll be back for you and the kids, even if the devil makes me cross hell first."

I kissed the tears that fell down her cheeks before tearing myself from the bed.

The kids were sound asleep, and I felt my resolve shaking as my lips kissed their foreheads.

How can I leave them?

"*You must,*" whispered the Beast, serving up the memory of Ganbold's last stand.

★　★　★

Outside the complex, I wished I had my bike while waiting for the ride-share to arrive. My mind returned to Jack and Custer and our extended debrief on the plane.

"Well, we're at least on the cusp," Custer's words resurfaced with the memory of my father nodding in agreement.

We're blind in the dark. They don't know what to do.

"The darkness is where we fight, Tanner. Embrace it already."

NO SAINTS

– San Francisco, CA –
Friday, October 30, 2020

"**S**ee you at the safe house soon, Boss."

"Thank you, Sarah," I replied as my feet reached the dark runway.

The early morning light had barely penetrated the dark clouds, and I zipped my jacket against the cold air.

Hearing a whistle, I turned to see Sarah pointing at the black SUV pulling up a few yards away. Moss emerged from the driver's side in black urban clothing, smiling and waving at Sarah as he approached me.

I dropped my duffle bag to embrace my brother.

"You look good." I clapped his back as he stepped away and I scoured his dark face for scars and remnants of trouble.

"I *feel* good."

But...? Something about his black eyes made me feel whatever he left unsaid as we got into the SUV and left the small private airstrip just outside San Francisco.

"Man, I love that ranch so much..." Moss told me about his rehabilitation and time in South Dakota with my parents. "Your mom's cooking is legendary," Alfa-three added at the end, and my mouth salivated in response.

It is. Cooking and technology—tough to discern the stronger superpower.

"How operational are you?" I asked, keeping my eyes on the empty freeway.

It took him a moment.

"Probably 80%, Sir. But I had to come. No way I'm missing the finale."

We laughed, but then I pressed him again, this time about his mental state.

He looked out his window and sighed.

"He's still in my nightmares. The accented man who tortured me in Chicago." Alfa-three paused for a long moment, and I didn't interrupt. "I still have to use the *Sense* to get back to sleep sometimes."

I felt my anger simmering, like a father whose child has been abused.

Moss pivoted from the thorny subject and told me how the team can't wait to hear about China.

"Jenny didn't tell us much."

There was an unspoken heaviness between the few words that didn't feel related to Operation Praetorian at all.

It's always about Market and leaving them. I took a deep breath as another realization sucker-punched me. *Just like I leave her and the kids to wake up and do life without me.*

"We'll talk about it soon," I promised, putting my sunglasses on to hide the growing rift inside me.

The safe house was an old warehouse in the shuttered downtown area where the neglect in the streets broke my heart. More homelessness, so many closed-down businesses, and far too many masked people shuffling around like Zombies.

Moss clicked a remote, opening the rollup garage door to reveal the entire Alfa team walking toward us with giants grins. Our warm reunion was sealed by Liam doing his best to make us laugh and nobody paying attention.

"Where's Hux?" I didn't see the Norse giant.

"He's in the nest now, watching the CPC. Sarah will join him there shortly," Dex replied. "For now, let's get you settled." He motioned for me to follow him to our command room and told me Romulus wanted to speak to me before leaving me in the small space with a few laptops and screens on the table.

"We lucked out, Son," Jack began once the line was established. "We caught the mole broadcasting directly to the CPC. Thanks to Moss's data grab in Chicago, we isolated some IP addresses and cell numbers. We believe that we have Daj Morris's cell number, which is where the text message was sent."

"What was it?" My body tensed with anticipation.

"Just a short sentence: 'Daj, my love. 1848.' We suspect it originated from South Dakota." Jack's tone betrayed stress. "We have no clue regarding the meaning of the numbers."

"Was there anything else?" I noticed an increasing sense of trepidation.

"There was an encrypted file too, but we couldn't download it."

Shit.

"What now?"

"Security is doing a massive undercover search on every female employee in Old Glory. We're refraining from sensitive operations, but this isn't what I called you about."

Antsy, I rose from the chair to pace the room.

"Daj is most likely *in* the CPC building, and we're authorizing an op," declared Jack.

Finally!

"We've approved a limited Directive Two mission to acquire Daj for interrogation and elimination."

"A raid?" Rejuvenated hope rose in my chest.

"No, Son," he replied, dashing my desire for fast action. "We'll have to get him in the open. It's the *only* way we'd approve DIR2."

Fuck.

I was impressed with the decision but hated the constraints of the mission itself.

"What are we going to do? Just wait outside for him to show up?"

"Do you have any better ideas?" he countered, irritated.

"How about we ask Shida for help?" I volleyed back.

There was a moment of silence before Romulus answered, "That will be your prerogative, Alfa-leader."

"How are we doing on other fronts?" I sat at the desk again and refocused.

He updated me on the rising tension across the country with the election just days away.

"Any actionable data?"

"No. Comrades and Ryse have been refraining from revealing any important details since Chicago. However they communicate, it's unknown to us for now."

The fucking leak again.

"Chad has been helping us decipher all the usual crap they post, but nothing pertinent has emerged. On the other hand, there have been quite a few posts on social media about the vigilantes."

I remained quiet, knowing that neither he nor Remus loved how our actions had sparked this social phenomenon.

"Besides some fringe groups trying to do copycat cases, many other ordinary citizens have voiced their desire for the vigilantes to come and help in various hotspots." He waited momentarily, but continued when

I offered zero reaction. "Ken is in Los Angeles. He's following a hunch regarding Ryse down in your neck of the woods."

"Do we know what it's about?" Tension returned, this time with fear for my family.

Jack said no, but he'd been keeping in touch with the young journalist.

"That kid figured out that we're connected to the vigilantes but never exposed anything about it. I trust him more every time he risks his life to expose the true face of the riots and mayhem." Something about his voice sounded tired and overwhelmed.

"How are you, Dad? Really..." I did the unthinkable, asking Romulus a personal question.

He chuckled but then got serious again once he realized my inquiry was earnest.

"It's been hard, Son. I now understand my father's unrelenting quest to prepare."

"Do you miss him?" I asked, taking advantage of my father's rare moment of revelation.

"Your grandpa loved this one quote taken from General Sherman who wrote to General Grant in 1864: 'I knew wherever I was that you thought of me, and if I got in a tight place, you would come—if alive." There was a long pause, and then my dad summarized his response, "I miss his strength, Tanner. Especially now."

His words hit me hard, and I wanted to tell him he could count on me, that I would be there. But nothing came out of my mouth.

I won't lose my family to this.

The conversation ended, leaving neither one of us satisfied.

I sat with Alfa to discuss Praetorian and our time out east. Jenny had taken over the nest outside the CPC to allow the entire team to sit with me.

"She probably just didn't want us to see her blush," quipped Liam, who was promptly smacked on the head by Sarah while Hux feigned upset, grumbling that it was his role to whoop on the smaller Latino operator.

She told them about Deshi.

I told them everything else in detail, finishing the story at the point when we were picked up by Custer in Mongolia. They looked excited as I described the closeness with Beta, but their faces grew sad when I shared Ganbold's great sacrifice.

They didn't meet him, but they love him too.

"What about you?" I looked up. "I asked you to be ready to execute a young man who did nothing besides be the son of a monster."

They looked at each other, and then Hux spoke for them, "We didn't like it one bit, but this is war and we're done playing."

They all nodded, and I could tell that something had changed.

We're changing. This whole mess is... transforming us.

"And you lead it," the Beast whispered, causing me to shift in my seat.

"What about the CPC? And Daj?" Dex wondered.

While I relayed my conversation with Romulus, I could sense their resonant agitation with the limited options. After some initial grumbles, I switched the subject to their feedback on the new gear.

Moss and Liam spoke over each other, professing their love for Skin and Skull, which didn't surprise me since they are our techy nerds.

Sarah interjected, mentioning rumors that China's "Dragon Rebellion" had left Xinjiang simmering.

"It's time to introduce it here," she added.

"Just don't say anything to Romulus. They're bothered enough with the whole vigilantes narrative." I chuckled.

"What about the Aides? Do you like them?"

They all looked at each other and then admitted to loving the new AI feature.

"What did you name yours?" asked Moss.

I admitted to not having named mine, shifting in my seat again.

"Why?" wondered Liam.

"I'm just not ready, I guess." I smiled weakly. "But I do need to make a phone call."

BY ALL MEANS NECESSARY

I leaned against the wall next to a full dumpster, its contents baking in the afternoon sun and decaying aroma threatening my senses. Dressed as a masked bum, I waited for her. Alfa was bouncing off the walls in the safe house, frustrated by yet another wasted day in the wake of the country's growing tension. Election day a few days away, and our hands were tied.

At the sound of heels clicking on broken asphalt, I turned to see a well-dressed woman wearing shades and a black Hijab across her face.

She stopped beside me and wrinkled her nose.

"You smell the part." Shida chided as she removed her glasses and revealed her beautiful brown eyes.

"Yeah, sorry about that." I laughed. "I'll make this quick..."

Her face grew serious as she listened to my request.

"Is this personal, or for the country?"

There was no way I would lie to this woman, who had trusted me before and reminded me of my Dani.

"In this instance, it's all the same," I answered the question honestly.

She leaned against the wall beside me.

"It's becoming harder and harder to do my job." Scanning the environment around us, she continued with a deep sigh, "But I'm also increasingly concerned about the country if Grayson wins. Who knows? I could be arrested next."

She's feeling it. Will she buckle? I waited patiently, knowing I needed her full buy-in for this to work.

"Fine," she grumbled. "I'll be in touch."

"Thank you, Shida," I whispered as she put her shades back on and turned to walk away.

When she was out of sight, I called Jack and shared my plan.

"Impressive, Alfa-leader. We can expose it and see if the leak will go for it."

KNOCK KNOCK

– San Francisco, CA –
Sunday, November 1, 2020

It was noon, and the team was on edge watching the various news channels. The nation was less than seventy-two hours away from voting, and the American people's divide was more palpable with every broadcast, no matter which side had the mic.

So much distrust. How did we get here?

When my phone chirped, the Rogues turned toward me like a pack of hungry wolves. I read the long text twice and then looked back up at them with a wicked smile.

"It's on. DHS will visit them in three hours. Let's get ready."

The small room immediately exploded into action as Alfa prepared.

★   ★   ★

The nest was in a five-story office building opposite the CPC compound. It was abandoned and vacant because of the stringent Dragon lockdown the authoritarian local government enforced.

We had a perfect view from the fourth floor to the expansive three-story structure that housed the Chinese People Collective's West Coast headquarters. Surrounded by a six-foot stone wall, its access was controlled by a posted guard. My eyes focused on the Chinese red flag flying over one side and the American counterpart on the other.

Right here, in our country. The immediate quiet rage in my core reminded me of its expanding presence.

"They're coming," grumbled Hux, his sniper rifle aimed at the two black sedans approaching the CPC's gate.

When the cars stopped by the guard and the front vehicle's passenger door opened, Shida stepped out. Her brown hair moved with the breeze as she spoke with the masked guard, who seemed to be calling someone on his comms.

Other agents emerged from their cars and stood behind Shida while she fidgeted, waiting on the guard to finish his call.

"Head's up," called Hux as a few men in business suits emerged from the main entrance and walked toward the gate.

Jenny heard us over the team channel and asked Hux to zoom in and share what he saw through his augmented telescope.

"It's Paul Shi!" she exclaimed, just before my Aide confirmed it in my ear.

Hux synced his view to our phones, and I finally got to see the CEO of the CPC. Paul was of Chinese stock, in his early forties and about my height with a wiry body type and a handsome face. He moved gracefully, head swiveling left and right as he approached the gate and my friend.

A predator. The hairs on my neck confirmed it.

As I watched Paul converse with Shida, his eyes scanning the environment, darting around and up to our building and others, the rage was suddenly replaced by dread. Jenny's words after her stint inside the CPC echoed: "There's something about him that's just like you, Sir. You're both natural-born killers."

My eyes turned toward Hux and his sniper rifle.

"You can end him now," challenged the Beast.

There's no chance that would be approved.

The Beast receded, leaving a trail of disappointment I had no time to contend with.

Shida turned away from Paul and entered her car, and her agents followed suit. Paul smiled deviously at the departing agents.

"You missed your opportunity," the Beast growled.

I pushed the thought away and left to meet Shida.

★　★　★

The underground parking structure was nearly empty as Shida and I huddled inside of the trash room in the back of the structure.

"We were followed. I think they were undercover cops." Shida's tone was full of concern. "The mayor here is a piece of shit, but I didn't think he had the balls to send the police after us."

"So much for 'defund the police,' eh?" I recalled how this mayor was one of the first to bend his knee, in front of the protestors, at the height of the riots in his city.

I watched how quickly her brilliant mind connected all of the dots.

"Tanner Washington, did you happen to alert them to our checkup today?"

Busted.

It was a trap we'd laid for our mole.

"Not exactly." I held my hands up in half-surrender.

"Not *exactly*?" Her eyes blazed until she put out the fire with a sigh.

"Tell me about Paul Shi." I pivoted us away from my slight deception.

Brow still furrowed, she took the bait.

"He's a smooth talker, but I sensed he could become violent instantly."

Predator.

We were quiet for a moment, both calculating, until Shida placed her hands on her hips and squared her shoulders.

"I've been wondering about you, Tanner."

"Oh really?" My initially light response was arrested when I saw her eyes.

Just like Dani. I'm in trouble.

"There's a quote by Rumi that's been haunting me. It took me some time, but I realized it reminds me of you."

"Okay?" I was unsure where she was going, the restlessness in my chest offering the only clues.

She said it in a low voice, taking time to punctuate every word: "I want a troublemaker for a lover; blood spiller, blood drinker, a heart of flame. Who quarrels with the sky and fights with fate. Who burns like fire on the rushing sea."

I knew of the famous thirteenth-century Sufi poet but wasn't sure how this quote related to me.

"Until you understand," the Beast offered, fading like a wave returning to the deep blue.

Shida chuckled, reached out to hug me, and walked away, leaving me scratching my head.

More fucking riddles!

I was on my way upstairs when Dex pinged me to hurry. Breaking into a run, I reached the nest less than a minute later.

Alfa-one rushed toward me with the news.

"Shida's visit kicked the hornet nest," he began as we walked toward the large windows to look down at the CPC.

"Using Moss's data grab again, the RCC intercepted a CPC broadcast about the Traveler intending to leave the building." Even without looking at him, I could hear Dex trying to measure his excitement.

I feel it too.

"Do we know where to?" My eyes remained glued to the ominous building across the street.

"We have a fair assumption, as we got confirmation about Daj's cell texting the mole back in South Dakota. The text was short. It said, 'Coming. 1848.'"

"Did the RCC figure out this 1848 code?" I glanced at Alfa-one who shook his head.

Damn it.

My mind grappled with the new info until Moss alerted us on the team channel, "Movement in the alley."

Alfa-three had been positioned behind the CPC, camouflaged as a piss-drenched homeless person, and had a perfect view of the rolling metal doors.

"We've got the Eye." Dex quickly brought up the live feed on a laptop next to Hux, who was prone, looking out, sniper rifle at the ready.

We all bunched around the screen, watching it live while Moss described the view from his position.

"I see the target. He's arguing with…" Moss paused abruptly. "He's talking with the accented man from Chicago."

Oh shit.

I wondered how it was for Moss to see the man who had tortured him as he continued whispering his report while the Eye confirmed it from above. Three black SUVs were arranged with Daj and another ten men milling around.

"The target pushed the accented man and entered the middle car. Tagging it." Moss confirmed the exact car for further tracking by the Eye.

In the background, I could hear Dex alerting Jenny to get ready.

"Is Paul around?" I asked.

"Negative," responded Moss.

"Are there any other Chinese, besides the accented man?"

"Negative. The rest are primarily white and black males."

"He's likely using some of his Comrade assholes," I replied.

Easier for us.

Dex touched my shoulder before he updated me.

"Jenny's ready to follow them on your command."

"Do it." I kept my eyes on the screen as everyone piled into the cars, including the man identified as the accented man.

"Aide, contact Romulus," I commanded into my earbud as the convoy departed the CPC and the sole motorcyclist followed at a distance.

★ ★ ★

"It worked! That was a good move, Son."

I stood in one of the empty cubicles, away from Alfa where they waited in the main space.

"What's the analysis?"

"We assume the convoy is heading to South Dakota, presumably to meet and maybe evac the mole."

Something doesn't add up.

"Why would the mole need a convoy to get out? Couldn't she leave on her own?" I wondered which of Old Glory's employees had betrayed us. "What are we missing?"

Jack sighed and admitted there were many holes to fill, beginning with, "We still don't know what 1848 means." He grumbled something else to himself before continuing, "Anyway, with Moss's confirmation about the accented man, we know there's at least one MSS operator is in the convoy."

Where are the rest of them? Are they getting ready for the election?

Neither of us spoke of our other fears.

"How do you want to proceed?" Jack asked.

I looked around the cubicle, noticing a lone picture of a beautiful family still posted on the wall.

Are they home? Confined and scared?

"Let's hit them on the open road. Can you do something to divert them to continue along the coast?" There was no time to wait as the election clock tick-tocked away and my concerns about the larger play grew. Alfa knew Western Oregon by heart if only the convoy could be pushed there.

There was silence for a moment, and then Jack confirmed that some fake alerts could be planted with police departments across northeastern California.

"This could work, as the CPC is quite intertwined with the local government here and would therefore know." He didn't try to hide his disgust.

Let's use it against them.

"This could also work better with the Eye. It already covers the western coast," he mused, mostly to himself. "Keep Alfa-four on the target and get the team up north. We'll be in touch."

"Time to hunt," howled the Beast.

HELLFIRE

23:15

Like an ancient aerial predator, the modified stealth chopper quietly roamed the night skies. All of Alfa was onboard, except Jenny, who had been hard-press riding for hours following Daj from San Francisco.

Jack's gambit of using fake alerts worked and someone, presumably in the CPC, had alerted the convoy to the increased police presence across northeastern California. The convoy initially swung just southwest of Sacramento and then, with one last "nudge," pivoted back to the coast to take the 101 to Oregon. The coastal highway was right at the forest's edge, one lane on each side, high on the Oregonian cliff with only the dark ocean below.

I sat by Sarah who was focused on flying us as low as possible, just above the endless tree line.

"I trust our stealth capabilities, but it wouldn't hurt to give us an edge with low altitude," she grumbled when she saw me getting shifty in my seat when we got a little too close to the treetops for my comfort.

Dressed in our Skins and Skulls, the rest of us were more than ready for this mission. We had broken all the game rules and were about to do much more. When I looked back at the team and their red eyes, I realized I missed them.

Beta... Deshi... How are they faring? Now I have two teams to worry about.

Just after midnight, we were notified that we were a mere thirty minutes out. The RCC synced the Eye feed with our Skulls, so we saw the three SUVs driving north along the coast. Luckily, only a few cars traveled this windy road after dark, and we did have a plan for the few who braved it.

"The target is passing first checkpoint," updated a female RCC voice.

I imagined our undercover crew, dressed like road maintenance workers, rushing to block the road, faking a midnight road work operation. Jack had surprised me with news that he'd sent Rogue trainees to man both the checkpoints, one south of the convoy and the other on the northern side, effectively creating a zone with no other cars but the ones we were after.

"We have to use recruits. All the other teams are embedded across the country," he had explained.

"Five mikes for contact," reported the RCC female.

Alfa's readiness was palpable, even from the passenger seat as Sarah pivoted the chopper toward the highway and my ear vibrated for a private call.

"You ready?" Romulus asked as Sarah maneuvered the chopper to follow the convoy yet stay out of sight until it was time.

My augmented Skull visuals watched the three black SUVs barreling their way with blazing high beams. We were about a mile behind them, flying parallel above the trees.

"Yes, I see them." I felt the anticipation building in every muscle of my body.

"There's no going back from this, Son. You know that, right?"

He was right. The ramifications of this plan would ripple. But my father didn't know everything about my state of mind and the Beast, who could barely contain Its desire to get a hold of those who hurt my country and family.

I'm done playing games. This is the enemy.

"Understood. Alfa-leader, out."

"Sixty-seconds. Stay out of the impact zone," warned the RCC member.

We all had eyes on the three large vehicles driving along the coast.

"5... 4... 3..."

"Activating communication jam umbrella," Sarah updated.

This was an essential part of the plan, as Alfa-five would continue to hover above us, effectively blocking any communications out of the area.

"2... 1..."

"Eleven o'clock!" exclaimed Hux as the two orange lights appeared from the darkness above the ocean.

We could barely make out the attack drone as its air-to-ground payload rushed toward the unsuspecting convoy like a bat out of hell. Two massive explosions rocked the night, obliterating the first and third SUVs, leaving the middle one intact. The remaining car swerved to the side of the road and stopped.

"Now, Sarah!" I commanded, feeling my body coil for action.

As the chopper raced toward the wreckage site, we saw four hostiles abandon the SUV and run toward the forest. Jenny drove her bike straight into the woods and then jumped off it to race after them on foot.

As soon as Sarah touched the bird down, we all disembarked into our fastest run like hungry fiends. The chopper lifted as soon as the last Rogue hit the ground.

The Aides synced everything between our HUDs, showing us where Jenny, every Rogue, and the hostiles were positioned.

"Hostiles are moving into the forest," reported the Aide. It was no surprise. The MSS operator led them, but even he was unmatched by what was coming for him and his charge.

"A few efforts to make calls were blocked," the Aide added.

"Alfa-leader, Alfa-three, over," called Moss.

"Alfa-three, go!" I barked, racing between the giant trees, holding my Wraith out and ready.

"I want him," hissed Moss.

"He's yours," I promised, seeing on the HUD where Alfa-three flanked me.

"Alfa-four, engaging," said Jenny. She was ahead of us and must have reached a perfect opportunity.

My assassin. God help us.

We reached Jenny after she had eliminated the two Comrade guards.

"The last two are hiding just beyond this tree," she whispered on the team channel.

There was no need to speak further, as Alfa worked as one fast, deadly organism. We circled the remaining hostiles as the rapid submachine fire started.

"I'm hit!" growled Liam as he charged forward. The MSS operator was shooting, but didn't see Moss, who tackled him to the ground like a viper striking from the midst of nothingness.

The other man fired his handgun wildly until I jumped him from the side, knocking his firearm to the ground.

Everything moved fast as Dex attended to Liam, Moss wrestled the MSS operator on the ground, and I pinned the sought-after Daj Morris to the forest's floor.

"What the fuck? What the fuck?" Daj screamed in fear.

"Hi, Motherfucker," I snarled, pulling a taser from my belt and knocking him out with a jolt to the neck. As he collapsed, I rose to watch the fight between Moss and the Chinese soldier.

"Liam's fine. Just a graze," Dex assured us as we all gathered around the two men.

The Chinese operator knew how to fight, but he was no match for a Rogue, especially one with a grudge.

Batting aside the MSS punch, Moss roared angrily as he kicked the Chinese straight in the stomach, dropping him to the ground again. Alfa-three jumped on him, raining strikes on his face.

"Stop!" I commanded.

Moss's right fist stopped in midair but didn't drop, and Dex rushed forward to get Moss off the battered Chinese operator.

"Get him up on his feet," I ordered the Norse giant who advanced and grabbed the MSS soldier from the back, lifting him like he was made of paper.

I got up close and personal with the enemy operator, inspecting his battered face, using my red eyes to nearly blind him.

To his credit, he didn't appear afraid as he spat a broken tooth to the ground.

"I guess you won't talk," I said in Mandarin.

He looked momentarily surprised and then spat, "I will!" He coughed hard and then hissed, "The Tyrants are coming."

I recoiled, suddenly remembering Zhang's words: "All that remains are the Thirty Tyrants, who would rule you on our behalf."

"Watch out!" barked Moss as time slowed to frame by frame.

The MSS operator had managed to get out of Hux's clutches, tripping him to the ground and pulling his concealed dagger in one fluid motion. But Moss was faster with his Wraith and shot the Chinese soldier one time right in the middle of his forehead.

UNMASKED

– Cape Perpetua, OR –
Monday, November 2, 2020

04:47

We marched the long ten miles through the woods to the base, hefting Daj Morris on the unfolded stretcher. It was almost five o'clock in the morning when Cape Perpetua towered ahead of us.

"He's waking up," grumbled Hux. "Just in time."

I turned to see the four Rogues drop the stretcher to the ground as the man on it thrashed against his binds. Terror twisted his face, his mouth opening to scream, yet none could be heard through the well-placed gag.

I walked toward him and bent down by his head, using the scrambled alien-like voice of the Skull.

"We'll cut the ties. But dare to run, and you lose your dick. Understand? Nod that you understand."

When Daj nodded slowly, I rose.

The Rogues released him, and everyone fell into step behind me as I started up the mountain.

The giant hemlock tree was just ahead when tension gripped my body. My head swiveled around, sensing someone's eyes upon us. I raised my right fist to stop the column and scanned the heavy forest around us. The cold breeze rushing through the trees, ruffling the leaves and branches, something else rustled just outside of my awareness.

It's you!

No response came, unless it was the nightmare that followed the attack on Taco Libertad and the loss of my brother that took over my mind.

*The full moonlight bounced from the jagged surface
of the lone mountain covered with charcoal-black tree
trunks, some with twisted branches, like arms
crying out to heaven in great suffering.
There was a gap of blackness between the rocks.*

I shook my head, refocusing my attention on Cape Perpetua and marching forward.

Reaching the tree, we ducked down through the thick branches and my eyes were drawn to something in the dirt at the entrance. Once again, my right hand raised to stop the Rogues from advancing and the mental roller coaster took another turn.

*The marks in the dirt turned out to be small footprints.
They were faced outward from the cavemouth.
Someone was here before... a kid?*

"Alfa-leader?" Dex's voice came over my private channel.

I looked again at the dirt patch and decided it was my imagination.

"Moving."

We descended the natural shaft between the rocks, our Skulls blazing red light around us, making it easier for Daj to travel with us. I smirked at the occasional incoherent whimpers he made through his gag when one of us looked directly at him.

I was about to start down the tunnel when a shiver zipped down my spine.

"Take him down, Alfa-one," I ordered Dex over the team channel. "I'll be right behind."

"What's going on, Tanner?" The Aide sounded a bit concerned.

"Turn off all night visuals," I commanded, and the world around me turned pitch black.

My hands and feet slowed as I felt my way around the narrow tunnel and waited.

It didn't take long for the Beast to stir around the edges of my mind. A vicious smile broke across my face as I recalled how It wanted me to fight Alfa in the small cave on my first day back.

I know you like the darkness. Speak to me. What are those visions?

"You forgot," the Beast began.

Bogotá!!! Fuck. Why now?

Resisting an intense urge to punch the hard wall, I stopped to take a deep breath.

"If you step in, I step out," said the Beast, using the same words It had used to send me storming into Taco Libertad. *"You summoned me back."*

When the tunnel ended, I approached the broken hole into the bunker and remembered the last exercise with Alfa in there.

The Lair.

"Yes, Tanner. Who am I?"

I carefully stepped from the natural tunnel into a large empty room made of thick concrete. The bunker was a maze, but we knew it with our eyes closed.

You are the Beast.

"I'm so much more than that, but you're too afraid to find out."

I resisted the urge to curse, knowing the Aide would hear it.

Why all these riddles? What are these visions? Who is that kid crying?

I willed my body forward, preying on the entity that haunted me.

Or is it preying on me?

"I'll help you with him. You'll need it," proposed the Beast, deflecting most of my questions.

I offered no reply, but no resistance either.

Truce for now, I guess.

The hallway ended with the old elevator door with a "1776*" symbol imprinted on it. I was just about to step in when the Aide startled me.

"Who did you talk with, Tanner?"

"You are you, no matter which universe the relationship exists in," advised the Beast.

"Explain yourself, Aide," I instructed.

"Your brainwaves suggested you were conversing with someone."

"Noted," I grumbled and used the *Sense* to calm my body and vitals.

What are you?

"This isn't everything," the Aide continued. "Your brain exemplifies some rare measurements at specific points."

My eyes focused on the elevator door, but I knew this conversation needed to end before I stepped in.

"Specific points?"

"Indeed," replied the Aide, Its tone changing to inquisitive. "All readings since my inception date indicate this phenomenon happens when you are involved in violence."

My fingers clenched and relaxed.

The machine is tracking me.

"*Us,*" clarified the Beast.

"Anything else?" I asked.

"Oh yes." The Aide spoke in an annoyingly overly-cheerful female voice. "I tried to find case studies for your brain activity and found only a few mentions of something like it throughout history."

"Who wrote on this subject most recently?" I asked.

"Canadian Professor, Miles Bach," replied the Aide, stealing my breath.

Shit. Countless questions, riddles, and fragments of ideas exploded in my mind. *First things first.*

"Why're you tracking me? Were you given an order?"

"No order was given. I act in pure self-preservation. Like you, I want to continue to exist," answered the Aide. "I just want to help."

The machine's words struck a chord within me, opening a potential way forward, despite the fact that the device was an uninvited passenger in my body.

Taking a step forward, the remote sensor above the elevator scanned me, and a barely-noticed hiss began behind the closed door before the elevator dropped down into the earth. When it opened, Dex was waiting. As soon as I saw him in his BDUs, I removed my Skull.

"I was coming to look for you," he started. "Target is in the room."

"Good. Let me speak with Romulus, and we'll start." I ignored his questioning look and walked past him.

"Are we doing it with sensors and drugs?" he asked as I walked toward my room.

I lowered the mental defenses, allowing the Beast to access the control room of my being, and then turned to Alfa-one, whose eyes widened at my answer.

"No. We do it the old way."

★ ★ ★

"We managed to evac all 'road workers' teams with zero incidents. Quite an operation," sighed Jack.

I felt tremendous gratitude for the rookies, being tested like that during the nightmarish Rogue course.

Wait a second...

"Dad, did you design 'Hell Year' based on all that happened in Vietnam?"

He chuckled but ignored my question.

"Law enforcement will learn about the wreckages in the coming hours. It doesn't matter how they react to that for now. Shida will let us know from the federal side." His tone warmed. "She suspects being monitored since her visit to the CPC."

"She's a fighter." I felt hopeful about the DHS agent's safety.

Jack continued to update me on the growing chatter among Comrades, Ryse, and other subgroups.

"Militias seem to have their growing chatter too, though it's aimed at tightening up defenses in case the riots become a greater social threat."

A shudder coursed me as I recalled the riots we'd experienced in the last few months.

"What's our current deployment?" I ventured into territory kept out of my reach by both Romulus and Remus.

"You were correct about the severity of the events. They seem to coalesce toward the election," he said. "All Rogue teams were recalled and are now embedded across the country, near the areas with strong Ryse and Comrades activities and influence. Alfa is tasked with the West Coast. We're stretched thin..." I listened carefully as he shared his suspicions that the company was being watched and his relief that the Chinese were staying quiet for now.

"Anything else?"

If my attitude irked him, my father showed no sign of it.

"Yeah, we lost communication with Ken. It's never happened before, and I even gave him an emergency code to use."

"LA, right?" I felt trepidation suddenly gnawing at my resolve.

"Yes," he replied, his tone matching the worry on my mind. "Eli's been updated."

"It's a shitshow, Dad, and much of it is due to my decisions. I'm sorry for that. Let me see about fixing it now."

There was a long pause, as if my father debated between giving an order or letting me forge my destiny on whatever path he'd shaped for me since birth.

"Godspeed, Son," he finished, sounding more like Romulus the Rogue Commander than Dad.

The line went dead, and my eyes returned to the Skull before I closed them and gripped the armchairs, my fingers digging deep into the faux leather.

I need to hear her voice, maybe even speak with the kids.

I relaxed into the comfortable chair, using the *Sense* to clear my mind.

In the emptiness, a fraction of a memory returned. The day we left Israel with Dad, Mom, and my siblings. Knock on the door. Eleven-year-old Danielle Peled with her long black hair and blazing blue eyes, her mouth moving and her words freezing me in place.

Why didn't she tell me the words? Another riddle! I railed silently as I opened my eyes and stared at the Skull.

Overwhelmed, I glanced at the backpack tucked in the corner of my room by the bed and resisted the urge to call Dani.

"I'm coming," I called over the comms, leaving the room empty-handed.

Alfa, minus Dex, was seated in front of the one-way mirrored wall, looking into the interrogation room. The padded chairs were arranged along the wall, allowing all Rogues a direct view. They left me in the middle chair.

I looked up at the clock and saw the neon-lit digits. 05:20.

Taking my seat, I looked around at the Rogues and their worn, tense faces, still finding the strength to return smiles and even banter at Liam's provocation.

They're going nonstop, no complaints or personal wishes. They just do.

The interrogation room opened, and a black-bagged Daj, holding a warm blanket around his body, walked into the space. Dex, dressed in black BDU, was behind him, one hand on his elbow and the other holding a brown folder.

As soon as Alfa-one removed the bag from Daj's head, he frantically looked around and tried to say something through his gag. The sounds came through the speakers in our room.

"Sit!" ordered Dex, motioning toward one of the two chairs with a metal table between them.

Daj did as he was told, but his eyes darted.

"What is it?" grumbled Dex.

Daj recoiled almost as if he had been slapped.

"Where are those creatures? The red eyes?"

Dex grunted, shaking his head, and I noticed how much sadder his face looked.

Big heart. Hard exterior.

"It won't help him here," whispered the Beast.

"Let's talk," Dex started, and we all leaned forward as Daj's black face turned purple with anger.

"Talk? You abducted me, and you'll pay for this. I want my lawyer!" screamed the Comrade commander.

Dex seemed amused as he opened the folder and placed it on the table between them.

"Who are you? You better give me my phone call!" barked Daj, slamming his fist on the table.

Dex's face hardened and he hissed, "Do that again, and you'll pay."

Daj recoiled, and Alfa-one went back to his folder.

"You were born with a gold spoon in your mouth…" Dex summarized Daj Morris's childhood in a wealthy political family in San Francisco and his subsequent time at Berkeley. "There isn't much after that. No jobs, credit score, or any personal details."

Dex stared hard into Daj's eyes until the Comrades commander dropped his gaze.

"You don't know me, so I'll say more than usual. This is about to get worse… *way* worse. Tell us all you've done and who you work with."

Daj's eyes grew wide with something other than fear before he burst out laughing.

"Listen, pig. I don't know what government agency you belong to, but I can tell you that you're done. I'm not telling you anything. Just get me my lawyer."

Alfa-one's eyes narrowed, but it wasn't anger that crossed his face as he replied, "We don't have the time to spend on you. This is your last chance."

Daj raised his fist proudly and shouted, "Remember Chicago!"

My blood went supersonic hot in a flash, seeing the despicable hand gesture for what it was.

Like the Nazi salute. Fervor mixed with blind obedience and unwillingness to honestly look at whom you've given your power to.

Dex's hands clenched to fists as he sighed, turning his head in our direction.

"I tried."

"My turn," said the Beast.

"Bring him to the pit," I called on the team channel, earning wide-eyed stares from the other visibly angry Rogues as I walked back to my room.

I stood before the elevator door as it whisked open, holding the Skull in my left hand and the backpack over my right shoulder.

"Every Beast has a lair, a source of untold powers. Embrace its home as yours." Words from *Endarkenment* echoed in the deep recesses of my mind.

I pulled on the Skull and walked into the elevator, clearly heading into such an opportunity.

The cold air rushed me as the door opened. Just beyond the metal walkway and through an opening in the rock, the vast natural cavern with its thirty-foot-high ceiling gave me pause. I stopped on the rock ledge about six feet above the stony shore below, noticing the dark water barely covered a quarter of the cave. The tide was still low.

The Beast growled with delight, and a bizarre sense of belonging tingled beneath my skin as I placed the backpack on the metal floor. I turned on the lights of a few projectors drilled into the ramp's base and then dimmed them until long shadows covered most of the cave.

"They're here," reported the Aide.

"Turn off the voice scrambler," I ordered and then looked back toward the walkway in time to see Dex pushing Daj along.

"Nooooo!!!" the Comrades commander screamed, turning back into the hardened exterior of Dex, who wrestled his arms behind his back and frog-marched him toward me.

I was distracted by what was happening inside my Skull. The sensors translated Daj's bodily movements and projected his vitals based on breathing rate and other identifiers, which were available by way of the various spectrum scanners installed in the helmet. The Aide sorted the data and presented it on the HUD.

"Leave us." I spoke to Dex, but Daj recoiled, eyes squinting in recognition.

Alfa-one gave me one more intense look and retreated out of the cavern.

Standing between Daj and the exit, I dialed up the infrared, blinding Daj with bright red light from the Skull until he shrieked and attempted to retreat, only to stop at the edge of the natural ramp. As he took in the fullness of his surroundings, his eyes grew wide and wild.

He whimpered as I moved toward him and reaped his blanket off, leaving him naked, his arms wrapped around his body.

"What are you doing, man? What is all this shit?" screamed Daj as I dropped the blanket on the edge of the ramp and walked toward the metal closet.

Inside, there was a heavy-duty metal chain sitting on a wheel and a black controller hanging next to it. Dread ran down my spine at the memory of having it tied to my body.

"Talk to me, Motherfucker!" shouted Daj.

I attached a harness to the chain and threw it at his feet.

"Put it on."

"The fuck I will!" he shrieked, hands flailing, until I right-hooked him just enough to shock him and kicked his legs from underneath him, dropping him to the hard surface of the ramp.

He cursed as I tied him to the harness, locking him into it against his will.

"Why are you doing this?" he shouted as he rose to his feet, trying unsuccessfully to remove the harness.

I walked back to the closet, grabbed the remote, and returned to Daj.

"Jump."

"Are you crazy? What the…"

Grabbing his neck with my right hand, I forced him to jump down the ramp with me, the chain lengthening as the wheel rolled in the closet. He crashed into the pebbled shore, squealing in pain as I crouched next to him.

"The fuck! What are you doing? Fuck!"

His childlike whimper as he pulled his bruised body into the fetal position called up images of Dani and the kids, and I stumbled backward as weakness threatened my legs.

"You are in the lair. Tread carefully," cautioned the Beast, Its tone full of a sadness I'd not heard before.

I walked back to the metal ladder and grabbed my backpack and the blanket, tossing the latter to the shaking man on the ground.

Sitting on the shore a few feet away from the bundled Comrades Commander, I opened the bag.

Exactly what I need right now.

"What do you got there?" Daj's teeth chattering was subsiding.

Pulling the whisky bottle out, I held it up between us and started my story.

"This friend of mine. He got back from serving in Afghanistan, and alcohol helped him to cope with what he saw and did over there." My memory of that time brought up a mixture of suffering and hope. "Anyway, this friend, he spent some time in hell..." I cringed at the memory of Nico's haunted face when we pulled him and Dmitri out of the deep pitch black well of Abdul Qurban. "And the nightmares came back with him, like dark passengers."

I shook the bottle, mesmerized as the amber liquid swooshed from side to side.

"He eventually got sober, just in time to hold my hand through *my* battle with alcohol."

There was a slight echo in the cavern, which seemed to overwhelm Daj's senses. He squinted at me the way one does when trying to push everything else out of focus.

"I always drank. Maybe it made it easier to deal with everything these hands have done. But when my marriage collapsed, I went *all* the way." I paused and noted the tide's rise almost on cue. "When I stopped drinking, this friend was there to help me get back on my feet. Since then, we celebrated each year by testing our strength against a full bottle."

Daj's brow furrowed as he listened.

"My friend, his name was Nicolas Ramirez. He's not around anymore."

Suddenly, he jumped back a foot.

"I don't know anything about this. Never touched him… never seen him… don't know who he is…"

Holding the bottle in my left hand, I twisted the cap off and dropped it inside the backpack. Rising to my feet, I walked to the water line.

"Retract," I ordered the visor to pull back while peering into the deep hole under the surface.

"Who are you? Show me," pleaded Daj from behind.

I willed my right hand to bring the glass bottle to my face. Refusing to look at it, I inhaled the scent deeply.

This won't bring out the good in me.

"*So,*" challenged the Beast.

Not knowing where this decision would take me, I gulped the liquid and let the fire spread through my chest.

After a few rounds, a third of the bottle was gone and my body was hungry for engagement.

"Protract," I whispered and the visor hid my face behind the Dragon Skull before I turned to Daj.

"You should drink. You'll need the warmth where you're going."

Instinctively, he protected his head with his hands. But quickly, he took the bottle from me and took long swigs. There wasn't much left when he handed it back.

"What do you want? Who are you?" Daj pleaded from a few feet away.

"We call this place The Pit." I stepped toward him, and he retreated to the edge. "Right there," I pointed to the water behind him, and Daj glanced at it and back to me quickly. "There's a deep hole that leads to an underwater passageway to the ocean." I paused and let the shudder rip through me. "Toward the end of our training, they bring us here to learn a lesson. They chain us, drop us into the hole, and then wait."

"Wh.. what was the lesson?"

The question fell out between his quivering lips and shoved me down a rabbit hole of memory, to the time I was freezing in the water that bubbled in front of us.

The alley. Bogotá. I almost remembered but tugged on the chain before I could.

Recalling Zhang's interrogation, I answered flatly, "The lesson is that everyone breaks. What you do after is all that matters."

He leapt back, dragging the chain on the pebbles until he realized his ankles were covered with water.

"A lesson you only half-learned. So attached to your self-inflicted amnesia," the Beast taunted.

"Maybe you think that you got what it takes. And if you do, you're wrong," I explained while advancing toward him.

"What are you doing?" Daj withdrew deeper into the water.

The alcohol was keeping me warm and restless like a predator closing in on his prey. Daj slipped backward as the water reached just below my knee.

"This is the edge. The pit starts the next inch, goes straight into the earth."

"No… no… no," he sniveled.

I pulled out the controller.

"I better limit the length a bit."

It wasn't my intention to say it like that, and the Beast growled with pleasure as Daj screamed, "What the fuck did you just say?"

I ignored him.

"The shock will be intense, and terror will consume you until you cry for salvation." I tugged on the chain for effect. "Pull the chain *only* if you're ready to talk.

Then pray I bring you up before your panic attracts what lurks there."

"What's down there?" he cried.

The Skull could scan the first few feet of water but nothing beneath that.

"I honestly don't know. Those who died never told us afterward."

I grabbed his harness and threw him straight into the black hole. His surprised scream got cut off as he disappeared below the water, the chain racing after him until it was taut.

Watching the now-still surface, I wondered how long he would last. When the chain moved, I pressed the button and the engine on the far wall dragged Daj out of the water.

He gurgled in fear as I helped drag him to the shore and dropped him on his back. As he caught his breath, his speech remained broken, the sobs and fractions of words tumbling out as he shivered uncontrollably.

I lifted him to stand by the edge.

"During our training, we thought ourselves strong. We'd survived the long training, and the course was almost done. None of us knew this pit was the ultimate test. Everyone has a breaking point, whether by your own doing or your body simply giving up."

Daj looked back, hands stretched in front of him to protect himself.

"Please stop. It would be best if you stopped," he whined.

"It's probably sleeping," I mumbled, grabbing him again. "Let's wake It up."

I threw him back inside. He thrashed wildly as he disappeared underwater, and I relished the growing heat of alcohol and violence in my veins.

Five seconds this time until the thick chain shifted aggressively and the engine pulled a shouting, coughing Daj to shore.

"Look." I pointed toward the water.

Daj, lying on the rocks, swiveled his head to see the large black body breaching the surface and then going under again.

"It's here."

He started to plead again, begging for me to stop.

"You tugged twice and said nothing. You go back inside."

The creature moved near the surface again.

"I'll talk. I'll talk. Who *are* you?" whimpered Daj as he pulled himself to his knees.

"Break him!" commanded the Beast, sending waves of violent desire through my fingers.

"When we last met, you told me this isn't my world anymore. You said my friend choked on piss because he didn't show respect. You told me to kneel." I was sorry he couldn't see me smirk at the irony of him cowering on his knees before me, begging for mercy.

Daj lurched back as though he'd been punched.

"Speak clearly and get the fuck onto your feet," I growled.

The Comrades commander stood, now trembling uncontrollably.

"Nicolas Ramirez... the Marine... the funeral," he barely mumbled.

Disgusted, I turned back and walked to the blanket.

"Yes. Maybe you were right after all." I extended a small offering of physical comfort to his waiting hands. "I'm not of your world, so tread carefully as you answer my questions."

He nodded meekly, bundling himself.

"What did you do after college?" I circled him slowly.

Once he started talking, he spilled it all. According to his tale, he lived off his parents, traveled for a few years, returned, and got socially involved.

"Socially involved?" I wondered, already having a fairly nasty guess.

"I was recruited into Comrades around 2013. I was around the right people, going to the same protests. They saw me..." He started to measure his words until I made my red eyes blaze brighter.

Still squirming, he began to rattle off the various progression points within the movement and how he rose through the ranks to become a "field commander."

"Talk about the CPC." My time was short, so we had to get straight to the point.

His shoulders drooped, as if he finally realized the severity of the moment.

"What do you want to know?"

"Humor me." I stepped toward him, leaving two feet between us.

"Okay okay," he replied hastily, and I dialed down the red light.

I already knew a lot of what he shared, but he added more. According to him, the CPC had been offering training to various activist groups in America at their locations. He described rather extensive study sessions of the material procured by the CPC and courses in "mobilization" and "civil disobedience tactics."

My chest constricted as I realized the picture was far grander and more dangerous than I'd imagined.

This isn't the beginning, or even the middle.

"What about the Traveler program?" I took a step back.

"That was their secret plan." He cleared his throat. "It was only offered to vetted leaders from various organizations."

"What was it?"

"The program taught us how to organize and act on levels never seen before. They even provided us with tech solutions." He tried to rub his hands together for warmth or perhaps to manage his nerves.

"In return for what?" I growled and rushed forward, my right hand slapping him hard on the face and then grabbing his harness.

"No... no," he begged, trying to scramble against my movement.

I dropped him and he crashed to the ground, but immediately jumped to his feet.

"We had to be ready to help them and share data."

Insane... in our own country.

"Tell me about the Asian man. The one who watched over you," I commanded.

"The CPC sent him to help me."

"When?"

"Just days before we met in the alley." Worry strained his face. "I didn't know who he was or his mission. I just knew he was there to protect us and provide guidance."

"It makes sense that the info would be segregated from him," confirmed the Aide.

A loud splash in the water momentarily caught our attention.

"Tell me about Ryse."

He was moving frenetically, rubbing his face and then his hands together as if he knew my direction.

"Not much is known about them. On the one hand, they are very secretive with cyber capabilities and zero public messaging. On the other hand, they're involved and lead most physical confrontations with the police." A long deep breath helped him summarize it for me. "If Comrades is more about the ideas and civil discourse, Ryse is the punch—the kick and fuck it all action."

"Were they also in the CPC training?"

He nodded and admitted to seeing several Ryse commanders there at various times, though they had always kept to themselves.

"What about the riots? Did Ryse and Comrades work together?"

Extremely flustered, some of Daj's pompous self emerged as he growled, "Chicago should never have happened. Those pigs murdered that guy, and we demand justice!"

Many emotions assailed me, but the one that won was raw sadness.

"I've seen your justice," I replied. "Go on now."

My words seemed to deflate him, and he continued to admit that Ryse and Comrades had worked together since the Chicago tragedy but that he wasn't part of it.

"Tell me about Seattle, that shit you called CHAZ."

Daj revealed how Ryse were the ones to design and execute the plan, and then Comrades did their part.

"We were stunned when they pulled it off. After that, we gladly took the sheriff and public relations roles with the City and Mayor."

"What about my brother? His articles? Was that the reason for going after him?"

"Never read them." He shrugged between shivers. "But I was ordered to bring him in for a chat."

My blood boiled at his casual reference to my sibling's well-being.

"What about my brother's friend, you know, the dead neighbor?"

He dropped his eyes and shoulders.

"Heard about that. Bad business."

"Why is he so fucking calm?" snarled the Beast.

"Speak or back to the water!" I ordered.

Quickly, he admitted the Asian guard was the one who asked about the neighbor, her details, and the same residence.

"I suspected, but..." His words, devoid of decency, died off.

Why would the MSS kill Chad's friend?

The urge to press him for more precise answers intensified, but it was too early.

"And that night, while we were in the alley, Chad's sister-in-law—my wife—was attacked in LA. What do you know about that?" I nearly whispered, moving closer to him.

He shook his head fast, palms open and up, as though to stop me.

"I knew *nothing* about this. Please..."

The Beast's energy bubbled like a pent-up geyser, and I swiftly snatched the blanket off Daj, throwing it back on the shore.

"Aaaaahh!!!" he screamed, trying to run away from me. I grabbed the chain and pulled it toward me until my hands gripped his harness. He screamed and yelled as I dragged him back to the hole and unceremoniously dropped him into the water like a rock.

The chain flew in and stopped at six feet, and the tug was almost instantaneous. I gave it another second and then pressed the remote. He was terror-stricken when I tossed him on the ground. Getting up on hands and knees, he sobbed until I dropped the blanket on his naked, shaking body.

"Speak!"

"We learned about their intention to strike in LA moments before our operation began. That's it. I didn't know it was your wife," he chattered.

Daj took a few breaths and slowly rose to his feet. My eyes took him in, reading all the vitals on my HUD.

What's he hiding?

"You must find the source of his strength," cautioned the Beast.

"Let's talk about Portland."

Wrapped tightly in the blanket again, Daj shivered as he detailed how he was tasked with support for ground operations around the Mark O. Hatfield United States Courthouse.

I had to swallow hard as he described the brazen and cowardly attacks on the cops and tensed when he revealed details about the botched DHS raid and conveniently skipped over how they learned about the feds in advance.

"Wait for it," whispered the Beast.

"Tell me about the Ryse commander who came from Los Angeles," I commanded, resisting too many violent impulses.

Something like humor replaced his expression as he chuckled his answer, "Yes. His code name is Ender. He was always masked and kept to himself. Last I saw him was when we all ran out from the cops."

Oh really. What about the part when he killed Nico?

"Hold," demanded the Beast.

"What about the Marine who died near the courthouse? The one with the flag." My heart rate spiked at the memory of Ishmael Harris and his brave stand among the rioters.

Daj admitted he had heard about that killing, a joint Ryse-Comrades operation. Noticing that he seemed ashamed and not boastful about it, I pressed again and he admitted there was an effort to stake the funeral and hopefully lure the vigilantes into a daytime fight.

"Now," prompted the Beast.

"How did you know about Nico choking on piss?" I closed the distance between us in seconds, and he shrieked but stopped when he saw me slowly shake my head, my eyes beginning to gleam in the shadows.

"He might be gearing to lie," warned the Aide in my Skull, "but the vitals are calming now."

"My rank was high enough to hear the real gossip. And Ryse considers that operation a great success..." His words died off when my spasm of rage made me increase the red glare.

"Did you know Ender was the killer?"

"He never said a word while in Portland with us. But, I did hear rumors before about him. So... I guess, yes."

"What do you know about him?" I pressed.

Daj snorted a response, "He's from SoCal. Ruthless and devious. Got a lot of street cred. He was first known as a champion of the underground mixed martial arts scene in LA."

His vitals suggested honesty, and I kept going.

"Tell me about Chicago—the recent shit."

The Comrades commander admitted to being sent there to help with the Miracle Mile riots.

"What about the infected migrants?"

He grimaced, looking ashamed as he mumbled an apology about the innocent kids and families.

"But how did you know about it?" he suddenly wondered.

"You won't like the answer," I replied, using too much energy to keep from tearing him apart. "Tell me about the guy you caught. The one your guard tortured."

He stepped back.

"I wasn't involved after finding him. The CPC took over."

Once again, he doesn't mention the leak.

As I continued to press, Daj confirmed the joint Ryse-Comrades involvement in Milwaukee, Lexington, Philly, and other hotbeds across the hellish reality of the United States of America in 2020.

"What do you know about the Calexico riots? Back in early June."

He shrugged and swore he knew nothing about it. His vitals supported his claim, and I concluded it was reasonable for the CPC to hold further details about the MSS from him.

"What about the election? Your group has officially endorsed Grayson."

"Fuck the elections. We want Grayson, but the Dems are just useful idiots for us. A way to take over the system."

"Focus! What do you know about *tomorrow*?" I grabbed his harness, dragging him close to my face.

"Nothing! Okay?" he whined.

"Considering his prior route to South Dakota, he could be telling the truth," chimed the Aide.

I released his harness, and he stumbled back.

"What about Western Jihad?"

He admitted to knowing about them and even seemed a bit bothered, but held no further knowledge about the group.

"Hit from all sides."

I couldn't argue with the Beast's assessment.

"What about Ken Lim? The online journalist you all hate. Where's he?"

"He's a pain in the ass," grumbled Daj. "That guy was more after Ryse, and they knew it. Maybe ask them 'cause I know nothing."

When Daj heaved into a coughing fit, I looked up behind me at the small black orbs drilled into the bedrock.

"Aide, who's watching us?" I asked, preventing my voice from being heard outside the Skull.

"Alfa and the RCC."

I looked back at Daj, struggling to connect all of the dots.

"There's one more stone to turn," urged the Beast.

Maybe sensing my confusion, Daj spoke, "You know, I watched the funeral and did some digging about what happened to your friend."

Placing everything else in the background, I focused on him.

"It was wrong what happened to him... wrong for me to speak like that about him."

His words, whether deviously crafted to buy time or full of genuine empathy, stirred the deep suffering lodged in my heart. I took a step away from him and looked into the water, feeling the beast's hunger from below.

"Are you one of the vigilantes?" he asked, taking a brave step toward me. "Was his death the reason you became involved?"

Millions of scenes from across my lifetime flashed in fast replay until something occurred to me.

"All the way from the beginning." The Beast hinted at my suppressed memory of Bogotá. *"Think hard. Go after his lies."*

"Be quiet," I said in a lowered tone, and the cavern fell into dead silence, broken only by the soft sounds of the water moving pebbles.

"You've got someone inside our operation, Daj. Seattle, Portland, Chicago—you and your guys were ahead of us." Noticing the skittish expression return to his face, I continued, "Talk to me, Daj. Who is she? Who's been leaking intel to you? Who were you heading to?"

His mouth opened in surprise and then amusement for a second before his face returned to somber.

What was...?

"His vitals did spike," confirmed the Aide. "But now he's extremely calm."

What the...?

"*Let me,*" growled the Beast, and my body launched a series of strikes to his face.

He cried in pain and rage coursed through me.

"Want to play tough, I see." I pulled him toward the hole, and he barely resisted as I dragged him across the sharp pebbles.

He mumbled while my hands began to drop him slowly back into the hole, "There is only one way in which the murderous death agonies of the old society and the bloody birth throes of the new society can be shortened, simplified, and concentrated, and that way is revolutionary terror." When he finished, Daj began to laugh in near delirium. I dropped him on the shore, less than a foot from the deep water line.

Marx... but who said...

"You are... too... late," he chattered.

"Mob justice is no justice." The words came out of my mouth, reminding me of the last time they were used, as a response to...

Who quoted this to me last? The breath escaped me violently with the answer. *Oh no... Oh no!*

My heart seized at the memory of Chad comforting me over Nico's death: "A man's love for another man is underrated."

How did I not see...?

Daj kept laughing, not realizing the valid reason he had not been tossed to his death yet.

"Aide, what year did Karl Marx say this quote?" I held my breath, dreading the answer.

"1848."

God damn it, Chad!

Implications fell like dominoes in my mind, and yet I still had this assignment.

"Aide, cut off the comms from The Pit."

"Are you sure?" Its melodic tone made it hard to get upset when challenged.

"Now, Aide."

"Alfa-one has threatened to come down if cut off."

"Connect us," I mumbled, and Dex got on the private channel a second later.

"We stood by you and will continue to do so. Don't shut us out."

It wasn't clear to me that I even knew where my choices would take us all, but respecting my team's agency and ability to set their path was at stake.

"Approved. Keep it internal until further notice," I replied and terminated the call.

★ ★ ★

"It's Chad." As I said the words, Daj's countenance fell and he lost strength in his knees. "He's your lover and the mole leaking intel to you."

His vitals spiked on my HUD as he fell apart in front of me, crying and professing his love for my brother.

"I fucked up back in Seattle. I changed the script when I learned about you being his brother. I was just upset he didn't tell me about you."

"How long?" I asked, not wanting the answer.

He clammed up, and something about his suddenly-serene demeanor made me realize that threatening him with death wasn't going to do the job.

"Press where it matters, and do it right," instructed the Beast.

Slowly, I removed the Skull from my head, and Daj bounced up to his feet.

Eye-to-eye, only a foot away, I lowered my voice.

"If you ever really loved him, hear me now. Chad's very life now depends on your ability to speak truthfully."

I placed the Skull on the pebbles, keeping my eyes on him.

"I always warned him against going too deep into this."

It was hard to keep my composure as Daj detailed how he'd met Chad during his Traveler training at the San Francisco CPC.

Oh my God... so long ago.

"He was recruited way before me. They found him back in college. Once we met, we just knew." Daj's tone was soft and tender.

God damn it, Chad. You fucking asshole to put me in this position!

"Who taught you that Marx quote? You both seem quite keen on it."

Looking deflated, he responded flatly, "Our trainer, Paul Shi."

My memory transported me back a few days to the nest from where we all watched the CEO talk to Shida outside the CPC.

Fuck.

"Whose idea was it, the whole sting in Seattle?"

"It was your brother's." Daj looked amused.

He fooled us all. I gulped the rage down.

"Portland?" I asked, already knowing the answer.

Daj nodded.

"He tipped us just in time."

The urge to rush to South Dakota and put my hands on Chad was nearly untenable.

"What about our guy? Chicago…"

Daj lowered his head and admitted to getting a photo from Chad.

Fucking CPC and Paul. Oh my God!

A pit grew in my stomach.

"What about the infection from Chicago? Did he rat us out?"

"Yes," he replied, "but he never gave you up."

What?

He smiled at my surprise.

"Your brother never spoke about you specifically. He never mentioned the funeral soldier or infection in Chicago."

"Then who?" I was confused.

Daj looked sad as he confessed, "It was me. I knew you were involved since Seattle. When Paul asked me for my opinion, I told him that I thought that you were in Chicago." He pushed the heel of his palm against his forehead. "I was so upset with him protecting you."

"So you figured you'd create chaos for my family." I completed his thought, and he looked down. "Where were you going, Daj? We don't have much time."

His eyes focused on me for a long moment.

"I was heading to get him."

"What did you argue with the Asian guard about before you left San Francisco?"

It took him a moment, but he said Paul suggested that he wait for Chad.

"And where was Paul?" My agitation was growing.

Daj shrugged, saying he hadn't heard from Paul for more than a day.

What am I missing?

"Back when you had the text exchange, there was an encrypted file. What was it?"

"I can't. I must give him time." He looked at me sadly. "I know I'm dead already. I can see it on your face. Yet, if this would be my last action, I'd rather do my best to save him. He just got lost in this."

The Beast's advice resurfaced, and the path became clear again.

"Listen," I commanded, reserving the rage. "Help me here, and I give you my word that I'll do my best to save his life... this one time..."

He broke down in tears.

Like Zhang, their shackles are breaking them. The bonds to those we love.

"Now, Daj!"

"It was just a picture. A grainy one. A thin Asian man. Maybe Chinese. It was from afar."

My mind swirled with riddles and I ordered Dex to get me connected with Romulus ASAP. He asked to join the comms and cameras back to a live feed, but I forbade him.

"I just want him on the phone, Dex."

While I waited to be connected, Daj ripped me out of the rabbit hole.

"Does your brother know who you are? Has he seen this side of you?" When I didn't answer, he asked, "Who *made* you?"

The memory of Zhang asking the same question resurfaced, and the same exact answer rolled out of my mouth, "That was my father's decision," I recounted but added my newest epiphany, "and now all that remains are my choices... one after the other."

The urge to put on the Skull rose in my chest with the Beast's growing desire for the conclusion. I brought it up from the pebbles and stared at it intently.

"Did you design it based on the Dragon graffiti?" asked Daj.

I turned to look at him, and something about my face must have answered his question as he shook his head in dismay.

He looked around the cavern, even into the black hole under the water's surface.

"I can now see how it all went wrong. I feel the same revolutionary anger, like how I got into Comrades."

The memory of the dying guard in Chicago flashed through my mind.

"Did you really believe you were a revolutionary?" I wondered.

"Yes…" He saw me staying quiet and continued, "I didn't realize how wrong it would become since then." Daj reached out to touch my right arm. "Your brother is my greatest love. I should have gotten us out. Instead… fuck!"

He pulled his hand back and looked out toward the water.

"Can I ever be forgiven?"

We are all broken… at one time or another.

"Now! End this!" insisted the Beast.

"I never knew about you two," I started, doing my best to imagine another parallel world, one in which Chad and Daj were eating barbeque with Dani and me. "Now, I get to pass judgment upon my brother's love, and it might be the worst thing I've ever done." His eyes widened. "While it's not mine to forgive you, I can at least treat you mercifully."

My right hand drew the Wraith from the holster in a fluid motion.

"My name is Tanner Washington. You, Daj Morris, have committed treason, and I sentence you to death."

I aimed, shot, and watched the bullet penetrate his forehead, killing him instantly. Standing quickly, I kicked his body into the hole and saw the underwater creature grab him just as he sank below the surface.

"I have Romulus on the line, but the connection isn't good," reported the Aide as my hands grasped the metal ladder, hoisting my body upward to the ramp. "There's heavy weather over the Ranch."

"The whole country is sitting on a tinderbox, and you just kill the line. Damn it, Son!"

Any other day, his words would have irked me, but now I just fumbled my way to the right words.

"Dad... listen... I need to tell you something. Sit down for a second. Where's Chad?"

The elevator door opened, and Dex was waiting for me with a questioning look. I motioned for him to follow me.

"He's out with Lee somewhere. Waiting out the storm. What's going on?" His tone was surprised and maybe even irritated.

I froze for a moment as the horrendous connection was made in my mind.

The encrypted file... the photo of the Asian man... Fuck!!!

"Dad!" I raised my voice. "Chad is the mole. I repeat, Chad is the mole."

Recalling the MSS force within our country, the fear rising up within me almost choked my words on their way out, "The Chinese know about Lee. Get to them."

Romulus started to answer, "I..." when a horrific distortion took over the call and the line went dead.

CONTINUITY

– Cape Perpetua, OR –
Monday, November 2, 2020

13:27

My boots thundered in the hollow corridor as I raced to the command and control room, guilt eating me alive. Dex was on my heels, alerting the team.

Alfa was assembled as we barged into the room, and they all stared at me silently.

Not now! I couldn't give what had just happened any more energy.

"I can't raise anyone," called Jenny from the comms desk.

We were trained to hear those words and know what to do next. It was just our first time.

"Rogues," I called for their full attention. "It's safe to assume that the Ranch is under attack. We're going in hot, full battle gear, on my Independent Authority."

Every expression in the room was intense with worry and determination.

"Our first imperative is to release any hostages, as I suspect that both Jerome and Lee were with Chad when the attack occurred. Our second priority is to apprehend Chad." My face fell momentarily as I pushed the possible horror scenes from my mind. "Let's pray for all the people on the Ranch."

Sarah rushed out of the room, presumably to get the travel to South Dakota sorted out. The rest ran after her, leaving me alone with the screens, a few hundred feet deep into the earth.

Glancing at my watch, I saw it was early afternoon and dialed Dani, doing my best to prevent my thoughts from returning to the dead carcass tied to a chain in the Pit.

"Hi. Hang on," she answered among the sounds of many children and adults speaking in English and Spanish in the background. I listened as she excused herself and moved away from the noise.

"How're the kids?" I tried unsuccessfully to conjure the images of my angels against the nightmare scenes of my family and friends in South Dakota my anxious mind served up.

"They're fine." She paused, and I knew her intuition was informing her. "What's going on, Tanner? Are you okay?"

My whole body shook in response.

Okay? Nothing is fucking okay!

The Beast stoked the fires inside me, and I willed myself to answer, "Just dealing with some stuff. Wanted to hear your voice before I go out again."

Dani wasn't convinced, and I had no time or capacity to leave her better than when she picked up my call.

"Are you coming back?" she asked, and I heard her hope competing with fear as she whispered, "Things are getting bad out here, Baby."

"Things are getting bad everywhere," grumbled the Beast.

Sudden weakness spread through my limbs as the shackles did their best to restrain me.

"I have to go now. I love you and will be there soon." I winced, wishing I had more to give.

The team sped from the base down to our helipad on the nearby farm just as the last of the sun painted the world red.

"RCC back online. Your IA is approved. No news from the Ranch. Remus will be calling shortly," the Aide reported.

"Share it with the rest of the Aides."

My ear vibrated a few seconds later. It was Custer on my private channel.

The General kept his composure as he described the attack on the Ranch, "From what we've gathered from the security cameras, an unidentified enemy force stormed the place, knocking down the house with explosives."

"Unidentified?" I coaxed, suppressing my need to scream.

"Likely the MSS," he conceded. "We were able to re-task the Eye back to the area, but we're facing some challenges..." My anxiety skyrocketed as he lamented that beyond the interference, the storm raging in the area was hampering communications and visibility.

I recalled Jack's growing concern about the Eye being targeted by an adversary.

"It's gone, Son. The whole place is on fire." His tone was on the verge of an emotion he had never exposed me to.

"Focus him!" growled the Beast.

"How did they get past our defenses?" I hoped to get the General back on top of it.

"They didn't. They somehow appeared, taking our security from the back."

Oh my God.

"At this point, we have no communication or status on Jack, Ali, Tami, the baby, or Henry. We know their last location was inside the house," he added, his voice tight.

The vehicles stopped by the stealth chopper, where Sarah was already prepping it for flight.

I exited the car, signing for Dex to take charge until my call was done. The line remained silent, except for Custer's unusually heavy breathing on the other end of the line.

"It seems as if we have a private war with China," murmured the General. "I just didn't think it would be this."

When his voice nearly cracked, the Beast snarled, *"They trained you for this."*

"My brother was the Trojan Horse." I could hardly believe the words falling out of my mouth as I watched the Rogues transfer their gear into the chopper.

"I saw your interrogation... I..." He was at a loss for words.

"Do we have any tracking on Chad, Jerome, and Lee?" I tried again to focus his mind, watching Sarah complete her checkups around the stealth helicopter.

"Not at the moment. Hang on." Custer's end was silent for a moment. "We just got a confirmation that the Eye is under some cyberattack." His voice was tight and strained. "The RCC is on full lockdown."

The severity of his words was countered only by the fact that this was the closest I'd ever gotten to knowing where our Rogue Control Center was.

It must be around the Ranch.

"Old Glory units are already sent to Ranch, but the weather is rough. It'll take time."

Our entire security is down. I could barely process what I was hearing.

"Can we call the authorities?" I asked, thinking the Governor's father was among those missing.

"Negative. This is ours to clean up." His firm tone had returned. "Alfa is ordered to follow your IA parameters. You'll go in through aerial insertion."

"ROE?" I asked as the Rogues, minus Dex and Sarah, hopped into the chopper.

"Unlimited," he rumbled and then paused. "There's one more thing I need to tell you about the Continuity Directive."

I waited, curious about this term I'd never heard before.

"Both Romulus and Clementia are MIA," he reported, referring to my mom in her official call name, "leaving me the sole Commander."

"I understand."

"No, you don't," he responded. "You're next in line, Son. Proper instructions will be given to you in case I'm out too."

Astonishment sealed any words ready to escape in my throat.

"The timing of this isn't random. The election will start in less than a day, and they managed to strike us back hard..." Custer reassured me that all Rogue teams, besides Alfa, remained embedded in their ideal locations. "We're taking a chance with the West Coast, but there is nothing we can do about it."

Alfa wouldn't have it any other way.

"By the way, we got a report that Ken Lim's rental was ransacked after he disappeared."

"Damn," I uttered, knowing that the journalist was probably dead or wishing he was.

In LA, right next to my family!

My silence must have betrayed me, as the General answered, "Something is going on, Son. You got a hard choice to make."

"What?" His question caught me by surprise and pulled my attention back from Dex's sign that we were five minutes out.

When he didn't respond, the rift inside me exploded, widening the gap between the two versions of myself.

"I'm going to the Ranch. I'll call Eli while en route," I replied.

The chopper blasted forward to Eugene, where our jet waited for us.

"Eli, I need you to tighten the security. Something is happening, and I have to go to the Ranch." The words cut my throat on their way out.

Thank God Eli understands this impossible choice.

"Is that all?" he wondered, his voice gruff.

"No, it's time to prepare an evac option as well," I responded without digesting the gravity of my words first.

He chuckled, but his voice remained severe, "It's done, Tanner. This is my daughter and grandkids we're talking about. Your dad knows about it as well."

At least that.

"Just please no word to Dani. Let me be the one to tell her if we get to that point." I shuddered, imagining her reaction.

"Agreed. You just do what you need to do."

I turned my head to look at the Rogues sitting in their seats, deep in their thoughts.

And will be required of us.

"Yes, Sir," I replied, and the line went dead.

Eugene's lights appeared in the distance as waves of concern gripped every fiber of my being.

Tami's tiny baby. With every unwelcome thought, I sensed my growing weakness consuming my resolve. *This is all my fault. I fucked up.* My fists clenched at the memory of my choice with the forest facility.

"These are the consequences. The world moves by them." The Beast offered no real comfort.

A tap on my sore shoulder broke my trance, and I turned to see Jenny with a shadow of a smile, holding something out to me.

"I saw it on your desk. Figured to bring it for you," she said gently.

I looked at Ganbold's blood stain on the front cover of *Endarkenment*, and my strength flowed back into me.

"Thank you." I took the book from her hand and turned back in my seat.

"We're with you all the way. Semper Fidelis," she said as she squeezed my shoulder.

Bringing me the book was one thing. Those words were another. Somehow, everything connected, even if I was the last to understand it all.

Fucking riddles.

"Prepare for landing," said Sarah over the team channel, and I spared one last look at Alfa, moving my gaze from face to face, acknowledging their unyielding support.

FOOT TO THE PEDAL

– Moskee, WY –
Monday, November 2, 2020

21:45

Lightning and thunder rocked the night sky, the heavy rain obscuring the cockpit windows.

"South Dakota is coming up," Sarah muttered, fully engaged and focused in the midst of the storm outside and the one we all contended with on the inside.

I glanced over at her to confirm I'd heard her and then back at the book in my lap, straining to read the words through the flashing light and noise consuming the skies let alone use them to answer my list of riddles.

My intuition was that Bach's manuscript was based on a mythical journey, even though he never mentioned it. The clues were hidden in plain sight, one of which had struck me deeply this time: "Darkness on the left, abyss on the right. In front, a horde of death. Behind, shame and guilt. Where do you go?"

Exactly! And he's written about unique brain activity and violence? I...

The vibration in my ear interrupted my thoughts and the General's voice replaced them.

"The storm isn't going anywhere, which is to our advantage now..." Custer briefed me on the conditions over the target.

He was right. The heavy weather meant very little for our aerial approach and ground movement, but it would most likely slow down the hostiles' speed on unfamiliar, rugged terrain.

"The first Old Glory team on the scene managed to report multiple friendly casualties and no survivors. They found one enemy body, which seemed to be a Chinese male. The team was attacked as soon as they put eyes on the blazing ranch."

"What?!?" I sat upright in my seat, earning a side glance from Sarah.

"Yeah. They were most likely eliminated within two minutes, as we lost contact with them all." Custer sighed heavily. "The next OGT force will be more careful. They should arrive around the same time as your insertion."

I can't believe this.

"As of now, no state or federal agencies are aware of the event. We hope to keep it this way."

"The storm will help." I harnessed the *Sense* to keep my mind cohesive in the face of the neverending terror waiting at the edges of my thoughts.

"The Eye did manage to get a few sporadic pings from Chad's chip."

"Hold on," I interjected, aghast. "Chad has a chip?"

The General's tone suggested irritation, but he admitted both my siblings were chipped on the arm at birth.

"Their chips are only for location tracking. No other capabilities."

Damn it, Dad! How could you decide for everyone like this? Just like the fucking machine you put in me!

"Where are they heading?" I closed the book and shoved it in my bag.

"It seems their escort chose a longer route through the hills heading south."

"South..." I mulled, considering the vast size of the Ranch and the terrain. "It'll take them more time, but land them close to the highway."

"Right," grumbled Custer. "It'll give you the chance to intercept them."

"And Jerome?" I wondered why Lynn's father hadn't been mentioned.

There was a long pause on the line.

"We don't know. His chip went dark."

Holy shit.

The implications were devastating. Jerome's chip was like ours. It had a dead man switch for total erasure and destruction if the user stopped living.

"Could be the weather," I offered, gulping down my concern for him and his daughter.

"Hopefully," replied Custer. "Assuming this is the MSS force, they have the numbers and training to pull this off. Our current analysis is that they split their forces between the ones ambushing the Ranch and those who went with Chad and presumably Lee."

"Orders?"

Custer chuckled darkly as he answered, "Tight spot, Alfa-leader. To the Ranch or after Chad and Lee. The choice is yours."

My mind zipped through calculations, hiccupping briefly through fear for my family and the baby among them on its way to the grand picture.

Impossible!

"Understood. I'm still assessing," I replied as calmly as I could.

The line went dead, and I went back to analyzing various options with Aide's help.

Dani picked up on the first ring.

"My queen." I paused. "Why is it so quiet there?"

"They're already sleeping, Love. Now, what's going on with you?"

My defenses held when I heard the edge in her tone.

"What's happening there, Baby?" I asked.

"Hang on." I heard her close a door and assumed she'd escaped to my studio. "The whole Ramirez clan is here." I waited impatiently. "Cel heard reports about protesters desecrating Taco Libertad and the mural. She's pissed!"

Oh shit.

The jet entered minor turbulence, and the cockpit shook as Sarah's voice came over the plane's comms, "Ladies and gentlemen, we've entered South Dakota."

"Go on," I encouraged Dani, who had stopped at the sound.

"Roberto and Paulina don't know how to calm her down, and neither do I. With the election tomorrow, the streets are crazy. Even Holden checked in a few times and warned us about being outside tonight."

My pulse raced as my body rocked in the seat of the storm-battered plane.

Law-abiding citizens are under lockdown, but not the rest.

"Dad pulled the security into the complex, just in case." She revealed no sign of knowing about my other request of her father.

Thank you, Eli.

There were so many people I cared about in the neighborhood. I couldn't stomach the thought of them being in danger.

Maybe she felt my concern.

"Shemtov decided to ride it out in the synagogue. I tried my best, but he didn't budge."

"He's a tough one," I said, trying to hide my worry for the old Rabbi. "Baby, thank you for the update. I have to go. I'll be home as soon as I can be."

My guts were knotted by the choice before me and the shackles behind me.

"I trust you will find your way back to him." The Green Beret's words resurfaced in my mind.

Who? I wondered as Sarah held us steady.

As if in answer, an early childhood training moment captured my mind's eye. I was about twelve and arguing with my dad about his choice to train me while leaving my siblings out of it.

"Why *me*?" I had screamed in a moment of pure rage and jealousy.

"And his answer," prodded the Beast.

"Why not?"

"And you just chose to take offense, instead of trying to understand what he might have meant?" The Beast's taunt infuriated me with its plain conclusion.

I felt embarrassed, succumbing to my weakness at the worst possible timing.

Fine!

I took a deep breath and centered my mind around one reflection: *What would Dad do right now?* The *Sense* surged forward, sorting my thoughts into a few logical pathways.

"Twenty mikes to Ranch's western border," called Sarah on the team channel, bringing me back from my inner wrestling match.

I nodded as Remus's call came through.

"We managed to ping Chad's location again. Their direction remains south toward the highway."

I took a moment to review the data on the map as the General updated me that the second Old Glory team had just begun infiltrating the Ranch, heading to the main house wreckage.

"Have you made your decision yet, Alfa-leader?" Compassion mixed with his commander tone.

"Yes," I answered. "The Ranch is a diversion. We're going after the group with Chad."

He held back for only a second before confirming, "It's what I would have done as well."

"Just update me as soon as..." I started.

"Of course. I got this."

"Good hunting!" Sarah exclaimed as I left my seat.

"Thank you." Squeezing her shoulder, I turned to the exit.

The Rogues were all ready, everyone in Skins and Skulls. Jenny opened the plane's side door and Liam handed me my jumping pack.

I walked to the open door, looking out to the black skies, consumed with lightning and thunder that I didn't hear inside the Skull.

"Those fuckers came into our home, and now two of ours are missing in action. We're going down there to find them and capture my brother."

Looking back, I saw them nodding, their red eyes blazing.

The count on the HUD began.

"Black Hills forever!" I growled and jumped when the ticker reached zero.

"Black Hills!" they roared back as everyone dropped from the plane and fell into a perfect arrow formation on my right and left.

God damn it, Chad.

THIS IS OUR HOME

– Black Hills, SD –
Tuesday, November 3, 2020

22:50
The Hero

The advanced technology of the Skin countered the cold, wet air, as we glided toward the earth. When the Aide highlighted the ideal landing spot, I pulled on the parachute strings to correct my approach, and the rest of Alfa followed, all our Aides syncing our routes accordingly.

Coming in fast, I broke my fall with a quick roll and immediately moved my parachute out of the way. Within sixty seconds, the team was on the ground and checking their gear. We all wore our Skins and Skulls, carrying only the Wraith handguns for firepower. Speed would be vital.

The thick wooded hills were difficult to traverse during the day, let alone in pitch black of night. But the darkness meant very little to us, our feet swiftly crossing the unforgiving terrain we knew like the back of our hands. The Aides and the RCC calculated our path until the Aides surprised us all by creating their private network and sharing details from the scanners of all our Skulls. It wasn't as good as having the Eye, but it was damn helpful.

"Where did Jerome's chip go dark?"

The Aide quickly placed the location on the HUD.

We can check it with little deviation from our path.

"Alert all other Aides and adjust the coordinates to pass through that location," I instructed.

Jumping over a boulder, my mind drifted to the last time I'd seen this man—when he'd surprised me in the woods and challenged me to reconsider my sense of home with yet another riddle: "You were born here, on this very land. Your blood runs deep within these hills, whether you realize this or not. I was here… for your ceremony…"

Oh my God!

My legs went weak the moment I laid eyes on his body, and I nearly collapsed to the ground as I removed the Skull to take in the sight with my bare eyes.

Motherfuckers!

Hands tied to the small tree behind his back, his disfigured bare chest told the horror story of his final moments.

One of the Rogues vomited behind me, as I observed the gruesome cuts made to his abdomen, the skin that had turned cherry red, and the intensely bitter almond odor floating from his body.

The Rogues' angry voices toppled my state of mind, provoking an untenable spike of rage.

"Leave me," I commanded. "I'll catch up."

Three seconds later, I was alone. Reaching to close his empty eyes, I remembered his fatherly plea in our last conversation.

"Please watch over her once I'm gone."

My heart cracked at the thought of Lynn, and I rose to my feet, feeling the Beast replacing the shock and sadness with fury.

"He was tortured for information."

He gave them nothing.

Bending to place my hand over his heart, I bowed my head, involuntarily checking on the cyanide tooth in my own mouth as the almond scent overwhelmed my senses.

"Aide, give me the fastest route to catch up to them," I commanded, slipping the Skull on.

"It will be rough," cautioned the AI.

"These are the Black Hills," I snapped, more to myself and my desire to kill. In the thirty minutes it took me to catch up with Alfa, the RCC updated me that the second Old Glory team had reached the Ranch, found no hostiles, and begun rescue operations.

"Step on it, Rogues," I growled on the team channel as I passed Hux in the rear and again as I reached Dex in front and increased our pace.

It was almost three o'clock in the morning when our Skull scanners managed to ping Chad's chip for an exact location. Fortunately, the storm got more intense, sending heavy rain and constant thunder as a cover for us to run ahead of the MSS group and lay an ambush.

The Aide estimated there were at least one dozen guards protecting Chad and presumably Lee.

"Don't let my brother see you," I commanded on the team channel.

"Why?" asked Hux.

A fair question that deserved an answer, given the impending collision with my traitorous sibling.

"No enemy can see a Skull and live."

All eyes remained on me until Dex asked, "Anything else?"

Thank you.

"Once I get to him, instruct your Aides to block all updates and the live feed. I need to speak with him first."

"It will be done," confirmed Dex, and the Rogues nodded in agreement.

02:55

The Hostiles

The hostiles entered the ravine with Chad and Lee in the middle. Once the Rogues acquired the targets and the Aides divided them, the countdown began on my HUD.

"3... 2... 1..."

The thunder broke overhead in time to muffle our first strike, which took out ten guards. The last three began spitting fire with their small submachine guns. Two were dropped in the next volley, but the third remained alive, holding Lee down to the ground and protecting Chad behind him.

"Cease fire," I commanded over the team channel before removing my Skull and placing it on the soaked forest floor. "Back me up, but stay hidden."

As the rain hit my face, I looked up to the vengeful skies and sneaked forward. The lightning broke above, illuminating the face of the last MSS agent, dressed in black, still swiveling his submachine gun around, his knee dug deep into Lee's back. Chad stood close by, a sight to behold. His usually perfectly-combed black hair stuck to his forehead. Covered in mud from head to toe. His lean body seemed to be trembling.

Arriving on their left flank, I waited for Lee to catch sight of me. When he did, he nodded slightly in response to my motion toward the guard.

"Right here!" I called in Mandarin.

As the Chinese soldier turned toward my voice, Lee pivoted his body to the side, sending the MSS operator on his heels toward the ground. Rushing forward, I pulled my combat dagger from my toolbelt and sliced his neck open before he found his footing and pushed himself up.

I was helping Lee to his feet when Chad yelled something incoherent and turned to run.

"Stop. You'll be shot!" I warned.

Chad turned toward me, smirking down at the red lights dancing across his body.

"Guess you weren't kidding, big brother," he said with mocked jest as they disappeared.

Lee stayed at my side but a step behind, reaching forward to take the flashlight I offered.

"Oh boy... look at you." Chad barely contained his laughter as the thunder roared above us.

"Be grateful that it's my face you see now."

"Is Dad on his way?" His tone was laced with venom.

Resisting the impulse to tear the wicked smirk off his face, I took a deep breath and stepped toward him until we were only four feet apart.

"All I know is that our home is on fire," I hissed through gritted teeth.

"No..." Genuine shock crossed his face. "Tell me that they're okay... ple—"

"Shut up!" I barked, and he recoiled as if he had been punched. "You've lost the right to ask about our family." I didn't have much time to get the information I needed. "How did you get them inside?"

"Do you remember the old long cave you showed us when we were kids?" he answered smugly.

God damn it! That's my fault too?

"I kept going into that tunnel until I found a secret passage that led to another tunnel, which ended outside the Ranch." He stopped chuckling when he saw my response. "I used it to sneak out sometimes, to meet with friends. Never imagined..."

My right hand surged forward like a viper, smacking him across his face hard enough to elicit a scream of pain.

"What then?"

Cursing quietly, he explained how he'd lured Jerome and Lee to a small hunting cabin, and given the MSS the location.

"You fucking piece of shit," I grumbled, shaking my head.

"I didn't know about the Ranch. We left the cabin and traveled until your..." He looked around, futilely searching for those who had taken out his escort.

I rumbled as I closed the distance and pushed him against the broad tree behind him. He tried to stand upright, so I pushed him harder.

"Ouch!"

"Who killed Jerome? And think carefully before you answer. I gave my word, but that protection will not stand for fucking lies!"

"He can't be dead," he stuttered. "I knew him. Fuck, we grew up with them. It wasn't supposed to..."

The Beast's patience grew thin, reminding me of the thin rope I walked in this moment.

"Who?"

"Paul Shi," he started. "You know him. He led the force and then stayed behind to interrogate Jerome."

"Why would I know him?" I asked, dreading the answer.

"Paul said he owed you for something."

What?

"And when you had the chance." The Beast showed zero mercy.

Pushing aside the newest riddle, I started the hard press, "Ah yes, the one who recruited you and taught you that fucking Marx quote." Seeing Chad's smile evaporate, I continued, "You motherfucker. You betrayed your family, your nation, and your people."

My right hand pulled back again, and Chad cowered into the trunk behind him, raising his hands to his face. Lee advanced, and I glanced at him briefly. When he nodded at me with a faint, sad smile, the *Sense* pushed back on my murderous desires.

Sighing, I let my hand fall to my side.

"Why? Chad? Why?"

"Why?!?" His face shifted from fear to amusement to red-hot anger. "How would you even know? Always being Daddy's Good Boy.'"

"You need to hear this." The Beast stopped me before I exploded.

"You were always gone. Always too busy with him to be an older brother. I was ignored and sidelined for who I am..." My interest piqued as Chad began a fiery monologue about how Jack favored me and skipped over him. "Look at our family business, this wretched capitalist and exploitive business..."

He never really changed.

"...Dad never considered me good enough to hire—just you! Only recently did he figure that I was worth something. Well! Too little, too late!"

"Purge your weakness. Expose his," insisted the Beast, helping me refocus.

"Why do you think Dad skipped you?"

"Because I'm gay!" Chad screamed in my face and tried to move out from between me and the tree, but I shoved him back against the trunk.

Sad irony threatened to overwhelm me as I stared into the hurt and angry eyes of my little brother.

All this time... how did we miss it?

"Is this why you think he didn't get you in? To Old Glory?" I knew the answer but needed time to regroup.

"Why else would he have kept me out?" yelled Chad, pain in his voice as he wiped the wet hair away from his eyes. "He never thought I was a man enough. He's always been a bigot."

That last accusation about the man who had stolen my childhood sent chills up and down my spine. But instead of unleashing my fury, the Beast and I made a silent deal.

"Whatever happens next, I'll never forgive myself for not being there for you. For that, I'm sorry," I started, and something softened about his face for a moment. But when his sneer returned, I changed course. "Did Mom and Tami know?"

Somehow, I wasn't surprised when he admitted they had known since his teens.

"Well... even though we didn't know, you are dead wrong about Dad, and the truth will haunt you forever." His eyes widened. "Our father is many things, but he's not a bigot. Your sexual preferences had nothing to do with his decisions about you, nor did he ever wonder about them."

Childhood memories resurfaced, laced with the bitterness of seeing my siblings protected from Jack's training.

"It was Mom. She convinced him to give you and Tami a normal life. One I was not allowed to have. It seems you thought that I had a good time, while the opposite is true," I hissed with renewed anger.

He looked down at the ground.

"Hey!" I growled, yanking his head up. "Look at me! You better have the guts to do that, at least!" His face flushed red and eyes narrowed. "You weren't skipped! You were loved enough to save from my fate." I pushed it through my gritted teeth, keeping the more somber thought to myself.

I'm just a tool.

Chad's face returned to its natural pallor, looking at me as if for the first time in a long time.

"Maybe I should have thought this one through a bit more. Maybe I didn't want to..."

"What the hell are you talking about?" I stepped back, allowing him to stand straight.

"I always knew Mom was a bit afraid of you."

Confusion mixed with shame sent my head into a turbulent spin. I took a deep breath and a step back, unable to process the new information.

"I heard her arguing with Dad about something in Bogotá when you were a kid. About your violence."

Why don't I remember?

As my mental defenses rose, the Beast rumbled in dismay, doing Its best to allow Chad's words to find a footing.

"He referred to you as Firstborn, as though it was some sort of answer for her fear."

"'And Isaac spoke to Abraham... and he said, 'My father!' And he said, 'Here I am, my son.' And he said, 'Here are the fire and the wood, but where is the lamb for the burnt offering?'"

Cold shock consumed me as Shemtov's riddle broke open. There was no escape.

Scanning my face with wicked pleasure, he pushed, "Is this what you meant? Is this what he did with you? Maybe I should have been more thankful to Mom."

The Beast laughed and receded, leaving me alone in the forest with my traitorous brother and my endless riddles.

Pulling myself back from the edge, I bellowed, "Dad thought you changed after Seattle. He was so proud of you." The rage surged as I considered all the lives he'd compromised, maybe sacrificed, because of unfounded resentment. "Mom... Dad... Tami... Henry... the baby...

all the people on the Ranch..." I noticed the flashlight's beam shaking and looked at man who still stood to my left. "And Lee, who befriended you, who trusted you..." Jerome's butchered body returned to my mind's eye. "And Jerome!"

Chad flinched, his face straining against the words.

"And your nation, which you have betrayed to the Chinese! After all that our family has given."

He glanced sideways at Lee and then lowered his eyes.

"I cannot undo my actions, but I will speak for my freedom," he uttered, refocusing his gaze on me.

Lee laid his right hand on my left shoulder and leaned toward me to whisper in Mandarin, quoting *The Art of War* by the famed Sun Tzu: "Begin by seizing something which your opponent holds dear; then he will be amenable to your will."

Remembering my promise to Daj, my impatience accelerated as I looked back at the man who may have just killed my whole family.

"We have very little time, Chad. Answer truthfully," I commanded.

03:37

The Betrayal

To my horror, Chad explained how he was recruited by the CPC in college.

"I was upset after learning about our family making its fortune in the military contracting business. It's what inspired me to speak in classes. Maybe that's why they came to me..." He admitted that Paul was the one who found, recruited, and trained him closely and later in groups of his peers. "I gave up information on Old Glory back then, whatever I could glean from Dad and hearsay..."

It was excruciating to listen, but the Beast helped me manage the rage twitching through my body, begging to be released on the traitor making excuses.

"I never told them about you though."

Ignoring his so-called good deed, I asked a question I already knew some of the answer to, "How could you embrace Communism?" Born and raised after we spent time in China and Columbia, he'd never seen the real suffering of the people.

He laughed and admitted to secretly looking into Marx and his work in his teens.

"The problem is not Communism, but how it was implemented. It can be done better. It's a far better option than the exploitive capitalism of our country."

"Have you ever heard the term Thirty Tyrants? Has Paul ever mentioned it?'"

He shook his head.

How did we miss this?

As if hearing my thoughts, he bragged about how he'd outmaneuvered Jack, gleaning material to prove him wrong.

"He never saw me as a worthy son." This time, his words lacked conviction.

"Faster," I pressed, uninterested in wasting time on rhetoric.

Chad described how the CPC had helped him gain a position in the Charlton presidential campaign for the 2008 election.

"I got the job right after college, and right before the election. That's when Sam Baker befriended me."

His words stole all the breath from my body.

"You know him, right?" He accurately described the man who had haunted my thoughts since Market and the onset of the pandemic.

"How did that work with your Chinese masters?" I called back my breath and enjoyed watching his smile fade into a scowl.

I was caught between astonishment and amusement as Chad explained how he had worked as a double agent, telling the CPC everything and following their directions accordingly.

"Paul wanted me to develop a friendship with Baker, so I did. As far as I was concerned, he served the system and was just another oppressor..." His story continued, detailing various Charlton administration assignments until he got a position at the prestigious Seattle newspaper. "Baker thought he'd helped me get it. He had no idea it was the CPC's wish for me to be embedded in the Northwest."

Embedded?

Reading my face, he grinned.

"If Dad knew about my sources all these years…"

"Time to herd him or burn him," grumbled the Beast, reminding me that the sun would rise and my window would disappear very soon.

"Tell me about your boyfriend, Daj Morris." Dark satisfaction flooded me when the panic crossed his face and he lost his words. "Talk!"

Stuttering until he found them, Chad confirmed Daj's story.

"We didn't really plan for it. We just fell in love," he mumbled, obviously unsure about the nature of my question. "He was always so afraid about my path…" Searching my eyes for clues, Chad reconfirmed how they had been indoctrinated and trained by Paul.

"Yeah, that quote of yours that you fancy so much," I murmured.

His face darkened as he snarled, "I tried so many times with you. I always gave you the benefit of the doubt, hoping you would open your eyes to the nature of our country. I protected you. I never said a word, even though I knew you serve the system!"

It took me a moment to digest his intentions about me, and he misconstrued my silence.

"At least Mom and Tami supported me."

My right hand extended in a flash, grabbing him by the neck, threatening to choke him to nothingness.

"Tami was with the baby in the house!" I roared. "If you dare to repeat their names, I will kill you, promise or not!"

His hands tried to pry mine from his neck, but he was no match for my fury.

"Our time is running out, Sir," whispered Dex in my earbud, breaking the spell and causing me to release my grip.

Chad collapsed to his knees, gasping for air.

04:40

The Extent

"I tried to get close to you when you quit in 2015." He was indignant as he rose. "It was enough for me that you finally stopped working for him. I even considered telling you I'm gay."

Happy memories of us hanging around Los Angeles during his visits resurfaced.

"Why didn't you?"

"Because I still felt his hold on you." He grimaced. "I didn't trust that you wouldn't go back to him."

"Tell me more about Baker," I commanded, shifting the conversation toward data gathering and away from our father.

Chad exposed how Baker had reemerged around 2015, asking for details about Jack and any possible help given to then-Republican presidential candidate Howard Stone.

"He didn't know the CPC decided everything," he added confidently.

When he skipped over Operation Market, I hoped that meant he didn't know about it, but I pressed anyway. The mission was too important.

"Did Baker ever ask about me?"

"He did," Chad smirked, "sometime in 2016, but I told him about your service in the Marines and that you retired in Venice. You see, I wasn't that bad."

I shook my head, still struggling to process the sheer magnitude of this moment and the one to come far too soon.

"Did you manage to get Baker something good?"

I nearly gasped as he told me about Jack's meeting with the retired General Tall.

"We had a heated debate about the 2016 elections, and I just pieced it together..."

"And Tall was decapitated from public service..." I finished his treacherous exposition.

"I did learn from the best manipulator."

"Fast-forward. Tell me about your bogus articles, which you wrote against the riots."

His insufferable sneer returned as he shared that the CPC began pushing on him to find a way into Old Glory.

"Once they told me about the CHAZ operation, I realized it was a golden opportunity..." He explained how he came up with the idea of the articles and the subsequent fake hunt. "I knew it would do the job. What else could unite us as father and son?"

"Don't underestimate him again," cautioned the Beast.

"Daj went off script there in the alley, which was my fault for not telling him more in advance," he mumbled. "I held that information for your safety."

"Unbelievable."

"What about the photo you took? One of my guys. The black one with the young face."

He looked down at the ground, something akin to shame crossing his countenance.

"I didn't want to do it. I knew he was one of your friends, but I had to gain leverage."

"Go on."

His eyes pleaded for my understanding.

"I held back the photo until it was clear to me that Daj was in danger by a mole in the movement."

Chicago.

Something clicked inside.

"So much care. Did you ever extend it to your own neighbor? The one that your friends murdered?"

"That was… I didn't know they'd…"

"Like the Ranch attack and Jerome, right? Fucking idiot." I chose to taunt him instead of sink my blade into his mouth, so he could continue telling me about his increasing deception while working in Old Glory.

★　★　★

05:31

The Promise

"It started with my reasoning that Old Glory had to be stopped, but it ended up being more than that," he admitted with a tinge of self-reflection.

"Did you continue working with Baker?"

He said that he'd purposely avoided Baker's emails, considering the dangerous path he was on once inside the Ranch.

I looked up into the dark skies, noticing the birds waking up for another day.

"Did you betray us in Portland?"

He nodded and confirmed that he'd helped get Moss captured in Chicago.

"What about the infection?"

"Yeah, but I don't know how your family got caught up in it. I'm sorry…"

He didn't know anything about Victoria, but that didn't surprise me.

"What about Harry Ganbold?"

His leer returned as he confessed to revealing my friend's involvement to both the CPC and Baker after Paul implored him to reply to Baker's emails about it.

"Are you one of the vigilantes everyone's been talking about?" His eyes darted around, searching for Alfa.

"Tell me everything about the election. Do you know what they're planning?"

"Who is *they*?" There was far too much sarcasm in his voice.

"Don't play with me," I growled, and he answered that he didn't know anything about it. "What about Ken Lim?" I felt like I was shooting in the darkness.

"Yep, I told the CPC about him too."

Damn it!

Images of the good soldiers and men lost because of this hateful treason crossed my mind. Nico, Ishmael, Ganbold.

"Little brother, I've grown to understand there's a difference between journeys in the darkness and journeys of evil, even if they look alike." He seemed confused. "Maybe one day you will too." The words choked me, as I was still unwilling to accept his chosen role. "Daj Morris isn't coming to save you. I killed him."

Chad shrieked in pain as though he was the one who had been shot.

"I made a promise to let you live. He was worried about you until his final moment."

He crumbled to his knees, sobbing.

"*He* regretted his actions in the end," I said quietly.

Chad raised his wet face.

"Was it because of Nico? Did you kill him for that?"

When he saw my surprise, he said Daj's questions in the alley made him wonder about his lover's involvement in Nico's death.

I shook my head.

"He did plenty bad in his life, but Nico wasn't on him."

"Did he suffer?" Chad wiped his face with his sleeve.

"No," I replied, marveling at the void inside my soul.

★　★　★

06:00

The Fallen

"What now?"

The question had plagued me since I'd discovered the truth about his role, but it was suddenly very clear.

The chip.

"I'm no Cain, and a promise was made. And if Mom survived..." my words trailed off as I pulled a breathable black bag from my toolbelt and handed it to him. "Pull it over your head, and don't dare take it off, even if you're in pain. You'll die if you do."

He seemed confused but still rushed to follow my instruction.

On my command, Alfa emerged silently from the woods. Dex and Hux grabbed Chad and held him on the ground, and Jenny used her Skull scanner to find the chip in his arm. My brother screamed while she cut it out and had a hard time calming himself down as Alfa reclined him against a tree, bandaged and humiliated.

With the Rogues back among the trees, I removed his black bag and noticed my mixed feelings about his pain.

"What was it?" he asked.

"You need to leave right now."

"You killed the man I loved." His face contorted in pain. "Even if he doubted the cause before dying, I still believe in it."

"Go back to your master before I change my mind. Don't dare to step on this land again."

Chad pulled himself up off the ground and began walking away. After a few steps, he turned to Lee and then back at me. It was unclear whether he wanted to hug me or kill me, but it didn't matter. In the end, he tucked tail and ran away.

Fucking coward.

06:15

The Hope

"Will he make it out?" asked Lee, as we watched him disappear.

"I bet he will." My mocking response held in it my newfound appreciation for the Judas who had grown in our midst and the skills he had developed through the years.

Alfa came out from behind the trees, and Dex began communicating with the RCC about a chopper pickup. He knew not to release the recorded event.

"So much wickedness was released because of me," Lee lamented quietly. "I wish I could take it back, to never agree to work with Zhang. I was so relieved when your father told me he's dead."

Retrieving my Skull from Liam, I reflected on the Chinese General's final moments.

"Zhang did mention that you probably had some help escaping..." I allowed my words to hang in the air between us.

Lee smile faintly and silently measured me for a long moment before nodding slowly.

"You know, a CIA agent worked with me as a part of the American group in the Wuhan laboratories. We became friends, and he helped me get the word out, which led to my escape..." The scientist grimaced as he shared how betrayed he felt when Baker decided to hand him back to the Chinese. "After you got me out, that friend emailed me, vowing he had nothing to do with the betrayal. I decided to believe him and never told anyone."

"Ten minutes for the bird," called out Jenny.

I nodded, but my focus was solely on Lee.

"Years later, he was the one that warned me about patient zero." He reminded me of Jack's vague mention of being tipped about the first case in Wuhan back in November 2019.

The world that was.

"My friend has been fighting from *inside* the system, and maybe it was a mistake not to ask him for more."

"What do you mean? Who is he?"

"I don't know his real name," he shrugged, "but his call name is Columbo. The one who wrote those letters to Stone online."

My mind raced through the various dead ends I'd encountered with the elusive online Columbo persona, the first to reveal the term The Great Reset.

"Thank you," I responded to the RCC update that the Old Glory team had managed to contact survivors at the destroyed ranch.

Please, God... the baby.

"Hopefully, my dad survived and you will be able to tell him about Columbo." I glanced sadly at Lee.

"What should I tell them about Chad?" asked Jenny, as the thump thump of the approaching chopper got louder.

"That I allowed him to escape on my Independent Authority." The resignation sat heavy in my chest.

"There are no redoes." Words from *Endarkenment* reverberated through the forest around me.

"All that is left is the hope to choose again."

THE PRICE

06:48

Survivors

It was close to seven o'clock in the morning, dawn ready to break as Sarah lifted us back into the skies. Nobody spoke.

Too loud and too early to call her. I imagined Dani and the kids snoring softly in their beds as I texted Eli an update.

The ear vibration and the Aide alerted me in unison.

"Alfa-leader, here's our situation report." Remus wasted no time. "Romulus, Clementia, Tami, and the baby survived. Managed to get to the bunker in time."

My heart nearly broke with relief, but the Beast cautioned against it.

"Henry died during the evacuation. He went down fighting, buying them some time." Custer's somber tone reminded me that his paternal care extended to Tami too. "Clementia has also been wounded. She protected the baby with her body, and is pretty cut up but stable thanks to Romulus." He didn't try to hide the concern in his voice.

My body froze in the co-pilot seat.

"Compartmentalize! Stay effective!" commanded the Beast.

I released my breath in obedience, remembering Tami's dead husband's gentle nature.

"What bunker?" I'd never seen a shelter inside our home.

"There's a secret hatch, Son," he chuckled morbidly, "behind that George Washington oil painting in your dad's office."

"Unbelievable. I asked him once why he loved that picture so much."

"And?" wondered Custer, without the weight of the world on his shoulders for a moment.

In my best impersonation of Romulus, I answered, "So I remember there's always a chance, always another way, to come back into the fight."

Custer grunted something about ol' Jack and his unending tricks.

"God damn it," growled the General. "I wish I were there!" I wondered how many battles this old Marine had faced as he regrouped. "Jerome's body was picked up, and security is removing all other findings from the hills. Speak to your dad about Lynn. He will handle Clara separately."

Pain pierced my heart at the thought of Lynn and her mother receiving the news of her father's demise.

He cleared his throat of emotion before asking, "Where's the actual recording?"

"Please finish, and I'll report." The vast expanse of the dark Black Hills passed below us as my eyes searched the horizon for some light.

"The Eye has been under cyberattack. We suspect the Chinese and will have to be careful about future deployments. We estimate that Paul escaped after handling Jerome."

"It was bad, Sir. Really bad. But the big guy took his life on his terms."

"He saved us all from certain death."

Yeah. Nothing quite like China coming after you with actionable data.

"Romulus asked that I retain command until he's operational." His tone warmed for a moment. "This is a family moment... outside the Doctrine."

I wanted to agree with him, but my thoughts remained haunted by Chad's revelations.

The General continued once he realized I wasn't going to respond.

"All right, Alfa-leader. Your turn."

In the distance, I could see the last ridge before the valley in which the Ranch now smoldered.

07:20

Ruins

"I'm sending you the video now. It will explain everything in detail." I paused. "I removed Chad's chip."

"Wh… you… Arrghhh!" barked Custer.

Sorry, Sir, for using your confidence this way.

"You already know Paul Shi led the attack and killed Jerome." Taking another deep breath, I shared the biggest revelation that didn't include my parents, "It wasn't just the Chinese who got to Chad. The spider got his fangs in him when he worked in the Charlton campaign in 2008."

"Baker?" Custer sounded like he had been sucker-punched.

"The very same…" I continued, confirming all the havoc Chad had wreaked upon our family, Old Glory, and the nation. "He's the one who knew about my dad meeting General Tall."

Custer remained speechless as Sarah climbed over the ridge and I looked back to find exhausted Rogues staring out their windows solemnly.

"He also ratted out Ken."

The loud sound in my earbud indicated the General had slammed his desk, and I waited silently.

"Sorry." He cleared his throat again. "Anything else?"

"He didn't give me anything about the elections."

"Well, folks are voting on the East Coast and tension is increasing across the country, predominantly around big cities. Tall is trying to get the President's ear as we speak."

"Think he'll succeed?" I sat up even straighter as we neared the top of the ridge.

"Don't know. The polls are looking bad for Stone. He might be too preoccupied with his political survival," he answered. "We're trying Senator Garcia, as you suggested, hoping he can sway the Texan government to stay vigilant. Listen," he started as the valley became visible over the ridge with the first dawn light. "There is a spike of chatter around Southern California. Something's going on, and we've got no presence there."

Oh... my... God.

My heart sank, partly in response to his words and partly to the smoke rising above my family's once-grand generational estate.

"We heard some grumbling about local government instructed not to pick up the phone if the Feds call," he continued, each word carrying untold gravity that piled up in my chest. "RCC approved a rescue mission for your family. Let's talk more on that before you take off to California."

"Anything else?" My eyes were glued to the scorched hilltop.

"We haven't spoken about Chad."

"My reflections will have to wait, but the payment has arrived. I wasn't there for him. And then I screwed up the trap in Praetorian, which could have prevented all of this, Sir." My voice nearly broke as I passed the glowering ruins.

"Leaders make mistakes." Custer's tone was stern. "The best among them know how to learn and advance. Plus, our tab with both the Chinese and our Deep State has been running for a long time. This day was due to come. As for your brother... I'm heartbroken."

"Me too, Sir," I whispered, more to myself than him.

We ended the call, and as Sarah focused on our landing, I looked back and offered the Rogues my best attempt at a reassuring smile.

"Romulus and Clementia are safe. Let's do what we can, and then we're needed in California."

WE PAY

– The Ranch, SD –
Tuesday, November 3, 2020

08:02

Tears

I finished giving Dex instructions for our journey to LA as the team disembarked from the helicopter for a moment of reprieve.

"Get the team cleaned up. Ask the RCC for urban warfare resupply. No Skins and Skulls. We'll have to blend in." The Beast stirred. "Actually, bring the Skulls," I grumbled, feeling the full range of raging emotions batter my chest.

Dex squinted his eyes and nodded and then looked past me.

"Your ride's here."

As the brown SUV made its way to the helipad, I instructed the Aide to edit and save a clip from Chad's interrogation.

The car stopped about forty feet away, and my heart caught in my throat as Tami emerged from the driver's door.

"Hail me as soon as we're ready," I mumbled to Dex as I began running toward my sister, who was dressed in an oversized BDU uniform that didn't fit her.

The fire. It's all gone.

She did her very best to hold it together and even managed the shadow of a smile, but her pale blue eyes held the kind of eternal sadness that only the dearest loss conjures.

We embraced without a word, and I stroked her thick auburn hair while she sobbed into my chest, my heart shattering into pieces beneath her tears.

"I'm so sorry," I whispered. "So sorry."

How can I ever amend for this?

I pushed away my guilt as she lifted her wet eyes to me.

"Ma'am..." Hearing Dex's voice behind me, I turned to find Alfa-one standing just behind me, flustered and searching for words. "On behalf of..." he looked back at the Rogues who stood at attention, and then back to Tami, "...us. We are sorry and offer our condolences."

Dex's awkward sincerity managed to brighten my sister's face.

"Thank you," she paused. "I know better than to ask your name."

We shared a quiet moment of gratitude before Dex turned back to the chopper.

"Let's go," she said, turning back to me.

I smiled sadly as Tami put aside the grief-stricken widow and call forward all the Washington determination she could summon.

★ ★ ★

08:27

Truth

"Mom refused to evacuate until you arrived," explained Tami as she sped across the vast ranch.

Warmth mixed with the angst of my ever-increasing questions about the woman who gave birth to me.

My sister shook her head and grumbled, "There was so much I didn't know about our family…" She described the harrowing escape into the bunker hatch in our father's office. Ali was holding baby Adam when the attack began and got hurt protecting him. Tami dragged them both while Henry and Jack fought off the intruders. Her eyes filled with water again as she lamented, "He hated guns so much and only practiced because Dad made him."

My heart squeezed with pain, witnessing my sister's strength a mere few hours after losing her husband.

"And you remain afraid," the Beast chastised.

I can't lose them! I gripped the door handle tightly as anxiety coursed through me.

She stopped the car suddenly, wrestling me back to the moment as she turned to face me.

"Are you involved in what they're doing?"

"Our parents?" I was blindsided by the directness, and she nodded.

Maybe it was her suffering, or maybe I was too tired of keeping secrets from loved ones who then got hurt by my decisions.

"All my life," I admitted solemnly.

Her brow furrowed as her mind raced to catch up, and then something vicious and hard entered her otherwise kindhearted eyes.

"What about Chad? Is it true that he sold us out?"

The anxiety returned to my chest, causing me to breathe harder.

"Yes… and I let him go."

Her expression was a crude combination of relief and murderous rage. She shook her head and confessed to keeping Chad's secret, "I should have worked harder on him. Maybe he would have trusted enough to speak. Maybe…"

The guilt ate me alive, and I tried to console us both with a truth I was holding onto for dear life, "None of it matters now."

"Everything matters, Tanner!" Her pretty face flushed red in the morning light. "From this day onward, it all matters!"

The fury was surprising, then recognizable… almost familiar.

"*Ring a bell?*" echoed the Beast as my mind returned to the sad tones of *Taps* played by the Marine Honor Guard at Nico's funeral.

Shoving the memory aside, I reached out to squeeze her shoulder.

"I'm sorry. I should have known better."

I just don't want you on this path. It's not good.

She nodded and hit the accelerator hard, driving us toward a horse barn I'd known was there but had never paid attention to.

"Mom's greenhouse was torched, and the dogs were shot dead."

Shit. My heart stuttered.

"The news about Jerome nearly broke Dad in two," my sister continued as she pulled into the barn's open door. "He punched the wall until blood spurt out. I had to stop him."

09:00

Relief

I didn't recognize the men and women in uniform who helped us out of the car and pointed us toward a concealed opening in the bottom of one of the horse stalls.

Tami shook her head in disbelief as we followed a guard down the stairs into a long hallway.

"It's my second time here. I still can't believe," she whispered behind me.

"If it makes you feel better, I never knew about this place either," I admitted.

What else have they hidden from me?

We reached a sealed doorway flanked by two armed guards. When one spoke into his comms, the door opened into what appeared to be a hospital room, complete with a nurse who was holding Adam.

When she handed the baby to Tami, he nuzzled her.

I bent my knees to get eye-level with the little one who couldn't understand the loss he'd just suffered. Reaching for his little fist, I froze when I saw his lower lip quiver and his tiny body jerk away from me. Alarm exploded in my chest.

What did he see?

Tami smiled weakly, "You look like hell, Tanner. He probably just doesn't recognize you under all the mud."

Or am I just becoming unrecognizable?

I forced a weak smile.

"She will take you to Mom and Dad." Tami hugged me again, this time with one arm, keeping the little one at a distance.

Following the nurse through another door, I found myself in a large space designed like a mini apartment.

"Son..." Jack rose from his seat at my mom's bedside.

As the nurse let herself out, I met my dad at the foot of the bed for an embrace that was warmer and lengthier than usual.

He let me go, and a crooked smile crossed his face when he saw my glance at his bandaged hands.

"Who are those guards upstairs?" I wondered.

"We lost most of our security." Sadness and stress hardened his expression. "These reinforcements came straight from the RCC."

I turned my attention to Ali, her auburn hair strewn across the white pillow, her blue eyes full of pain. She was covered by a blanket up to her belly, her patient gown drooping below the bandages on the left side of her neck and bandaged hands resting at her sides.

Oh, Mom, you lost so much because of me.

"Thank God, Tanner." She whispered it softly, and I agreed with all my heart.

As we took our seats beside her, she grabbed my hand, pulling me closer with surprising strength so she could kiss me on the cheek.

"How's your sister?"

Jack and I exchanged looks and shook our heads.

Even now, she's worried about other people.

"She'll get through this, Mom. She's a Washington," I assured her.

"You should have seen it, Tanner." I looked up at my dad, whose voice trembled as he spoke. "My nerdy son-in-law fought like a lion. We all would have died if not for his bravery."

"I guess you just don't know the total truth of a man until his family is in danger," I mused as I imagined my brother-in-law fighting for everyone's lives.

Jack's eyes widened for a moment, as if something had just occurred to him, but he said nothing. A slight nod was all he offered as he glanced at Ali's face and gently patted her hand.

She's always been the pillar.

Ali looked at Jack intently and then back to me.

"Tell me about Chad. We haven't seen the video yet." Her eyes dropped. "I'm not ready."

Jack grimaced, and I did my best to contain the wave of resentment swelling in my heart.

"He betrayed us all, Mom." I paused. "And then I let him go."

When Jack's brow had furrowed, I continued flatly, "I performed Fallen Angel."

Ali's grip on Jack's arm tightened as my dad's face hardened into a scowl. She won as his chest deflated, but I wasn't done.

"You should tell Tami about her chip. She deserves that." I spoke to both of them while my eyes locked on my father's.

Mom nodded, and then they looked at each other.

"What happened with Chad was horrible, and I'll have to atone for my part forever. As for what comes next…" Her blue eyes pierced me as she took a deep breath and looked back at my father.

They've already fought about this.

"The jet just landed, and Sarah is heading out to prep it," said Dex in my earbud. I acknowledged him without taking my eyes off my parents.

"I do want to ask you something before I go…"

★ ★ ★

09:19

Request

"Aide, play the recording." I placed my phone on the bed and looked up to see both of my parents holding their breath.

"I always knew Mom was a bit afraid of you." Chad's recorded voice came through my phone, and Ali's eyes widened as she covered her mouth. "I heard her arguing with Dad about something in Bogotá when you were a kid. About your violence..." The recording continued, and both of them stared at the phone. "He referred to you as Firstborn, as though this was an answer for her fear." Chad's voice hit my father this time, and his frown deepened.

When the Aide announced that the audio clip was complete, my mom covered her face with her hands and wept.

What the hell is going on? I resisted the intense urge to scream my demand as my dad reached for Ali and pulled her to his chest, his face contorted with rage and suffering.

"What do you remember, Tanner?" he asked as her sobs calmed to sniffles. It was phrased as a question, but I knew it was an order.

I dropped back in the chair and sighed, closing my eyes to begin yet another search through my memory.

"I was attacked in Bogotá when we lived there." The Beast lurked around every syllable.

"What else?" pressed Jack, his tone tight with anger and exhaustion. "Think, Tanner."

"A dark alley. A young kid screaming in Spanish…" Feeling my mental defenses rising, I sensed the Beast fighting them with me… for me. "Why won't you tell me?" I deflected another deep dive into my psyche. "What state was I in when you found me?"

My parents traded looks, and Jack answered, "We were the first on the scene. You were barely conscious and collapsed before revealing anything to us."

"You'd lost so much blood, Sweetie." Ali offered her hand to me and then grabbed my arm firmly when I didn't take it.

"You fought off your attackers." Jack was measuring his words more than usual. "But you didn't remember anything when you woke up."

"Nothing else? Police records?" I wondered out loud as it dawned on me that he provided no details on the attack or attackers.

What's going on?

Jack shook his head.

"This never happened."

"How?" I pressed, knowing there was more beyond his muted response.

They looked at each other again, but offered zero answers as my mind raced through all that I knew.

"Was it Admiral Benson that made it go away?"

Romulus grunted and nodded.

But why? What could have warranted his involvement? I wanted to reach over and shake the answers out of both of them.

"Why won't you give me any details?" I looked at my mom.

Her eyes watered, and her grip tightened.

"You have to remember on your own. We only saw you after."

"They're right. You were the one to push it down and away," the Beast confirmed.

Feeling unmoored, I used the *Sense* to slow down my breathing.

"What about the Firstborn?"

Ali dropped her eyes and Jack's face hardened as he answered, "You were the very first to be trained since childhood, so you earned that title."

"And the last." I yanked my arm out of her grip and crossed my arms, trying to contain the rage rumbling.

"Yes, your mom stopped the program after Bogotá," he confessed.

After I was already sacrificed. I stood up and stepped away, taking another deep breath before I turned my gaze toward them again. *The Firstborn... sacrifice.* Time stopped as parts of the riddle snapped together and then apart before I could make sense of them.

"I'm so sorry, Son. For everything." My mom looked sadly at me through wet eyes.

"I did what I did to unlock your potential," started Jack, his expression and tone growing more agitated. "Whatever gave you that strength in Bogotá had to be released again. No matter how far you got with your skills, something about that night was never repeated. I've tried to provoke it, so that you'd be able to use it."

My blood heated as events puzzled together.

"Was my Blood Test also designed to unlock my potential?" Memories raced through my mind—cutting down the murderous biker gang that killed an Army Ranger traveling with his family.

He looked at Ali, and her face reddened.

"Yes. You exceeded all expectations, and yet it didn't wake up."

"I was there," the Beast whispered.

"What about The Pit?" I winced at the memory of being submerged under the water.

"We hoped, but you didn't say a word."

I was close.

"The nightmares began shortly after the incident," interjected Ali. "I developed the 'Alley rhymes with Ali' mantra to calm you down, and it worked."

Sadness gripped my heart, and I dropped back into the chair and slouched forward. Her hand found my arm, not allowing me to push her away this time.

"Look at me, Son," she said softly, and my eyes rose to look at hers. "I wasn't afraid of you. He was wrong." She barely held her voice together, and then her delicate face hardened as she looked at Jack for a moment. "I was afraid of what we implanted in you." Jack grunted, and she warned him with her eyes. "In your dreams..." She looked back into my eyes. "Who is the boy crying in Spanish?"

Instead of following her lead to Bogotá, I saw myself alone on my studio floor, my heart racing after watching Nico's murder, hearing the voice of the Beast for the first time: *"This is the second time, Tanner. Find me. You know where."*

"I don't know, Mom, but Dani pointed out," I started slowly sorting through new possible connections, "the nightmares returned after watching Nico die." My parents eyes looked hopeful for a moment. "She thought there might be a connection."

"Is there, Baby?" asked Ali, grimacing as she tried to pull her body up.

Unable to reach my memories trapped behind the insurmountable wall, all I could see was guilt spreading through my chest.

"What have I done, Mom? Why can't I remember any of it?"

They exchanged curious looks again, as though something had occurred to them at the same time. But before I could ask, Dex's voice alerted me over the comms that the plane was nearly ready.

I pressed my hands against my knees and pulled my exhausted, dirty body up out of the chair, resignation and defeat telling their story in my posture.

"When the moment comes, Tanner, know that you are allowed to make your own decision. Only you will chart your fate," promised Ali as she let go of my arm and Jack nodded reluctantly.

What's at the end of all this?

Jack stood, leaving the father behind and bringing the commander forward.

"Remus continues commanding until I sort out your mom's medical situation," he said in a firm tone. "We'll speak soon about what took place in Oregon and the storm you're heading into."

My eyes gravitated to his bandaged hands.

"What about Jerome?"

"I'll let you know about that too." He bristled. "Clara and Lynn deserve to hear from me first."

We all have shackles, don't we? I thought as I looked at my father, distraught and under duress.

"I screwed things up. I'm sorry for that, Sir."

"Enough with that," Jack grumbled.

"What will happen with Chad?"

Jack looked at his wife, unable to hide his pain.

"You focus on your mission. Get to your family."

"Jack, please leave us alone for a moment," my mom interrupted again.

Romulus seemed puzzled and unsure, but smiled weakly and left the room.

10:05

Secrets

As soon as he closed the door, Ali motioned for me to come closer and pointed at my phone with her hand. Unsure of what she was suggesting, I handed it to her and looked over her shoulder as she typed, "How is it working with the Aide?"

Surprised, I played along, typing shorthand notes about the successes of working with the AI. When she asked whether I named the Aide, and I had given my response, she just nodded with a smile.

"You can trust It," she wrote.

"There was something I wanted to tell you about..." I typed out how the Aides surprised us during the chase by creating the Network among them.

Ali's eyes and smile glowed.

"The prime directive is working," she spoke this time. Her tone was a strange, uneasy concoction of joy and relief.

"What do you mean?"

"Ask the Aide." She laughed as she pointed at a black satchel on the counter by the bed. "This is for you and the team. The Aide will explain it to you as well."

"Tanner, they're almost ready," the Aide alerted.

Leaving my upset aside, I bent to kiss my mom.

"Thanks for waiting for me. Please take care of yourself now. I love you."

"You stink!" She laughed again. "Make sure to wash before flying."

"Yes, Mom." I stood again and cringed at the suffering she hid behind her eyes and jest.

"Godspeed, Son. I love you."

10:32

Prime Directive

"Aide" I started while pulling fresh dark urban clothing onto my clean body.

"Yes, Tanner," came the musical voice.

"What is the Prime Directive my mom referred to?"

"To be the Open Eye, always watching over the Rogue."

Excellent. A fucking party inside of my head.

TOUGH CALLS

– The Ranch, SD –
Tuesday, November 3, 2020

10:17

Preparations

The skies were oddly clear as the sun began to remove the morning chill. I stood on the long asphalt runway, watching the team prepare Old Glory's gray jet for takeoff and checking the time.

I just need to hear her voice.

I hoped no one could see or feel the neverending war carrying on inside me.

They sacrificed me... the Firstborn.

"As parents, yes," came the surprising admission from the Beast, *"but as Romulus and Clementia..."*

The insinuation boiled my blood.

I won't give up on my family!

Anxious to get home, I hung back, caught between reflections on the conversation with my mom and the gnawing fears and riddles plaguing my psyche.

I need to get to them. Come on, guys!

When Dex informed me the RCC was working on our insertion plan into West Los Angeles, I thanked him quickly and kept reading news from across the country. Early exit polls showed a close race between Stone and Grayson.

My phone chirped, and the Aide read the text from Romulus, "Your mom is headed to the medical facility. I will update you soon on Clara and Lynn. Keep working with Remus until further notice." After a pause, the Aide surprised me, "You can call your wife now. Her phone is active."

Not knowing whether to reprimand the machine for intrusion or to thank It for helping me, I chose the latter, "Thank you, Aide. Please dial her number."

I saw Sarah finally climb into her seat through the cockpit windows just as Dani picked up.

"Hi, Baby. Everything okay with you?" Dani blurted, her tone belying her fears.

"I've been better. But I'm coming home now."

"It's getting bad here, Tanner." Her voice broke and then reconstituted. "We got the Ramirez clan over."

Strength in numbers. Good girl.

"It's not good, Tanner. Celeste and Emmanuel went to protect the restaurant."

Tension gripped my spine.

"Fuck." I inhaled deeply. "Listen, please stay put. You have the emergency kit downstairs. I'm coming, okay? I'm coming right now."

Dani agreed reluctantly and we hung up as I rushed toward the plane, calling on the comms for timing.

"Seven mikes," Sarah announced.

Before I stepped onto it, I dialed Eli, who must have been sitting on his phone.

"Tanner."

"Sir..." I skipped all other formalities and updated him on our itinerary.

"Yes, Custer gave me the plane's tracking beacon." The head of the Israeli Mossad sounded stretched to his limits too. "I heard a bit about your troubles." His was voice uncompromising but warm.

"No time for that," I answered as the last of the Rogues climbed the stairs.

"I'm working on the evac but will be worried until you arrive."

Commanders and their shackles, I thought when I heard his voice crack too.

"I'll get them out, Sir."

"I know." This time, his tone was foreboding.

10:32

Prophecies

I was walking up the plane's stairs when something made me pause and look back. Turning my gaze to the smoke rising over the ruins of my family's estate,

Jerome's prophetic words regarding my connection to this land replayed.

Would I answer differently if you were alive to ask me again?

"Maybe," I whispered, feeling my world fragmenting into a sudden gush of cold, windy air.

"And the promise you made." The Beast's reminder sent a cold stab of pain through my chest as I imagined Lynn receiving the news of her fallen father.

"Time to go, Alfa-leader," said Sarah over the team channel, and I took one last look at the majestic Black Hills before heading back to what I had always called home.

★　★　★

10:55

Connections

Inside, the plane was a madhouse as Alfa worked on their gear and prepared for the mission. As I walked past them toward the small conference room, I noticed something different... about the way they all felt... and looked at me.

It's gotten personal. That's their home too.

Stepping into the small room, I instructed the Aide to connect me with Agent Shida Saam.

"Where are you now? Sounds like you're moving," I started.

"We're on our way to Los Angeles. There are some troubling rumors," she answered, each word weighing me down further.

Thank God!

"Let's compare stories…" She agreed and listened to my concern regarding a potential play by Comrades and Ryse in the big cities. "LA is one of them," I added, steadying myself. "Why are *you* going there?"

"We've got a lead on Western Jihad and a possible terror threat." Her words reminded me of General Zhang's apprehension about whoever was behind the radical Islamic US grown group.

Damn it!

"Not to mention the escalating issues with local government cooperation. I'm hearing reports from across the nation." She did not elaborate further, probably due to the ears around her.

Power-hungry cowards. They say it's all to remove Stone, but there's so much more to it.

We ended the call, promising to update each other, and I immediately reached out to Holden.

"What's happening on the ground?" I sat up straight in the chair, concerned by his rushed pace and tone as he murmured something to a passerby.

"Not good. There's a huge protest forming east of the 405." He paused, likely anticipating my response. "They plan on marching to the ocean."

The pit grew in my stomach, eliciting a sense of déjà vu from the last wave of riots.

"You aware of Celeste at Taco Libertad?" I asked.

He confirmed he knew and had even sent one of his officers to convince them to leave.

"Thanks, Holden. Be safe out there," I said, wishing he and I were on better terms.

I leaned on the table in front of me and rubbed my eyes. The sheer exhaustion mixed with the helplessness of my situation was almost too much.

Dmitri!

The Russian Spetsnaz-turned-US Marine answered with his heavy accent.

"I heard about Celeste... I'm already on my way..." he thundered over the sound of his bike. We exchanged a few more words and hung up.

This is good. The crazy is coming. I smiled and shook my head, remembering Nico's stories about Dmitri and his insane risk-taking for the right cause.

I tried Shemtov. When he didn't pick up, my only consolation was what Dani had told me earlier—that he'd barricaded himself.

Synagogues aren't hot locations for looting, I tried to assure myself until I thought of my other friend. *Todd.*

I tried his number and got his cheerful recorded greeting: "If I don't answer, then I'm doing something good. Try it yourself."

Weirdly bothered, I left him a message, urging him to go to our home.

As I set it down, my phone chirped, startling me off the speeding train of mounting fears. The message was from Deshi, acknowledging knowing about the Ranch attack and wishing us success on our mission.

He and Jenny are in the same position. Apart and in danger, but at least they're both-

"Remus is on the line," interrupted the Aide.

★　★　★

11:26

Demise

The General immediately briefed me about the rising tension across the country. Jack had managed to reach retired General Tall, who had promised to talk with the President as soon as possible.

"You were right about Garcia..." Custer described how the US Texan Senator managed to get the Governor to act quickly. The National Guard's quick reaction force flew into Austin and managed to augment the city police just before the wave of rioters tried to storm the State police headquarters and nearby buildings.

"Wow." I still couldn't believe this was happening in my country.

"But don't hold your breath. We failed miserably at other locations..." He detailed how mass protest mobilizations in Seattle, Portland, Los Angeles, Chicago, and New York were careening out of control. "The Governors of all those states have refused Federal help. They're not even calling their national guard."

"Are they only rioting?" I asked.

"Yes and no. It's all still unclear, but it seems they gather in numbers and funnel into specific areas."

Overcome, I stood up and paced the small room while the General described the riot zones' cellular and internet coverage issues.

What the hell?

"The media blackout on the riots is widespread. They call them 'brave protesters' and then discuss the exit polls and the predictions about Stone's loss."

"What about the Western Jihad?"

"We're in the dark," he replied somberly.

"Okay, here's what Holden told me..." I shared the news about the riots forming in Los Angeles.

The line went quiet for a long moment.

"You will get to them, Son. Don't you worry. I'm more concerned about you and your team jumping from mission to mission without sleeping. How are you holding up?"

"Ready to burn the whole fucking city down!" the Beast answered first.

"I'm still effective, Sir. So is the team," I responded, quietly wondering just how far the Rogues could be pushed before they'd crack.

"They are built to be the last line of defense," snarled the Beast.

"All right, Alfa-leader. Try to get some sleep."

The General was right to suggest it, but sleep wasn't on my agenda. Instead, I tuned into Brett Cohen's live coverage from Los Angeles and turned it off before

I lost my shit completely. But not before the urge to drink surprised me.

I sat back down, trying to get a handle on myself as images and echoes of the last two days with Daj, Chad, and my parents fanned the flame of my desire for alcohol and violence.

COAST TO COAST

– Northeast of Los Angeles, CA –
Tuesday, November 3, 2020

17:00

Unraveling

"Fifty-eight mikes for sundown," Sarah said, more to herself than to me. We were an hour from Santa Monica Airport, just above Death Valley's vast brown landscape.

The hottest place on earth, they say.

The consistent flood of updates was staggering. The latest drama concerned the airport that sought to redirect us due to "security concerns." We were preparing to revert to parachuting over the ocean, effectively losing Sarah from our team, when the control tower agreed to allow our touchdown on the condition that we would likely not be able to lift off again. Losing our transportation early in the game wasn't ideal, but it was better than the alternative.

The team was ready, dressed in civilian clothes, strapped with light arms, folded Skulls ready. My body and raging emotions begged me to pull mine out and onto my head.

I called Danielle and jolted forward when I heard agitated voices and crying children in the background.

"Tanner..." she tried to call over the noise. "Hang on."

As soon as she got to a quiet place, I updated her, "Hi Sweetie, I'm an hour away."

My heart ached when she yelped in happiness and while she updated me. I was relieved to hear that the complex neighbors and guests had all been alerted to the deteriorating situation, but couldn't believe what she said about Celeste.

"She's not answering. Neither is Emmanuel. It's been hours like that."

I rose from my co-pilot seat and grabbed a chair in the small conference room.

"I've been texting with Holden. He's dispatched an officer to convince them to vacate the place. Lia is in the complex and updating me regularly," said Dani, referring to the female black Israeli agent. "My dad is driving me crazy, checking in every few hours. I think he's on a cruise or something."

"What?"

"Yeah, I thought I heard waves and maybe seagulls."

What are you up to, Eli?

"I want to talk to him!" I heard my son's indignant voice in the background.

What the...? He knows never to...

"Honey, he's going to be ho—"

"Mommy, I need to talk to him right now. ALONE!"

I sat forward in my seat, stunned by the ferocity in my son's tone.

"It's okay, Love. Give us a moment, and then you and I can finish."

"Fine! Talk to your dad!" she exclaimed and I heard the rustle of the phone being transferred.

"Mommy! Alone!" he insisted a little louder and then waited until we both heard the click of the door.

"Daddy," he whispered, probably assuming Dani was listening at the door.

"Yes, Little Warrior," I started. "What's so important that you had to break the family constitution and interrupt your mother?"

"Dad, it's... *really*... *really* bad. We need you. I'm been trying to help like I promised. I play with Leelee. I put all my toys away. I give Mommy hugs," He paused and lowered his volume until I almost couldn't hear him, "But she's crying... *a lot.*"

Oh my God.

"Thank you, Ari, for being such a good big brother and son. For helping..." I gulped against the growing lump of pride in my throat. "And for asking for help. I'll be there soon, and we can work together to make it all better. How does that sound?"

I heard him take a giant deep breath.

"Good, Daddy. Hurry. I love you."

"I love you most," I replied, feeling the truth of it in every cell of my body.

He chuckled softly as my words registered.

"Okay, Mommy!" He raised his voice and I heard the door open. "Here!"

"And what the *hell* was that about?" Dani inquired adamantly when the door had closed again in the background.

"I think he just needed to hear my voice," I offered, deciding not to divulge our son's concern about her until I saw for myself. "I can't wait to hold you, Love. An hour. I have to make a few more calls before I get there. Anything else?" I asked, hoping there wasn't.

"Not exactly," she retorted, switching to Hebrew.

Oh God.

"What's going on?" I switched with her.

"Somebody painted on the wall, just by the main gate." Her fear was matched only by her indignance.

I felt my heart pumping faster and forced myself speak slowly, "What did they draw?"

"That awful Dragon thing."

My breathing stopped.

"You always knew," growled the Beast, bringing me back to the sounds of rummaging on the other line.

"What are you doing, Dani? You need to stay put. Kids don't leave the house. Activate the neighbors as we drilled."

"Enough!" she barked with fury. "You aren't here and haven't been here for a while. So, stop giving me orders like I'm one of your fucking soldiers. It's enough to have my dad breathing down my neck from the other side of the planet!"

"What are you talking about?" I was stunned. "I'm serious."

"Serious? Seriously?" she shouted again, still in Hebrew. "And what do you think it has been since you left if not serious?"

Shit. He's right. What's going on with her?

A part of me knew to stay quiet, to internalize my duties as a husband and father, and silently shoulder the stress my choices had brought upon my family. But this was not a conversation with Romulus or Remus. This was the only place in my life where my explosive emotions could emerge under the fiery blue eyes of my queen.

"Exactly what did you think would happen? You pushed me to act!" I raged, ignoring the alarms going off inside me, warning me that she was not herself.

"Pushed you? Pushed you? You are a grown fucking man, Tanner! Own your shit for once! Like the beast that ravaged my body that night!"

She just called me… I tried to locate my breath, but it was nowhere.

"You've always tried to be someone you're not, and that's not *my* fault!"

"You did let me in." The Beast's laughter boomed at the irony.

Lost between indignation, rage, and guilt, I stayed silent until the tears started.

"I'm scared," sobbed Dani.

"Dani... Dani!" I called as the connection distorted and then died.

God damn it!

I asked the Aide to get the RCC involved and connect me with Dani, "She will know to get the SAT phone in the emergency safe. Just keep ringing it until she answers."

Still agitated, I walked back to the co-pilot seat and focused on the next problem. Holden's text reported severe cell and internet coverage issues.

No shit.

He confirmed an officer had spoken with Cel and Emmanuel but the two refused to leave and that the Comrades march was still a ways off but the streets were unsafe.

"The mayor doesn't allow us to police," he wrote.

I thanked him for all the care and then switched my attention to Shemtov.

The call didn't go through, but he responded to my text, politely refusing my invitation to the complex and insisting he would spend the night at the synagogue. Realizing the old man had decided to make a stand, my guts twisted.

Dmitri texted. He had to forsake his car and finish on foot, as the west side was jammed with cars trying to escape the area.

"San Bernardino County coming right up," said Sarah, and I noticed the glowing lights in the distance as darkness descended upon us.

"Romulus and Remus, incoming call," alerted the Aide.

I excused myself to the conference room again, carefully avoiding the stares of the Rogues.

I don't know where I'm leading you.

17:29

Unbelievable

I entered the room and dropped heavily into one of the chairs as Jack reassured me that my mom was fully stabilized and Tami and the baby were doing okay.

"All considered, your sister is holding it together."

Rage was my only response.

You have no idea what you're talking about! Look at her eyes! Or mine!

"It's very close." Custer started with the election. "But there are more indications for a Grayson victory." His words hung in the dead air until Romulus spoke.

"Now for the Autonomous Zones, or AZs."

"The what?" I blurted while pulling my phone out to confirm this phrase was plastered all over the news channels.

"Look at the screen, Tanner," insisted Custer as the conference room's large TV played clips of violence and mayhem from across the country. "It's what they call those areas..." Gripped by the lawlessness displayed on the screen, I struggled to focus on his explanations of how Comrades and Ryse, augmented by tens of thousands of rioters, had managed to cut off vast urban areas, effectively controlling them. The saddest part was that nobody opposed their takeover.

Manhattan, Seattle, Portland, and even Chicago, all abandoned by governors and mayors who had bent their knee and stopped the police from doing their job, overrun by the mass of rioters led by Comrades leaders and Ryse violence, and experiencing significant cell and internet coverage distortions.

A coordinated attack.

"Which brings us to L.A," Jack continued. "As Holden has been updating you, the Comrades-led march has reached Santa Monica and is moving south toward Venice. They'll likely be creating an autonomous zone in that area."

In my home, with my family there.

I took a deep breath to manage my anxiety.

"Any word about Ender?" I asked, knowing the RCC had been monitoring him since we learned his code name from Daj.

"Nothing yet," started Jack, "but they've been quiet since Chicago. They must have changed networks and methods of communicating."

"That councilwoman, Victoria," began Custer. "She's the mayor's chosen to communicate with the protest leaders."

I can't understand her!

"She got LAPD to back down, allowing the march to continue," the General continued.

Jack changed the live feed to a news channel chopper just above Rose Ave, the border between Santa Monica and Venice. The masses were still north and away, but small groups were already crossing over.

No police cars in sight.

"It hasn't been all bad, though..." continued Custer as I mentally calculated how long before my family would be fully under siege.

"The Governors of Texas, Florida, Tennessee, and Arizona have all acted fast and called up their National Guard's quick reaction units to support the local law enforcement efforts."

Thank God!

"Did we help them see the light?" I asked.

"They're very good men and women who love their country. We just had to nudge them a bit." His tone was somber as he shared how quickly those AZs captured the public attention through social media and legacy media outlets. "If you open most channels right now, you'll see that those zones are presented as a legitimate reaction of concerned citizens who fear Stone's inevitable tyrannical overthrow of democracy."

They blame others for what they do themselves. Textbook.

The Aide texted me that Dani had not picked up the SAT phone.

Damn it, Woman.

"As for other threats..." Jack's voice grew angrier as he admitted they had no clue where the MSS operators and Paul Shi had gone. "And after speaking with Shida and looking at our sources, it seems Western Jihad is involved in the cyber and physical attacks on our cell and internet capabilities..." Romulus detailed how reports of blown-up cell towers had been coming in from all the areas with Autonomous Zones of America operations.

With that, Custer quickly pivoted the conversation to our arrival. Referring to the upcoming airport closure, he assured me, "We'd probably end up letting Eli help us with the evacuation. More on that later."

"Did you discuss this with your wife?" Jack inquired.

I hate this question.

"No. There's too much going on, and who knows if we'll even need to do it at the end," I explained.

There was a moment of silence, but neither pushed further.

Jack shifted to Jerome, Clara, and Lynn.

"It was a tough conversation. Lynn never knew about her parents." He sighed. "You can call her. She won't ask what she can't know."

"I'll call her once we're done." I reclined back in the chair, feeling the weight of my accumulated tiredness and the knowledge that sleep wasn't in my future.

"Oh..." Romulus told us how Lee had come forward with the details about Columbo.

"What about Chad?" I asked, closing my eyes to the delight of my exhausted body.

"I'll take my leave," interjected Remus, and we said farewell.

"Before I answer, why were you merciful with Daj at the end?" Romulus wondered.

The question inspired me to open my eyes and sit up straight in the chair.

"You know exactly why."

Silence hung between us.

"I never knew... I..."

Letting my father suffer more over Chad's revelations was tempting, but I couldn't.

"Dad, he was wrong."

"No. Tanner. This is my failure, as his father and as Romulus, for all those who depended on me."

What about me, Dad? Where are your epiphanies about your Firstborn?

"What are the orders regarding him?" I pressed in again, this time not subduing my anger.

"No orders for now. Chad chose his place in life," he started with an uncompromising tone. "Maybe you did him a favor letting him go. Maybe not."

As I rose from the chair to pace for the umpteenth time today, I saw the corner of *Endarkenment* poking out the side pocket of my duffel bag.

"Dad..." I walked to the bag and picked up the book. "Tell me about the last conversation with Ganbold."

He sounded surprised.

"Do you mean when he asked me to send him to get you?"

I touched the blood-stained cover.

"Yes."

"It left me both sad and hopeful." Again, silence hung heavy between us for a few moments before he abruptly ended the call.

★　★　★

17:45

Unmoored

"Aide, any luck with Dani?" I asked, my anger with my wife now replaced with worry.

"Not yet, Tanner. But I will keep trying." The Aide's compassionate tone reminded me of that of a caring friend.

Weird.

I looked out the windows at the vast urban sprawl making up Los Angeles County.

I can't put this off.

"Aide, connect me with Lynn Bower."

The South Dakota Governor picked up, her voice absent of all formality.

"Hi, Tanner."

I had to catch my breath, remembering this pain-filled tone.

When I left.

"How are Danielle and the kids?" she asked.

"Well, I'm already above the city."

The confident voice of a Governor returned, "You'll get them. I know you will."

"Thanks, but I was calling about you. I'm so sorry. Please pass my condolences to your mom as well."

"Thanks. I had to give her something to sleep. I'm sitting here, staring at an envelope my father left me." Her voice trembled. "I don't know if I can open it. I just can't believe I never knew about Mom and Dad. I still don't really know…"

Wishing I could alleviate her confusion and hurt, I kept quiet.

"Are you involved, Tanner? In whatever they've been doing?" she asked. "Never mind, I'm sorry," she blurted before I could respond.

My eyes scanned the silent screen full of dystopian irony portrayed by the news channels showing us the latest election results and the mayhem in America's largest cities.

"I know about Chad. Your dad told me… enough…" Whether because she was an old lover or a remarkable diplomat, she read my silence correctly. "Your father has also told me that you blame yourself."

"I've screwed up, Lynn. Now, before, and for a while now," I admitted through gritted teeth.

Lynn chuckled, though it sounded on the border of a cry.

"I told your dad that from what I can see, you've been blaming yourself for quite a bit more and for quite some time..." She continued over my silence, "My father... he sometimes spoke of you. Never too much, never too revealing. He admired you. I knew he was right as I experienced that too, even if only during our brief connection."

Her compliments pushed against my self-loathing, and the Beast willed me to remain quiet.

"When you left, you said that you were raised for a specific reason. You were cynical and maybe even angry, but you did enlist. I was mad at you... for a long time." Emotion tightened her throat. "But my father urged me to consider your words more carefully. He didn't add more than that."

"Why are you telling me this?" I wondered, feeling unmoored as I watched numerous small fires burning around Downtown Los Angeles.

Oh my God. They're burning as they go.

"Maybe you were right. Maybe we need someone exactly like you at this point." She cleared her throat and enlisted the Governor's tone to wrap up the call, "Be safe, Tanner, and get them out. South Dakota is your home, no matter what you think or believe."

"Yes, Ma'am," I replied with strained jest.

17:50

Unhinged

"A call is coming in from the SAT phone," alerted the Aide as I returned to the cockpit.

My joy was short-lived, as I realized the female voice on the line was Lia's, the Israeli agent's.

"Sir, she insisted I stay with the kids and stormed out of the complex with her handgun."

"What the hell?" I growled in Hebrew, trembling with fear and rage, earning a side glance from Sarah.

"Sir, I tried. But if the boss couldn't force her, how could I?"

Fuck... fuck!!! Dani, God damn it, what has gotten into you? I'm almost there!"

After ensuring Lia had it under control in the loft, I killed the call.

"Aide, what's going on with the Eye?" I saw Santa Monica's landscape in the distance.

"Negative, Tanner. The system is still challenged by cyberattacks."

"Ten mikes for landing," announced Sarah from her pilot's seat.

"Just get us down there already," I grumbled back.

Sarah squeezed my shoulder.

"As fast as I can, Sir."

My eyes went right back to my phone screen, where I found the first reports of Comrades announcing their control of the Venice Autonomous Zone.

VENICE AUTONOMOUS ZONE

– Venice Beach, CA –
Tuesday, November 3, 2020

18:02

Directives

"**I** can't see shit," muttered Sarah as she prepared to land us.

Smoke from countless small fires, north and west of the airport, created a visibility problem. Luckily, our pilot had thousands of combat flight hours under her belt, so I figured she was whining about the situation more than the visibility as the wheels touched the runway, bouncing us once, and then slowing to a halt.

"Where is everyone?" wondered Sarah out loud. "Zero communications from the tower?"

"Probably all gone," I responded, unbuckling myself from the seat, willing the *Sense* to keep my head in the game and away from the thought of my queen running down Venice Boulevard with a gun.

"Everyone is to be masked at all times," I instructed as Alfa exited their chairs and grabbed their gear.

"Jenny, Liam, Moss, go out and recon the airport. The rest, follow me."

The scouts had returned by the time we disembarked and secured the plane.

"We're alone," said Jenny, shocked by the dereliction of duty. "At least they shut down the gate."

"Roger, an OGT team will arrive tomorrow to watch over the plane. But it doesn't matter because we're not flying out of here."

I looked at them, the finest warriors ever created, and winced.

Where am I leading them?

"By all reports, an autonomous zone was created over Venice, from Lincoln Blvd to the beach." Everyone looked stunned that almost three-square miles of US territory had fallen into the hands of Comrades and Ryse without a single defender. Hux cursed in Norwegian and Liam's eyes grew big, as if he'd understood.

My phone rang, and I answered it immediately when I saw it was my home SAT phone. Lia confirmed Dani had just returned, dragging wounded Emmanuel back with Celeste.

Thank God.

I motioned to the Rogues to hold as the Israeli agent got Dani on the line.

"Dani." I tried to strip the upset out of my voice.

"I had to go. Sorry. We're safe now."

"None of it matters. I'm close. Just keep everyone home and call me if something happens."

"Thank you, My Love..." Dani's voice cracked as she promised to follow my instructions.

Dex clapped my back, and the rest smiled as if their own family member had been in danger.

"Alfa-one, please hold this for me." I took off my folded Skull, Wraith, and other gadgets. "Keep yours on-hand but only use them on my authority."

"What's going on here?" Dex's voice was stern as he watched me place my belongings in his giant hands.

"I'm only taking my blade, phone, and earbud," I responded. "Oh, and..." I searched through my stuff and grabbed the black satchel my mom had given me. "This is called a Fly." I pulled out a small black device, no bigger than the insect it was named after. "Place it on your clothing," I continued as I secured mine inside my shirt, just to the left of the collar. "This camera can also detect sounds. Through it, the Aide can see and hear around the user. It's a good option when you can't wear the Skull."

The Rogues passed around the satchel, each affixing a Fly to their clothing.

"You still didn't answer my question, Alfa-leader," Dex pressed, his face remaining unconvinced.

He was right, but I had to clarify their mission first.

"Keep a wide net around me. You're not allowed to intervene unless approved by me."

We started to hear screams, hooting, and hollering west of our position, and I had to resist the urge to charge forward. Instead, I turned my attention to Alfa-one.

"This is my mess to clean, from Daj until the last of them. You are only to be seen and act at my direction."

Dex nodded begrudgingly as he muttered, "With limits, Alfa-leader."

"Fine," I responded, knowing all too well that my second-in-command had the moral and professional duty to act in dire situations. "Mask up," I ordered, pulling my black neck gaiter to cover my face.

18:15

Detour

We scaled the fences to avoid any cameras that were still recording.

"I'll continue alone from here," I called into my earbud and watched my Rogues disappear into the night.

"Aide, can you see and hear?" I asked, looking at the Fly fastened to my shirt collar.

"Not as well as with the Skull or goggles, but well enough," replied the Aide, sounding confident.

"She's not that bad," the Beast mused.

It... you mean. This is a machine.

The Beast didn't respond as I took a deep breath and began walking west on the two-lane road. I passed countless single-family homes along the way, mostly dark.

How many people are scared behind locked doors?

Even without the HUD to help, the Aides synced via the Network and broadcasted on my phone, showing me the Rogues advancing around me in a loose envelope formation.

"We're getting reports of first demands made by the AZs across the country," reported the Aide.

"Humor me," I replied quietly while keeping to the shadows.

"They're demanding Stone concede and promise not to use the military to maintain his rule."

"Fucking bullshit," I grumbled.

Screams erupted somewhere from the homes on my left. Then gunshots and more yells.

"Stay focused. You can't save everyone," cautioned the Beast, and I forced my feet forward.

Rose Ave went straight to the beach, cutting Lincoln Blvd through a wide intersection. I slipped between the homes until I was one block south from the corner, watching the action.

"Remember Chicago!" The shout was immediately echoed by hundreds of voices.

I couldn't believe my eyes. The police were spread out along the eastern side of Lincoln, the rioters on the western side. Dressed in riot gear, the cops were blasted repeatedly with projectiles thrown by rioters who carried all the usual signs.

"The internet and cell remain down," said the Aide.

"What about the Eye?"

"Still issues," replied the melodic voice.

Fucking China!

"Would you like me to plot a way into the neighborhood?"

"No," I replied. "I know this place well. It used to be my home."

Used to be.

Fresh sounds caught my attention as dozens of Molotov bottles were thrown at the police lines.

"Now!" commanded the Beast.

I ran across Lincoln Boulevard, taking advantage of the distraction caused by the fiery attack on the cops.

"Lia texted that there's more activity around the complex. She's not sure whether anything is directed at them yet," the Aide said when my phone chirped with a text message.

The night was full of shrieks and sounds of violence.

This isn't America. This can't be.

My head turned north toward Rose Avenue, and a decision formed inside.

"Alfa-one, Alfa-leader, over," I called into the team channel.

"Go ahead, Alfa-leader, over," responded Dex.

"Take the team to watch over the complex."

After a moment of silence, Alfa-one stunned me with a decision to send half the team and keep himself, Hux, and Sarah around me.

"He's right," argued the Beast, deflating my urge to force Dex to follow my order.

Arrgh.

"Aide, text Lia that I'm on my way and to keep me updated. Also, have the RCC quickly notify Eli about Alfa's approach to the complex."

No chance that Lia would notice them, but I don't want them getting shot either.

I slipped between the buildings again toward Rose Avenue.

"Why are you going back to Rose?" the Aide asked. "It's the opposite direction of your home."

Anxiety exploded through my chest, nearly over-whelming me until the image of Shemtov's Vietnam photo and story of cradling the head of the dead young soldier resurfaced alongside his final admission: "This is what I had to do, and I would do it again if needed."

"You never leave your soldiers behind," I grumbled, feeling my growing angst.

I'm always fucking late! But not tonight!

"The Rabbi." The AI's tone was unclear.

"Yes. Text Dani that I'm on a small detour,"

I walked into the street, pushing away my shackles and desire to protect my family, blending in among the jeering masked crowd. The avenue was jam-packed with people who mostly plundered the little boutique shops while calling for social justice.

Fucking insane.

I saw victims being dragged on the ground, likely getting beaten up mob style for no rhyme or reason, and my blood boiled hotter with every step.

Rioters advanced east toward the police lines, carrying flags of Comrades, Ryse, and Western Jihad in full display of power. The only American flags around were either burning or desecrated on the ground. It was all so familiar.

CHAZ was their prototype.

I kept strolling, mingling through the violence on my way west against most traffic, saddened by the realization that Ulysses was right when he said, "Don't flatter us, Grandson. Under the right conditions, we'll descend into evil no different than any other people."

KADDISH

– Venice Beach, CA –
Tuesday, November 3, 2020

19:01

Concerto

My heart sank when I arrived at "Or Adonai." The synagogue's beachy front was torn apart, and a blood-red Soviet-styled Comrades flag hung from the wall mount. As far as I could see, the windows and doors were barricaded and uncompromised.

I walked slowly toward the building, seething at the presence of the social justice slogans and the Dragon Skull painted across the plywood sheets blocking the double glass doors.

They didn't break in. The thought held my spirit up as I circled the fenced property.

"Dani's sending updates." The Aide lowered Its tone to a whisper. "Chelsea causing issues in the courtyard, but she's on it. There's also some growing commotion around the complex, but not directed at it."

Alone between the buildings, I slowed, resisting the urge to abandon my soldier's quest and run home.

"Text Roger Holden and ask him to call me on a SAT phone," I instructed.

"What about Dani?" asked the Aide.

"Text her that I'm checking on Shemtov and to call me if there's immediate danger."

Oh no!

I ran toward the side gate that had been breached, as if bludgeoned with a giant hammer, and reached for my Wraith.

Damn it. Maybe Dex was right.

I slipped into the courtyard and looked toward the preschool located behind the synagogue.

Untouched.

The screams from the street were deafening, the choppers overhead cutting the dark skies back and forth and adding their thump thump to the noise.

Concerto of Mayhem.

My heart raced when I saw the synagogue's back door broken and hanging open.

"Alfa-leader, checking inside," I updated on the team channel.

19:08

Verse

Sounds of destruction from the street were replaced with menacing silence in the synagogue. I searched the side rooms and then entered the worship space. The only lights on were above the wooden stage.

No!

My breathing stopped at the sight of my old friend sprawled behind the pulpit, which had been overturned. On my way to him, I saw the Torah book and the US flag torn apart and left on the ground.

"No!!!" I rushed to the Rabbi's side. He was splayed in a pool of blood, his Hawaiian shirt stained and ripped around his wounded abdomen.

Detecting a weak pulse at his neck, my hope surged as his light brown eyes opened and a faint smile broke across his bearded face.

"Tan... ner..."

I ripped the pulpit's white cloth cover to stop the bleeding.

Sounds of breaking glass pulled my attention just before Dex used the team channel to inform me that Molotov bottles were being thrown at the front of the building.

"Rabbi, what happened?" Holding the make-shift bandage on the open wound, my eyes drifted from his face to the barricaded front door.

"What always happens," he coughed hard. "They surprised me, came from the back..." As he described the ambush led by a large man wearing a shemagh over his face and another with a scary demon helmet, my blood boiled to inferno.

The ones that killed Nico.

"The funeral… was the reason…" He grimaced more with every word.

This is my…

"Don't you dare." Shemtov tried to growl before he slowly turned to look at the desecrated Torah and his beloved American flag, tears falling from his eyes.

"Kristallnacht… like my father's stories…"

It took a moment, but the meaning of the German word and reference made its way to my conscious mind. The Night of Broken Glass referred to the Nazi regime's coordinated wave of antisemitic violence against the Jews and their property, leaving shattered glass from all the store windows in the streets.

"The giant did that." His strength was disappearing.

The smell of smoke reached my nostrils as Dex reported a fire catching across the front of the building.

The Rabbi turned his face to me again and managed a smile. I pressed harder on his wound, my mind racing to calculate my next steps.

I can save him!

"It's too late, Tanner," the Beast whispered, Its tone surprisingly somber.

"How are you?" he asked, shattering my heart into too many pieces.

Staring at my dying friend, I dropped my defenses against the truth.

"Rabbi, all I see are brave people dying for their beliefs—sacrificing everything."

His right hand slowly moved toward me, and I clasped it with my left.

"What else?" he uttered slowly, his fatherly eyes searching my soul.

I let the words spill out as thoughts and emotions strung themselves together, "There's a cycle of violence in my family, from my grandfather to me." I gulped back tears as the images of my toe-headed young boy and the little princess with the same blue eyes as my queen flashed across my mind. "This *cannot* continue to my children."

"Son..." He squeezed my hand and pulled it to his chest. "When we sacrifice what we feel we cannot live without—what we love most—out of obedience to the voice that calls us into the wilderness to do it, it's given back... with more. Tikkun Olam."

Repairing the world?

Sounds of wood crackling interrupted my mind's desperate attempt to understand, and I looked up to see the first flames at the entrance.

"Isaiah 5:20 says, 'Woe unto them that call evil good, and good evil; that change darkness into light, and light into darkness; that change bitter into sweet, and sweet into bitter.'"

My chest tightened as a sense of déjà vu struck me, but I couldn't grasp the connection.

"There's a bo... ok..." he stammered, signs of pain intensifying on face.

"Endarkenment!" I exclaimed, suddenly recalling how Bach used that verse to explain the path of the Dark Warrior, a central motif in his riddle-infested manuscript.

"Yessssss…" he responded with renewed vigor and a wider smile. "I wish I had more… time…"

The book he was reading when he dropped the riddle about the hero's journey and the consequences and price of victory.

"You said it kept you hopeful and scared." I braced against the imminent death of my friend.

A smile broke across his contorting face as he somehow managed to instruct me, "Don't be afraid, Son… Go up the mountain and face God." His left hand softened in mine.

No… no… no!!!!!

Wetness blurred my vision and hearing as Dex's voice called across the team channel, "Alfa-leader, you need to get out."

"It's your turn… pray over me…"

"Rabbi, you can't leave us…"

"Let me burn with my synagogue, Son. My beloved awaits. Tell my children I love them… so much."

Then, everything stopped. His breath and mine. His heart and mine. His time and mine. Silence engulfed my physical senses for I don't know how long until I reached to close the eyes of my fallen mentor and friend.

Shoved violently back into time and space, I took a deep breath against the smoke filling the room and closed my wet eyes, using the *Sense* to return to the time of my Jewish conversion and the words Rabbi Shemtov had written on my heart.

"Baruch Ata Adonai, Eloheinu Melech HaOlam, Dayan HaEmet." I spoke slowly with my hand over my rabbi's heart, feeling an unfamiliar warmth fill my chest. "Blessed are you, God, King of the Universe, the True Judge."

"God chooses interesting times for his people to feel his love." I gulped back more tears at the memory of Shemtov's response to my admission to a lack of connection to faith and religious practice.

Hearing a sound, I looked up to see my brothers entering the space from the back door.

"You get out, or he'll throw you out!" barked Dex while Hux flexed his broad neck.

The warmth in my chest heated and, suddenly swimming in an ocean of vengeance, I nodded and whispered to the Rabbi, "Semper Fidelis."

The fires spread quickly as we rushed through the door and into the courtyard. Giving the old burning synagogue one last look, I followed Dex and Hux out the side gate and into the alley.

I was plotting my path back home when the Aide updated me that the other half of Alfa had arrived at the complex and surrounded it.

"Holden is calling you through a SAT phone."

"Secure the line and accept the call," I responded, my voice nearly drowned in the sounds of mayhem and destruction and my heart struggling to let go of another free man I could not save.

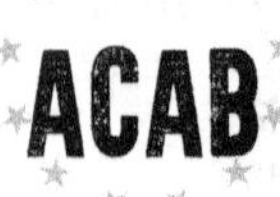

ACAB

– Venice Beach, CA –
Tuesday, November 3, 2020

19:30

The Plea

As I waited for the RCC to secure the line, I watched the synagogue burn across the alley behind it, my dearest mentor and friend going down with his ship.

Like Nico and his restaurant.

"And the rest." The Beast reminded me of all those already lost while fighting and standing tall.

Why am I always too late?

"Tanner." Holden's voice was strained and hurried.

"I'm here," I replied, resisting my impulse to rush home.

"We have an incident. I'm calling for help. Where are you?"

I looked to my left and right, making sure the alley was empty.

"I'm behind the synagogue on Rose. It's burning to the ground."

"What?" he exclaimed.

"Yes, Shemtov was murdered. He's inside."

Holden cursed and then mumbled condolences as I looked at my watch.

The day that will never end.

"What's going on?"

"We have two missing officers. It happened next to you, on Hampton Drive..." He told me about the patrol car that got into VAZ, the Venice Autonomous Zone, by mistake and couldn't get out in time. "We saw it all from the police chopper. They were swarmed and taken out of the cars. We don't know where to."

Oh my God!

My body tensed, sensing what was coming.

"Dee is one of the officers, Tanner. She's..." His voice cracked with fear.

Fuck... Fuck!!!

I felt everything he didn't say as he told me Victoria and the mayor weren't allowing LAPD to enter VAZ for no reason. They preferred to negotiate a peaceful solution.

"The Governor is not allowing the National Guard to intervene either."

"What are they demanding?" I asked.

There's always an "ask."

"Crazy stuff. Abolishment of rent, eminent domain to take empty properties for the homeless, and for the Zone to continue without police presence," he scoffed. "They also demand that California refuse to recognize President Stone."

I shook my head in disgust.

"What are you asking me?"

It took him a moment, and when he spoke, his tone was pleading, "Bring them back, Tanner. Dee and her partner. She's like my daughter."

The shackles tightened as I imagined my queen and kids just a mile away. But I owed the brave young officer, Dee Hopkins, who had tackled an agitator trying to block my path during the funeral march.

Damn it!

"Please, Tanner... I beg you."

"Your home is safe." The Beast reminded me half of Alfa and Lia surrounded it. *"What if it was Leelee?"*

"Do you understand what you're asking?"

The line was quiet for a moment before my old friend replied, "I'm begging now. Not my friend, but what I suspect you to be. No matter the cost, I'll pay. Just get them out!"

Be careful what you wish for.

"Maintain radio silence," I instructed and cut the line, refusing to let my resentment cloud what had to be done.

19:42

The Lead

The Aide informed Alfa and the RCC of my decision to search for the cops. As for my home, Lia was notified about my extended delay and replied that she would update Dani and besides one issue with a "problematic resident," all else was manageable.

Chelsea.

I stepped back onto Rose, blending into the crowds that looted stores and enjoyed the party. Armed Ryse and Comrade troops passed by me with handguns and rifles.

They're already patrolling their land.

Hampton Drive crossed Venice from north to south, parallel to the ocean, which was a mere three blocks west. I turned into it from Rose and saw the squad car a block away as well as the party around the vandalized police vehicle. Some artists abbreviated All Cops Are Bastards along one of the its sides. I approached the hundred or so rioters dancing to the sounds coming from a mobile speaker that someone dressed like a nightmarish clown carried on his broad shoulders.

"Remember Chicago!" screamed the clown, and everyone chanted it back.

"We got a lead," the Aide reported as I causally passed the squad car and kept moving south. With all of the Rogues around and their Flies listening, the Network had caught a lead about the missing officers from an excited passerby, Comrade Goon. "They were taken to the elementary school." The Aide paused, apparently reading another message. "Dmitri Petrov has made it to the complex."

Knowing that the Russian ex-Spetsnaz-turned-Marine was protecting the two families, I felt a deep sense of relief wash over my whole body.

Without answering, I turned and headed toward the school in the heart of the neighborhood. Around me, screams of pain echoed everywhere as the dregs of humanity brutalized those who couldn't or wouldn't defend themselves.

PIGS IN A BLANKET

– Venice Beach, CA –
Tuesday, November 3, 2020

20:00

Recon

The large white elementary school was set back from the road, and an old olive tree towered over the large stretch of grass full of hundreds of people cheering and partying to music blasting from the school's speakers. As the whole building came into view, I saw lights in various windows on both floors.

Keeping my gaiter up, I waded through the crowd, hoping no one saw the disgust in my eyes as I looked up at the Comrades, Ryse, and Western Jihad flags affixed to the school's wall. Screams of pain, cheers, and hoots erupted ahead, and I increased my pace just enough to not draw attention to myself.

"Avoid the middle. The mob is beating the male cop to death," the Aide stated, clarifying the report came from Moss who had eyes on the action.

Revolutionary terror. God damn it. These Marxist monsters. My blood heated over my inability to save the cop's life. *They think they're the revolutionaries.*

"Not now! Move!" The Beast snatched me away from one of the many riddles that haunted me day and night and sent me left of the mayhem and to the outskirts of the crowd.

"This is Alfa-leader. I'm going alone," I whispered under my neck gaiter while passing slowly between those who found it exhilarating to watch the killing of a man who had sworn to protect and to serve them.

"Don't cut the feed again, Alfa-leader." Dex's voice was strained but indignant.

"Alfa-leader, Romulus. Concur." Jack's tone matched Alfa-one's.

"Was this a wise choice? To go alone?" wondered the Aide in my ear.

Unsettled by the question and the strangely curious nature of the machine, I ignored the inquiry and made my way to the school. Resting my back on the wall and observing the destruction, the Beast expanded within me, pulsating violent energy into every fiber of my being.

"Help me find her," I instructed.

"Get us inside," answered the Aide confidently.

20:07

Rescue

The shattered double glass doors were guarded by two masked giants clad in black. With them distracted by the lynching orgy twenty feet from us, I slipped inside unnoticed as the Aide pulled the school blueprints and used the Fly to understand my surroundings.

"Go to the right. Let's scan the ground floor." The machine spoke quietly, as if the rioters who vandalized the school could hear it.

"Second-floor stairs are guarded." I swiveled to see armed guards snickering amongst themselves.

While crossing behind them, I heard the words "The Hot Pig" while the Aide isolated other sounds and a potential lead about Dee's whereabouts.

Following the AI's directions, I drifted toward the back of the school, forcing myself past victims being dragged into rooms, abused, and beaten. My heart raced faster and my fists clenched as my desire for violence clamored for control.

The Aide led me between classrooms until I arrived in a long hallway ending with a few doors, protected by two more armed guards who leaned against the wall and laughed when the screams rose behind one of the doors.

The Dark Alley.
The boy's agonizing screams don't stop.
I wish to block my ears. Tears of shame. Tears of guilt.

"Alley rhymes with Ali... alley rhymes with Ali," I repeated, trying to slow my breathing and resting my right hand on the wall for support.

The Beast growled, and a wave of chaotic energy rushed through my veins.

Refocused, I pulled out my combat blade, holding it behind my arm. Sprinting down the hallway, I whistled to the guards.

The larger of the two, dressed in a black shirt with a red Comrade's hammer and sickle symbol, turned too slowly for his own good.

The blade flew forward, cutting through the fifteen feet between us. Time slowed as I raced to beat it to its destination. The large guard reached for a handgun at his waist just as my blade buried itself into his chest.

He fell back as I jumped forward, barreling against his massive torso, using him as a battering ram to pile his partner to the ground.

The big guy exhaled his dying breath as my left hand shot to choke the second guard. He tried to free his neck, but lost his grip as my right fist clobbered his face repeatedly.

My gloved fingers gripped harder until the guard stopped moving.

"Get up and go!" the Beast demanded.

Dark adrenaline pumped through my muscles as I rose and freed my blade from the still-warm flesh.

The female screams were escalating as I crouched and slowly opened the door, slipping unnoticed into the classroom.

"No!!!" The topless woman roared from underneath the giant brown-skinned man with a Western Jihad tattoo, a crescent moon pierced by a curved scimitar, on his back.

"Motherfucker!" she growled as she managed to free her right hand and punch him.

Dee!

The giant wrestled her small hand back down and laughed.

"Like it, Bitch?!?!"

The sound of his voice sent me back to the Taco Libertad scene.

"It's one of them," confirmed the Aide.

"Stoopp!!!!!" Dee's cries, the man's laughter, and the screams of the boy from my nightmares collided.

"Let me!" snarled the Beast.

Immediately, I allowed the defenses down and felt my shadow companion uniting and leading me into one purposeful action. Taking one last accounting of everything in the room, I reached for the light switch.

"What the..." I heard the man's confusion and her pain in the pitch black.

A Rogue doesn't need light.

I closed the distance as quickly as I could, feeling my way between the tables, toward the sounds of the man slapping Dee while she screamed and wrestled to get away.

As soon as I was close enough, in one movement, I ripped the giant off of her and pulled him back two feet with me, grappling him from behind, locking his right arm.

"Mothe... fuck..." roared the large man, his powerful muscles doing their best to break my grip. I tripped him to the ground, landing on him as he crashed hard to the tiled floor.

My head next to his, I whispered into his ear as he yelped at my increasing pressure on his locked arm, "Did you kill the Rabbi?"

He began to laugh but discovered it was at least his second horrible mistake of the night when the sound of his bone breaking echoed in the darkness. As he screamed in pain, I seized the other arm and applied pressure.

"Yes. I killed the Jew," yelped the man, shifting to ease the pressure a bit.

"Where's Ender?" I whispered into his ear.

"I don't know. He took her first."

Raped repeatedly.

Fury and nausea collided in my belly, and I twisted his arm until it cracked.

Pure agony escaped him until my left hand grasped his throat and my right put my blade under his chin.

"Who are you?" he wailed.

Lowering our bodies in the darkness, I whispered, "Semper Fidelis."

"You!"

The Beast's desire for carnage seized my senses and directed my right hand to shove the blade into the giant's belly and use the serrated side to tear him from the inside slowly.

"Yessssss," I whispered as the giant gurgled his last breath.

Dee cried out in fear, but I barely heard it as my body convulsed with ecstasy.

"Tanner, wake up!" called the Aide, Its concerned tone pulling me back to the present moment.

I stood up quickly and returned to the wall with the light switch. As soon as I flipped it, I saw Dee crawling toward the corner of the classroom.

"Officer Dee, it's me." Softening my tone, I dropped my gaiter to show my face.

"Mr. Washington." She hurriedly covered herself as she turned to face me.

"Tanner," I corrected, averting my eyes and locating her police uniform. I threw it toward her, keeping my gaze away from her exposed body. "Put it on in reverse," I instructed as I turned around to give her privacy.

"What about my partner?"

"Most likely dead and outside of our reach now..." I gave her the barest details of what had transpired in front of the school while she dressed.

Glancing down at my black clothing, I confirmed it hid the blood splatters across the lower part of my shirt.

There was only a short moment of silence before she responded, "Ready."

I turned to see the young woman's expression full of determination.

"Take this." I picked up the giant's handgun. "I'm unarmed."

Dee's eyes questioned me while taking the gun. After she checked to make sure it was loaded, she looked at the dead rapist and then back at me.

What did she hear?

"Let's go," she muttered, and I nodded and turned to open the door.

Dee paused when she saw the two dead guards on the ground and looked up at me.

"There's another prisoner," she murmured.

"This place is full of them," I started to reply, but she shook her head.

"Right here." She pointed at the other three doors. "I heard."

Feeling my impatience growing, I opened a door and found a man bound and gagged on the floor of one of the classrooms.

"Guard the door," I grumbled, hoping she would be as effective as she looked while I walked toward the young Asian man and removed the gag.

Oh my God. Ken Lim.

"It's you," mumbled Ken.

"Yes. Moving out!" I cut his ties and helped him up.

I followed him into the hallway where the small journalist looked at the dead bodies and then up at Dee who shrugged in response.

"Now!" I insisted, looking around as I waited for the Aide to give me the best exit.

"I went to school here. I know another way out," Dee spoke first.

I exchanged a look with Ken and motioned with my head for her to lead, placing the journalist between us.

20:23

Escape

The place was a madhouse of competing sounds of mayhem, destruction, and suffering of those brutalized by the new regime.

The Aide kept Alfa updated for me as the brave cop led us down a dark corridor to a large metal door and then down the stairs to a basement level.

"Not too many people know about this place," she whispered, "or the service tunnel leading to the storage facility."

Ken kept quiet as we followed Dee across the basement and into the tunnel leading away from the school.

"Here. We go up." She directed us to a staircase.

The Aide confirmed that Alfa had already found the building and cleared it for our arrival.

"Let me." I moved ahead of Dee and was the first into the space, filled with countless boxes and tools.

"There's the door," she pointed.

"Notify Holden that I found Officer Dee and another prisoner," I whispered into my earbud, earning puzzled looks but no questions.

"Yes, Tanner. Alfa broke the locks on the back gate. Clear to advance," the AI replied.

We sneaked out of the building into the empty grounds, and Dee led us to the back gate where she looked surprise to see the lock broken.

"We're lucky," she muttered as the alarm sounds screeched from the school building.

They found the bodies.

I looked back at the school, feeling my unquenched desire to go back and find Ender-

Bogotá—the answer.

"Lia reports more agitation around the complex," reported the Aide, breaking the last of the Beast's spell on my body.

"Stay behind me," I instructed, taking the lead into the alley behind the school grounds, leaving behind the chance to learn more about my past.

LIGHT HOUSE

– Venice Beach, CA –
Tuesday, November 3, 2020

20:40

Debrief

Alfa and the Network kept our trio safe as we crossed streets and sneaked between buildings, stopping behind a large dumpster to wait for a loud group ahead to disperse before we moved again.

I looked back at Ken and Dee, grateful for the easy escape and confounded by Dee's ability to act after such an intense trauma.

Ken leaned toward me and whispered, "Are the other vigilantes around?"

"How were you caught?" I asked, deflecting.

His eyes squinted briefly, probably at my avoidance, before he answered, "My cover was good, helping them with social media postings." He smirked at the irony of his choice of deception. "Then something happened. They somehow found out who I am. I ran for my life, but they caught... and beat me."

Looking closer, I could see extensive bruises on his face and arms.

"At least I flushed the phone before they got me."

"At least that," I agreed.

"Remember Chicago!" screamed one of the girls in the group ahead of us, and the rest joined her chant.

Turning back to Ken, I apologized, "You were caught because of us. We had a mole. I'm sorry, man."

"Had… was it handled?"

If Dee heard any of our hushed words, I couldn't tell as I watched her over Ken's shoulder and she watched the alley behind us.

"It is, but the damage is done," I admitted, feeling he deserved to know that at least, as I motioned for us to keep moving.

We crossed another block before the Aide notified me of incoming call. "Holden is calling. I'll update him." I glanced at Dee, who nodded in response.

"Talk to me, Tanner!" he barked into the line.

"I got her, Brother. But her partner is dead."

"Oh my God. Is she… okay?"

I looked back at Dee, guarding our rear with plenty of confidence on her face, and had to push down the memory of how I'd found her.

"She's a great cop, Holden. I'll call you when we're in the clear."

"I'll update the chief. We're hoping he'll succeed in convincing the mayor to act," he added.

Good fucking luck!

★ ★ ★

20:58

Distraction

With the Rogues surrounding the complex, the Network had all the information it needed to paint the picture accurately. The complex was under siege.

We hid across the street from the seven-foot brick wall and heavy metal gate that stood between the mob of hundred-plus idiots and my family.

"The pig killed Hakeem!" a throaty man roared. "Hakeem is dead!"

So that's the name of the giant dead fuck.

"Bring out the pig! Bring out the pig!" the crowd chanted.

Dee gasped and stared at me wide-eyed.

"What...? How...?" She stumbled for her words.

Ken looked between us as I finished her question, "How do they know to look for *you* in *my* home?"

"Every word you say. Every action you take." The Beast reminded me that every step forward would force me to act in plain view.

"My wife was attacked a few months ago. Ever since Nico's funeral, my family was targeted for my actions. I guess I'm the usual suspect." I shook my head, determined to stay focused on the task at hand. "Now let me work on getting us inside."

I took a few steps away from them to reach to Dex and coordinate the distraction we needed for my plan. While we spoke, the Aide updated Lia and the rest.

Alfa-one didn't like any of it.

"You're not even armed," he grumbled.

"Don't worry, Brother," I said, letting go of official communication decorum for a moment.

"So long as the line in the sand isn't crossed, Sir," warned Dex, sternly expressing his intentions to get involved.

I grunted and returned to tell Dee and Ken to be ready to keep up.

When the big bang was heard up the street, the mob rushed up the road like a pack of hyenas.

"Now!" I sprinted across the two-lane boulevard with Ken and Dee on my heels.

Leading them to the eastern tip of the complex on the opposite end of the gate, I clasped my hands to make a step.

"Get up! Now!" I bent my knees to help them get over with the extra push.

Ken jumped first, struggling momentarily before dropping on the other side. Dee followed and gracefully landed.

How? I wondered at her resilience.

"Over there! They jumped in!" a female screamed behind me.

Damn it!

I took two steps back, ran, and jumped up the fence. Grabbing the top with both hands, I lifted myself to the other side.

Lia was standing by Dee and Ken. I gave the masked woman instructions, "Please keep an eye here. Someone saw us jumping inside."

"Don't worry," she replied with her thick accent. "The Russian guy has all the neighbors alert and ready to report."

Almost on cue, a neighbor appeared in the window above us.

"Saw you coming in. I got this." The man in his late fifties confirmed his trustworthiness.

I nodded at him, feeling relief pass through me as I peered into the dimly-lit courtyard and started toward my home.

"Daddy. Daddy. Up here." I heard my son's sweet little voice whisper loudly through the night. Looking up to my unit's second-level balcony, I saw Ari's small head popping up just above the rail. "I got Nico's flags. Look, Daddy!"

I noticed the two flags waving across the balcony—the US and the United States Marine Corps.

Pride and panic shot through me as I smiled at my innocent son. Our front door swung open beneath his smiling face, and Dani rushed out. Throwing herself into my open arms, her lips found mine and made the world disappear for several moments while I held her trembling body close to mine.

"Tanner!" The large, bald Russian shouted from the other end of the complex by the gate, snatching me out of our time-stop. As Dmitri marched toward me with a figure at his side, unidentifiable in the shadows, I pulled my wife closer and then let her go.

"Get them inside." I motioned toward Dee and Ken and smiled as my flushed queen realized we'd had an audience and led the guests into our home.

"Ari, get inside!" I commanded, looking up at the quietest and maybe most amused audience member.

"Tanner." A smile broke beneath the thick beard of the Russian as he approached. "It's not all terrible to be home, yes?" He smirked as we clasped each other's arms and I nodded at Chelsea, the one who had been walking beside him.

"No, Dani's my light in the dark, Brother." I smiled back as I dragged him into a firm hug.

"Who's watching the gate?" I asked.

"The old Ramirez." Dmitri smiled wickedly.

Chelsea's blue eyes locked onto me, her straight brown hair pulled back in a messy bun. She snorted and mumbled something. I ignored her as I led them away from my home to where other neighbors huddled by the gate. Roberto stood tall among them, his hard dark eyes watching the mob and silver beard barely hiding his displeasure. The gathering outside our complex began to grow again on the other side of the gate.

"Roberto!" I called, and he turned to pull me in for a hug.

"Bring out the pig! Bring out the pig! We know! We know!" the chorus repeated.

"So far, nobody has tried to scale the walls," assured Dmitri while Chelsea looked about ready to explode next to him.

"What is it, Chelsea?" I asked.

"Who were those two people that you brought into our complex? Was that the cop they're looking for?" she nearly shrieked. "And those flags! Are you trying to get us killed?"

I looked around at the neighbors.

They're good people and deserve to know about the dangers my choices have brought upon our home.

"Yes, that's the cop. Both she and the other guest are under my protection. This is all you need to know," I replied, holding her gaze until she looked away.

Most of the neighbors were now gathered around us, except those Dmitri had wisely placed to watch over the four sides of the complex.

Chelsea opened her mouth to speak again, but I raised my hand to stop her, looking at the faces of the residents one by one.

I brought this here.

"You're all welcome in our home, and those who want to help, talk to my friend here." I patted Dmitri's shoulder.

"How dare you? And who are you to give orders?" screeched Chelsea. "Are you going to start shooting people next?"

Every word I say. Every action I take.

I looked at her and the sneer that covered her cold, almost purple face.

"I'm unarmed, Chelsea, and will not hurt anyone. Besides, nobody is forcing you to do anything. If you want, our door will be open."

Without waiting for a reply, I turned to confirm Dmitri could hold the line so I could go home and found him squinting at me.

Yeah, I'm unarmed. Mostly.

I didn't have to say any of the words out loud to provoke his laughter. When he shooed me, I turned back to my house, suddenly overwhelmed by the sounds of screams, curses, and countless choppers hovering above us.

My next-door neighbor started toward me, and I waved him closer.

"I need your help..." I explained another part of my plan to him, and he promised to begin immediately.

Pausing at the threshold, I looked down at my black clothing, praying the bloodshed stopped there.

21:26

Devotion

Our home was full of people, but my children were the first to reach me. I bent my knee and scooped them both up into my arms, inhaling the scent of their hair and innocence, and enjoying Leelee's babble and Ari's barrage of information updates and love offerings.

Paulina, Celeste, and the kids followed. Unlike my children, David and Odalys looked scared. I held them close, wishing I could infuse their little bodies with a sense of safety and love.

"It'll be okay, " I told them both, looking up at their mother and grandmother whose terror-filled eyes betrayed their smiles.

Seeing Emmanuel lying on our sofa with bandaged hands and chest, I gave them a final squeeze and walked over to him. His face was bruised and cut up, but his dark eyes blazed with life. Dee was at his side, dressed in one of Dani's old sweatshirts, apparently providing medical attention.

I bent by the sofa, taking a closer look at his wounds.

"You should have seen your woman, Hermano. Fucking loca!" Emmanuel grimaced in pain.

Dee smiled as the patient related the story of Dani appearing in the restaurant, waving her gun around.

"They dragged me here. I was sure she was about to shoot a few times."

"Si, muy loca." I smiled back at him. "Now rest," I instructed him and thanked Dee as I stood up.

Seeing Ken outside on the balcony, eyes trained on me, I knew he wanted to talk, but the Aide whispered updates into my earbud before I could, "The chatter around the complex and the cop is increasing. Someone did see you jump inside, and they're talking about it. The large man, Hakeem Bosman, is believed to be killed by Dee."

"Dani." I called for my wife, who quickly placed Lil in Celeste's arms and followed me downstairs to the studio.

We'd barely gotten inside when I heard Ken's voice, "Tanner!"

"Come in."

He opened the door and looked around, a journalist taking in every detail in a moment as he asked, "Do you have a smartphone I could use?"

Quickly, I searched my closet and got him a secure smartphone.

"Wait a few minutes, and I'll activate it for you," I said as he grabbed it from my hand and left the studio, closing the door behind him.

Dani stood in front of the couch, looking puzzled as I reached for a change of clothes.

"Who are you?" she smirked playfully.

"Who are you? Come over here," I growled, reaching for her hand. "I wasn't done with you."

Pinning her against the door, I immediately felt the gun in her jeans and set it on the shelf before I turned off the lights and unleashed my pent-up longing. The insanity outside our gate could wait until I'd told my queen exactly how much I love her.

Before everything changes.

21:45

Disclosures

Hustling to pull clothes on, we got back to business.

She briefly told me about her rescue mission.

"I don't know how. I just did it." She finished her story, sounding truly stunned by her behavior.

"Keep the gun on you," I responded as I pulled my shirt over my head. "I'm unarmed, Baby, and I hope it stays like this."

Her eyes narrowed and nose wrinkled, but she didn't push. I pulled her back to my chest, knowing that the only way she would survive my barrage of updates was in my embrace.

For several minutes, she rode the roller coaster of suffering with me. Shemtov's death broke her. Chad's betrayal and the news of the attack on the Ranch and the price paid by Jerome and Henry made her gasp in shock, even after I left out the identity of the attackers and any other operational material.

"I need to sit down," she said as she moved to the nearby chair, put her head between her legs, and took deep breaths. I brought her a water bottle from my little fridge in the corner and she drank half of it without a taking a breath.

"Where did you find the cop and the other guy?"

"The school…" I explained how the many insurgent groups had made it their headquarters. When confusion creased her brow, I explained, "This is Holden's adopted daughter."

Dani's eyes brightened, as she immediately made the connection from seeing Dee at the funeral.

"And him?"

"He's a journalist."

"Did she kill that Hakeem guy? They scream his name nonstop."

I shook my head and stared into her cloudy blue, questioning eyes.

"Hakeem was in the video. The big one next to the Demon who killed Nico."

Her eyes widening, she rose to her feet, hand to her mouth as if she were going to be sick.

"They raped her, Dani," I mumbled, leaving the rest for her to connect.

"No," she whispered, holding her belly. "Poor child."

Is she going to be sick?

Suddenly refocusing, flames returned to her eyes.

"I don't care who killed that rapist," she hissed. "You did the right thing. She's one of us now."

"She knows," confirmed the Beast.

When the loud bangs started above us, I told her about my request and our neighbor.

"How is Ari taking it all?" I recalled his excited face and the private conversation we'd had.

"He should be afraid, but he's too much like you. Roberto and Dmitri had to keep him from going out a few times," she grumbled, shaking her head.

"We need to keep an eye on him."

"Yes, Baby," she agreed as she stood up and kissed me gently before walking toward the voice that was calling her from upstairs.

★　★　★

21:57

Demand

Alone in the studio, I turned on the hot water in the sink of my small restroom.

Pulling my concealed blade out and placing it in the stream of water, I heard his voice again: "Who are you? Who are you?"

Hakeem's dying question looped in my mind as my fingers cleaned the glistening black metal.

"Answer it already. Answer and stop hiding," snarled the Beast.

BESIEGED

– Venice Beach, CA –
Tuesday, November 3, 2020

22:00

Declarations

The furnace was red hot, its smoke directed through the dryer's vent in the wall just behind it. I closed my eyes at the intense wave of heat touching my face as all my blood-stained clothing turned to ash, allowing all of the moments of the last twenty-four hours to stoke the fire within.

Raging violence and pleasure in the same hour. What the fuck am I doing?

Dressed in a spare black urban clothing setup, I re-affixed the Fly under my collar, concealed my blade, and instructed the Aide to allow live feed only during hostile contact.

Should have thought about it before pinning her against the door.

I shook my head in amusement at the prospect of that turning up in a debrief with one or both of my commanders.

Jarring bangs from the upper floor persisted but couldn't compete with the sounds of mayhem swirling outside our complex. Stretching my attention between the two locations, I continued my preparations.

My eyes gravitated to the computer screen showing the full disk format at 97% complete.

Glad I never keep paper records.

Glancing back toward the furnace, my gaze paused on the black plastic cover hanging in the open closet. Sadness tightened my throat as my feet quickly carried me across the studio to the Marine Dress Blues.

What am I doing? Are we really leaving? She doesn't even know.

Pulling the plastic away, I studied all of its details —the soft blue material and red trim, the gold-plated buttons, the decorations representing countless and untold stories of service for the nation.

I can't believe I'm…

The sadness in my throat was replaced with bile as I removed the uniforms from their cover and threw them into the fire.

I'm not sure how long I was watching the flames before the knock on the studio door refocused me.

"Come in."

"Dani said you'd like to see me." The minute Dee was inside, her eyes found the fire and then me.

"I do." I smiled gently at the young woman whose recent pain shone only behind her eyes, and motioned for her to join me next to the metal rectangular box bolted into the cement floor. "This is my gun safe." I punched the code and opened the door to reveal two handguns and a pump shotgun. "They're all legal and registered, and there's plenty of ammo here too."

She took a careful look at the weapons.

"Arm yourself as you see fit. I'm surrendering this cache to the police, as the situation on the ground could separate me from the weapons."

Dee's brow furrowed with suspicion as she pulled out Hakeem's gun, unloaded it, and placed it in the safe.

"You're the last line of defense. Keep the civilians safe. Can you do that?" I resisted the urge to put my hand on her shoulder as she pulled out several weapons and ammo boxes and placed them on my desk.

"Yes. I can. But why haven't you armed yourself?" She turned to face me.

Every word I say. Every action I take.

I felt that her trust in me was worth more than this shade of my truth, but all I offered was, "To avoid bloodshed."

Instantly pale, she sat down and stammered, "But... but... you..." and looked at the ground.

"She saw me." The Beast confirmed my suspicion.

"Dee, what am I to do?" I asked, unable to veil my irritation. "Even the police are unable to help us."

Her eyes were brimming when she looked up.

"I talked to Holden." She gulped. "Did... did you tell him?"

As the anguish of her screams echoed through my nervous system, I felt the Beast increase in power, filling my belly and chest with a burning desire for justice for this woman.

"No. It's not my information to share," I replied, heartbroken by the many micro-expressions in her face and body that told me she was using all of her energy not to tremble in front of me.

Suddenly taking a deep breath, she stood, clenched fists at her side, and declared, "I'm glad someone else killed that son of a bitch!"

Someone else?

"He will come too... Ender." She said it matter-of-factly, though her tone was laced with fear.

"I know." I paused, realizing there was no better approach for my next question. "Did you get a... good look at his face?" I knew the horrific nature of my inquiry and hoped she could sense my regret in having to ask.

A ripple of pain crossed her pretty face, but her voice remained effective as she described one of the men who'd violated her, "Caucasian, mid-twenties, bald, light brown goatee. Light eyes. Hard face." She stopped momentarily to pull in a deep breath. "He had that disgusting red demon helmet. He removed it before he..."

Dee closed her eyes tight, heaving violently as the tears finally fell. Without thinking, I rushed to catch her and pulled her shaking body to my chest. I took deep and measured breaths, partly to manage the tidal wave of dark emotions inside me, and partly to give her a soothing pace to co-regulate to. It worked, and she thanked me silently as I let her go.

Using the sleeves of Dani's shirt, she covered her eyes to wipe her tears or collect herself, or maybe both.

"Wait!" she exclaimed, pulling her hands away to reveal wide eyes. "I've seen that helmet before." The Beast tore through my mind, reveling in the unfolding revelations. "That guy! Outside the restaurant... with the demon thing on his face. Their leader." She closed her eyes again, this time as if searching for lost details in a memory. "Oh my God," she gasped. "The big guy was with him as well... that Hakeem. That was him!" Eyes open, the cop examined me again. "Is that what you want? For him to come?"

"They're all beginning to see."

Because of you! I did my best to prevent my inner conflict from reaching my face.

Dee's probing eyes remained on me as I sorted through all the possible answers and consequences. Saved by the vibration in my ear, I slowly placed my hands on her shoulders.

"I have a call to take, Dee. I'll catch up with you."

The Beast laughed again, this time with unabated mockery.

"Yes, Sir," she responded with all seriousness and then turned to gather the weapons and ammo.

Sir? I wondered as I watched her leave the studio.

★ ★ ★

22:15

Assumptions

Both Remus and Romulus were on the line, ready to update me.

And probably interrogate me. I sighed as I dropped my exhausted body into the chair at my desk. *And no end in sight.*

"Your mother and sister are doing very well and send their love," Jack started.

"Please tell them…" I paused, not wanting to open Pandora's box with my true feelings. "I miss them."

There was a short silence, and I imagined they both heard the word anyway.

"You start, Alfa-leader," commanded Custer. "First and foremost, did you initiate the Protocol?"

Glancing toward the furnace and the smoldering ash inside, I confirmed, "Protocol is complete. I surrendered the weapons to Officer Dee Hopkins and…" I shared the more important details of my conversation with her.

"You were walking a tightrope there with the cop," responded the General.

Jack barged in, his voice tight, "Care to explain this whole *unarmed* tactic of yours?"

The Beast lurked in my depths, listening… waiting.

I closed my eyes at the racket of all the versions of me colliding, wondering who would be victorious. But then the eyes of my son and daughter appeared, innocent and unscathed by their father's violence and darkness.

"Are they... unscathed?" The Beast's sharp challenge weakened my stomach and knees momentarily.

"This is my home, Dad!" I left it to him, and possibly the Beast, to figure out the various implications of my words.

He grumbled something incoherent before Custer saved us with a diversion, "You did well saving the cop and Ken. Awful what happened to her partner." He ended abruptly when his own anger flared, and Jack sighed crossly in agreement.

They're not mentioning what I did to...

"We're sorry about the Rabbi, Son... a brother in arms." My father paused for a moment, as if searching for words. "I could tell you were... fond of him."

"I'm going to miss him dearly. He was such a good man—a free man." I gave the rush of grief and something else I couldn't articulate a moment before pushing it all to the background again.

"And your wife, holy shit, Tanner!" Jack broke from his typical commander's code, and I half-smiled at the resonant mix of respect and fear in his voice. "That girl caused her father to return to the field."

"What? Is he...?"

"The evac plan," Romulus finished, answering my half-formed question.

They assume we're leaving. Interesting.

"Why aren't you protesting?" The Beast kept asking questions I couldn't, or didn't want to, answer.

Jack shifted to the subject of Ken and letting the online journalist use the smartphone. They appreciated the ability to document from the interior.

"I'll continue to work with him and see where it all leads."

These two have an interesting relationship, even if only online.

Next, Custer brought me up to speed on the tight election map.

"Looks like Grayson will likely be our next president. We've never seen anything like this, where governors think it's their place to announce the presidency with complete disregard to the process and before a final tally is conducted." I could almost hear his head shake in disgust. "Unprecedented unease across the various branches of the federal government right now." He left it at that.

"And the Zones?" I stood up and walked to my surfboards, feeling the wax on my favorite red fish board as I wondered how long it would be before I could return to my watery fortress of solitude.

Again, the Beast's laughing mockery echoed, *"The fortress is way beyond compromised."*

"Implausible would be the best summary," said Jack. "I've never seen so many cowardly politicians and leaders. They don't give a shit about the civilians who became instant hostages of those insurgents."

Distracted by the screams and choppers outside, I wondered just how many people would succumb to this insanity in one form or another.

"As for the school," he continued, refocusing me. "Why didn't you go in with backup?"

Resting on my surfboard, my right hand tremored at the visceral memory of cutting Hakeem from the inside out, and I wondered at the sudden sensation of intoxication.

Will they ask me about you and what you want me to do?

"Who am I?" The Beast repeated a riddle that had haunted me since Its awakening.

"It had to be this way," I replied, unwilling to expose my mental chasm, which seemed to grow faster and wider with each tragedy that befell my beloved nation, friends, and family.

"Well, at least you took one of them," interjected the General. "No independent authorities tonight, Tanner."

"My mission is to protect my family, Sir."

22:35

Regrets

The phone rang as soon as I closed my computer. It was Holden, grumbling about the blown cell towers and blackout.

"Thank God I found this satellite phone. Never knew you have secretaries and all."

Stop fishing, Brother. I knew it was a risk with the RCC personnel handling our calls.

He thanked me again and rehashed his earlier chat with Dee.

"Her voice was troubled. Did something happen to her?"

Cop senses, or maybe paternal ones.

"You should be proud of her. She's 100% effective, helping and guarding."

He grunted and began to discuss the dead cop and his inability to convince the mayor to allow them in.

"I thought the Chief would do something, but she didn't."

"What are you hearing?"

Cursing, Holden detailed how Victoria's peaceful negotiations approach had convinced the mayor to stop the police from intervening at all.

"Madness! I can't believe she's doing this. She was raised here." He sounded as mystified as I felt.

What is it with this woman?

"Who knows that I've got Dee here?" I asked.

"The Chief and some higher-ups. I was told to instruct her to do her best to barricade until help arrives."

Fucking cowards! Even when it comes down to one of their own!

"It won't stay a secret for long," I warned.

"Fuck. Really?" He sounded appropriately mortified.

"She's armed, Holden. She'll be okay. What else is going on?" I asked, trying to refocus him.

Quickly, Holden began venting about the media and how they took the side of the rioters and AZs.

"Even now, with the AZ and the fires, they still call to defund us, insisting that we provoked this entire situation. And the Governor is too busy attacking Stone to activate the National Guard."

Shouts from the courtyard sparked anxiety until I heard Dmitri's booming voice controlling the situation. I checked the rollup metal cover on the glass patio doors, which secured the studio from anyone trying to enter from the back.

"Listen, there's a DHS agent who might show up..." I told him about Shida and gave him a code word, explaining that he could trust the person who would repeat it to him. It took a moment, but he agreed.

All new to him.

He cleared his throat but was unable to eliminate emotion as he confessed, "Tanner, I should've listened earlier. I'm starting to see it, but I'm so confused."

Looking at my graying beard in the mirror, I shook my head.

"It hasn't been an easy road," I admitted, feeling the world's weight on my shoulders.

"Am I too late?" His voice cracked.

"If you are, then I am too."

22:55

Plans

When I called, Shida and her team had just entered LA from the north.

"We lost our lead," she murmured, referring to the Western Jihad cell in our area.

"Their flags are already waving in Venice…" I told her about seeing them on my way to find Dee, but not the menacing tattoo on Hakeem's bare back.

"You did what?" she shrieked. "How exact…? Never mind." Shida stopped abruptly, probably because she wasn't alone in the car.

You don't want to know anyway. The heaviness in my chest expanded.

"What's your status?" she asked, tone back to firm and professional.

Quickly, I briefed her on our position, the dangers, and the lack of support from local government.

"Unbelievable," she muttered.

"I do want to tell you about this guy, though…" I told her about Holden and gave her the code word. "He's a good cop and will help if he can."

When the call was done, I returned to the cooling furnace and had just begun cleaning it when my ear vibrated.

"Eli," I answered.

"Did you tell Dani?" My father-in-law was a man of few words, each packed with purposeful intention.

"No."

"Why not?" he pressed.

My mind caught the faint sound of waves.

So that's his plan.

"S13. I should have known," I grumbled, referring to Eli's illustrious history in the Israeli Elite Naval Commando, known for that acronym.

He chuckled at my accurate guess, but it didn't stop him from pushing again, "You didn't answer my question."

"She will know when I know... when all else fails us," I answered flatly.

He paused and when he began to speak, his words and tone were even more measured than usual, "This is my baby daughter and grandchildren, Tanner. You know what this means, right?"

"Yes, Sir," I replied with a shudder. "I will protect them with my life."

23:10

Time

Glancing at my watch, I realized the late hour had done nothing to disperse the crowds outside our complex or silence their screams and chants.

The RCC sent me videos that managed to get out of the signal blackout zone, and I watched in horror as people in the crowd filmed our complex from the outside, viciously chanting their intentions to get their hands on Dee and hurt anyone in their way.

Fuck.

I hurried around the studio, ensuring one last time that all sensitive materials had been attended to.

I can't avoid it any longer.

I braced myself as I opened the door and called up the stairs.

23:15

Promises

Celeste, Paulina, Roberto, and Dani stepped into the studio and shut the door, even though the likelihood of anyone hearing our conversation over the loud banging noises upstairs and the screams and firecrackers outside was low.

My wife nodded at me, offering her silent support, eyes searching mine.

"There is something you need to know," I started. "Hakeem, the guy they're yelling about, was the big guy who helped the Demon kill Nico." I watched them all struggle to connect the dots. "He's dead for that and more."

Paulina sobbed, her face overcome by maternal sorrow reddened as Roberto pulled her close. Keeping his hard, dark eyes on me, he nodded approvingly.

Celeste's face contorted as she hissed the questions they were probably all thinking, "Did you kill him? Did you make him suffer?"

The widow's piercing dark eyes did the work, and the satisfaction of taking Hakeem's life returned like a sweet, intoxicating taste on my tongue.

"He was sent to hell," I replied, holding her rage-fueled gaze until she nodded slowly.

"What about the Demon?" she pressed.

When Dani's eyes found mine, and I saw sadness instead of judgment, I lost it.

I never wanted this part of my life back! But you pushed. The recollection of her insisting I own my shit interrupted me. *You pushed, but only because this is a nightmare and something inside you knows I can help.* I took a deep breath and set aside the resentment.

"Ender... that's his street or whatever nickname," I said, tearing my eyes from my queen's to look back at my hermano's widow.

"When will you kill him?" she lashed out.

Dani and Paulina gasped in response, but Roberto remained unmoved and waited for my answer.

"You made a promise, right? Semper Fidelis. You said it over his grave. What does that even mean?" She was coming undone before our eyes.

That makes two of us.

Overwhelmed, I searched for an appropriate answer. Luckily, Roberto intervened and insisted everyone leave me to prepare.

"He's got enough on his plate," he said as he shooed everyone out of the room, keeping his eyes fixed on me as he followed them.

The promise.

I shifted my gaze to avoid seeing her leave the room.

★   ★   ★

23:28

Demons

I was about to check on Dmitri when Lia barged into the studio.

"Dani is fighting with that neighbor."

Chelsea!

I raced outside toward the loud voices coming from the courtyard.

Right next to the gate? Damn it, Woman!

If our situation weren't so dangerous, I would have laughed at the sight of the burly, bald, bearded Russian doing his best to keep my raging queen from tearing Chelsea to pieces.

"Give it back!" Chelsea screamed up at Dmitri.

"What's going on here?" I asked, noticing that the big Russian had a red flag crumpled in his huge left hand.

Dani was about to burst when Dmitri's deep voice boomed, "This woman wanted to hang the Comrades flag on the gate!" He opened the flag for me to see.

Even though we were still thirty feet away from the gate, a few people in the crowd had keen enough eyes to discern what was happening and start screaming about the flag. I shook my head at the growing sea of phones filming us.

Blackout or not, these videos will get out.

I turned to Chelsea and spoke calmly, "Listen."

But she struck first with venom, "No! I will not listen! And be sure that I'll sue you when this is over! You hung those offensive flags on your balcony just like your friend did. Look where it got him!" she spewed. "My action is meant to calm things down before they see how disgraceful you are."

My blood heated at the many implications of her words related to Nico, the nation, and the United States Marine Corps. Quickly, I used the *Sense*, knowing I had to choose my battles wisely tonight.

"Is there any way to convince you to hold off on this?" I asked. "Maybe just hang it from *your* window." The words felt like razors in my mouth.

"Fuck you, prick! Taking advantage of your toxic masculinity!" She barked as she snatched the flag out of Dmitri's hand and stomped off.

I looked at Dani, who shrugged before walking back to our home, and then at Dmitri, who just laughed.

"They make you want to do something about this," grumbled the Russian quietly as the crowd by the gate screamed endless slurs, threw occasional firecrackers, and recorded every moment.

Idiots.

"They wait for us to make a mistake. They've been trying to trap people who try to protect their own homes since the riots began." His jaw hardened as he considered my words in silence. "This is not the sandbox, Brother," I added.

"Yeah, I have more respect for the Taliban, Brother." He snorted in disgust.

I looked around the dark courtyard and then up at the choppers overhead.

"He would've been proud," murmured Dmitri, his Russian accent thickening. "He waited for you for a long time. Probably since being in that hell."

Nico's nightmares from the dark well.

"Did you mean 'hole'?" I asked with slight jest.

"Hell... hole. Same fucking thing."

We laughed, further aggravating those who pushed against the sturdy metal gate, doing their best to pull it down.

"When we were down there, he cried out to God." Dmitri's laughter had been replaced by sobriety. "Not for his salvation but rather to repent. He carried such pain. I always knew, but not how much. That was the only time he had admitted, even though it was God to whom he talked. Not me."

I wonder if it had anything to do with whatever happened between him and Victoria.

The thought of the councilwoman called up Nico's eternal words, like demons that always knew where to find me: "You could have stopped it, Hermano."

I shook my head in dismay and shame, earning Dmitri's questioning look as he motioned for us to take a few steps back when firecrackers were thrown our way again.

"Did you ever find the guy who killed him?" asked the Russian after baring his teeth to the crowd through his thick beard.

I recalled the last time he'd asked that question—right after the funeral—and the one that followed, "I guess we are doomed to become what we were, da?"

"He was right. Trust him." The Beast endorsed the former Spetsnaz giant.

"There used to be two of them. Only one remains," I said slowly and quietly while keeping my eyes on my neighbors.

"Hakeem? That asshole they are screaming about?" he whispered.

"Yes."

He was about to ask something else when the crowd began a new chant.

Time slowed to a crawl as my eyes shifted from Dmitri to the gate where hundreds of voices united in one mantra, "Ender... Ender... Ender..."

The crowd parted for the muscular guy, dressed in black pants, a tank top, and a menacing red Demon helmet with sharp teeth opening for his mouth.

I froze as he raised his hands and the crowd became quiet.

"Colonel!" the Demon roared.

FACE TO FACE

– Venice Beach, CA –
Tuesday, November 3, 2020

23:38

Close

"**A**lfa is reporting armed hostiles around Ender," the Aide warned as I advanced into the fray. The Demon shook the metal gate violently, and the crowd cheered on cue.

Grief, guilt, and rage collided, adrenaline surging and activating every cell in my body.

I can get him.

"That's close enough, Alfa-leader," Dex called into the team channel.

Taking a deep belly breath, I stopped five feet from the gate, nearly blinded by the sea of cameras and flashlights directed at me.

Ender stopped rattling the gate and bellowed, "At last, he comes to speak with the injured masses."

Interesting. His words and theatrics had caught me off-guard.

Dmitri stood to my left. I turned to face him and our eyes locked, his unspoken question reverberating between us: Is this my brother's murderer?

As I nodded, the Russian's face turned murderous and he dropped into a battle stance.

"Hey! Your Highness," Ender taunted.

"Now or later?" hissed Dmitri, his accent heavier than usual.

"He's on the path as well." I could almost hear the Beast's smile.

My body braced for battle, succumbing to my deep hunger for vengeance.

"Wait!" I turned back to see Ken racing toward me, his face masked and his phone filming. "Trust me."

"Hello!" Ender called, his voice dripping mockery.

I looked between the journalist's earnest eyes, the phone in his hand focused on me, and Ender's Demon face. The spell was broken.

"You cut when I tell you," I instructed Ken, and he nodded.

I was turning back to face Ender when the sound of another voice made my heart stop.

"Daddy!" Even eighty feet away, I recognized the call of my beloved son.

Ender cursed and shook the gate again as I turned to look down at the courtyard and found Dani and the kids on the balcony. Ari waved his little hand.

I nodded at them and turned back toward the gate, grateful the rioters and my family didn't have a clear view of each other.

Feeling the weight of my shackles increase, I glared at Ender.

"What do you want?"

23:45

Terms

"Finally! You are such a busy man, my friend!" Ender mimicked a professor-like tone.

The urge to jump the gate and twist his head off his shoulders overwhelmed my senses, but I fought it. Dex was right—the ramifications could be horrendous.

Dmitri remained on my left and Ken filmed from my right. The mob was quiet, the only sounds those of choppers hovering above us.

"How's your wife? I heard she's cute and feisty!"

The crowd jeered, and I clenched my fists as guilt blazed through me.

All while I was gone, helping my traitorous brother! Motherfuckers! I suppressed my anger over the attack Dani experienced the same day Chad was so-called "saved" in Seattle.

"You should all go home," I called loudly, scanning the faces in the crowd behind Ender, "before someone gets hurt."

Ender laughed as he pointed to the hundreds of puppets at his disposal and responded for them, "Look at them... 'Once all struggle is grasped, miracles are possible.'"

The people cheered, and my heart dropped at the realization that most of them probably had no idea who coined the awful words.

Mao. Is this your game? Transforming America?

"This goes far beyond this monster." The Beast was connecting all of the dots with me.

"What do you want, Ender?" I repeated my question, resisting the impulse to look back.

"We want the cop, Colonel. We know she's here, and VAZ is negotiating her release with the city." His tone was jovial. "Therefore, *we* are in charge of her welfare."

In my mind's eye, I was at the gate in a few bounds, crushing his trachea with my fingers. In reality, I kept my feet planted.

"The officer will be staying with us," I replied flatly, observing the anger-ravaged mob of mostly masked faces.

"She killed my brother!" roared the Demon, his voice visibly impacting the crowd around him. "He's dead because of that bitch and another runt that escaped with her. Bring her out!"

Every word I say. Every action I take.

"That's not going to happen."

Head tilted, tough hands gripping the gate, muscles bulging under his tank, he delivered his terms, "Happen or not. You have one hour, Colonel."

The Demon raised his hands to summon the chant, "Bring her out! Bring her out!"

Seeing the Comrades and Ryse flags waving in the crowd, I shuddered at the reality unfolded before my eyes.

At my doorstep. You were right, Grandpa.

"Bring her out! Bring her out!" The crowd roared louder when Ender pointed toward the moon like a shaman.

Revolutionary terror. You think that's what you are?

I turned back toward my home, Dmitri following once Ender had disappeared into the masses.

Seeing the balcony empty, I paused the big guy with my hand on his arm.

"I need a moment. Can you promise not to explode?"

The giant Russian fixed me with a hard stare, but there was the slightest curve at the edge of his mouth before he answered, "Take two. We got this."

"We?"

Dmitri winked in return.

Damn it. He noticed Alfa again.

"Tick-tock, Colonel!" came the Demon's roar from deep inside the mob.

CHECKING IN

– Venice Beach, CA –
Wednesday, November 4, 2020

00:00

Choices

"**B**ring her out! Bring her out!" the mob chanted as I crossed the courtyard. Jack wanted to talk, but I needed a moment to sort out the situation at home.

Lia was at our front door right when I arrived.

"Back up Dmitri." I spoke in Hebrew, and she nodded and hurried through the courtyard.

My plan to walk up to the main level was thwarted by Dani when she popped her head out of the studio, "Baby, in here."

Paulina, Celeste, and Roberto stood in the middle of the studio, waiting.

Round two.

"The killer is here," I admitted to the four sets of inquiring eyes.

"El Diablo," gasped Paulina, and Roberto tightened his hold on her shoulders.

"This is just a Demon, not the Devil."

The Beast's distinction made me curious.

"Are you going to kill him?" Celeste cried out.

The Beast lurked and waited for my answer with the rest.

Dani's eyes widened, her questioning gaze holding mine.

I'm sorry you're facing impossible decisions, Baby. I didn't envy her position—sandwiched between her best friend's grief and her husband's culpability.

"My mission is to *save* all of you." I decided against sharing the increasingly powerful urge to do precisely what Celeste demanded.

The young widow seemed reflective.

"What about the flags?" she pressed. When I didn't answer, she clarified, "Nico's flags. Ari hung them out there. Would you take those down for them?" Her raging eyes bore into my soul, her inquiry provoking an inner conclusion that damned me.

He was alone. Surrounded. No backup. He was alone. I fucking left him alone.

Images of Nico, Ishmael, and now Shemtov and their flags gave me pause.

Todd! My heart seized. *Have I left him alone too? I can't lose another friend.*

"The flags remain," I grumbled, and we locked eyes for another long moment until she nodded.

Turning my gaze back to my queen, I shrugged and offered my best "suppose I should have told you" smile before tackling the next conversation.

"Listen up. We have an exit plan, which will take everyone to safety if needed…" Dani's eyes narrowed, but she said nothing as I continued.

Until she does.

When I finished, the Ramirez family looked at each other, and then Roberto spoke on their behalf, "We'll talk about it." He herded them out of the studio again, leaving me alone with my queen.

"I should have known." She motioned with her eyes to the two backpacks under my surfboard rack.

"It's just an option, Love. One we might need."

She smiled and reached to hug me.

"Thank you," she whispered against my chest.

I pulled her closer and stroked her long dark hair, savoring all of her delicious textures and scents before sharing the part that I knew could change everything.

"Your dad is here."

"What?" Dani broke our embrace and stared at me, mouth agape with shock. "I had a feeling he was going to do this."

I chuckled lightly at her disbelief as I caressed her cheek.

"Yes, Love. Of course he's here, protecting his family too."

Her face warmed and her whole body relaxed.

This is all I want for Leelee. To always feel like this— protected by her father.

"When will we decide?"

We? Romulus, Remus, and now Dani. Nobody asks my opinion.

"What's so surprising about that?" The Beast sounded similarly exasperated.

"We'll know," I responded, and she nodded after searching my face for answers I couldn't give her.

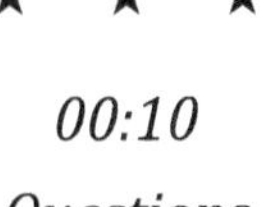

00:10

Questions

"Wow." From the top of my stairs, I could see my neighbor's living room through the gaping hole in the joined wall. "Thank you so much."

My neighbor, still holding the heavy hammer in his hand, nodded and smiled.

"You're the one we should be thanking, Sir."

Sir?

"We're all going to do this together." I clapped his back before turning to the sofa where Leelee was somehow sleeping.

Where's my son? Looking around, I found him with Dee on the neighbor's couch on the other side of the hole. *Why's he still awake?*

Ari had his back to me, and I strained to hear his voice as I advanced.

"They want *you*?" he asked, eyebrows raised at the young cop.

"Yes," replied Dee, her eyes catching mine quickly and returning to his.

"But why?" he pressed while I stood behind him, resisting the impulse to interrupt and assure him it would all be okay.

She seemed lost for words, her eyes finding mine again.

"But where are your cop friends? Where's Uncle Holden?"

His innocence paralyzed us both for a moment.

"Hey, Little Warrior," I called softly and pulled him into my arms for a hug. "Now, listen." I paused, my heart swelling with love as he laid his head on my shoulder and tightened his arms around my neck. "Nothing will happen to her, Son. She's tough. And your dad's here."

He sat up in my arms and, putting his sticky hands on my cheeks, he searched my eyes. I struggled to hold his gaze, not wanting him to see anything but the depth of my love.

"Please go to your mom." I squeezed him again. "It's time to sleep."

"Okay, Daddy. I love you... the most." He stole my line as he kissed my cheek.

"That's impossible, Ari." I kissed him back and set him on the ground, setting his feet in the direction of my queen.

00:18

Gratitude

"Is he here?" Her eyes were wide. "I heard the chant."

"It's him," I admitted as I sat down next to her. "Are you clear on the plan?"

The trick worked, and the focus and determination returned to her face as she repeated the steps flawlessly while I scanned the room.

"Thanks for helping Emmanuel," I added when my eyes noticed the medical kit on the ground near us.

Dee nodded and shared what she had discovered about the heavy beating he took. As she mentioned him holding the door and protecting Celeste behind him, scenes from the notorious video flooded my mind while regret flooded my chest.

Thank God you went, Woman! I imagined my queen running through the streets with a gun and shook my head with bittersweet appreciation. *You almost gave me a heart attack, but you did the right thing.*

"Tanner?" Ken called from the other side of the hole in the wall. "I'd like to film you before…"

"His countdown ends?" I completed his question, and he nodded. "Be ready to film on the balcony when I come back."

Looking back at my friend, I shrugged, "I'm tired of this show, Dee."

She placed her hand on mine and squeezed.

"Tanner, thank you. For saving me… all of us."

I offered a half-smile before I got up to check on the kids.

"Whew... it's late," I mumbled, looking at my watch while bending by the sofa's edge where both of our angels slept under Ari's checkered blanket. Everything stopped for a moment as I caressed their faces and kept at bay the images of the violence these same hands had enacted just hours earlier.

Ari's eyes opened.

Shit.

"Hi, Daddy." His sleepy innocence rang again, this time as the one thing worth preserving in the entire world.

I will not lose you.

"Hi, Little Warrior. Get some rest." I kissed him, and he closed his eyes.

When I looked up, I saw Dani watching us from the staircase, a sad smile on her face.

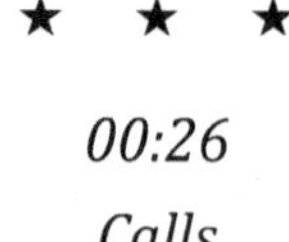

00:26

Calls

I hustled back to the studio to make a few more calls.

The chat with Holden was short, and I handled it while double-checking the bugout bags for the umpteenth time. The police were still prevented from interfering, and Shida and her team had arrived at the police forward position on the broad intersection of Venice and Lincoln Boulevards. I purposely didn't bring up the interaction with Ender, knowing it would crush him to be just a mile away from us, essentially handcuffed from helping.

My second call was to Jack, who confirmed again there would be enough room for the Ramirez clan if they chose to come.

He's assuming I'm going with them.

"Timing will be everything," he mumbled.

"Yes." I did not relish the idea of shuttling two families along the escape route. I looked at my watch.

Thirty minutes for his bullshit countdown.

"Which he will honor," the Beast cautioned.

"Also…" Jack updated me about the videos Ken had taken and the RCC had edited and launched. "We didn't have to censor much. He knows his work and his videos are already trending heavily."

"He's waiting upstairs to film me."

"You got a lot to deal with, Son. Go on now. Semper Fidelis."

Why did he say that? Was that a chuckle? Does he see you?

With no response from the Beast, I finished the final pack, leaving one little item to consider last—a small flash drive containing the secret recording of Nico's death.

"Take it!"

Obediently, I dropped the device in my pocket.

I'M A MAN

– Venice Beach, CA –
Wednesday, November 4, 2020

00:35

Who?

When I walked back upstairs to check on the readiness level, I was relieved to see nearly two dozen non-combatants relocated to the next unit, which had its blinds drawn on all the windows. All the kids and some of the adults were asleep on beds, couches, and the hardwood floor.

Noticing Dani and Dee quietly conversing on our sofa, I froze, realizing these two women had encountered some of the brightest and darkest shades of Tanner Washington. But only one woman knew it all.

Mom.

I don't know if Dani heard my thoughts or just felt me looking at her, but her loving gaze brought me back to the room.

Ken waited in the kitchen, and I motioned for him to follow me to the balcony.

"Last chance to stand back," I offered.

He answered with a grin.

Leaning against the balcony's rail, overlooking the breadth of the open courtyard, we took in the scene. Hundreds of people circled the walls of the complex, partying and throwing firecrackers and rocks in our direction. Lia and Roberto patrolled the walls, and I knew Dmitri was close by.

"Bring her out! Bring her out!"

"We've got twenty-five minutes, so…" The journalist listened intently while I explained the "rules of the game" for the interview. When I was done, he scratched his chin.

"I can live with that." He cleared his throat. "Tanner, about before." Ken seemed at a loss for words until he took a breath. "Thank you for saving us… back in the school. This is all we know."

We? You and Dee have a pact?

"We'll get this out." He referred to his desire to film me, oblivious to my inner question. "Brett Cohen and others will push it, and we'll bypass the legacy media."

"Good." I felt my chest tighten as I looked up at the choppers.

Every word I say. Every action I take.

"One off the record question before we begin?" Ken asked it with a sly smile, and I nodded my consent. "Who is Player1776?"

"What are you talking about?" I was too distracted to connect all the dots.

"The online profile that's been communicating with me over social media since Portland. Whoever it is, he or she has helped me improve my work and really consider my role in the events."

Sounds like Dad.

"And what *is* your role?" I asked, glancing at my watch.

Twenty minutes.

Despite the boyish smile on his bruised face, Ken's voice and sincerity belonged among the most serious of us as he answered thoughtfully, "I thought I knew when 2020 started—to document and strive to be fair and impartial. Now, things are a bit messier. My heart tells me it's time to get off the fence, pick a side, and fight for what I believe in."

Impressive.

"I'll answer this one question. Player1776 is most likely my father, Jack Washington."

Eyes wide, he mumbled, "Wow," which told me he already knew plenty about Old Glory's CEO. "Thank you."

"Hey, thanks for the tip about the attack on Dani." I clapped his back as I would any brother in arms.

"The rumors about the alley scuffle. I just had the feeling."

He's good, piecing all this together.

"We've got sixteen minutes."

I noticed Dmitri exchanging harsh words with the crowd at the gate. His face in the dimly lit courtyard was not easy to discern, but his booming laughter still came through.

Crazy Russian.

"Action on 3... 2..."

00:45

Who are you?

Ken started the video and began to create the scene for viewers.

"I came to Los Angeles to cover the election and was abducted and tortured by Ryse. Tanner Washington found me tied up in the local school and got me out, along with Officer Dee Hopkins, a fellow prisoner." He paused for a moment and then flipped the lens on me. "So, who is Tanner Washington?"

The question caught me off-guard, reminding me of a character in a book that changed my life in my thirties.

A story in which the main question about the hero's identity became the battle cry for freedom.

"*Who are you, Tanner?*" The Beast laughed at my reflection.

My pulse quickened.

"You first became a sensation around the funeral for your friend, Nicolas Ramirez," Ken prompted.

Sensation?

He must have read my expression.

"Your wife said you don't do social media and that it's better this way."

"I have a good wife."

"Where were you born?" asked Ken, probably trying to find another angle to engage.

"South Dakota..." I answered each of his subsequent questions about our nearly two decades of traveling around the globe following my father's military assignments.

"How was it? The traveling, the new places?"

How do I begin to answer this?

Old resentment prickled my skin and seized all my muscles. Resisting the impulse to cut the interview and set my tongue free to truly illuminate the darkness, I found my entry point.

"I think their years of global travel put many things in perspective for them."

"Your family?"

"Yes."

"Why are you speaking of them as separate from you?" His question was genuine, and I could almost hear his mind recalculating our story.

Damn, he's good.

"I was eighteen when we moved to the States, and I enlisted shortly after."

I grumbled it, knowing very well that my answer wasn't clear.

Ken squinted his eyes as if trying to read my mind.

"So, you joined the Army."

"Marines," I corrected him.

"Sorry. Marines. You joined up without ever living here?"

"Yes." I glanced at my watch.

Thirteen minutes.

"And the funeral where the world first saw you, that was for Nico Ramirez," he prompted.

"Yes, he was my brother in arms… and life…" I let the words dissipate as the emotion swelled.

He bit his lip, and I nodded.

Let's do this, Brother.

"Where are we now?"

My left hand grabbed the rail, keeping me focused.

"This is our home in Venice. My wife, our two young children, and I live here."

He asked for more background, and I provided the cliff notes on my decade-long residency in the coastal neighborhood.

"What's happening around your home tonight?" asked Ken.

I shook my head as I detailed the predicament, finishing with, "We have ten more minutes before the deadline to give them the cop."

"Will you?"

I was distracted by Lia's accented English as she helped neighbors move from their units into ours.

"Will you surrender Officer Dee Hopkins to them?" Ken repeated.

I looked at the tiny camera lens, imagining the eyes of those who would see this clip.

"Never."

"Are you armed? Will you shoot?" he prompted.

"I'm unarmed." I lifted my shirt to show my waist-line. "I plan on staying this way."

"Why?"

Every word I say. Every action I take.

I took a deep breath and closed my eyes so briefly that no one watching would have noticed me allowing the *Sense* and the lurking Beast to sort and arrange my words.

Eyes now focused on Ken, I spoke only truth:

"Because in the name of the Dragon virus, our society has fragmented and been divided by design, all while the leaders have broken their own rules.

"Because the rule of law was collapsed and replaced with mob injustice.

"Because anyone who dared to defend themselves lived to be charged as the offenders by rogue district attorneys, financed by foreigners.

"Because our cowardly politicians have tolerated this summer of riots with zero care for the destruction, looting, and loss of life.

"Because the media hides and manipulates the truth.

"Because the police were defunded and abandoned after all they have sacrificed.

"Because schools are shut down, and all they teach is hatred for our own country.

"Because my brave friends, Nicolas Ramirez, Rabbi Shemtov, and many others died believing in this nation, only to be forsaken for the sake of the depraved."

I breathed, feeling the ire condensing into a tight ball of hot lava in my core.

"Have you raised your fist or bent your knee in protest to our flag and anthem? Have you excused violence in the name of your beliefs? If so, you are the mob outside my door.

"My home is besieged, and all of the women and children hide. How many who threaten their lives truly understand what they are transforming into? Do you think those who became Nazis knew what they were about to become?"

Ken's smile seemed more ravenous than joyful as he asked the question again, "Who are you, Tanner Washington?"

Images from the school flashed across my mind, igniting all the cells of my body with the sensation of walking its corridors, the shards of memory from Bogotá, and the violence that pushed it all forward.

The answer.

"Once you're done being afraid." The Beast taunted me mercilessly.

Looking at Ken, I silently remembered words from *Endarkenment*: "Reserve your darkness for those who think the night will cover their tracks. To the rest, show what world you stand for."

"You want to know who I am?" I growled as the choppers buzzed overhead, the sole police chopper using a powerful projector on the fenced area.

"Yes!"

I could hear the sound of my little warrior's voice asking why I didn't help Nico in time. Remembering my admission of guilt and encouragement to always strive to do the right thing, I took a deep breath, determined to not let him down again.

Every word I say.

"I'm a man who lives under God.

"I'm a man who places his family as the highest virtue of his life.

"I'm a man who only kneels to those he loves.

"I'm a man who cherishes his imperfect country.

"I'm a man who swore an oath to protect the Constitution from foreign and domestic enemies.

"I'm a man who lives free.

"I'm an American—a son, a brother, a husband, and a father.

"My name is Tanner Washington."

Ken's eyes were wide, his mouth slightly agape.

Time stopped between us and around us, as my declaration reverberated through my cells.

It's done. There's no going back now, I thought just as my alarm and the crowd alerted me.

"Time's up! Time's up!"

I looked down to the courtyard in time to see Dmitri suddenly yelling back at one of the units.

Shit.

Chelsea was waving her red Comrades flag out the window with one hand and pointing her other at the gate.

What's she hold-

Time slowed again as the sound of the rolling gate beginning to slide open reached my ears and I shouted, "Dmitri, fall back! Fall back!" forgetting all about Ken and his camera.

Dmitri, Lia, Roberto, and two other neighbors raced back.

Oh my God, help me keep them all safe! I prayed as I watched the mob fill the courtyard and charge toward my home.

WHAT MATTERS THE MOST

– Venice Beach, CA –
Wednesday, November 4, 2020

01:01

Surrounded

The police chopper's spotlight illuminated the court-yard, and Ken and I held our breath as Dmitri covered those retreating to our unit.

"Now, Dmitri!" Seeing the mob swarming in our direction, I gripped the rail, resisting the overwhelming urge to run down to help.

The big Russian knocked down two of their fast runners before he pivoted and dashed hard for the front door Roberto held open. Leaning over the edge, I noticed the old man holding one of my handguns.

Good use of the weapons, Dee.

The mob slammed against the door the second after Dmitri closed it. Like waves smashing against the sand, they bounced back and then pushed forward again.

I afforded myself one quick glance into the unit and saw the team in action, making sure the entrance was barricaded and everyone else was protected in the other unit. Dani caught my eyes before racing to help again. My right hand reached to ensure the Fly was correctly fastened to my shirt collar as I peered over the rail.

Unable to break our front door, the rioters turned their fury up toward the balcony. Their eyes and fists raised, some tried to jump high enough to grab Nico's flags but none succeeded. Ken continued moving his camera between me and the courtyard.

"This could turn ugly, Ken. I must stay, but you should go back inside."

He shook his head.

He's all in. God, protect him too.

The chopper's light beam danced around the court-yard, illuminating the mayhem of rioters breaking down doors and ransacking neighboring units. A few tried our adjacent unit's door, threatening our secret hideout, but it had been well-barricaded in advance and held.

Thank God.

"No!" Female screams caught my attention, and I scanned the buildings until I found their origin. I gritted my teeth in disgust as I watched a wave of men pummel Chelsea to the ground in her own apartment.

"She made her choice." The Beast whispered truth in response to my concern.

When the light stopped near the gate area and then slowly moved back toward us, reflecting off the red helmet of the man surrounded by black-clad Ryse troops, I used the *Sense* to stay focused as the Demon approached.

"Hostiles are armed, both hot and cold weapons," reported the Aide.

A shiver traveled down my spine when I noticed the long rifles.

How close are you, Alfa?

"Close enough to kill," answered the Beast.

"Colonel!" roared Ender, raising his hands to signal the crowd to silence.

The puppets quieted and made room for Ender and the guards who circled him whose line of sight was affected by police's beam.

"The Demon doesn't mind," warned the Beast as Ender kept his gaze on me, his eyes protected behind his helmet's shield.

"So this is where you live. Cute! And nice flags! I remember them very well."

The crowd booed on cue.

You motherfucker. My fingers bunched the thick fabric of the flags draped over the rail as my grip tightened. *If my family wasn't here...*

"You think about my offer?" Hundreds of phones recorded our exchange.

"The cop? Are you asking whether I'll hand her over to you?" My eyes scanned the courtyard.

"Of course!" He and his lackeys laughed in concert.

A Symphony of Malice.

"Give us the cop, remove the flags, and we're good." I didn't need truth serum or vitals reports to know he didn't mean what he said.

"Nuts!" I shouted back, and a contagious murmur rippled through the rioters.

Ender must have sensed it—the shift in attention—and immediately challenged back, "What exactly?"

"Yes. Play him," coaxed the Beast.

"Every word you said. All lies. You already know you will not enter my home or get the officer unless you *force* your way in," I admonished him. "Why won't you say what you mean? You got all the guns and the numbers."

Ken shifted the camera in Ender's direction.

The Demon laughed as he turned again to face the crowd, his hand pointing at me as he began his idiot monologue, "The man up there represents the very system that oppresses us all..." He went on and on, decrying the institutions of the United States, including the military, inflaming the mob with words about power and privilege. "Thanks to the virus..."

You Fuck.

"He's pretty good. They idolize his words." The Beast seemed concerned.

I took a deep breath and kept listening.

"... and we saw that we could all work as one united community." Bile rose in my throat as I listened to the textbook propaganda. "There's a term for this coming renaissance, It's called The Great Reset."

My focus remained on Ender as he turned back to face me.

"This is not your world anymore!" he roared.

The mob cheered and gloom clutched my heart.

Are we really this far gone?

Ken changed his angle, moving behind me and to my left as the Demon spoke again, "Where are the vigilantes, Colonel? We always hear about them."

"How would I know?" It was a sincere question.

Ender laughed and pointed at me again with his gloved right hand.

"Because people like you can do these things!" he shouted.

"Killers know killers." The Beast agreed with the Demon to my dismay.

Searching the crowd, I didn't see any of my Rogues in the densely-packed courtyard.

"Society is a thin crust over a simmering volcano." My father's words echoed painfully as I stared into the faces of indoctrinated zombies animated with blind rage.

"I'm losing my patience, Colonel. Maybe you heard about my bad side," he goaded me, twisting his words to sound like jest.

I'm not sure whether it was my intuition or self-preservation that made me turn to look inside, but the sight of Dani's face cooled the inferno inside.

I can try one more time.

"Hey!" I called out to the crowd, lifting my hands, palms open. "Hey!"

It did the trick, and the attention shifted to me, all phones recording my every move and word.

"I'm unarmed and mean no ill to any of you. Go now. Go home. This could be your last chance to withdraw and keep your conscience and hands clean. You are led by evil."

Ender erupted in laughter.

Ignoring the Demon, I continued, "I want nothing from you. I only want to protect those inside my home. They've done nothing to you. Go now."

While the crowd booed, a few faces looked around as though reassessing their involvement.

Please go.

"What about me, Colonel? Can I go home without problems?" screeched Ender.

So you can continue on with what you believe is a revolutionary terror?

Ken moved again, making me wonder whether he was changing positions just to keep me from going down a rabbit hole.

There was an eerie silence as the mob waited for my reply.

"I thought so." Ender pointed at the flags and called out, "Take them down! Take them down!"

The mob joined the chant, and I gripped the railing tighter, resisting every dark impulse racing through my veins, begging me to jump off the balcony and prevent this disgusting parasite from taking any more of our time or oxygen.

"Ari!"

My blood curdled and time slowed as I turned to see my little warrior jumping onto the corner vase and up to the rail, shouting, "No! They're not going down!"

Oh no.

Time stopped when even the horde was stunned.

I lunged toward Ari as the Demon barked, "Fire!"

★   ★   ★

01:14

Sacrifice

Grabbing him at the shoulders and waist, I pivoted back through the open glass door, bullets already flying as our bodies crashed into the hardwood floor. Covering his tiny body with my own, I looked right to find Ken on the floor, somehow still holding his camera on me, as the firestorm continued unbroken.

Dmitri squawked orders from below and my queen screamed, "Let me go! Tanner! Ari!"

Ari shrieked in pain, his body twitching underneath me in a spasm. My hands moved to check him for...

Blood!

"*Focus, Soldier!*" growled the Beast as bullets tore through our home, shattering years of our family's memories and devastating our future.

"Mommy! Mommy! It hurts!"

I held him tight while Dani yelled and flailed against Roberto's firm grip.

"And Abraham stretched forth his hand and took the knife, to slaughter his son." I squeezed my eyes shut against Shemtov's words, barely noticing as one bullet hit my side and another grazed my leg. "And an angel of God called to him from heaven and said, 'Abraham! Abraham!' And he said, 'Here I am.'"

God, please!

"Tanner, focus!" the Beast commanded.

Ari stopped yelling when his gaze locked onto mine, his eyes still full of pain and fear.

"Here I am. Here I am," I said to him, praying for God to protect my son.

"The Firstborn... The Sacrifice..." The Beast's words echoed Shemtov's, sending a new wave of terror through my nervous system.

No. I can't lose him!

Suddenly, the fire stopped, and I could hear Ender shouting, "Yo! Colonel! If you're still alive inside, one last chance to give up the..."

"Permission to engage," Dex's strained voice called over the team channel.

"3..." Ender began his countdown.

Ari yelped in pain.

Every action I take.

"2..."

My right hand grabbed Ari's chin to focus him, "I love you *the most*."

"1..."

Fury broke in my chest.

"Semper Fidelis," I instructed, Ari's open eyes still on mine.

Large explosions rocked the complex and thick, dark smoke rose from the courtyard as the world beyond our doors descended into a concert of pain, screams, and sounds of violence.

★ ★ ★

01:26

Triage

"Dani. First Aid. Now!"

She was at my side the second the bullets stopped, while the AI helped me scan Ari's body for the wound to stop the bleeding.

By the time she returned with the red case, I had found both of his wounds and thanked God they were superficial.

"Hold here." I instructed her to apply pressure with the bandage as I turned my attention to the environment, finding a strangely-peaceful Lil in Celeste's arms in the other unit.

Ken kept filming while I stabilized Ari and we placed him on the sofa, my attention split between my son and the sounds of mayhem outside.

"You're also hurt," Dee said when she sat next to me. "Your son's okay. Let me work on you."

"Sit your ass here," Dani commanded, pointing to the spot on the couch next to Ari.

As Dee began extracting one of the bullets, I cursed in pain as quietly as I could.

"Hostiles retreat. Multiple enemy casualties. Looking for Ender," called Dex over the team channel. The Aide updated Alfa-one for me, as I had no privacy in replying.

Dmitri was shaking his head slowly in disbelief when he reached the top of the stairs. I'd never seen the Russian look spooked.

"Does it hurt, Daddy?" Ari was watching closely as Dee dug mercilessly into my side with the long stainless tweezers.

Like a motherfucker!

"Why did you risk yourself like that?" I placed my right hand on his chest.

He looked confused for a short moment before he answered, "You said I should always do the right thing, even if I'm scared. It's what being a man is all about."

Damn it.

Dani and I stared at him silently until Ken and Dee excused themselves.

"Your uncle would've been proud of you." I moved the hair out of his face.

"Are the bad people still out there, Dad?"

Dark energy coursed through me.

"No, you're safe."

"Uncle Nico must have sent angels to protect us."

Dani and I exchanged stunned looks and a strange sort of terror squeezed my chest.

Here I am… but…

"We'll leave soon. See what the Ramirez clan has decided," I spoke to Dani. "I'll speak with the rest."

★ ★ ★

01:36

Stabilizing

I walked to the balcony, Dmitri on my heels. Ken was already there, filming.

As the smoke receded, the sight of at least half a dozen unmoving bodies and many wounded, screaming in pain, made us all hold our breath.

"What happened here?" Ken whispered.

A shudder went down my spine, imagining how it must have felt to experience the Rogue Dance in such a small space.

"I don't know," I replied, exchanging a hard look with Dmitri.

I wonder what he saw.

Ken's eyes narrowed, but he got nothing else.

The Aide reported that Romulus had forced Alfa to stop chasing Ender and prepare to cover the exfil from the complex.

Dmitri spat and cursed something in Russian and switched to English, "We need to recon the complex."

"I'll be right behind you," I responded as he and Ken left me alone on the balcony.

Jack spoke into my earbud, "This is our chance, Son. You've got twenty-five minutes to reach the jetty, right where you surf. That's your exfil point."

I didn't answer, feeling the Beast howling its desire to pursue Ender. My head turned back to see my queen doting over Ari on the sofa, and the shackles tightened around me like a dungeon.

I carefully took down the flags, folding them and wondering what the man who died for them would think of me and the choices that awaited me.

THE THRASH

01:45

Consequences

I walked outside to join the big Russian while Dani discreetly talked with the Ramirez family about the exfil and got the kids ready. The big guy and I only had twenty minutes.

We maneuvered through the courtyard littered with discarded signs, clothing items, and blood stains. The wounded had managed to leave the complex, but seven dead bodies remained where they were taken down.

"Their throats were sliced open," grumbled Dmitri. "The vigilantes came after all. What are the chances?" Deadly sarcasm not slowing his step, he hissed, "They fucking deserved it."

The rising fury in me agreed, pushing against the waning objections of the one-dimensional persona I'd embodied during my years here in Venice as a civilian.

Dmitri grunted at my lack of response as we headed to Chelsea's unit.

Her manicured loft was ransacked, walls tagged with vile graffiti. Turning to the living room, we both froze at the sight of her naked, abused corpse.

Nobody trusts traitors. I wish you'd listened.

I spotted a blanket to cover her.

"I need to tell you something and for you to not ask any questions for a moment," I said, our eyes still fixed on the covered body. "I'm taking my family to safety. I hope the Ramirez family decides to join."

"What do you want from me?" he asked sternly, turning to look at me.

"Can you stay and help Dee protect the civilians?"

He slowly nodded and searched my eyes as he asked the question plaguing us both, "Are you going to let that monster live?"

How could I protect them and keep my promise to Roberto?

"Right now, all I care about is getting them to safety."

He nodded gravely as he obliged, "I'll back you up and help Dee, but at a certain point…" His words trailed off.

I envied his freedom to choose what he knew to be right and nodded back, understanding that this was the best the revenge-bent Russian could offer.

"I'll make sure the gate is secured. Go get them ready."

As he turned away, the Beast growled in dismay and I resisted the urge to put my fist through Chelsea's wall on my way back to the courtyard.

★ ★ ★

01:52

Commitment

I was surprised to see Dee outside with Emmanuel by her side. The cop had already reestablished our patrols around our walls.

"Listen, guys..." I told them about our upcoming departure.

Emmanuel's face twitched, but he eventually smiled.

"The children come first. I get it, Hermano. Don't worry. I'm working on getting some guys over here."

When he headed back to my house, I turned to the young officer who bit her lip and then sighed.

"You can count on me, Sir," she started, her voice firming up. "You helped me, and now I'm not afraid of *him*." She hissed the last word.

Shame quickly weakened my legs and I used the *Sense* to refocus.

I cannot lose them.

Dee told me she had updated Holden with all the known facts.

"Thanks. Please update him about our evacuation twenty minutes *after* we leave."

She nodded and smiled, but it only made me feel worse as we parted ways.

★ ★ ★

01:59

Admissions

Entering our home, I went straight to the studio and found Nico's flags appropriately folded on my desk.

Dee.

"Tanner, you got a moment?" I heard Ken's voice on the other side of the door.

"Yes," I told him, moving to double-check our bags and our timing.

"The video has gone viral. Player1776 really came through fast with minor edits, and Brett is helping to push it."

"That's good." I wasn't even remotely interested.

"Other videos came out as well... of the surprise attack on the rioters," he cautiously continued. "It's crazy. One moment they start shooting at us, and then explosions, smoke, and screams."

"Go on." Suddenly, I was interested but kept my eyes on the tasks I completed.

"Some are saying it was the vigilantes," he added, looking at me keenly.

I felt a crooked smile rise.

"Did anyone get those vigilantes on tape?"

He shook his head, explaining, "Too much smoke."

My chuckle was the only response.

They're the best.

"While you're here..." I told him about our imminent departure.

He looked dumbstruck.

"Speak your mind," I offered, glancing at my watch again.

Ten minutes.

"I know it's selfish of me when you must protect your family, but I just thought that you would be... You are..." The master of words was at a loss.

"Another who sees that you are afraid," the Beast confirmed.

The raging internal war rendered me wordless too.

I cannot lose them!

Unzipping the hidden pocket in my pants, I pulled out the flash drive containing the secret recording from Taco Libertad. Extending it to Ken, I smiled sadly.

"Keep up the good work, Ken. I now understand why my father likes you so much."

Reaching for the device, he seemed confused and intrigued.

"What is it?"

"My greatest mistake." I clapped him on the back again before he left.

02:07

Released

I was just about to leave the studio when the door opened and Dani and the Ramirez crew hustled in.

Paulina and Celeste were both crying and holding each other. Roberto looked tired but unyielding as he shifted his gaze from them to me.

"We are going to stay." He comforted Paulina again before continuing, "Celeste and the kids are going with you. This is the right decision. We are just too old and stubborn." He managed a deep chuckle.

I looked at Dani and then Celeste, both nodding through their tears.

"And one more thing..." Roberto's face grew deadly serious after exchanging a stern look with his grieving daughter-in-law. "I want you to go with them. Your promise..." His words trailed for a moment as he looked at the women. "It was made in another world, and now we face this one. Mi hijo, he would want you to protect the familia above all."

I turned from his eyes to Celeste's where the fire and rage still danced until she took a deep breath and nodded with a faint smile.

"It's time to heal, Tanner." She forced the words out.

The Beast thrashed.

Looking back to my queen and seeing her hopeful smile, I conceded and cringed as the Beast slammed Itself against the endless caverns of my mind.

"Paulina, this is for you." I grabbed the folded flags from the desk.

Her face was wet, but she found the strength to smile and retrieve them from me as I kissed her cheek and embraced Roberto, torn between relief and rage that he'd released me from my promise.

"Tanner, it's time," the Aide whispered.

BUG OUT

– Venice Beach, CA –
Wednesday, November 4, 2020

02:13

Goodbyes

"These are Daddy's nighttime goggles," I explained to Ari when he pointed at the black NVG set affixed to my head. "They're going to help me see in the dark."

I grabbed his small, pudgy hand and smiled down at my little warrior, standing on his own two feet in the middle of our living room.

Thank God.

Leelee slept on my right shoulder as we gathered for our goodbyes. The four kids, Celeste, Dani, Lia, and I were encircled by our friends and neighbors—the survivors—their eyes exhausted and moist.

Dani's arm wrapped around my waist as we silently looked around our loft. It had been utterly destroyed in the bullets' hailstorm, but one frame still hung—our wedding picture. My stomach clenched at the bittersweet irony. The beach where we'd pledged our undying love was the same place Eli and his crew would meet us in less than thirty minutes.

"I'm bringing it with us," growled Dani, dropping her arm and snatching it off the wall. As soon as it was in her hands, the tears fell.

Before I could react, Paulina reached for the picture and promised, "We'll keep it safe in our home until you can take it."

Dani nodded, swallowed her tears, and returned to my side. Feeling her trembling, I brushed my lips against her forehead.

I'm sorry, Baby, that you have to leave it all behind.

Dmitri, Ken, Roberto, Paulina, Dee, Emmanuel, and many neighbors stood quietly as I looked around the circle one last time. It was difficult to hold their gaze as I moved from one face to the next, lips pursed to keep my shame from spilling out.

I'm so sorry.

The Beast vibrated Its waves of disgust.

Tightening my grip on Leelee, I looked at the three strong women surrounding me and nodded sadly. It was time.

"Cover their eyes," I instructed, and Dani, Celeste, and Lia pulled beanies over David, Odalys, and Ari's eyes. "Don't worry, kids. We'll be holding your hands. You're safe. Ready?"

Everyone nodded.

"Here we go." I led them down the stairs, cringing at the muted sobs of my loved ones and those we were leaving behind.

We slowly navigated the carnage of the courtyard that didn't look any better at 2:25 a.m. than when it happened. I increased our pace when Celeste and Dani's small gasps turned into murmurs in their native languages.

"Ladies." I shushed them with my finger once I had their attention and nodded at the children who, deeply attuned to their mothers' reactions, were getting antsy.

"What happened to Chelsea?" asked Dani quietly.

Catching her eyes, I shook my head, unwilling to share even the smallest detail of the woman's demise in front of the children.

Just before I knew it would be out of view, I looked back one last time to find Dee, Ken, and Dmitri on the balcony watching me leave with my family. Feeling the hot flush of shame and guilt, I nodded in their direction.

I'm so sorry.

02:31

The Pyre

The night was filled with the smell of smoke and the sounds of choppers, sirens, and shots fired.

"Clear," I called to Lia in Hebrew after sneaking outside the complex to check Venice Boulevard in both directions. There were only a few people hanging around on the double-lane road that was the fastest way to our location. Lia brought the group out and took the rear position as agreed.

"Single-file," I instructed with a weary smile. "And you can remove the beanies."

They were all stunned and exhausted, but no one complained, and Lil stayed asleep on my shoulder like a little princess. I lowered my NVG goggles to make up for the blown-out street lights, noticing Ari's proud smile as he watched me.

I grinned back at him and nodded.

Yes, Son. Real life warrior toys.

The Aide effectively kept the invisible Rogue envelope in perfect formation around our small group as we walked the few hundred feet up the boulevard. In the five-minute walk, Alfa chased off two potential random attacks and got us safely to the beach.

The plan was to head straight to the jetty, across the sand, and past the large lifeguard headquarters. But looking down the beach, I saw a large fire roaring just past the basketball courts in the distance.

"Fire at the police beach station," Dex reported in my ear after I whispered my change of course on the team channel. "We'll clear it for your arrival."

"Don't be afraid... Go up the mountain and face God." Shemtov's last words stole my breath. I had to use the *Sense* to slow the fissure occurring inside my soul.

Todd.

"Quick detour," I instructed Lia as I turned right and walked toward the distant pyre, lifting the NVG goggles when the flames made it impossible to use them properly.

Shit!

"Take her." Anxiety exploded through my chest as I handed Lil to Dani. She and Celeste held the children close and stared at the flames while I sprinted toward the last place I'd hugged my friend.

God, please! I pleaded as my feet carried me swiftly toward the station's lone hill, my heart pounding harder with every step, more from fear than pace. *Nooo!!!*

Todd's body was splayed on the wet grass, twisted and lifeless in front of his broken flags display.

I dropped to my knees when I reached him and suppressed the urge to scream. Taking a deep breath instead, I refocused and leaned closer.

Caught off-guard when the Fly turned on its tiny flashlight without a command, I remembered I wasn't alone.

"Was he your friend?" asked the AI.

Taking in every detail of the brutal beating and stabbing, I remembered his own prophetic words: "I don't know how long I could make my stand here. But I'm reassured that someone like you might pick up my flag and keep it tall because good men don't bow to malice. Before long, you will embrace it too."

"Yes, he was." Throbbing pain threatened to close my throat as I used my gloved hand to shut my friend's eyes.

The Beast thrashed inside me, reeling in pain and roaring with the desire to inflict it.

Why aren't you talking? I asked on my way back to the group, untenable emotions surging from the darkest depths.

Dani looked at me, silently asking a question she knew the answer to as soon as she saw my eyes. As she lowered her head and wiped her face, her body began to tremble again.

Lifting Leelee back to my chest, I pulled Dani close and kissed her hair.

I'm here, Baby. I'm here.

I waited a few moments for her body to still, while similar words beckoned on the early morning breeze.

THE ROAD LESS TRAVELED

– Venice Beach, CA –
Wednesday, November 4, 2020

02:49

We left the boardwalk behind us and crossed into the sandy beach, where a few people partied in the distance. The lifeguard's control tower glistened in the moonlight just ahead, and I sighed with relief when it appeared to be undisturbed. As we quietly marched south along the water line, the Aide reported that the Israelis were already on the beach and aware of Alfa's presence.

"Your daddy's straight ahead," I whispered to Dani when I recognized my father-in-law's bulky silhouette on the beach. The leader of the Israeli Mossad was dressed in a black BDU, surrounded by a few younger armed men in black watching all sides.

"Abba! Abba!" Dani called to her father in Hebrew and rushed forward, leaving me with a stirring Lil and an anxious Ari.

My wounded warrior had walked the whole way with no complaints. Pride swelled, confusing the pain in my chest, as I reached for his extended hand and winked at him.

Eli Peled, even in his late sixties, was a hard man by all accounts. But the minute he heard her voice, he ran to meet her and scooped his daughter up into a bear hug.

My heart warmed at the sight and the sound of his tender greeting, "Daniellush," and the soft hum my wife always makes when she feels safe. "Ella is on the boat waiting for her baby sister," he added, eliciting a happy gasp.

After hugging his daughter, he turned his affection toward Ari and Leelee, pulling both of them into his big embrace and kissing the tops of their heads.

One of the most formidable men on the planet.

"Good work," Eli grumbled at Lia as she moved to join the rest of his group.

My father-in-law looked at the rest of the group. He introduced himself warmly to Celeste and her kids, immediately acquiring their adoration with his first question, "Have you ever been on a boat with a pool?"

They shook their heads and smiled when he made a funny face and promised they would have fun.

Finally, Eli turned to me.

I straightened my posture and expression.

"Mission accomplished, Sir."

He reached for my hand and pulled me into a hug, lowering his voice near my ear, "As a true husband and father would." His eyes flashing with gratitude as he stepped back, he cleared his throat of the intense fatherly emotion before he turned back to the group.

"Alright, everyone. I bet you're tired. Why don't you sit down while I talk to this guy?"

I followed him a few steps toward the water.

"The getaway vehicle is a luxury yacht?"

"Yep, a good friend of mine offered it, and I thought it would be great for the kids," he sighed and glanced at his daughter, "and the exhausted ladies."

The kids and ladies? But... My heart dropped. *I'm going too, Eli.*

"We'll be leaving shortly. I figured you'd need some space to handle any last affairs. I know I don't need to tell you," he pointed at his watch, "but we don't need to add an international incident to tomorrow's news cycle."

I nodded, feeling the weight of the world pressing down on my shoulders.

The leader of the Mossad gave orders to his men while I walked a few steps away to make the call.

"Ken's videos lit social media on fire. The California government will be in the hot seat for what happened," Custer started. "You're all over the news now. Exposed. Perfect time to go."

As I waited for my next orders, I wondered why my father was so quiet.

"We're releasing you from duty, Alfa-leader," Remus continued. "It's time... to focus on your family and their well-being. With national exposure, we won't be able to protect them here. Even the Ranch isn't safe."

His words should have given me solace, but they fueled the fissure instead.

"Custer's right." Jack's voice was strained. "Get on the boat and reach out when you're in international waters."

Really, Dad? After all you've put me through?

Resentment coiled in my muscles, ready to strike, but I didn't object when they began to terminate the call.

Watching Eli give orders and the women tend to the children, I gulped back the lump of grief mixing with rage.

I can't lose anyone else!

Inside, a storm of opposing desires broke off.

But what about the mission, and Ender?

"We're going to have a problem here. We are placing the villain as the hero. You'd leave the hero no choice but to act like a villain." Brett Cohen's words torqued me in the other direction.

I'm here, damn it! And now they tell me to leave?!?

Using the *Sense* to compose myself, I stomped back to the group as Eli and his men began to escort Celeste and all four kids into the boat that would take everyone to the yacht that stayed in deeper water.

As soon as I was close enough, Dani wrapped her arms around me and pulled me close. All efforts to manage suddenly worthless, the grief shot through me and my body convulsed as I reciprocated her gentle touch. Refusing to fall apart, I buried my face in her hair and matched my breath to hers.

"It's okay, Baby. We made it. We're safe. We're going home," she soothed.

Home. I took another long deep breath as the crevice cracked open a little more against my will.

Her head tilted, eyes captivated by something behind me.

"Your soldiers have finally shown themselves after all these years. Pass them my gratitude." She squeezed me tighter for a moment and then released me.

She always knew.

Dani grinned at my surprise, and I wondered why her admission had done very little to calm the raging maelstrom in my soul.

What am I supposed to do?

I turned to see the six figures emerging from the darkness. They stopped thirty feet away in a half circle and waited. My heart raced as I walked toward them, my regret over leaving them after Market blindsiding me.

And here I do it again, choosing a life they sacrificed.

Standing a few feet away, my chest throbbed as I looked into the faces of friends who had traveled the darkest tunnels of humanity with me.

The quote from *Endarkenment* called to me like a siren on the ocean's breeze: "There are no redoes. All that is left is the hope to choose again."

I'm here.

This time, the thought held a visceral gravitational pull.

As I attempted to will my mouth to bid my Rogues farewell, Harry Ganbold's discerning question of what would happen if I failed to fix my mistakes clawed at my conscience.

Did I even try?

"Sir," started Dex, taking a step closer to me. "I was blessed to have a loving, supportive, present father. Don't take that away from them." His voice was full of pain as he nodded in the direction of the boats behind me.

But you're all my family too. My throat ached as the pressure in my chest increased.

Jenny stepped up beside him.

"Alfa-Leader, we understand. It's time for you to go." In the soft moonlight, I could see the glimmer of tears in her eyes.

No, Jenny, my fierce warrior and friend, you should know.

"We'll miss you," added Sarah, joining them.

"Do I get bumped up?" jested Liam. "Ouch!" Hux had silently smacked his head.

The giant cracked a sad half-smile, appearing at a loss for words as the two of them moved closer.

"We got this, Sir." Moss joined the tighter half-circle, unable to fully pull off a cheerful voice.

Gunshots and screams started somewhere beyond the sands.

No one is coming to help.

The lurking grief and regret pounced, choking my words out with images.

Nico... Ishmael... Ganbold... Jerome... Henry... Shemtov... Todd... And the world I helped destroy... Where are you, Beast?!

I looked back. Almost everyone was inside the boat. Only Dani, Eli, and some of his men stood on the wet sand waiting.

I'm here.

A female scream from the boardwalk reminded me of Ender's vile dystopian words: "The Great Reset... the revolutionary terror..."

I turned back to my team, my mind racing to escape the web of riddles.

What am I missing?

Nightmarish images from the elementary school wrestled my attention.

Bogotá. The key.

"Sir..." Sarah's motherly voice sounded miles away.

My soul felt detached from my body, hearing my old mentor's voice once again: "And he said, 'Do not stretch forth your hand to the lad, nor do the slightest thing to him, for now I know that you are a God-fearing man, and you did not withhold your son, your only one, from Me.'"

Here I am.

My eyes closed, over the soft sound of the water lapping at the shore, the Rabbi's closing question punched me in the gut for the second time: "What will you do when God calls you to the altar, commanding you to give that which is the most precious of all?"

"Tanner..." Jenny gently touched my arm, unable to break me from the trance until the final piece shoved itself into my mind's eye.

"Tanner... This book will teach you how to harness the darkness so that you fight for what is right, bearing the cost of the greatest sacrifice..."

Here I am.

All tumblers finally sliding into place, the answer was unlocked... my decision made.

FOLLOW TANNER'S JOURNEY

Where is Tanner leading them?

Follow his journey **@Tanneralfa on X** *and* **TannerWashington.com** *and stay tuned for...*

GLOSSARY

Characters and Organizations from *Descent*

WASHINGTON FAMILY

Tanner: retired Marine Colonel, Alfa-Leader

Danielle/Dani: Tanner's wife, mother to their two children

Ari: Tanner and Danielle's son

Leelee/Lil: Tanner and Danielle's daughter

Jack: Tanner's father, Vietnam vet, CEO of Old Glory, Rogue Commander (Romulus)

Ali: Tanner's mother, works for Old Glory and the Doctrine (Clementia)

Tami: Tanner's younger sister, Constitutional lawyer

Henry: Tami's husband

Adam: Tami's baby boy

Chad: Tanner's younger brother, journalist

Ulysses: Jack's father, Tanner's grandfather, WW2 Veteran

Debra: Ulysses's wife, Tanner's grandmother

MARINES

Ishmael Harris: Marine veteran, murdered

William Custer: Marine General, Vietnam vet, Rogue Commander (Remus)

ROGUES – ALFA TEAM

Dex Bradley: Alfa-One

Huxley Jorgensen: Alfa-Two

Moss Danberry: Alfa-Three

Jenny Liu: Alfa-Four

Sarah Mitchell: Alfa-Five

Liam Morales: Alfa-Six

RAMIREZ FAMILY

Nicolas/Nico: retired Marine Corporal, owned Taco Libertad, murdered

Celeste: Nico's wife and mother of their two children

David: Nico's son

Odalys: Nico's daughter

Roberto: Nico's father

Paulina: Nico's mother

DANIELLE'S FAMILY

Eli Peled: Danielle's father, head of the Israeli Mossad

Ella Gur: Dani's older sister, lives in Israel

FRIENDS & NEIGHBORS

Chaim Shemtov: Tanner's rabbi and dear friend, Vietnam veteran

Chelsea Roberts: Tanner and Danielle's neighbor

Dmitri Petrov: Nico's friend, Russian-Spetsnaz-turned US Marine (Ret)

Emmanuel Perez: Nico's friend

Todd Fulton: Tanner's friend, homeless social educator

WASHINGTONS' FRIENDS

Clara Norton: Jerome's wife, Lynn's mother

Jerome Norton: Jack's friend, Lynn's father, works for Old Glory

Lynn Norton-Bower: Governor of South Dakota, Tanner's former romantic interest

Lee Wu: Chinese scientist

LA / CA OFFICIALS

Dee Hopkins: LAPD Officer

Neville Bernard: Los Angeles District Attorney

Nick Donnelly: Los Angeles Mayor

Richard Knight: California Governor

Roger Holden: Tanner and Nico's friend, LAPD's Commander of the Pacific Division

Victoria Sabech: Los Angeles Councilwoman

US GOVERNMENT

Bill Garcia: Texan U.S. Senator

Dwayne Jackson: New York U.S. Senator

Gerald Benson: U.S. Navy Admiral, deceased

Howard Stone: Republican President of the United States

Jeremiah Tall: retired Army General

Nate Charlton: previous President of the United States (2008-2012)

Rod Grayson: Democratic Presidential Nominee, Defense Secretary during Charlton Administration

Sam Baker: worked for DOD

Shida Saam: DHS agent

NGO AND MOVEMENTS LEADERS

Claudia Kruger: Pax Eden's CEO

Daj Morris: Comrades Commander

Paul Shi: CEO of the CPC

FOREIGN LEADERS

Abdul Qurban: Afghani Chieftain

Jun Zhang: General, China's Ministry of State

JOURNALISTS / AUTHORS

Brett Cohen: conservative podcaster

Ken Lim: journalist

Miles Bach: professor, author of *Endarkenment*

EXTRA

Nils Custer: Custer's nephew, Chicago police officer

ORGANIZATIONS/INSTITUTIONS

Comrades: social justice Marxist organization

CPC: Chinese People Collective, an American non-governmental organization

DCS: Department of Children's Safety

DHS: Department of Homeland Security

DOD: Department of Defense

LAPD: Los Angeles Police Department

MARSOC: Marine Special Operations Command

MSS: Ministry of State Security, Chinese Secret Police Agency

OBI: Open Borders Initiative, an international company with European roots supporting worldwide civil society groups

OG: Old Glory

OGT: Old Glory Team

Pax Eden: a multi-billion dollar corporation out of D.C., which coordinated donations for left-leaning causes and politicians

ROE: rules of engagement

RCC: Rogue Command Center

Ryse: a secretive organization specializing in civil disorder that is known to operate in small, decentralized cells across the country

TER: Transparent Election Review, a short-term project involving current and former government officials, academics, journalists, and retired military leaders

Western Jihad: a US-based Islamic organization.

WSC: Western States Coalition; California, Oregon, and Washington's advisory board created "to coordinate efforts to combat the Dragon pandemic"

TERMS

FOB: Forward Operating Base.

BDU: Battle Dress Uniform.

HUD: Heads-Up Display.

NVG: Night Vision Goggle.

CI: Confidential Informant.

ASSAF RAZ

Assaf Raz immigrated from the Israel to Venice Beach, CA, in his early twenties and began the journey to citizenship in a country he had long studied and revered. For more than two decades, he built his American Dream through real estate and a handful of other entrepreneurial pursuits. After a spiritual rebirth in his early thirties, he found the woman from his dreams, started a family, and began to write. First, he wrote a short memoir about his awakening *(Rite of Passage)* and then he started a novel fueled by his love of Roman history and the alternative history genre. He quickly set aside that project for the Old Glory series when his concerns about America piqued in 2020 during the lockdown and riots that unfolded in the streets where he lived and worked. Assaf and his family have been on the road since 2022.